LIFTING JULIE OFF HER FEET, LYON PINNED HER AGAINST THE CLOSED DOOR.

He rubbed his body against hers, letting her feel his arousal, thickened and hardened with need. He was a big man, and there was no mistaking his carnal state.

Julie gasped in shock. She pressed her shoulders against the door in a futile attempt to pull away from his touch and succeeded only in lifting her breasts higher against him. Her entire form quivered with rage.

Lyon had never known a woman could feel so unbelievably delicate and small-boned. Even in his frenzied state he was aware of her heart-stopping fragility, and his mind shouted a warning to his ravenous body. Honor and lust dueled within him.

Suddenly the point of Julie's knife was pricking the vulnerable underside of his jaw. "Put me down, *veho*," she ordered with cool deliberation, "or I will slit your throat from one ear to the other."

He considered forcing a kiss before setting her free. He could take the knife and the kiss by brute force, but he knew she'd fight him with every ounce of the considerable courage she possessed.

And if the knife slipped and cut her, he'd never forgive himself.

Other AVON ROMANCES

BY LOVE UNDONE *by Suzanne Enoch*
HER NORMAN CONQUEROR *by Malia Martin*
HIGHLAND BRIDES: HIGHLAND SCOUNDREL
by Lois Greiman
THE MEN OF PRIDE COUNTY: THE OUTSIDER
by Rosalyn West
PROMISED TO A STRANGER *by Linda O'Brien*
THROUGH THE STORM *by Beverly Jenkins*
WILD CAT CAIT *by Rachelle Morgan*

Coming Soon

THE BELOVED ONE *by Danelle Harmon*
THE MEN OF PRIDE COUNTY: THE REBEL
by Rosalyn West

And Don't Miss These
ROMANTIC TREASURES
from Avon Books

A RAKE'S VOW *by Stephanie Laurens*
TO TAME A RENEGADE *by Connie Mason*
WHEN DREAMS COME TRUE *by Cathy Maxwell*

KATHLEEN HARRINGTON

ENCHANTED BY YOU

AVON BOOKS ◆ NEW YORK

This is a work of fiction. Names, characters, places, and incidents either are the product of the author's imagination or are used fictitiously. any resemblance to actual events, locales, organizations, or persons, living or dead, is entirely coincidental and beyond the intent of either the author or the publisher.

AVON BOOKS, INC.
1350 Avenue of the Americas
New York, New York 10019

Copyright © 1998 by Kathleen Harrington
Inside cover author photo by Debbi DeMont Photography
Published by arrangement with the author
Visit our website at **http://www.AvonBooks.com**
Library of Congress Catalog Card Number: 98-92769
ISBN: 0-380-79894-8

First Avon Books Printing: October 1998

AVON TRADEMARK REG. U.S. PAT. OFF. AND IN OTHER COUNTRIES, MARCA REGISTRADA, HECHO EN U.S.A.

Printed in the U.S.A.

WCD   10 9 8 7 6 5 4 3 2 1

With warm affection to my dear and special
friends and colleagues,
whom I've worked with through the years
at Los Altos School:
Linda, Annamae, Sally, Judy,
Nancy, Silvia, Sue, Bernie,
Mary Ellen, Betty, Cathy, Kay,
Janet, Katie, Yvette, and Carolyn

Your friendship and support
have brightened the good times,
your kindness and compassion
have sustained me through the bad.

You are the salt of the earth.

I would like to thank Duncan Murray for generously sharing his knowledge of the Gaelic language and correcting my numerous errors. Any that may have slipped by are strictly my own fault.

"If, maiden, thou wouldst wend with me,
To leave both tower and town,
Thou first must guess what life lead we,
That dwell by dale and down.
And if thou canst that riddle read,
As read full well you may,
Then to the greenwood shalt thou speed,
As blithe as Queen of May."

"With burnished brand and musketoon
So gallantly you come,
I read you for a bold dragoon,
That lists the tuck of drum."
"I list no more the tuck of drum,
No more the trumpet hear;
But when the beetle sounds his hum,
My comrades take the spear.

"And O, though Brignall banks be fair,
And Greta woods be gay,
Yet mickle must the maiden dare,
Would reign my Queen of May!

"Maiden! a nameless life I lead,
A nameless death I'll die;
The fiend whose lantern lights the mead
Were better mate than I!
And when I'm with my comrades met,
Beneath the greenwood bough,
What once we were we all forget,
Nor think what we are now.

"Yet Brignall banks are fresh and fair,
And Greta woods are green,
And you may gather garlands there
Would grace a summer queen."

SIR WALTER SCOTT, "BRIGNALL BANKS"

Prologue

12 September 1886
Edinburgh, Scotland

You could hear the shouts of their war cries from the hillsides. The jarring clatter of sword against sword echoed up and down the glen. Great, double-edged broadswords severed hands and arms, their polished steel blades sharp enough to cleave a man from his head down to his buckled brogues. Blood flowed, rich and red, soaking the blue and black plaids of the besieged men, turning their brilliant colors to a dull, sodden gray.

Now and then a pistol shot rang out, and a man would topple from his saddle to sprawl in a twisted heap on the ground.

The trapped horsemen were valiant warriors. Caught by surprise and hopelessly surrounded by a much larger mounted force, they fought with the courage of lions.

The attackers hacked and stabbed at the doomed circle with swords and dirks, the delicately muted colors of their lavender and pink kilts an incongruous contrast to the methodical butchery.

No quarter was given.

The injured and dying were executed with a calculated thoroughness that chilled the deepest recesses of the soul.

When the fighting was over and the last man had been

1

dispatched to his maker, the victors gathered their wounded and retreated, leaving only three of their own dead amidst the carnage.

Then silence fell along the valley floor.

The rustling of aspen and larch on the rocky cliffs above murmured a hushed death chant over the unburied corpses. Clouds swept in from the mountain peaks beyond, gray and laden with moisture. Lightning lit up the darkened sky, and the thunder that followed boomed like artillery brought up too late to the battle.

Rain poured down, washing the blood into rivulets, leaving the faces of the fallen Highlanders scoured clean and fresh as the purple heather on the hillside.

The very heavens seemed to weep in shame at the merciless slaughter . . .

Juliette came awake with a breathless start. She stared at the ceiling overhead and fought the impending sense of doom that always followed her vision. The gruesome dream had haunted her since she was fourteen.

Trembling and disoriented, she shoved the plush comforter aside and slipped from the ornate brass bed. Her feet were cold, in spite of the thick rug that covered the floor. Her fingers shook as she lit the gas lamp on the night table and watched its rosy glow illuminate her unfamiliar surroundings.

"Hesc!" Although she spoke both English and French with ease, she always reverted to the Cheyenne of her childhood in times of stress. It was the language of her father's people.

Juliette looked around the floral-papered room in bewilderment and waited for her heartbeat to return to its normal, steady rhythm.

Hehe! Yes! She remembered now.

She was in Edinburgh, in the house that Uncle Benjamin had rented upon their arrival from Liverpool less than a week ago. Her twin sister, Jennifer, was in London with

Grandpapa. The letters she'd written to them before falling asleep were still lying on the stand beside the bed.

Juliette moved to a low, carved chest that stood beneath the curtained window. She raised the lid and lifted out the blanket she'd brought with her from Canada. Carrying the folded length of wool reverently across her forearms like a shaman's robe, she crossed the room and sat on the edge of the goose-down mattress. The lamplight fell across the plaid's muted pattern of lavender and pink. She stroked her fingertips along its frayed edge, and the comforting feel of the worn fabric soothed her jangled nerves.

The blanket was very, very old. It had belonged to her great-grandfather and to his father before that.

Juliette's mother, Rachel Rose Robinson, had been born in the Cumberland Mountains of eastern Kentucky, and raised by her maternal grandparents, Nehemiah and Matilda McDougall. Their people had emigrated from Scotland. This faded piece of material was the only thing of her grandfather's that Rachel, called Little Red Fawn by the Cheyenne, had brought out west with her.

Now it belonged to Juliette. Her mother had insisted that she take the heirloom with her to Scotland, certain it would help in the search for the meaning of her frightful dream. No one in her family doubted the importance of Juliette's quest, for the twins had inherited the second sight from their Scottish ancestors. From their father, Strong Elk Heart, they'd received the ability to interpret visions sent by the Great Powers.

In the aftermath of the dream, Juliette felt once again the overpowering conviction that she alone held the key to some grave mystery. That she was the only one who could right a terrible wrong.

Juliette had also inherited her father's gift for languages. She'd studied Gaelic, as well as the Celtic ballads and folk tales, hoping the ancient language and stories would help her unlock the elusive riddle. Finally, she'd come to the

conclusion that the answer could only be found in the Highlands of Scotland.

She buried her face in the blanket and inhaled the tangy
scent of juniper. Cheyenne women were inordinately fond
of perfumes. They always packed their clothing and sleeping robes with herbs, wildflowers, or pine needles. The
fresh, woodsy aroma reminded her of the Canadian forests,
and a bittersweet feeling tightened in her chest. She wondered if Jennie felt as equally homesick in England.

With a sigh, Juliette replaced the wool plaid in the cedar
chest and lowered the lid. She opened the drapes that covered the diamond-paned window and looked out.

It was nearly daylight. A dense fog shrouded the deserted
street below. The faint, high-pitched keen of a bagpipe
could be heard moving steadily closer and she smiled in
anticipation, certain it was the young war veteran who'd
greeted the dawn every morning since she'd arrived in Edinburgh. The strapping man in his kilted uniform, his chest
covered with medals, had become a welcome sight. Her
sister, Jennifer Morning Rose Elkheart, would have declared it to be very romantic.

Juliette wasn't given to dreams of romance. She was far
too sensible to yearn for a handsome warrior to come charging up on a painted pony and carry her away. Still, she had
to admit that a lusty Scotsman in kilts was a sight to warm
any girl's heart—even a sensible one.

She eyed the rumpled blue comforter with a frown. The
prospect of going back to bed, only to toss and turn until
breakfast time, seemed far from appealing. Urban civiliza-
tion definitely had its drawbacks. Being cooped up inside
a house was pure torture to a girl who'd raced her sister on
horseback across the high plains of Alberta day after glorious summer day.

Juliette decided to go for a walk. Although it was far too
early for a proper young lady to be strolling about unchap-

eroned, the heavy mist would conceal her from curious eyes. If she was very quiet, she could slip out of the house and back in again without Uncle Benjamin or Mrs. Meighan, the housekeeper, even realizing she'd been gone.

Chapter 1

⁓⟨෧⟩⁓

The laird of Strathlyon hated the sound of bagpipes.
He hated the accursed piping almost as much as he hated the sight of a kilt.

Swearing a blistering oath, he sat up in bed and threw his legs over the edge of the lumpy mattress. His old injury throbbed like a new wound. The bullet shard lodged in his left elbow was a souvenir of the British Expeditionary Force's disastrous campaign in the Sudan. He grimaced as he massaged his arm.

Damnation.

Who in hell would be playing "Highland Laddie" at this blighted hour of the morning?

Despite his best efforts to keep the image at bay, the sight of his brother's broken, mutilated body wrapped in the blood-soaked MacLyon plaid rose up to haunt him. He covered his face with his hands and squeezed his eyes shut in a determined attempt to block the memory.

His efforts were useless, of course.

The wailing of the pipes always reminded him of James.

Lyon grunted in disgust at his own weakness. He rose and crossed the floor of the small room, his bare feet soundless on the worn planks. Thrusting his head out the ancient inn's second-story window, he spied a stable boy in the courtyard below, nearly obscured by the fog.

"You! Lad!" he bellowed.

The groom looked up, and, recognizing the chief of Clan MacLyon, tugged politely on his cap.

Lyon scooped a pile of coins off the nearby bureau and flung them in a shower at the boy's feet. "Go tell that damned piper that if he doesn't stop his infernal screeching, I'm coming out there and ramming those pipes down his throat."

"Aye, laird!" the boy called with a delighted grin. He snatched up the coins with nimble fingers, then met Lyon's gaze once again. "But I dinna think it'll make much difference what I tell 'im, sir. Geordie Ferson's been paid by the town council to don his old regimentals and greet the city's visitors. He's been strutting up and down Princes Street every morning this week like some great cock o' the north welcoming the sun."

"Hell."

Lyon slammed the window shut with a bang. Walking over to the washstand in defeat, he poured water into a basin and splashed his face. He'd never get back to sleep now, but a dose of fresh air might ease the pounding in his head. He'd drunk too much the night before, which wasn't exactly rare. Lyon drank too much every time he came to Edinburgh.

That's why he *came* to Edinburgh.

That and the Golden Dirk's plump, dimpled whores.

He rubbed his numb face with a towel. Last night's romp must have turned into an out-and-out orgy. The sheer, unadulterated agony of this morning's headache proved it. But while he had only a vague recollection of a buxom redhead's sly, come-hither smile and a pretty brunette giggling uncontrollably into his pillow, all the drinking and whoring in the world couldn't erase the memories that plagued him.

Lyon clenched his teeth as he pulled on his shirt and trousers, steadfastly refusing to coddle his stiff elbow. The joint ached like a rotten tooth on the best of days, but the brawl he'd purposely provoked in the inn's common room before retiring upstairs for more amorous activities had left it almost unusable. He shook his head at his own stubborn perversity. He had to stop picking fights just for the fun of it.

A walk in the damp air might not do his elbow any good—nor his head either, for that matter—but it couldn't do any harm. And if he was lucky enough to happen upon Geordie Ferson, late of the Forty-second Highland Regiment, the satisfaction of breaking those odious pipes over the idiot's skull would act like a tonic.

Enticed by the lilting tune of the pipes, Juliette turned down a narrow street. She'd thrown a voluminous cloak over her walking dress before leaving the house and now pulled the hood up to conceal her unbound hair. The fog grew thicker as she walked, but she hoped the morning light would soon penetrate the gloom.

The houses of Edinburgh were built of gray stone, many of them rising over four stories high. As she looked up at the gloomy facades that loomed above the winding lane, the sensation of entering a blind canyon made her glance cautiously over her shoulder.

No one was in sight.

Releasing a pent-up breath, she touched the carved handle of the weapon sheathed at her waist beneath the cloak. Her father had taught her how to throw a knife with pinpoint accuracy when she was only a child. Any man foolish enough to accost her would quickly learn that a Cheyenne warrior-woman made a dangerous adversary.

Juliette rounded a bend in the roadway and halted in her tracks. A smothered gasp of shock lodged in her throat, and she stiffened her spine. Only a short distance down the street, three sinister thugs with stout cudgels were attacking a lone man. Wielding vicious blows across his head and massive shoulders, they'd backed their prey up against a wall, cutting off any chance of escape. Not content to just rob the unlucky gentleman, they meant to administer a sound beating as well.

The beleaguered gentleman was a giant—but a crippled one. Though he fought valiantly, he kept his left arm tucked tight against his side, nearly immobile.

Juliette hurried toward the one-sided confrontation.

Lyon raised his good arm to ward off another blow. He'd stupidly left his pistol back at the Golden Dirk. Disabled and without a weapon, he wouldn't last long against the three of them.

Using his left shoulder as a battering ram, Lyon slammed his full weight into the closest attacker, knocking him off balance and into the second. The nearer man, a stocky, thick-chested brute with a puckered scar beneath his bristly eyebrow, dropped his stick and gave a strangled grunt of disbelief at his victim's aggressive tactics. Arms flailing wildly, he staggered backwards.

Lyon grabbed a handful of his opponent's stringy black hair and jerked him sideways, pulling him over his hip. As the swarthy man toppled, Lyon crouched and reached for the fallen club.

By the time the second man lunged aside to avoid tripping over his beefy accomplice, Lyon was ready. He struck the skinny, flint-eyed bastard full across the shins. The fellow dropped to all fours on the paving stones and howled in rage.

But before Lyon could spring away from the wall, the third assailant, who'd been hanging back out of the way of his cohorts' flying clubs, swung his oak truncheon in a wide arc and landed a savage hit squarely on Lyon's bad elbow.

Lyon dropped to one knee. Jolts of excruciating pain speared through his arm like bolts of lightning, and the club fell from his hand. Clutching his elbow, he gritted his teeth to stifle an agonized groan. His head fell forward, and a black haze floated before his eyes as he fought desperately to remain conscious.

Juliette watched in horror as the evil-doer raised his cudgel over his victim's bowed head for a final, lethal blow.

She knew, instinctively, she was witnessing a ruthless, premeditated murder. The wicked man grinned victoriously, so intent on his kill he wasn't even aware of her presence, though she now stood less than twenty feet away.

"*Veho*! White man!" she called out, unsheathing her knife.

The assassin looked up at the sound of her voice. In that split second, Juliette hurled her weapon. The razor-sharp blade struck him in the throat, neatly severing a carotid artery. Blood spurted like a geyser from the fatal wound, as the club fell from his nerveless fingers to bounce twice on the cobblestones with a hollow clatter and roll harmlessly away. His eyes wide in blank disbelief, he dropped like a lodgepole pine beneath the ax.

The other two thieves belatedly clambered to their feet and backed slowly away. The cowardly pair took one long, incredulous look at their dead crony, turned, and raced down the street, where they quickly disappeared into the fog.

In delayed shock, Juliette stood frozen in her tracks and stared at the man crouching on one knee in front of her. His hair was longer than fashion decreed, and golden waves glinting with coppery strands fell over his forehead and partly obscured his face. But she caught a glimpse of angry eyes the deep, rich green of cottonwood leaves in the springtime.

Lyon regained his feet, still cradling his injured elbow. He shook his head to clear his clouded vision. Through the swirling mist, a young woman in a green velvet cloak watched him with dark, solemn eyes. He glanced hastily about, searching for the man who'd just saved his life, then back to the diminutive female in wonderment.

Little more than five feet in height, she appeared completely unruffled by the fact that a dead man lay in a pool of blood on the walkway with a knife buried to the hilt in his throat. Despite the mayhem she'd just witnessed, an aura of angelic serenity seemed to shimmer around her.

"Did you see who threw the knife?" Lyon gasped, his throat constricted with pain and shock.

"I did."

"Where'd he go?"

The slightest hint of amusement touched her lips, as though she found his predicament humorous. Her deep brown eyes glowed with calm self-assurance. "Do not look so concerned, Scotsman," she replied in a husky contralto. "You were in no danger from me. At this distance, there was no chance I would miss my target. And my target was not you."

Lyon frowned at her puzzling remark, but kept his over-taxed patience in check. She was a wee, bonny thing, and he didn't want to frighten her. If he shouted in his usual fashion, she'd probably dissolve into tears and run away without telling him who'd just saved his life.

She didn't seem very frightened at the moment, however. The cloak's fur-lined hood framed her face, its soft, white trim highlighting classic features of such arresting beauty, he blinked to be sure he wasn't hallucinating. With slightly almond-shaped eyes, high cheekbones, and a wide, generous mouth, she seemed as out of place on the drab streets of Edinburgh as a belly dancer from Cairo or a veiled harem slave from the bazaars of Marrakech.

For the space of a moment, he felt the sultry warmth of the Egyptian sun spread through him, as though he'd been transported to a place of mystery and enchantment.

Hell. Maybe he *had* been knocked out and was still unconscious.

He shook his head again and scowled ferociously. "How long have you been standing there, lass?"

"Long enough to see that you were in grave danger, sir. I had no choice but to act quickly. If there had been time to reflect, I would have merely wounded the scoundrel."

She spoke in a precise, deliberate manner with just a trace of a French accent. Or was it French? Whatever her origins, it was clear she hadn't fully understood his questions. Lyon tore his gaze away from the dark eyes watching him so intently and looked up and down the street in confusion for his rescuer.

There wasn't another soul in sight.

His senses told him no one but the dainty lassie could have hurled the blade, but his mind refused to accept such an incredible feat. He repeated the question slowly and distinctly, as though addressing an inattentive child.

"Who threw the knife?"

Chapter 2

At the lass's brilliant smile, Lyon's breath caught high in his chest. Her eyes fairly danced with elation.

"I did," she replied.

"What the—"

"Call the police!" a man yelled from a gabled window above them. "Someone call the police!"

A butler and chambermaid stepped cautiously from a nearby doorway to investigate the commotion. At the sight of the corpse, the ruddy-faced woman flung up her hands, shrieked to high heavens, and scurried back inside the house.

"Murder!" a housewife screamed at the top of her lungs.

Two constables came racing around the corner. They hurried over to the lifeless body sprawled on the cobblestones, then stared at Lyon. Despite his disheveled appearance, it took them only a moment to realize he was a member of the upper class, and they simultaneously touched their hats in a sign of respect.

The taller policeman rolled one end of his enormous handlebar mustache thoughtfully between his thumb and forefinger. "I'm Constable Findlay, sir." He motioned toward his partner. "This is Constable Beathy."

"What happened, sir?" the shorter constable asked.

"I was attacked by three robbers," Lyon answered, calmly dusting off his trousers. "Two of them escaped."

He jerked his head in the direction they'd taken as he straightened the cuffs of his ruffled linen shirt, then glanced down with indifference at the corpse in front of him. "This man wasn't so lucky."

While the policemen gazed inquisitively at the gruesome remains, a crowd of onlookers surrounded them, pushing and jostling one another to get a closer peek.

"Weel, sir, at least you got one of 'em," Beathy said. He scratched his pug nose complacently. "That's one miserable cutpurse who'll no' be stealin' again."

"I . . ." Lyon paused. Given that the homicide was justifiable, there was no need to involve the young lady in a police investigation. He'd thank her privately after the crowd dispersed. "Yes," he agreed with a humorless smile. "I was fortunate enough to have my knife on me."

Lyon reached down and retrieved the weapon, wiping the blade clean on the dead man's shirt. Its bone handle was carved with intricate figures. He looked out over the heads of the bystanders for the mysterious lass, only to find she'd vanished. Swearing softly under his breath, he shoved his way through the cluster of gawkers and glanced up and down the street.

Where in hell had she gone?

"We'll need to take a statement from you, sir," Findlay said. He paused, waiting politely for Lyon to introduce himself.

"MacLyon of Strathlyon."

"We'd greatly appreciate it, laird, if you'd come with us."

Lyon nodded absently. He scanned the houses, hoping for some clue to her whereabouts. She must have entered one of the nearer buildings, which meant she probably lived on this street. Or had come here this morning to visit a friend. She shouldn't be too hard to find, once he finished with the police. He'd get the formalities over with and then come back and thank her properly.

He slipped the strange knife into his pocket. Her skill

with the weapon had been nothing short of amazing. Yet what kind of female would be carrying a knife in the first place? Or have the courage and expertise to kill a man? Not a genteel young lady, that was certain.

As he accompanied the officers to the station house, Lyon wondered idly if the bonny petticoat was married or single. The memory of those velvety brown eyes brought a renewed sense of brightness and warmth, as though she'd carried a ray of sunlight concealed in her pocket.

What a peculiar thought.

He must have taken a harder knock on the head than he'd realized.

"Thank you so much for coming, Dr. MacDougall," Juliette said. "It is a pleasure to meet you at last." She shook his hand warmly, then sank down on the sofa, motioning for her visitor to sit beside her. "I feel I know you already from your wonderful letter."

The bluff, sandy-haired man who'd been ushered into the drawing room by her uncle returned her smile. His years in the desert sun had etched deep creases at the corners of his eyes. "The pleasure is all mine, Miss Elkheart," he replied as he took his place next to her on the sofa. "I'm happy to be of assistance."

In his mid-thirties, Dr. Keir MacDougall retained the posture and bearing of a soldier. Juliette's uncle had told her that he'd been an officer in the Army Medical Service and served in the Sudan, before resigning his commission to practice medicine in his home village of Strathbardine.

"My niece is very anxious to get started on her journey into the Highlands," Dr. Benjamin Robinson said, "though I surely do hate to see her leave." Born and raised in Lexington, he spoke with a soft Kentucky drawl.

Juliette met her uncle's perceptive eyes and immediately looked away, hoping he wouldn't notice how nervous and flustered she felt. Although her heart had finally returned to its normal rate and her racing pulse had slowed, she was still shaking inside. She clasped her trembling hands together, attempting to concentrate solely on the task of serving tea.

Ahahe! The Cheyenne exclamation of woe echoed in her mind. How could she possibly forget she'd killed a man?

"My mother sends her regrets that she couldn't come this afternoon as she'd planned," Dr. MacDougall said. "My sister's two girls have recently contracted the mumps, and Mother hopes to spend as much time with her grandchildren as possible before returning home. But we'll both meet you at Waverly Station on Wednesday morning, as we'd originally planned. Mother says to tell you that you're more than welcome to stay with us in Strathbardine. We've plenty of room."

"That is very kind of Mrs. MacDougall," Juliette replied. "But Lady MacLyon has already invited me to stay at the castle while I complete my research. She wrote to offer me unlimited use of the library there. I understand it is quite extensive."

"It is," he said. "Lady Hester has spent the last forty years studying the history of the clans. You'll find the dowager marchioness an expert on genealogy. And she knows everyone in the Highlands."

Suddenly, the image of the fierce Scottish warrior intruded on Juliette's thoughts. Was the man a Highlander? He hadn't worn a kilt. Still, Lady MacLyon might know him. The possibility of meeting the tall Scotsman again brought a shiver of anticipation.

Somehow, Juliette managed to pour the tea without spilling it all over Mrs. Meighan's freshly baked scones. And to her relief, the fragile, hand-painted china didn't rattle embarrassingly as she handed it to her guest. "Please express my thanks to your mother for her kind invitation, Dr. MacDougall."

"I wish you'd call me Keir." He smiled engagingly as he stirred the sugar and cream into his tea. "After all, you're probably a long-lost cousin."

"Very well," she said with a laugh. "But only if you will call me Julie."

"Done," he agreed. "I'm looking forward to introducing you to my fiancée, Miss Annie Buchanan." He took a sip, then set the cup and saucer down on the tea table in front of him. "Annie's also interested in the history of the Highlands. We both belong to the Scottish National Society, as does Lady Hester. The association has been planning a gathering of the local clans for months. You'll see more tartans in Strathbardine in the next few weeks than you'd normally see in a year."

"A gathering of the clans," her uncle repeated, clearly impressed. "Now that must be something to see."

"Could you come with us?" Juliette asked hopefully.

Dr. Robinson shook his head. "I wish I could, dearest. But I've come to Scotland to study the latest techniques in surgery, not to gallivant all over the countryside. I'm afraid you'll have to research your family tree by yourself."

"Well, no one knows more about Scottish genealogy than Lady Hester," Keir told them. "If anyone can help you trace your forebears, she can."

Uncle Benjamin came over to the cherry tea table and took the cup and saucer Juliette offered him. He dropped into a wing chair across from the sofa. "How long do you plan to be gone, dear?"

Juliette pursed her lips and shrugged. "For as long as it takes to trace my great-great-grandparents, I suppose. I do not expect to be away more than two or three weeks, at the most. It will depend upon where the trail leads me." She smiled gratefully at Keir MacDougall. "Thanks to you and my uncle, I have a place to start and every hope of succeeding."

Her guest's friendly eyes glowed with pleasure. "I've done no more than any MacDougall would have. I was just fortunate enough to be the one asked."

Uncle Benjamin had written to his future colleagues at the medical university in Edinburgh before he and Juliette had sailed from New York with her sister and grandfather, Senator Garrett Robinson. In his letter, he'd asked the doctors if they were acquainted with anyone named McDougall.

Keir had responded, writing that the spelling of her great-grandfather's name was probably an Americanization of his own surname, MacDougall. If such were the case and Miss Elkheart wanted more information about his clan, he could put her in touch with the knowledgeable Lady Hester MacLyon.

Juliette hoped to establish a connection between the lavender and pink blanket she'd brought with her, and what she'd seen in her terrifying vision—if there was a connection. Sometimes the true meaning could be misinterpreted, so the dream might have nothing to do with her ancestors. Still, she had to try to find out, if only to quiet the ghosts that haunted her.

"Dr. Robinson tells me that, besides genealogy, you're also interested in medicine," Keir said.

Juliette leaned closer, unable to conceal her excitement. "I am to begin my studies at the University of Pennsylvania in the spring. Once I receive my four-year degree, I hope to be accepted as the first female student in their school of veterinary science."

MacDougall's sandy brows lifted in amazement. He'd probably expected her to say she wanted to be another Florence Nightingale. "Veterinary medicine! That's quite an unusual goal for a young lady."

"I was raised on a horse ranch in Alberta," she explained. "I have helped my parents deliver colts and fillies, calves, and lambs since I was a youngster." At his incredulous stare, she chuckled. "Women healers are not uncommon among my father's people, and working with horses comes as second nature to us. I also learned a great deal about medicinal plants and herbs from my great-grandmother, Porcupine Quills."

"You don't say," Keir murmured, his pale lashes shielding his downcast eyes. He took a bite of scone, then washed it down with a gulp of tea, his prominent Adam's apple bobbing comically. The Scottish doctor seemed so astonished by what she'd just told him, Juliette was afraid he'd choke on the pastry's fine crumbs.

"Julie has a special gift for treating sick animals," Uncle Benjamin said, coming to her rescue. "We're hoping that with her grandfather's influence and mine, we can succeed in enrolling her in the veterinary school in Philadelphia. Of course, she'll have to complete her undergraduate work at the top of her class, but I've no doubt she can do that."

When Keir started to cough, Juliette and her uncle jumped to their feet. Their guest politely waved them away. His eyes watering, he looked up and met their worried gazes. "I'm really quite all right," he assured them. "I was just thinking what a lovely addition you'll make to our Strathshire Gathering, Julie. I can hardly wait to introduce you to everyone in our village . . . and at Strathlyon Castle, as well."

Juliette sat back down beside him. There was something in Dr. MacDougall's strangled voice . . . some secret amusement she didn't quite understand. *Hesc!* When had she ever understood the *veho* and his curious, unpredictable ways?

After saying good-bye to their visitor, Juliette walked arm-in-arm with her uncle down the narrow hallway that led to the back of the house. "I have been wanting to talk to you alone since this morning," she said as they entered his study. "But I did not wish to disturb you while you were reading your medical journal."

"What is it, sugarplum?" he asked. Sensing her hesitation, he peered at her intently. "Is something wrong?"

"Nakhan," Juliette began, addressing him with the respectful Cheyenne title that meant her mother's brother. "I . . ." She took a deep breath, exhaled it slowly, and finished in a rush. "I killed a man this morning."

Clasping her shoulders, Uncle Benjamin turned her to face him. "You . . . *what*? Are you all right?"

"Yes," she assured him, his shock deepening her sense of guilt. "I am perfectly fine."

He gestured to the window seat nearby. "Let's sit over there, and you can tell me exactly what happened."

They sank down on the leather cushion together, and he listened in stunned silence as she related the morning's extraordinary events.

"You were very courageous, Vehona," Uncle Benjamin said. The pet name, meaning "princess," had been bestowed on Juliette by her father because of her serene Cheyenne ways.

"But that does not assuage my feelings of remorse. I should have merely wounded the evil-doer and let him face whatever punishment such a crime demands. But for some unexplainable reason, the despicable attack on such a brave fighter wiped out every other thought from my mind. I had to save his life."

Her uncle touched the tip of her nose with his finger admonishingly. "You did exactly the right thing, Julie. Don't ever think otherwise." The admiration in his voice made it clear he approved of her actions, no matter how uncertain she felt. "If you hadn't acted instinctively, an innocent man would be lying in his coffin right now."

She gave a half-hearted smile as she traced a flower on the printed material of her skirt with the tip of one finger. "I hope you are right, *nakhan*. The moment I heard the tall Scotsman say he'd killed his attacker, I slipped away in the fog." She looked up and met her uncle's sympathetic gaze. "I did not want to contradict the man's story. Not when the officers appeared to believe it."

"If the gentleman chose to take the blame, why quibble?" Uncle Benjamin said, patting her hand. "It was undoubtedly his way of repaying you. I think he wanted to shield you from any further unpleasantness."

"I was quaking inside afterwards," she confided, "but

Cheyenne women do not scream in the face of danger and scamper away like frightened rabbits. So I pretended to be unperturbed by the entire confrontation.''

His hazel eyes twinkling, Uncle Benjamin grinned at her. ''I've seen you at your most aloof, unflappable self, sugarplum. The fellow you saved must have been positively discombobulated by your composure.''

Juliette laughed in agreement. Even as a little girl, she'd had the ability to hide her inner feelings behind a wall of unfailing self-control.

''The disbelief on the Scotsman's face *was* rather amusing,'' she admitted. ''As my mother would say, he looked more confounded than a passel of preachers caught in a boardinghouse brawl. ''

''It's a shame you didn't learn his name. What did this brave gentleman look like?''

Juliette tipped her head to one side thoughtfully. ''The man was truly magnificent. He fought the evil-makers with the courage of a Red Shield warrior. If it had not been for his previous injury, he could have easily vanquished all three of his attackers without any help from me. He was like a wounded mountain lion,'' she added, half to herself.

''A mountain lion?''

''Yes. Ferocious, in spite of his impairment. His hair was a dark reddish-gold, the color of a lion's fur. And he had the greenest eyes imaginable. Until this morning, I had never seen anyone as tall and massively built as my father. But in spite of his great size, the Scotsman moved with the effortless grace of *nanoseham*, the mountain lion.''

''A veritable conquering hero. Why didn't you tell me about all this before now?''

Juliette met her uncle's quizzical gaze and smiled sheepishly. ''I was afraid you would change your mind about letting me visit the Highlands without you.''

''Good Lord, I have no worries about your going with Dr. MacDougall and his mother,'' Uncle Benjamin said. ''I trust your common sense, Julie. I know you'll always behave in a prudent, practical manner."

"Everyone in the family takes it for granted that I will always behave in a responsible manner," she replied with a frown. "But walking alone down a deserted street in a strange city was not a very prudent, practical thing to do."

"Your family also knows that in a crisis you'll react with an unerring instinct for survival. Which is exactly what you did today." He slipped his arm around her shoulders and gave her an affectionate squeeze. "I'm very proud of you, Vehona. Your parents would be proud of you, too."

A feeling of relief spread through her. "Thank you, *nakhan*."

"Maybe you'll see this mountain lion again," he suggested with a chuckle. "The poor fellow's probably wandering the streets of Edinburgh right now, wondering who the devil you are and where in blue blazes you disappeared to. I'm sure he'd like to thank you for saving his life."

Juliette shook her head. "The foolish *veho* did not even believe it was I who had thrown the knife. He kept looking around for his rescuer, but could find no one on the street except one small, helpless female. Me."

Uncle Benjamin threw his head back and laughed. "Obviously the big Scotsman's never met a Cheyenne warrior-woman before."

Juliette grinned. "Obviously not."

Chapter 3

~~~~~~~~~~~~~~~~~~~~~

"**T**ell us again, Uncle Lyon!" Jamie shouted as he raced into the drawing room. "Tell us about the lassie who saved your life!"

Neil followed on his younger brother's heels. "Yes, please! Tell us!"

Setting the newspaper aside, Lyon ruffled Jamie's thick black hair, then lifted the boy up on his knee. "Shh," he warned them softly. He put his arm around Neil's shoulders and drew him closer. "You two try to be quiet, for once. Nana is sleeping."

Six-year-old Neil shot a dubious glance at the dowager seated in a wing chair nearby. Her snowy head was resting against its high back, her eyes closed. The pair of half glasses she wore to do stitchery lay in her lap.

Neil leaned closer to whisper in his uncle's ear. "We want to hear the story again, please."

Lady Hester opened one eye and peeked at them. "I'm not asleep in the middle of the day," she announced, as though she'd been accused of stealing flowers from the kirkyard. "There's no need to whisper. And all of you should be speaking Gaelic."

Lyon smiled indulgently at his grandmother. The eighty-year-old matriarch insisted that her family converse in Gaelic whenever they were within the confines of Strathlyon Castle. It was her way of insuring that their Celtic

23

heritage wouldn't die out. Although there were still villages scattered throughout the Highlands where the ancient tongue was spoken, each succeeding generation used it less and less.

"Nana is correct," Lyon instructed his nephews. "Both of you scamps should be upstairs in the schoolroom right now practicing your lessons with Mr. Dittmar. And you've heard the story of the mysterious lady at least three times, if not more."

At that moment, Lyon's younger brother strolled into the room. Tossing his riding crop on a side table, Rob sprawled his long limbs on the sofa. His high jockey boots were covered with dust, his bright red hair disheveled from his recent gallop. He grinned as he brushed the unruly curls off his forehead. "You must admit, Lyon, the whole tale seems a mite unbelievable. You can't blame us for wanting to hear it all over again, just to be sure we've got it right."

Neil tugged impatiently on Lyon's sleeve. "Tell us again what the lassie looked like."

"She was small."

Jamie squirmed, his five-year-old body quivering with excitement. "Didn't you see her throw the knife?"

"No."

Neil studied his uncle with skeptical eyes. "Then how do you know she threw it?"

"It had to be her," Lyon explained succinctly. "No one else was there."

Jamie braced his hand on Lyon's shoulder and gazed up in fascination. "Was she beautiful?"

"Aye, she was bonny," he admitted with casual indifference.

Rob snorted, clearly enjoying his older brother's discomfiture.

Since that day nearly a week ago when she'd saved his life, Lyon hadn't been able to get the remarkable lass out of his mind. The image of her dark eyes, shining with amusement at his expense, haunted his dreams. Only last night he'd awakened, his sex swollen and heavy, to experience an intense frustration at finding himself alone in bed. His heart pounded unaccountably, and he could have sworn he'd heard her husky contralto murmuring his name.

He remembered with vivid clarity the few words she'd spoken in her odd, yet enchanting, way.

"Did you try real, real hard to find her?" Jamie queried, although he already knew the answer.

"I spent three days searching house-to-house, up and down half the streets of Edinburgh," Lyon told his nephews. "I couldn't find a single soul who knew her whereabouts. I even put an announcement in *The Scotsman* with no results."

Propping his elbow on the arm of Lyon's chair, Neil rested his chin on his palm and gave a low, exasperated whistle. "I wish you'd found her, Uncle Lyon. She could have taught me how to throw a knife."

"I wish I'd found her, too," Lyon acknowledged ruefully.

The thought that he'd never see the lass again left him more and more irritable each day. He felt as though he'd been cheated of something. Something he had the right to possess. After all, she *had* saved his life; she should have stayed around long enough for him to thank her. And learn her name. His mental tension had spread through every muscle in his body, till he was one tight knot of male aggression. Several members of the household were beginning to tiptoe around him, certain his war injury must be to blame for his increasingly foul mood.

One family member didn't appear the least disturbed, however. Untroubled by Lyon's scowl, Rob folded his hands behind his head and relaxed against the tufted sofa pillow. "I'm not surprised that she was so lovely. All ladies in fairy tales are supposed to beautiful. How could we expect anything less of yours?"

Jamie bounced up and down on Lyon's knee. "Is she a fairy?" he demanded. "Cook says your lassie's a fairy,

Uncle Lyon. That's why she disappeared right from under your nose. Cook says your spry, wee lassie is a fairy.''

"First of all, she's not my lassie," Lyon said. "And secondly, there's no such thing as fairies. They're an ignorant Highland superstition, the same as planting rowan trees beside a cottage gate to ward off evil spirits. If you two boys are going to learn your lessons from the kitchen staff, I'm going to dismiss your tutor and pocket the money for his salary, myself. I could use a new hunting rifle.''

"Yea!" Neil shouted. His blue eyes glowed in exultation. "Let Mr. Dittmar go and buy a new gun, instead.''

Jamie giggled ecstatically at his older brother's cleverness. "Let him go! Buy a gun!"

"Stuff and nonsense," Lady Hester admonished as she settled her glasses on the bridge of her nose. "Mr. Dittmar has the patience of a saint to put up with you rapscallions.'' She picked up the embroidery hoop that had fallen to the floor while she napped, then paused and eyed the boys thoughtfully. "Where's your mother, by the way?"

"Mama's lying down in her room," Neil answered. "We gave her a headache.''

Lyon exchanged a knowing glance with the dowager marchioness. His widowed sister-in-law suffered from what genteel ladies called the megrims. The plain truth was Flora spent more time moping over what she couldn't have and didn't need, than most people spent completing their daily chores.

"She'll feel better tomorrow," Lady Hester assured them. "Dr. MacDougall's going to bring us a special visitor, and you know how your mother loves to have company.'' She glanced over at the spindle-shanked man who'd appeared in the doorway only moments before. "Ah, Mr. Dittmar. Looking for your two charges, I suppose.''

Colin Dittmar threw back his narrow shoulders and ran his fingers through his thinning hair. "Yes, Lady Hester, I am. I turned my back for no more than a second, and they were gone. I mistakenly went to search the stables first.''

"Go with Mr. Dittmar now," Lyon ordered his nephews. "I'll tell you the story of the mysterious lassie again after supper."

"Promise?" asked Neil.

"Promise!" insisted Jamie.

"I promise."

"And if you work very hard at your Gaelic this afternoon," Lady Hester added, "you may join us at tea time tomorrow to meet our guest." She smiled as though she were offering a bag of rock candy or a fistful of licorice.

The boys exchanged looks of mutual disgust and bounded out of the room, their tutor in hot pursuit.

"Hah!" Rob said. "That'll guarantee their absence for the entire day. They'll sneak out to the stables first thing in the morning, saddle their ponies, and won't be seen again till dusk."

Lady Hester pursed her lips in disapproval, but didn't bother to argue the point. The only person the boys ever listened to was their Uncle Lyon. Though he was their legal guardian and head of the family, he rarely admonished James's two sons.

"Just who is this visitor Keir's bringing tomorrow?" Lyon questioned with mild interest. He picked up the paper once again to check the box in the lower corner of the last page.

> Seeking young woman who lost knife with uniquely
> carved bone handle on the morning of 12 September
> in Edinburgh. Please contact editor of this newspaper
> for its return.

"Nana's invited a woman from America who's come to the Highlands in search of her Scottish ancestry," his brother replied.

Lyon peered at his grandmother over the top of his paper. "Some idiotic matron who's financing her interest in genealogy with her rich husband's money?"

"Whether she's rich or not, I haven't the least notion," Lady Hester said, unruffled by his cynical tone. "She is, however, not a matron, but an unmarried lady." She gazed at her eldest grandson through narrowed eyes. "And as chief of Clan MacLyon, I expect you to be here to welcome Miss Elkheart when she comes."

Lyon rose to his feet, the folded newspaper secured beneath his arm. "I'll let Robbie do the honors." He favored his brother with a smug grin. "You can show our American guest around the castle. Give her a whirlwind tour of the battlements, a fast peek into the armory, and send the spinster on her merry way."

"I'm afraid that won't be possible," his brother replied with an equally complacent smirk. "She'll be staying with us for several weeks."

"Whatever for?"

Their grandmother looked up from her stitching. "Miss Elkheart is going to do some genealogical research in our library. Naturally, I extended an invitation for her to stay at the castle. There's no sense in her traipsing back and forth from Strathbardine every day. I trust you have no objections?"

"Hell, I don't care if she spends the winter," Lyon said. "Just don't expect me to entertain her."

Knowing it was useless to argue, Lady Hester looked pointedly at Rob, who threw up his hands in surrender. "All right! All right!" he conceded with a laugh. "I'll uphold the reputation of the MacLyon clan and extend our gracious hospitality. Besides, I've never met a Yankee spinster before."

"I have," Lyon said. "In London. The old battle-ax had a voice that could cut glass and a chin nearly as pointed as her inquisitive nose."

"Ah, well, who's to say?" his brother replied with an easygoing shrug. "This particular American might turn out to be quite charming."

"Charming or not, she's your responsibility," Lyon

stated. "Just let me know when she's finally gone. And by the way, I'll be leaving for Edinburgh the day after tomorrow."

This time his grandmother couldn't conceal her exasperation. "You just came back from there."

Lyon suspected she knew exactly what he did when he visited the city. "I left some unfinished business," he told her lamely.

Rob chortled. "And we all know what that business is."

Lyon shot him a warning glance.

His brother's eyes glinted with mischief. "I assume you're going to continue the search for the missing lady."

"As a matter of fact," Lyon retorted loftily, "I'm going to see a surgeon at the university. Keir asked a colleague to take a look at my elbow and see if he thinks the fragment can be removed."

Lady Hester's face crinkled with joy. "At last!"

"Don't get your hopes up," Lyon warned her. "This is only a preliminary examination."

"Keir told you months ago it could be removed," she scolded. "I don't know why you've refused to have a surgeon so much as look at you."

Lyon started for the door. He had no intention of seeing any bloody quack. He'd had enough of doctors and their torturous, bungling ways. And what right did he have to become a whole man again, when James lay rotting in the ground? His hand on the latch, he turned and looked back at them. The unspoken concern in their eyes only stiffened his resolve.

"Don't worry if I miss our visitor from America," he said, purposely misinterpreting their painful silence. "At least without me here, there's no one who'll tell her the brutal truth: that the Scots are a treacherous, cantankerous lot, who'd rather fight each other than nobody at all. This way, she'll return home with all her romantical notions about the Highlands still intact."

*   *   *

From high on a summit, the majestic castle overlooked the Vale of Ardchattan with its picturesque hamlet nestled against the sea loch. The castle's eight-foot-thick granite walls had been built in medieval times to withstand the siege of an entire army. Rounded turrets on the twin towers, gun loops along the walls, and banners flying from the battlements proclaimed its heroic past.

Juliette felt as though she'd stepped into the pages of a history book.

"Scottish castles were always built at strategic locations," Robert MacLyon told her with pride. The rays of the afternoon sun bounced off his coppery hair as he made a grand gesture across the length of the valley below to the range of craggy mountain peaks in the distance. "This site was chosen for its natural defenses. My ancestors knew that the family who controlled this castle could hold the entire area from Ben Meean to Ardmucknish Bay."

She listened in fascination as her host pointed out the architectural details of his family's home. She'd taken an instant liking to the handsome young man. His warm, outgoing ways reminded Juliette of her impetuous sister. Wishing Jennie could be there to share the day's marvelous adventure, she followed him down the winding stone stairway that led to a cobbled courtyard.

Dr. MacDougall was waiting for them at the bottom of the steps. "Well, what do you think of Strathlyon?" he asked with an expectant smile.

She tipped her head back and gazed up at the flag snapping in the breeze overhead. On its azure background, a golden lion with its front claws bared stood on hind feet and snarled ferociously. "The castle is truly marvelous. I only wish I knew more about the history of Scotland."

Robert MacLyon chuckled. His friendly eyes were the silvery blue of lupine shimmering in a mountain meadow. "After you spend a few days with my grandmother, you'll know more than you ever wanted to know about our violent past."

The trio walked through an opening in a boxwood hedge and into a flower garden profuse with tiger lilies, scarlet poppies, ox-eye daisies, and roses. The heavy, overblown blooms of late summer, with their fallen petals scattered across the ground, filled the air with a sweet perfume.

Juliette sat down on a stone bench with Keir, while Robert paused beside a doorway leading to a glassed-in summer room and spoke briefly with a servant.

"We're expected in the drawing room for tea," her host said as he came over to join them. "Lady Hester and Flora are there waiting for us now."

"Thank you for the wonderful tour, Mr. MacLyon," Juliette said.

His ready grin was contagious. "I insist that you call me Rob."

"Well, I—"

He held up his hand before she could say another word. "I heard you calling Keir by his first name earlier, and I won't allow you to stand on ceremony with me. You'll be treated as one of the family during your visit. We can't go around 'Mr.' and 'Miss-ing' each other for the next three weeks."

"I appreciate your kindness, Rob," she agreed, returning his smile. "But I do not intend to interrupt your schedule while I am here. I have taken up too much of your time already."

He waved his hand in dismissal. "It's always a pleasure to show a guest around this pile of old stones. Today, it's been more than a pleasure. It's been an absolute delight having such an avid and intelligent listener."

"I warned you he could be devilishly charming," Keir said, shaking his head indulgently.

"I can't help being charming," Rob countered. "I was born that way."

Juliette laughed at their friendly banter. "Well, your gracious and charming hospitality is sincerely appreciated."

*   *   *

Lyon tugged off his gloves and slapped at his dusty riding breeches. He'd visited several crofters that morning to discuss the coming harvest, then ridden through the fields of ripening oats and hay. When he'd left his hunter in the stables, he'd seen Keir MacDougall's bay mare and rig and knew their visitor from America had arrived.

Lyon made a beeline through the solarium, heading for the hallway that led to the back stairs. He'd change his clothes and join the visitors in the drawing room. In spite of yesterday's refusal to even greet Miss Elkheart, he couldn't disappoint his grandmother. One afternoon of polite chatter over tea, however, was all the American was going to get.

As Lyon passed an open doorway that led to the flower garden, he slowed at the infectious sound of laughter. Keir's hearty boom rang out, accompanied by his brother's carefree guffaws. But it was the feminine laughter, low and husky, that brought Lyon to a dead halt. Stunned, he stood and waited, unashamedly eavesdropping on their conversation.

"I apologize for my brother's absence," Rob told their guests. "The laird had to ride out early this morning to see about estate affairs and will likely be gone all day. He'll be sorry to have missed you."

"There is no need to apologize," the unseen woman replied. "I do not want to inconvenience anyone during my stay at the castle."

Lyon smiled as he recognized that tantalizingly familiar accent, and a mixture of joy and relief surged through him. That wasn't the spinster from America; it was the dark-eyed lass from Edinburgh who'd saved his life. She must have seen his notice and contacted *The Scotsman*. Instead of merely taking her name and address as instructed, the fool editor had sent her to Strathlyon Castle.

The bonny, wee petticoat was here.

In his home.

Lyon pivoted and strode into the garden. He hoped to

hell the tempting little morsel wasn't married. Suspicious husbands tended to complicate things.

Seated with her back to Lyon, the young woman held a folded parasol in one gloved hand, its point resting in the garden's rich, black earth. She was gazing up at Robbie, who hovered over her as though she were a speckled trout rising to the bait. An icy prickle of jealousy snaked through Lyon's gut at the unabashed delight shining in his brother's eyes.

Dammit, he'd nip *that* flirtation in the bud right now. He'd advertised for her in the newspaper. She belonged to *him*.

At that moment, Rob caught sight of Lyon. "Well, well, it seems as though I'm wrong once again," he said to the lass, making no effort to hide his amusement. "Here's the laird, after all. Julie, may I present the chief of Clan MacLyon?"

"How do you do," Lyon said as he moved to stand directly in front of her. "I'd almost given up hope of your seeing my advertisement."

At the sight of those dewy brown eyes, his heart reeled in eager anticipation. The delicate, ethereal quality he'd found so mesmerizing glimmered about her like a halo of fairy dust. It was all he could do not to reach out and touch her smooth cheek, just to be sure she was really there.

The lass sprang up from the bench and, for an instant, seemed to hover in midair, trembling and graceful as an arrow in flight.

Beneath a jaunty sailor hat, her braided chignon shone like polished wood in the sunlight, a dark, gleaming mahogany. She wore a stylish walking suit, and her figure, no longer concealed by a cloak, was every bit as enticing as he'd imagined in the dark, quiet hours of the night. She was lithe and firm and succulent as a ripe peach.

Lust seeped through Lyon's veins to pool in his groin. His entire body tightened in expectation.

God, she'd be a perfect little mouthful in bed.

Chapter 4

~~~~⟳⟳~~~~

Juliette was dumbfounded.

The laird of Strathlyon was none other than the magnificent male whose life she'd saved in Edinburgh! Up close, he loomed even larger and more impressive than she'd remembered. Despite her natural wariness of strangers, something inside her responded to his undeniable manliness. A tingling of excitement set her heart thrumming. She quickly hid her capricious emotions and tipped her head in polite acknowledgment of the introduction.

"Laird MacLyon," she said softly, "how nice to meet you, at last."

"I gave our guest a tour of the battlements as you suggested," Rob announced a little too loudly. He stepped closer, his elbow jostling MacLyon in the ribs. "We were just about to join the rest of the family for tea."

Lyon shot his brother a quelling glance. "Why don't you and Keir join the ladies, while the lass and I get better acquainted?"

Not the least deterred, Rob shook his head. "No, no, you go on," he cheerfully insisted, never taking his eyes off her. "You can change out of your riding clothes, while Keir and I escort Julie inside. We'll meet you in the drawing room."

Keir, who'd risen from the bench to stand beside the slender girl, looked from one MacLyon to the other, a smile of fascination hovering about his mouth. He'd never seen the two of them spar over a ladybird before. Although Lyon was usually pulsing and hot for whatever toothsome nymph happened to be closest at hand, the differences in the two brothers' ages had, until that moment, precluded their scrapping over territorial rights.

Lyon promptly switched to Gaelic. "Go away," he told his brother through a tight smile. "And take MacDougall with you."

"It's nice to see you, too," Keir replied in English. He knew exactly what Lyon had said. He'd shared lessons in the Celtic tongue with Lyon and James when they were boys.

Rob grinned pugnaciously and stood his ground. "I saw her first," he rejoined in Gaelic. "Besides, you said yesterday you didn't even want to meet the old battle-ax."

"What the devil are you talking about?"

"Our American visitor. Remember? You said I should do the honors. You didn't want to be bothered with some prying Yankee spinster who'd come to the Highlands with romantical notions of finding her Scottish heritage."

"Gentlemen," Keir interrupted in English, "don't you think you should—"

"This isn't the old maid from America, you ass," Lyon told his brother. "This is the young woman who saved my life."

"The hell she is," Rob protested. "Miss Elkheart's come here at our grandmother's invitation to study genealogy."

Taken aback, Lyon looked over at Keir for confirmation.

"That's correct," MacDougall said, switching to Gaelic at last. "And I suggest both you idiots shut up before the poor lass bolts and runs all the way back to Edinburgh."

Miss Elkheart stood rooted to the spot. Two red blotches stained her high cheekbones, and her dark eyes glittered dangerously. She clenched the parasol handle in both hands, as though she'd like to whack them over the head with it. She was clearly appalled at their display of bad manners by conversing in a language she couldn't comprehend.

The brothers met the young lady's stricken gaze and belatedly attempted an apology. "Please forgive our atrocious lapse in decorum," Rob begged.

"We had a slight disagreement," Lyon told her, "which it's just as well you didn't understand."

Juliette had understood every obnoxious word the man had uttered. Although she couldn't speak Gaelic fluently, she'd studied it enough to follow their conversation.

Haxc! The Cheyenne exclamation for annoyance echoed in her mind. How could she have thought MacLyon as admirable as a Red Shield warrior? He had the despicable manners of a rattlesnake.

She hid her indignation behind an aloof smile, and slipped her hand into the crook of Keir's elbow.

"I trust the disagreement has been satisfactorily resolved, gentlemen," she cooed. "But in any case, I think I shall have Dr. MacDougall escort me into the drawing room."

The interior of the castle had been renovated many times through the ages. In its present splendor, it looked more like a palace than a military stronghold. Juliette could see the influence of French Empire mixed with touches of the Jacobean and Regency periods. Here and there stood heavy carved pieces dating back to the Middle Ages. Whatever else MacLyon's ancestors had or hadn't done, they'd managed to hold on to their wealth over the centuries.

Lady Hester and Flora awaited them in a charming salon with sofas and chairs covered in brightly flowered prints, lamp tables stacked with magazines and books, and Chinese vases filled with bouquets of red, yellow, and white roses.

"I thought we'd explore the resources of our library tomorrow, Miss Elkheart," Lady Hester said, after the introductions had been completed. "This afternoon, I'd like you to get to know all the members of our family." She paused to study MacLyon over the top of her half-spectacles, taking in his dust-stained riding outfit with a lift of her thin white brows. "I see you've already been getting acquainted with my grandsons."

"Yes," Juliette replied. "Rob showed me the view from the battlements. And the laird was kind enough to join us in the garden afterwards."

She met MacLyon's bold gaze and sent him a sugar-coated smile. She was determined not to reveal her displeasure at what she'd overheard. Or the strange twinge of apprehension that had pinged down her spine as he'd followed her into his home. She'd felt his eyes scrutinizing her backside with a leisurely thoroughness that made her nerves tingle all the way to her toes. The moment they'd crossed the threshold, she'd had the uncanny feeling of stepping inside a trap and hearing the bolt snap shut.

The Scottish laird didn't take a seat like everyone else in the room, but continued to stand, one broad shoulder propped negligently against a tall cabinet. He folded his arms across his chest and watched her from beneath hooded lids. His thick, straight lashes, the color of dark rust, made his green eyes glitter like icicles. The rugged angles of his face seemed chiseled out of the same unyielding granite as his castle. His blunt-cut soldier's nose had been broken once, if not twice, and a scar was etched across the cleft of his chin.

At the irrefutable proof of his past drubbings, Juliette felt a flutter of relief. He wasn't as invincible as he'd like her to believe.

"We're so delighted to have you stay with us," Flora said with a contagious giggle. "I've never met an American before."

In her mid-twenties, the ebony-haired woman wore a rose satin gown fashioned in the latest mode with a poufed bustle riding atop her round derriere. She had the soft curves and milky skin so admired by gentlemen with walrus mustaches and fat cigars.

"Actually, I am a Canadian citizen," Juliette replied.

Lady Hester cocked her snowy head in surprise. "We understood that your uncle was originally from Lexington."

Juliette nodded. "Yes, both Uncle Benjamin and my grandfather, Senator Garrett Robinson, are from Kentucky. And my mother was born in the Cumberland Mountains. But I was raised in Alberta."

"Alberta!" Flora sighed dramatically. Her jet eyes took on a dreamy, faraway look. "That sounds so romantic."

"I grew up on a horse ranch near Medicine Hat," Juliette told the pretty brunette with a smile. "When I was fourteen, I was sent to Washington, D.C., to spend the winters with my grandfather. While I was there, I attended a school in the French embassy."

"That explains the slight trace of a French accent," MacLyon remarked.

Though his words were courteous and sociable, his gaze seared her. Juliette flushed beneath its scorching heat. She wondered if his family were aware of the sensuality that blazed in the green depths of his eyes, or if she was the only one conscious of the intense scrutiny he was lavishing on his guest.

"Yes. I learned to speak English from my schoolmistress, Madame Benét, who was born in Paris," she explained in a breathless voice. She tore her gaze from his and stared down at the kid gloves lying in her lap. Her chest felt suddenly heavy, as though he were pressing against it with his large, implacable hand.

The tall Scotsman's phenomenal effect upon her brought a surge of unfamiliar self-consciousness. Juliette prided herself on her serene detachment from any gentleman's unwanted attentions. How he'd discovered a crack in her composure astounded and dismayed her.

Thankfully, Lady Hester chose that moment to pour the tea, and Flora helped serve the raspberry tarts. The soft clink of spoons against china momentarily took the place of conversation.

"Here we are!" a child's voice called out in the stillness.

"We're all ready to meet our guest!" another one piped.

Juliette looked across the room to find two boys standing side by side in the open doorway. The taller one's eyes gleamed the pale blue of a robin's egg beneath a mop of red curls like his Uncle Rob. The younger boy, whose straight hair matched Flora's silken tresses, had the bright, inquisitive eyes of a black-capped chickadee.

They were dressed in their Sunday best, their faces scrubbed, their hair combed back from their high foreheads, their shoes shined to a waxy glow. She had the distinct impression that their spit-and-polish appearance was strictly for her sake; the two of them radiated boundless energy and unfailing high spirits.

"Uh-oh, here comes trouble," Rob warned with a grin.

"These are my great-grandsons," Lady Hester said, her voice ringing with pride. "Neil and Jamie, come say hello to Miss Elkheart."

"I'm Neil," the older one declared as he came over and blithely accepted Juliette's hand. "I'm six." He jabbed his thumb toward his brother. "Jamie's five."

Juliette shook Jamie's small hand in turn. "I have been looking forward to meeting you both," she said. "Dr. MacDougall told me about you."

Neil darted a quick glance at the physician, apparently surprised that Keir had found anything to say that would make her eager to meet them. Their uninhibited ways reminded Juliette of her own childhood. Her parents had taught their children by example and encouragement, not by physical punishment as the *veho* so often did. She'd heard white people say that to spare the rod was to spoil the child. That was not the Cheyenne way.

Jamie took the compliment as his due and crowded closer. He tapped her on the knee to get her full attention. "Neil's got a loose tooth," he confided. He tried without success to rock one of his own front teeth back and forth with his thumb. "Mine won't budge."

"Let me see," she said. When he opened his mouth, she attempted to move the tooth gently with the pad of her forefinger. "You are right," she concurred. "You will have to be patient and wait till you are older."

"Try mine," Neil urged.

Juliette complied, giving him a smile of admiration as she felt his wiggle. "Yes, I can feel it move. It will soon come out."

"Boys!" Flora gasped. She jumped to her feet with a swish of taffeta underskirts and fluttered about like a prairie hen ruffling its feathers. "Whatever can you be thinking of? Miss Elkheart isn't interested in your teeth."

"Please do not scold them," Juliette said. "I have a ten-year-old brother. I am used to checking loose teeth."

"What's his name?" Jamie asked.

"His name is Moxtaveano Eeveha, which means Black Hawk Flying."

Neil screwed his eyes up in deliberation. "What kind of a name is that?"

"Miss Elkheart is part Cheyenne," Keir told the boys. "She comes from Alberta, Canada, near the town of Medicine Hat."

They stared at her with a combination of awe and delight.

Juliette knew they had no idea what it meant, but they couldn't have been more impressed if the doctor had said she came from the moon. A quick glance at Flora told her their mother felt the same way. What the rest of the family thought wasn't nearly so easy to tell.

"Do you have any more brothers or sisters?" Neil queried.

"I have a twin sister, Jennifer. Her Cheyenne name is Vonahenene or Morning Rose."

"What's yours?" asked Jamie.

Juliette smiled at his frank curiosity. "My name is Hetoevahotohke, which means Evening Star."

Neil leaned against the arm of her chair and gave a long,

appreciative whistle. "Wow! I wish I had a name like that."

With a twinge of envy, Lyon watched his nephews charm Miss Juliette Evening Star Elkheart. She seemed to like everyone in his family.

Everyone except him.

And dammit, he liked everything about her, from the top of her saucy straw hat to the pointed toes of her button shoes. Those soft nutmeg eyes, framed by incredibly long ebony lashes, sent his heart rate soaring. The perfect correctness of her English enchanted him, the words sounding precise and aristocratic, and the soft-spoken Cheyenne language had a definite effect on his ability to breathe. If he didn't guard against it, he could easily fall victim to her undeniable charms.

Lyon knew Rob and Keir were vastly amused at his extraordinary reaction to the young lady. But Miss Elkheart seemed to have taken a sudden, unexplained aversion to him. If he didn't know better, he'd think she understood their earlier conversation in Gaelic.

What the devil did it matter whether she liked him or not?

His plans to seduce the little brown-eyed lass had just been blown to hell and gone. She was a guest in his home, a refined, educated young lady invited by his grandmother to conduct genealogical research on the Highland clans. It didn't matter if he woke up in bed every night as randy as a raw recruit on his first furlough. She was strictly off-limits.

And the sooner she left Strathlyon Castle, the better for both of them.

Lyon straightened and moved away from the high walnut secretary he'd been leaning against. He walked to the center of the room where he could command his family's full attention.

"I have a surprise for all of you," he announced. "Miss Elkheart is the mysterious lady who saved my life."

Everyone started talking at once, till he finally signaled for silence. "It's true," he assured them. He met Juliette's wary gaze. "I never thanked you properly," he said, moving to stand over her, where she sat on the loveseat. "That was an extremely brave thing to do."

He took her small hand in his big one, brought it to his lips, and kissed the smooth, oval fingertips. He caught the scent of wildflowers in his nostrils, and his body tautened with sexual need. A need he was determined to extinguish by whatever ruthless means were in his power.

A hush descended on the room. Not even the chink of cups and saucers broke the spell. She gazed up at him with utter serenity, and the unplumbed depths of her velvety eyes seemed to offer a man the balm of abiding peace and unending joy. Like a soldier mortally wounded on the field, Lyon felt the wrenching ache of what could never be. Cold dread knotted in his chest, as though foretelling the lonely emptiness to come. For he was a man who deserved neither peace nor joy.

As he released her hand and stepped back, Neil's clear, innocent voice rang out. "Uncle Lyon has your knife, Miss Elkheart."

"You do?" Her features lit up at the unexpected news.

"Aye. In fact, that's why I put a notice in *The Scotsman*," he lied. "I hoped to return it to you. I assumed you'd want the weapon back. The unusual carving on the handle makes it appear quite valuable."

"Thank you! My father made the knife for me. I was certain I had lost it for good."

"Will you teach me how to throw it?" Neil asked.

"Me, too!" chirped Jamie.

"I would be happy to," Juliette agreed, "if it is all right with your mother."

The boys whirled to look at the raven-haired woman, their sturdy bodies taut with excitement.

"Oh, well, if it's all right with Lyon," Flora answered hesitantly, "I suppose they may learn how to throw it."

She looked around the room for guidance, her brow puckered with doubt. "Though I don't know why anyone should want to."

"Highland lads have been taught to use weapons from time immemorial," Rob said. "The wee loons should learn how to defend themselves. And I'll gladly help with the lesson."

Neil and Jamie turned to stare up at their Uncle Lyon, eager faces aglow as they waited for the final decision.

The laird lifted one russet eyebrow and appeared to consider the matter. "Miss Elkheart may teach Neil and Jamie how to throw the knife," he stated imperiously, "under my close supervision."

"Hip! Hip! Hurrah!" Neil yelped.

"Hurrah!" chimed in Jamie.

Lady Hester set her cup and saucer on the tea table with a clatter and stared at Lyon. "I thought you were returning to Edinburgh tomorrow."

"I've changed my plans," he answered, his tone implying surprise that she'd even question it. "How could I leave when we're entertaining such an enchanting guest?"

Juliette averted her gaze from the man's perceptive eyes, determined to hide her breathless reaction to his offhanded flattery. A shiver of trepidation and some other emotion, yet to be identified, worked its way down her spine. He was purposely keeping her off balance, unwilling to let her recover her self-possession. The Lion was far more dangerous than she'd suspected.

For MacLyon refused to be ignored. His presence seemed to fill the room. She knew instinctively that he used his size, strength, and military bearing to dominate others. On the train ride from Edinburgh, Keir had told her that they'd served in the Royal Scots together, and the laird had held the rank of colonel when he'd resigned. The large, ferocious Scotsman was used to issuing orders and having everyone jump to his tune.

Haxc! He'd soon find that she wasn't so easily intimidated.

His show of gallantry hadn't fooled her, either. He was harsh, arrogant, and judgmental. He considered her visit to the Highlands the trifling errand of a starry-eyed simpleton. If he knew she'd come in search of the answer to a vision, he'd laugh in her face.

Juliette sensed that he was watching her now. She raised her eyes to meet his, determined to show him the calm, intrepid demeanor of a Cheyenne warrior-woman. She had come here for a very important reason, and no ill-mannered Scotsman was going to stand in her way.

"There is no need to change your plans for me, laird," she said with a resolute tilt of her chin. "I am sure Lady Hester will give me all the help I need during my visit."

A slow, predatory grin spread across his rough-hewn features. He was clearly amused at her misguided show of spunk. "Ah, but I insist on seeing that your stay at Strathlyon is all you hoped it would be, Miss Elkheart. We can't have you returning home disillusioned. Or thinking the Scots are inhospitable barbarians."

His burnished hair glinted in the light streaming through the window. His broad shoulders and wide chest stretched the tweed material of his riding jacket so snug it should have split beneath the pressure. Even his dusty breeches and riding boots proclaimed his blatant virility.

MacLyon's insolent green eyes held an unspoken challenge. With his feet planted wide, his hands resting on his hips, he was taunting her, telling her by his overtly masculine stance and his cocksure smile that she'd run like a scared jackrabbit the moment he made a move toward her.

Involuntary tremors quivered through Juliette's stiff limbs. Once again, she was reminded of a wounded, angry mountain lion stalking its prey. Her mouth went dry, and she swallowed nervously. She had the strange feeling he was trying to frighten her away. It was all she could do not to jump to her feet and fly out the door.

Keir had been right earlier in the garden.

If she bolted, she wouldn't stop till she got to Edinburgh.

Chapter 5

"**N**ow this book contains the history of Clan MacLyon," Lady Hester said, as she opened a gilt-edged tome that lay on the library table. She pointed to the Latin inscriptions on a page yellowed with time. "You can see that our family still holds the same lands that belonged to the chief of our clan when the parliamentary rolls were written in the sixteenth century. But of course, MacLyons ruled over an even greater area at the time of the Bruce kings."

Seated beside her, Juliette looked with interest at the feudal map. She recognized many of the geographical features from her stroll with Rob along the ramparts the previous day. The Vale of Ardchattan, the village of Strathbardine, and much of the region of Strathshire were only part of the present laird's far-flung holdings. She realized now that MacLyon territory spread farther than the eye could see, even from the vantage point of the castle walls.

"For the last forty years, I've made a hobby of studying the history of Highland families," the dowager told her. "It was my hope to one day publish a book on the subject, but there's still much more material to be gathered. Too much to be completed in my lifetime, I'm afraid. And unfortunately, Flora has no interest in such things."

Juliette could imagine the elderly woman's disappointment in knowing all her hard work might one day be forgotten. "It would be a shame if no one takes up the research where you leave off."

Her blue eyes sparkling, Lady Hester peered over the top of her reading glasses at Juliette, making it clear where Rob got his lively sense of humor. "My grandson's widow is far more interested in the latest fashions from Paris, but I haven't given up hope for a successor."

Juliette smiled with understanding. "Not everyone is intrigued with history. My sister teases me about being a scholar. Jennie would agree with Flora, hands down, that the stylish cut of a gown is far more important than the date of some forgotten battle."

Lady Hester chuckled softly. "It happens in every family, I suppose. Diversity is what keeps life interesting, even for a *cailleach* like me. That's Gaelic for 'old woman,' " she explained. "And *chaileag* means 'girl.' "

"My great-grandmother felt the same way about life," Juliette said, purposely skirting the subject of Gaelic words. "She had four husbands in her lifetime."

"Four? How impressive! And were her husbands all diverse?"

"I never knew any of them," she admitted, "so I cannot say. But Porcupine Quills told me once that, when it came to men, the only thing different about them was their names."

Lady Hester burst into a peal of laughter. "*Mo chaileag*, I can see you come from a long line of intelligent women."

The elderly lady was teasing, and Juliette knew that *niscem* had spoken in jest, as well.

Not all men were alike.

Some were a breed apart.

Juliette's father was one of the four head chiefs of the Cheyenne nation, a warrior renowned for his strength and courage. She could think of only one man who could match Strong Elk Heart's splendid physique.

MacLyon's size alone set him apart from the crowd. And the relentless determination conveyed in the Scottish laird's every gesture, every word, underscored the fact that he considered himself the unquestioned ruler of his own little kingdom. With another glance at the map, she silently admitted that his kingdom wasn't all that little.

Schooling her errant thoughts, Juliette returned to the document in front of her. "Have you collected all this material by yourself?"

"Most of it," Lady Hester said, turning the fragile vellum with care. "Naturally, I share information with other people interested in Highland genealogy. The chief of Clan Macfie has an extensive collection of papers going all the way back to the time of Wallace."

"Wallace?"

"One of our greatest heroes. Remind me to give you a book about him before we leave the library today. You can read it during your stay with us."

"I would like that," Juliette replied. "Does Laird Macfie live nearby?"

"Aye, he lives at the far end of the valley. Hamish is very active in the Scottish National Society. He's played an important role in organizing the upcoming gathering of our local clans. He's a member of the Standing Council of Chiefs—along with Lyon, of course."

Bagpipes—kilts—Scottish bonnets with feathers and badges . . . The thought of seeing such a marvelous spectacle gave Julie a thrill of anticipation.

"Dr. MacDougall told me about the gathering," she said. "I am looking forward to seeing it."

"I promise you, it will be quite impressive." Lady Hester closed the worn red cover, set the large volume aside, and opened another. "This book contains the MacLyon lineage, which shows that the present chief is a descendent in the direct male line of a Norse king, who raided our coast and established fortresses in this region in the twelfth century."

Juliette watched with curiosity as Lady Hester traced the branches of their family tree with the tip of her finger.

"Now here in the sixteenth century," the dowager said, tapping the page thoughtfully, "a MacLyon wed a Mac-Dougall heiress. She was the only granddaughter of a fearsome chieftain. As so often happens with headstrong MacLyon males, their courtship was notoriously stormy. The tale goes that he resorted to abduction in the end. But the marriage proved to be a happy one and produced many healthy bairns."

Juliette felt a surge of pleasure at the unexpected news. "Why, that means we may share a common ancestor!"

"Undoubtedly," Lady Hester agreed. "Although our two clans were once the bitterest of enemies, we have been allies since that first matrimonial union. Down through the years, more than one MacDougall has wed a MacLyon."

Lady Hester continued tracing the line of descent, pausing at the date 1771. "Here, at this point," she told Juliette solemnly, "there was only one living male heir to the chiefship. Over forty MacLyon soldiers were killed in a terrible massacre. The chief's eldest son, Colonel Gilbride MacLyon, a younger son, and three nephews perished in the space of a single afternoon."

"Ahahe!" Juliette cried softly. "How terrible!"

An ominous presentiment made her heart stumble. Could this have been the battle she'd seen in her vision? The fact that she was somehow related to the slain Highlanders made their images seem all the more haunting.

Unaware of Juliette's horror, the white-haired woman continued tranquilly. "Ours is a very bloody history, *mo chaileag*, but the line did not die out. At the age of seventy-one, the chief of Clan MacLyon took a young wife and sired a male child. That child was Lyon's great-grandfather, Aeneas. Lyon is the twenty-third chief of our clan and the nineteenth marquis of Strathshire. He is a member of both the Scottish and English peerage, but he prefers to be addressed simply as 'laird.' "

At that moment, Rob entered the library, and both women looked up in greeting. He came to stand directly behind them at the table. "You're not boring Julie with the grisly MacLyon saga, I hope," he said, resting his hand on his grandmother's shoulder. "Miss Elkheart's come to find the story of her own clan, not listen to ghost tales from our hoary past."

Juliette straightened in her chair. "Ghosts?"

Lady Hester patted her hand soothingly. "He's teasing you, dear." She shook her head at her grandson in mock disapproval. "There are no ghosts at Strathlyon, Robbie, and well you know it."

Juliette smiled up at him. "I just learned that we may be related."

"Only very distantly," came the reply in the twenty-third laird's deep, resonant baritone.

For a man of his size, MacLyon moved with the silent grace of a cat. His sensual mouth quirked derisively as he surveyed them.

"Has Miss Elkheart traced her lineage all the way back to a Celtic dynasty by now?" he asked.

"Oh, we haven't even started on the MacDougall bloodline yet," Rob informed him. "Nana's been extolling your royal pedigree for the last half hour."

MacLyon came to stand beside his brother. "Why would anyone be interested in such archaic blather?"

Lady Hester closed the cover with a snap. "Hmph," she sniffed. "Anyone with a brain in his head would know the importance of historical research." She pointed to a stack of books piled high on a shelf nearby. "Bring me the one on the clan tartans, please."

Lyon snorted in derision. "Clan tartans are a myth."

At Juliette's start of surprise, Lady Hester smiled reassuringly. "Before the rising of forty-five, tartans could generally be recognized by districts, since the setts and colors were determined by the vegetable dyes available in a particular area. And by local custom and preference."

"Then how can you say a particular tartan belongs to one clan?" Juliette asked in confusion.

Rob braced his elbows on the high back of his grandmother's chair. "After the wearing of tartans was proscribed by law in 1746, the only men allowed to wear them were Highland soldiers. Not an inconsiderable number, actually, for over the years, tens of thousands of lads enrolled in the government regiments."

"Prior to that," Lyon said, "the distinguishing marks of a clansman were the slogan he cried out in battle, usually in Gaelic, and the clan plant he wore in his bonnet." His hand brushed softly across Juliette's shoulder as he spoke, and goose bumps followed the path of his touch.

"In the years that followed," Rob explained, "marching and fencible regiments wore uniform tartan cloth to distinguish one from the other. Later, these setts were assumed to be the clan patterns of the chiefs, who'd originally raised the individual regiments."

"An assumption," Lyon interjected, "that has no basis in history. But when has that ever bothered anyone interested in creating a romantic myth?"

Despite his air of cynicism, the laird brought the large tome over and laid it in front of them. Juliette suspected there was a motive behind his sudden amiable cooperation. The Lion wanted her to find whatever she'd come looking for as quickly as possible. And then leave forthwith.

Lady Hester opened the timeworn leather cover and smoothed her hand lovingly over the page. "After the law was repealed, it became quite popular for chiefs and lairds, and others concerned with renewing interest in the old Highland ways, to wear tartan again. Many clans claimed as their historical tartan setts the patterns of the regiments bearing their names. The Argyll Highlanders' pattern became the tartan of Clan Campbell, while the MacLyon Highlanders' blue and black sett became our clan tartan, and so on."

Bracing his hand on the table, MacLyon bent over Juliette's shoulder to view the page. The fresh, tangy scent of his shaving soap engulfed her, and the delicious fragrance of balsam fir sent tiny bubbles of heat through her veins.

Her breath stalled, as his nearness brought an acute realization of her own small size in comparison to his massive frame. The feeling was far more intimidating than she'd ever have thought possible.

She looked down at the broad, scarred hand resting beside her forearm. The long callused fingers, with their blunt-cut nails, could crush the bones of her wrist with ludicrous ease. Her heart fluttered like the wings of a hummingbird. For the first time, Juliette wondered if she really had saved his life. Perhaps he hadn't needed her help at all.

"This book contains specimens of all the Scottish tartans," Lady Hester explained, as she searched through the pages. "Look, here is the sample of the MacLyon's."

Juliette gazed at the square of wool, and her heart plummeted. It was the very same pattern of black stripes against a rich azure background that had been worn by the murdered men in her vision. Without conscious thought, she touched the cloth. Her fingers trembled as though she were touching a shroud. Her voice sounded strained and hoarse when she spoke. "It is a lovely tartan."

"And very distinctive, too," Lady Hester added. "These thin lines of yellow running through the pattern identify the sept, or individual family in the clan."

"Show Julie the MacDougall sample," Rob suggested. "I'm sure she'd rather see what her own family's tartan looks like."

Complying, Lady Hester again turned the pages. "Ah, here it is," she said with a satisfied smile. She pointed to a swatch in the right upper corner. "Your ancestors' tartan, my dear. But then, you'll have seen it already in the doctor's house in Strathbardine."

Stunned, Juliette stared numbly at the scrap of wool. Until that moment, she hadn't given a thought to the tartan colors displayed in Keir MacDougall's home—brilliant red interwoven with broad stripes of dark forest green and narrow white lines.

Just like the one she was looking at now.

Not lavender and pink.

In the long moment of silence, Lyon sensed Julie's stupefying bewilderment. With her hands clenched so tightly that her knuckles showed white, she sat with head bowed over the open book, not saying a word. She looked as though she'd been struck a staggering blow that had left her dazed and speechless.

Then she raised a shaky hand to her brow. "There must be some mistake," she whispered, her gaze locked on the remnant of red and green wool. "This . . . this cannot be the MacDougall tartan."

"Oh, there's no mistake," Rob told her with a quizzical look. "You're sitting beside an expert. Nana can identify every tartan ever worn in the Highlands."

Julie sprang to her feet, her chair thumping against Lyon's thighs. He automatically stepped back to allow her more room, and she turned with a quick, jerky movement at odds with her usual grace. Before he realized her intention, she scooted round him and raced toward the door. There she paused to look back over her shoulder, her face drained of its inner glow.

"Please," she begged in a raspy undertone. "Please stay here. I have something I must show you." She made a stiff, awkward motion toward the hallway. "It is in my room. I will be right back." Not waiting for an answer, she hurried out of the library.

Incredulous, the three MacLyons stared at the empty doorway.

"Whatever could have upset her so?" Lady Hester asked. She wagged her finger at Rob. "It must have been your fault, young man, for talking about ghosts. You've obviously frightened her."

"I was merely joking," he protested. "I wouldn't scare

Julie for the world. You know that. And she seemed more unhappy than frightened.''

Absently massaging his left arm, Lyon stared down at the swatches of tartan and searched for some clue to her inexplicable behavior. The haunting sadness in Julie's dark brown eyes had ripped through his gut like a piece of shrapnel, and he fought the urge to chase after her. He wanted to take the darling lass in his arms, to hold her close and whisper that he would protect and cherish her. That she'd never be unhappy again.

The feeling of unprecedented tenderness staggered him. Until that moment, Lyon had never even considered the possibility of romantic love. He steeled himself, refusing to succumb to such demented thoughts.

"Women," he said gruffly. "They're all the same. Who could hope to understand them?"

Five minutes later Juliette hurried back into the library, her treasured heirloom folded over her arm. By then Flora had joined the others, who stood waiting for her beside the table.

"There you are!" Flora called, oblivious to the concern etched on the faces around her. "I was about to come look for you. I want to show you the new copy of *La Mode Illustrée*. Mama sent it to me from Glasgow."

"Perhaps later," Juliette answered distractedly. She smoothed her hand over the blanket she carried, then carefully draped it across the back of a chair. Taking a hesitant step backward, she met their inquisitive eyes. "This blanket belonged to my mother's grandfather, Nehemiah McDougall. She gave it to me before I left home."

"Oh, that's nice," Flora said, barely glancing at it. She fidgeted impatiently with her rings, anxious to leave.

No one else uttered a word.

MacLyon, Rob, and Lady Hester stared down at the lavender and pink wool for what seemed like a lifetime, then looked up in unblinking silence to meet Juliette's gaze.

She searched their faces, wondering what could have caused such blank stupefaction, and forced herself to stay calm. "What is it?" she asked. "What is wrong?"

MacLyon's answer stung like the lash of a whip. "Is this your idea of a joke, Miss Elkheart? Because, believe me, I don't find it amusing."

She held her ground, though the urge to escape from his penetrating stare was almost overpowering. "It is not my intention to be funny."

Although the dowager spoke calmly, her blue eyes were clouded with suspicion. "How did you come by this, girl?"

"This blanket is a family heirloom," Juliette said, growing defensive. *Haxc!* Did they think she'd stolen it? "My great-great-grandfather, John McDougall, brought it with him to America."

"And what the bloody devil was a MacDougall doing with it?" the laird inquired in a savage tone.

"The blanket belonged to him," she said curtly. "What do you suppose? That I come from a family of thieves?"

The sneer curling MacLyon's mouth told her he supposed exactly that.

Lady Hester lifted the lavender and pink wool from the chair and slowly unfolded it. She spread it across the books stacked on the massive table with consummate care, as though afraid it might fall to pieces in her hands.

"This is not a blanket," she said softly, her gaze fastened on the worn, frayed material. "This is a *feileadh-mor.*"

Juliette waited. She recognized the Gaelic name for the covering worn in the old days in Scotland, but she had no intention of giving away the fact that she understood their tongue.

Bemused, Rob stared at the lavender and pink plaid. "That means the 'big wrap' in Gaelic," he explained. "It was worn by laying a belt on the ground, then placing the plaid over the belt and folding it into pleats. The wearer laid down on top of the plaid and wrapped the material around him, then fastened the belt about his waist. The remaining plaid was draped over his shoulder. In time, it evolved into the *feileadh-beag*, the little kilt, which is worn now.''

That didn't explain their grim expressions. Juliette glanced at Rob, hoping he'd explain in his easygoing way. But he made no further attempt to come to her rescue.

''If this really is a family keepsake, Miss Elkheart,'' the laird said in a frigid tone, ''then your forebears never belonged to Clan MacDougall. For no God-fearing Mac-Dougall would have been found dead wearing the plaid of filthy vermin.''

''I . . . I do not understand,'' she said, recoiling from the venom in his words.

MacLyon's eyes grew as cold as shards of green ice. He grabbed a fistful of the blanket and lifted it up from the table. ''I mean that this belonged to an outlawed clan. This is the plaid of Clan Danielson: allies who betrayed us, who surrounded us in a trap and cut us down like hay beneath the scythe. Those treacherous bastards were hunted with dogs throughout the Highlands. Any male over twelve caught wearing this despised plaid was killed on the spot. The very name of Danielson is reviled to this day. They are now referred to as the Clan of the Clouds because they disappeared as if into thin air.''

MacLyon tossed the blanket to her, and Juliette caught it before it could fall to the floor. She felt as though he'd punched her full force in the stomach. Clutching the plaid like a lifeline, she fought back waves of nausea.

This, then, was the ghastly meaning of her vision.

Her own ancestors had perpetrated that foul, heinous deed. Now their spirits were crying out to her in their guilt and shame. But she couldn't change the past. By the Great Powers above, what was it they expected her to do?

Juliette was never more grateful for her ability to mask her emotions. Using every ounce of inner strength she possessed, she hid the staggering knowledge of her vision. She wouldn't reveal her anguish to this caustic, bitter man. Or the fact that she possessed what the Scots labeled the second sight.

He'd never believe her.

In his eyes, she was the descendant of a hated enemy.

She ignored the dizziness spinning inside her head and the bile that rose in her throat. "All of this took place a long time ago, Scotsman," she said, thankful her voice didn't crack beneath the strain and betray her humiliation.

MacLyon's soft words were laced with a scalding mockery. "Memories are long in the Highlands, Miss Elkheart."

Juliette squared her shoulders and met his sardonic gaze. "Then I shall curtail my visit at once."

Without warning, Flora burst into tears. "Oh, don't make her go, Lyon. Please, don't make her go! I never have anyone to talk to! Never!"

MacLyon didn't deign look at her. "Are you so desperate for foolish gossip, Flora?"

His sister-in-law glared at him. "My family is from the Lowlands," she hissed and stamped her foot in impotent fury. "What do I care about old blood feuds? Such things are barbaric!"

"Don't be a goose, Flora," Rob chided. He stepped closer to Juliette and gently pried the plaid from her stiff fingers. "Just because your great-great-grandfather may have been related to members of the Danielson clan doesn't mean you aren't welcome here, Julie. Your ancestor's name was MacDougall, for God's sake."

Lady Hester hurried to stand beside her. "Rob is correct, *mo chaileag*," she said. With a sympathetic cluck of her tongue, she slipped her arm about Juliette's waist. "Events that took place long ago, no matter how vile, shan't be held against you. Please say you'll stay. Think how disappointed the children would be if you left so suddenly. They haven't even had a chance to get to know you." She patted her cheek affectionately. "And neither have we."

At the dowager's kindness, Juliette's voice broke at last. "I . . . I do not think . . ."

Rob glowered at his older brother. "Tell Julie she's welcome to stay at the castle for as long as she pleases."

Lyon's throat ached with the need to beg her forgiveness. He choked back the words, determined to squelch the desire rising within him like the inexorable flooding of the Nile across the desert sands. Parched and thirsting for the promise of sweet consolation in her exotic eyes, he clenched his fists to keep from reaching out to her.

He didn't give a damn about Clan Danielson. He'd seen enough bloodletting in the Sudan to last him a lifetime. What the devil did he care about a massacre that had taken place a hundred years ago? He'd merely used it as an excuse to alienate her, to send her packing before he did something they'd both regret.

If she stayed, it was only a matter of time before his control snapped. Every blasted time he saw her, he was consumed with lust. He hadn't been able to take his eyes off her during supper the previous evening.

While his family had conversed politely with their guest from Canada, he'd spent the entire meal imagining what it'd be like to slowly peel away her gown, with its damnable peek-a-boo neckline, and bare her firm, small breasts to his lecherous eyes. As they'd plied her with questions about her childhood in Alberta, he'd mentally laid her naked body across his big bed and done everything but suck her toes.

Hell, if he hadn't tamped down the fire in his groin with repeated glasses of wine, he'd never have been able to get up from the dining table.

Then, blast it all, it'd happened all over again that morning. When he'd stood behind her chair and breathed her delicate floral scent, all he could think of was placing a kiss on the exposed nape of her neck. The desire to brush his open mouth across her silken skin and feel her tremble at his unexpected touch had raged within him. He felt like a randy sixteen-year-old lad desperate to lose his virginity and ready to explode at the least provocation. The hellish truth was that he was nothing but a burned-out old soldier who tried to combat his recurring nightmares with expensive whisky and even costlier women.

Now he'd succeeded in alienating his entire family, putting them squarely in her camp. Damn them. They had no idea of the hell they were putting him through.

But it was time to sound retreat from the battle, if not from the war. With an ingratiating smile, Lyon held out his hands in a show of conciliation. "Certainly, Miss Elkheart is welcome. I said before that our visitor from Canada can stay the entire winter, if she likes."

Julie met his gaze without a trace of the animosity he expected—and so richly deserved. The top of her braided chignon didn't even reach his shoulder, yet she stood as poised and regal as a princess, watching him with that wonderful air of tranquility that always seemed to surround her.

"I will be gone long before the first snowstorm," she stated in her smooth, gracious manner. "You may rest assured, laird, that it will not be necessary to cut more wood for the fireplace or stock up the larder on my account."

"Well, that's settled!" Lady Hester exclaimed brightly before Lyon could say another word. "Flora, why don't you take Julie with you. I think we've pored over dusty parchments long enough for today. Show our guest those new French fashions the postman brought this morning. You young ladies love to keep up with the latest modes."

"Oh, yes!" Flora said with relief. Wiping the tears from her cheeks, she sent Lyon a withering glance, then clasped Julie's elbow. "Come with me now, do. We can see if we shall be wearing bustles next spring."

Knowing he'd behaved like a first class prig, Lyon watched in brooding silence as the two women walked out of the library arm-in-arm.

The silence was short-lived.

"How can you be such an ass?" Rob growled. Not waiting for an answer, he laid the lavender and pink plaid on the table, turned on his heel, and left.

Lyon looked at his grandmother, waiting for her scathing denunciation with cold detachment. But she didn't lash out at him.

Instead, a tiny smile hovered about Lady Hester's mouth. Her intelligent eyes twinkled with merriment. "Well, I'd better get busy," she said, as she headed for the door.

"Busy?" he asked, in spite of himself. She had an entire army of servants to see to the castle's day-to-day routine.

"Why, yes," she told him cheerily. "I'll need to have more wood cut for the fireplace and more food stocked in the larder. Something tells me Miss Juliette Elkheart may be staying for a very long time."

"Dammit to hell!" Lyon roared.

But like the rest of his treacherous family, she'd already exited the library.

Flora led Juliette to a luxurious suite in the east wing of the second floor. She showed her guest the sitting room, dressing room, and bedroom, chattering gaily the whole way.

Juliette tried not to gape in astonishment. Yards and yards of pink and white striped satin covered the upholstered furnishings. The draperies, bed canopy, pillows, and comforter were made of pink satin as well. On the white and gold furniture sat Louis XIV figurines, Meissen porcelain, Wedgwood vases, Waterford crystal, and Watteau fans. Perfume decanters, pots of rouge, boxes of powder, and jars of cosmetic brushes lined the top of the dressing table. Tea gowns, morning dresses, traveling suits, and sable-trimmed capes with matching muffs—apparel of every description and color—seemed to burst from the several armoires. She'd never seen such a glorious display of feminine froufrou in her life.

"Do you like it?" Flora questioned eagerly, as they returned to the sitting room.

"It is . . . lovely," Juliette said, then added more truthfully, "it takes my breath away."

"I chose everything myself," her hostess confided with a satisfied giggle. "Whatever else Lyon may be, he's certainly not a pinch-penny."

Hesitating to comment on such a personal remark, Juliette wandered across the plush Turkish carpet and inspected a painting above the marble mantelpiece. She leaned closer, trying to decide if it really was a Vermeer.

"I hate him!" Flora cried.

"You do?" For a moment, Juliette thought she was referring to the Dutch artist, now long deceased.

"I think I shall die of unhappiness!" The volatile brunette plopped down on the settee and crossed her arms beneath her full bosom with a petulant frown.

Juliette marveled at the young woman's ability to move from heady exuberance to darkest despair within the space of a second. She knew she should redirect the conversation. She hadn't come to the Highlands to pry into another family's secrets. But her curiosity won out in the end. "Why are you so unhappy?"

"Why?" Flora's lower lip jutted forward in a pout. "I'll tell you why. Because Lyon keeps me here against my will, that's why!"

With a sinking feeling, Juliette realized the cause of the tension between the laird and his pretty sister-in-law. MacLyon coveted his dead brother's widow. Trying to ignore the quickened beating of her heart, she joined Flora on the settee. "How can he keep you here against your will?"

Flora's dark eyes filled with tears. "Lyon won't let me take Neil and Jamie to live with my parents in Glasgow." She placed one dimpled hand on her breast, her fingers spread in a melodramatic gesture of suffering. "He says I can go anytime I please, but the boys must remain at Strathlyon. He knows I'd never leave without them." She looked at Juliette beseechingly, the teardrops clinging to her long black lashes like crystal beads. "What kind of mother would I be to leave my two little sons? Whatever would people think?''

Juliette wondered if Flora was more concerned with society's opinion than how she'd actually feel herself. ''Can he do that? Can he keep the children here without your permission?''

''Oh, yes!'' Flora's high soprano quavered with indignation. ''Lyon is their legal guardian. James made him so in his will. But I'm sure if he'd known what a beast his older brother would turn out to be, my husband would never have done it.''

''Have you been at Strathlyon long?''

''Forever!'' she wailed. ''I came here when James and I were first married. The old laird was still alive, and it didn't seem so bad then. But ever since Lyon returned last spring, it's been horrible.''

''Why? What happened?''

''It's as though he's not the same person. When he came home, he had every scrap of tartan in the castle taken down and packed away. Why, he would have removed the portraits in the long gallery because of the MacLyon plaids, but Nana wouldn't hear of it.'' She looked at Juliette, her eyes wide with alarm. ''I've never heard such a terrible row. I warn you, these Highlanders have horrible tempers, Julie. They're not like my family, at all.''

Juliette squeezed her hand comfortingly. ''You're sweet and gentle and kind, Flora. Although the MacLyons may bicker amongst themselves, I am sure they love you dearly.''

''Not Lyon,'' she said with a shudder. ''I think he despises me for still being alive when James is dead.''

''How did your husband die?''

''He was killed in the Sudan when the natives overran his garrison. Everyone in the fort was slain. Lyon led a regiment of Royal Scots across the desert in an attempt to rescue them, but they arrived too late.''

"Was that when MacLyon received the injury to his arm?"

Flora dabbed her wet cheeks with a lacy handkerchief. "I suppose so. He's never talked to me about it. The whole family speaks to each other in Gaelic half the time. Even Neil and Jamie speak Gaelic, while I'm left in the dark."

"Have you tried to learn the language?"

Flora's head drooped. "Lady Hester asked me to join Neil and Jamie during their lessons with Mr. Dittmar. I tried, but it was just too hard."

"Gaelic is a difficult language to learn," Juliette agreed. When Flora looked at her in wonder, she added hastily, "At least it sounds as though it would be very difficult. I heard the two brothers speaking it yesterday in the garden."

"Well, I'm not going to let Lyon ruin your visit," Flora said with dogged resolution. "I've been looking forward to your coming for too long to allow him to spoil my happiness." She gave Juliette a trembling smile. "Come on, let's look at my new fashion plates and pretend he doesn't even exist."

Juliette returned Flora's smile as she nodded in agreement. But something told her that pretending MacLyon didn't exist wasn't going to be easy.

Chapter 6

"**Y**ou wanted to see me, laird?"

Lyon looked up from the papers on his desk to find Julie hovering on the threshold of his study. With a brief nod, he concluded the interview with his head game-keeper and rose to his feet. "Come in, Miss Elkheart."

As Woodburn turned to leave, his eyes lit up at the sight of the fetching lass framed in the doorway.

"Hello, John," she said, giving the grizzled man a bright smile. "How are you today?"

"Fine. Fine, indeed," he replied with an abashed grin. He crossed the room and halted in front of her. "And yer-self, Miss Elkheart?"

"Equally well, thank you. Cook says we're to have game birds this evening."

Woodburn turned his cap slowly round in his gnarled hands. His deep chest swelled with pride at her words. "Oh, aye, miss. I brought a brace of plump grouse round to the kitchen early this morning specially for your sup-per."

He left, closing the door behind him, and Julie crossed the room to stand in front of Lyon's massive desk. "Davie said you wished to see me."

"Davie?" For a moment, he didn't know who in the devil she was talking about.

"Your footman," she said with a quizzical look. "The

64

tall one with the dark brown hair.'' The amazement in her eyes told him she could hardly believe he didn't know his own servants.

"Ah, you mean Grierson."

"Yes, Davie Grierson."

Lyon scowled at her carefree reply. That particular footman happened to be tall and lanky and damn near as comely as a lass. "We usually address our servants by their last names, Miss Elkheart," he informed her.

That wasn't exactly the truth. The Scots were known for their disdain of class snobbery, particularly in the Highlands, where clansmen were often related through intermarriage to the chief.

A smile skipped about the corners of her mouth. Her dark eyes sparkled with impudence. "I am well aware of the customs of the landed aristocracy," she replied, "but you know how provincial we colonials are."

Lyon bit his inner lip to keep from smiling. He had no intention of encouraging such pert behavior, but her blithe raillery was so contagious that he grinned despite his intentions. "Let's consider ourselves on even ground, then, and reserve our ammunition for the next battle."

He motioned to one of the straight-backed chairs in front of his desk, and Julie sat down. She folded her hands in her lap and waited peacefully for him to explain what was so important as to require a summons to his inner sanctum.

The afternoon light from the tall windows splashed across her, illuminating her vivid coloring. The rich turquoise of her dress accented the shimmering highlights in the silken hair piled high in a loose chignon. Streaks of auburn and mahogany vied with darker chestnut strands.

The longing to remove the pins and bury his fingers in that tumbling mass created a fire deep in his belly. The steaming heat inside him stirred and rose upward, fogging his reason, making him forget why he'd insisted on this interview, when he knew all along just how dangerous it would be.

With her spine arrow-straight, Julie sat on the edge of her chair with an elegant, inborn grace. She was as serene as the evening star shining in the night sky. Her stillness called to him, promising a respite from all his guilt-laden memories, a sweet haven in which to tarry with delight. Her clear, innocent gaze spoke of a magical place of rest, where a man could sleep and dream of sea maidens combing out their long, dark tresses. And never think of war again.

Lyon was suddenly in no hurry to get on with the unpleasant business at hand. He searched his mind for a safe topic. "Did you and Flora finish playing with her paper dolls?"

Julie's full lips curved in a jaunty smile, but she spoke as though the question were of utmost consequence. "Yes, we did. We discovered that skirt silhouettes will be narrower next spring with only a slight pouf of draperies at the back. And loose, flowing bodices will be all the rage by summertime. In the early fall, short cashmere jackets will be worn over dresses of India mull, with high waists and long, full sleeves showing below the upturned cuff."

"What?" he asked with a derisive quirk of an eyebrow. "No hoops next year?"

"Not a hoop in sight," Julie told him. She lowered her lids with a sigh of disappointment he knew to be sham. Women hadn't worn hoops in fifteen years. "When I left Flora, she was trying to decide whether to purchase an ell of china crepe in terra-cotta red or a watered silk of cowslip yellow."

Enjoying her playful mood, Lyon sat down and drank in the sight of her. His gaze followed the enticing curves of her breasts to her tiny waist. The impulse to cuddle her in his lap and feel her soft, pliant form pressed against his big, hard body rocked him with its urgency. The startling force of his physical response was an immediate reminder of why she was there in the first place.

"And what was your advice, Miss Elkheart, or dare I ask?"

She studied her fingertips for a moment, then raised her lush, curving lashes to meet his gaze. "I suggested that Flora order both, since she'd be saving money by wearing last year's bustle underneath the new gowns." The laughter dancing in her nut-brown eyes dared him to cavil.

Despite the feverish heat that rushed through his veins, Lyon had himself well under control. This breathtaking attraction he felt was pure lust. Nothing more.

Pure lust—that was an oxymoron if he'd ever heard one.

Just why his body was reacting so traitorously, when he knew he could never have the bonny lass, he couldn't fathom. The lure of forbidden fruit, he supposed—though he'd never lusted after starry-eyed virgins before, and this was a bloody rotten time to start.

"Thank you for pointing that out to Flora," he said, "though I've yet to notice her making any attempts at frugality. I'm sure your counsel was all she needed to justify the purchase of two bolts of cloth rather than one."

Julie tipped her head in acknowledgment of the dubious praise. The naughty smile that hovered about her mouth was positively enchanting. "You're welcome, laird. I certainly tried my best."

"Yes, but to do what is the question," he said dryly.

Once more, she waited in tranquil silence for him to get to the point. She was unaware, of course, that when their conversation was concluded, he'd never see her again. Lyon planned to leave for Edinburgh in the morning, and before he left he was going to make damn sure she wouldn't be at Strathlyon when he got back. A man could withstand only so much temptation.

He'd chosen the site of this afternoon's meeting with deliberate forethought. Of all the rooms in the castle, this was the only place—outside of his private suite—they wouldn't be interrupted. No one entered his study without a personal summons. Not even Neil and Jamie dared to violate the stricture against it—at least, most of the time. Lyon glanced over at the door, wishing he'd locked it, just as a precaution.

It was too late now.

Juliette saw the laird's gaze dart toward the closed door and looked around her with growing unease. No wonder Davie Grierson had called this room the lion's den. The place fairly groaned with masculine accouterments. A leather sofa and two chairs stood in front of the fireplace. An eight-point rack of antlers hung above the mantel. A gun case displayed rifles, shotguns, and pistols.

She studied the ancient shield hanging on the wall behind MacLyon in fascination.

"That's a targe," he said. "The Gaelic embossed on the leather covering is the MacLyon clan gathering cry. 'Stand fast!' "

"And the sword next to it?"

"That beauty is a two-handed claymore," he replied. "Its large cross-guard ends in four-ringed quillons, typical of the fourteenth century."

"Could you actually fight with it?" she asked in disbelief.

He flashed her a crooked smile. "If I had to."

The thought of any man using such an enormous sword staggered her. Juliette doubted if she'd even be able to lift it.

Her wandering attention was recaptured when MacLyon opened a drawer, withdrew her knife, and laid it on the desk top in front of him. She smiled in pleasure at the sight.

"I promised to return this to you," he said. "I can understand why you're anxious to retrieve such a marvelous weapon. I was amazed at its accuracy. I hit the target every time." He cocked his head and looked at her speculatively. "Your father made this knife for you?"

"*Nihoe*—my father—is very skilled at making weapons," she explained. "Bows, arrows, knives, war lances. He also carves sacred peace pipes, courting flutes, and children's toys. Often, what he creates has a magical quality, which imbues its owner with special gifts.''

"Magic?'' The laird picked up the knife. Rising, he came around to the front of the desk and braced his backside against it. He balanced the weapon on the palm of his hand, scrutinizing the bone handle. "Is that the meaning of these strange designs? Are they supposed to be a wizard's incantations?''

Juliette shook her head. She leaned forward and pointed to the carvings. "This is the symbol of the evening star, which is my Cheyenne name. And here is my twin sister's, the prairie rose. On the other side, you will see stylized representations of an elk and a fawn. Those stand for my parents. And here is the flying hawk, for my brother.''

MacLyon turned the handle over several times, studying both sides intently. His cool tone betrayed his skepticism. "Where's the magic words?''

She took the knife and held it up in front of her, so the light from the windows bounced off the shiny blade. "The magic is within, made with each tiny cut carved by the artisan, and only for the person for whom it was created. Had you not returned my weapon to me, you would have experienced no mystical charm.''

"And hopefully no curse, either.''

She laughed as she carefully slipped the weapon inside the pocket of her skirt. "There is no curse on my knife, Scotsman. My father does not practice the art of black magic.''

"That's a relief,'' he said. "I've already been cursed enough to last two lifetimes.'' Though he spoke in jest, his words carried an edge of bitterness. He folded his arms across his broad chest, absently massaging his elbow. "But returning your weapon wasn't the only reason I wanted to meet with you.''

"Yes?''

"I'm afraid I have something a little more serious to

discuss than the latest fashions from Paris or the talismans carved on your knife.''

''And what is that?''

His forehead furrowed in a brief frown. ''You're not the first visitor who's come to Strathlyon hoping to trace their Scottish ancestry.''

''I should think not,'' Juliette said. She wondered why he'd mention such an obvious fact. ''Your library is a treasure-trove of genealogical data.''

''People come to Scotland with the mistaken idea of finding a mythical land of adventure, Miss Elkheart.'' Although his deep baritone remained cool and unemotional, a sudden tenseness about him sounded a warning. ''For some peculiar reason I've yet to fully understand, young women especially seem to expect every Scotsman they meet to be a romantic figure in kilts. They think every Highlander is descended from a clan of warriors who displayed ferocious courage on the battlefield and an undying loyalty to their chief.''

''A kind of Hercules in plaid?'' she offered.

He gave her a taut smile, not amused by her banter. ''Exactly.''

Juliette calmly waited for him to go on. Inside, a cold presentiment nudged her heart. She sensed that he had a lot more he wanted to say, and she probably wasn't going to be pleased with the half of it.

''I suspect Sir Walter Scott's ridiculous tales of chivalry are to blame,'' he said tersely. ''Once a myth becomes widespread, it's next to impossible to debunk it.''

''But I have a feeling you are about to try.''

Straightening, MacLyon moved away from the desk. He went to stand in front of a pair of double-edged broadswords with basket hilts mounted on the wall nearby. Beneath them hung a silver badge with the MacLyon clan slogan. *Duinealachd.*

He studied the badge for a moment, as though searching for some answer hidden in that single word that stood for manliness and so much more. Decision of character. Virility. Strength. Valor. Fearlessness. Honor. Resolution. Then he turned to face her, his rugged features harsh and uncompromising.

"The truth is, Miss Elkheart," he said, his words cold and clipped, "the Highland Scots were far from being the glorious warriors portrayed in popular fiction. Our history is one of violence and brutality. The clans warred against one another for centuries, until the invading Sassenachs provided us with a common enemy. And even then, we betrayed one another to our English overlords, nearly to the point of our own annihilation. Tyranny and treachery were a way of life. We weren't the chivalrous knights of old. We were sneaky, skulking cattle thieves, who preyed on our neighbors in the dark without a qualm or a trace of guilt."

"And what has all this to do with me?" she asked. Anger flared, churning in her stomach and shortening her breath. She prayed her dispassionate tone would conceal her indignation.

"To put it bluntly, Miss Elkheart, you're wasting your time and ours trying to dig up a romantic past to satisfy your own personal delusions of glory. There *is* no romantic past in the Highlands. There never was."

She stiffened at the insult, but he stepped closer and continued before she could object. "I'm not talking solely about Clan Danielson, though God knows, there's little there to recommend any further research, and you'd be a fool to pursue it." He swept his hand in a contemptuous gesture. "Nothing in Scotland's history merits your misguided attempts to glorify it."

Juliette rose, rigid with anger. She refused to let his menacing stance or his daunting size alarm her. "What do you know of the reasons that brought me here?"

"Oh, I know," he said with insufferable confidence. "I know all too well the childish, virginal dreams of romance cradled within that lovely young head of yours. All lassies invent lovers of heroic proportions. You said it yourself: *Hercules in a kilt.*''

She drew a shaky breath and lifted her chin. Her heart pounded so hard she could barely speak. ''If the motive behind these slurs is to frighten me away, you are wasting your time. I came to the Highlands to find the truth about my ancestors, and I will stay until I am satisfied that I have done everything in my power to discover it.''

''The truth? I'll tell you the truth, Miss Elkheart,'' he said, his low words filled with mockery. In his mounting wrath, his soft Scots burr became more pronounced. ''Your forebears were treacherous villains, whose tainted blood runs in your veins. Nothing, *nothing* you find will change that one immutable fact.''

Without another word, Juliette whirled and hurried toward the door.

Lyon followed her, his long strides quickly closing the distance between them. He caught her wrist before she could reach the latch.

He held her captive, careful not to hurt her but determined to finish what he'd started. When he moved a step closer, Julie turned her head away. It was the stubborn, willful movement of a child, as though she could ignore his presence if she chose to. Her artless naiveté infuriated Lyon.

Why in the hell did she have to be so young and innocent?

He moved closer to tower over her in a deliberate ploy to intimidate. At her sudden nearness, a driving compulsion to take her in his arms and kiss her in a way she'd never been kissed whipped through him like a lightning bolt. Every muscle and nerve in his body ached for her sweetness. Desire tightened his groin with its relentless grip.

Bending his head, he steeled himself against the floral scent that drifted from her hair and spoke with silky menace. ''You will change your mind about dreams of romance. I guarantee it. Like Flora, you'll come to realize that all Highlanders are barbarians.''

Her head snapped up, and she glared at him, her dark eyes furious. ''Not all Highlanders, MacLyon. Just one.'' She tugged on her arm in a fruitless effort to break free and the curve of her hip bumped against his swollen crotch in her struggle.

His tightly leashed control snapped.

Lyon caught her by the waist and spun her around. Lifting her completely off her feet, he pinned her against the closed door. He rubbed his body against hers, letting her feel his arousal, thickened and hardened with need. He was a big man, and there was no mistaking his carnal state.

Julie gasped in shock. She pressed her shoulders against the oak panel behind her in a futile attempt to pull away from his touch and succeeded only in lifting her breasts higher. Her entire form quivered with rage.

Lyon had never known a woman could feel so unbelievably delicate and small-boned. Even in his frenzied state, he was aware of her heart-stopping fragility. His mind shouted a warning to his ravenous body. His beleaguered senses told him he held a tiny, fluttering bird captured in his hands.

Honor and lust dueled within him.

Part of him wanted to fling her to the rug and pound his cock into her till they were both insensible; the other part was frantic lest he harm her in his wild, insatiable sexual hunger. Never had he felt so close to the brink of madness.

He bent his head, grazing her temple with his lips, and spoke harshly in Gaelic as he ground his hips against her. ''Can you not feel him, lass? Can you not feel him yearning for you? He wants to be inside your soft, honeyed flesh.''

Suddenly the point of Julie's knife was pricking the vulnerable underside of his jaw.

''Put me down, *veho*,'' she ordered with cool deliberation, ''or I will slit your throat from one ear to the other.''

Lyon drew back to meet her somber gaze. His hands

lingered on her waist, his thumbs tracing the bottom of her ribcage. In the heat of his need, his mind registered two facts. She had remained perfectly calm throughout, as though she fended off attacks from oversexed males every day of the week. And she wore nothing beneath her dress that could possibly be considered a corset.

He considered the idea of forcing a kiss before setting her free, but the look in her eyes told him not to try. He could take the knife and the kiss by brute strength, but he risked the chance of hurting her in the process. For there was no doubt in his mind: she'd fight him with every ounce of the considerable courage she possessed. And if the knife slipped and cut her, he'd never forgive himself.

Knowing he was about to pay for his transgressions with her complete and final rejection of him, he set her lightly on her feet. The moment he released her, she swung the door open and fled.

He knew that was the last he'd ever see of little Miss Evening Star.

The thought was so uplifting, Lyon locked the study door, found a bottle of Scotch whisky stashed in his desk, and proceeded to get blind, stinking drunk.

"Listen to this one, Julie. This ballad must be at least four hundred years old." Rob sang as he played the piano, pausing after every line to translate the Gaelic words.

Juliette hummed along, following the notes in the song-book while turning the pages for him. The ancient ballad told of fairies borrowing a kettle every evening from a blacksmith, who lived near their home beneath a sand bank. Using the power of a magic rhyme, the smith made sure the Little People always returned it before morning, so his wife could cook their porridge.

The lilting refrain faded to silence when MacLyon saun-tered into the room. He hadn't bothered with a jacket, but wore a pleated white shirt and gray trousers with disrepu-table elegance.

Rob stopped in mid-bar, his hands hovering above the keys, and stared at his older brother in surprise. "We thought you'd left for Edinburgh."

The laird dropped down into a comfortable upholstered chair. "What made you think that?"

"Well, for one thing," Rob pointed out, "you didn't have supper with us last evening. And for another, your bed hadn't been slept in. When you didn't show up for breakfast either, we all assumed you'd gone on that business trip you mentioned the other day."

"I slept on the couch in my study," MacLyon said. He met Juliette's gaze with a crooked half-smile. "I see you're still here as well, Miss Elkheart."

"Why wouldn't she be?" Rob asked with a suspicious frown.

For a fleeting moment, there seemed to be a haunting sadness in the depths of MacLyon's eyes. But he offered his brother no explanation.

Juliette managed a tepid smile for Rob's sake, while her heart skipped up and down her ribs like keys on a piano. "The laird must have had the mistaken idea that I was going to leave this morning. Though I cannot imagine what made him think so."

"Perhaps it was the same illogical reason that made me decide to postpone my trip to Edinburgh," MacLyon said quietly.

Juliette sat down on the bench next to Rob and flipped through the pages in front of her, pretending to search for a particular song. A blush scalded her cheeks. She felt as awkward and vulnerable as a quail dragging a 'broken' wing through the prairie grass away from her nest and her young.

Nanoseham was the hunter, and she was the prey.

"I find it hard to believe, laird," she said softly, "that you would do anything without a logical reason or motive aforethought."

MacLyon lounged back in his chair and propped one

ankle on the opposite knee. He scrutinized her with un-flinching candor. "That's *malice* aforethought, Miss Elk-heart. And even the most rational of us may do something insane when we're pushed beyond our natural limits."

As Rob looked from one to the other, Juliette forced herself to remain outwardly calm. Inside, she was quaking. Every shamelessly erotic suggestion he'd spoken in Gaelic was imprinted on her brain, as though burned there by a fiery brand.

Just the thought of what he'd said, his deep voice harsh and intense, set her heart racing. She'd awakened in the night to feel a warm ache pulsating through her. Lying in her soft, comfortable bed, she'd fought the memory of his large male body pressing against her, vaguely aware that the tingling sensation in her swollen breasts was the slow contraction of her nipples.

Yesterday, she should have felt dread and repugnance. But when he'd held her imprisoned with such ridiculous ease, she'd recognized the physical power he held firmly in check. And that leashed, shuddering power had revealed the extent of his pain. Some deep, primitive, female instinct told her MacLyon was not just afraid he might uninten-tionally hurt her, but also, for some fantastic reason, was afraid of her. And that fear made him rage inside.

"Please, don't let me disturb you," MacLyon said with maddening nonchalance. "Go on with your singing." He braced an elbow on the arm of the chair, rested his chin in his palm, and nodded for them to continue.

"Oh, we won't stop on your account," Rob assured him, only too happy to comply. Choosing another ballad from the songbook, he pounded away on the keyboard.

Every note his brother struck felt like a hammer crashing down on Lyon's aching skull. His entire head throbbed as though it'd been smacked on the floor repeatedly during the night. Even the damn hair on his head hurt. Not that he was complaining—he treasured the pain. In fact, he rel-ished every excruciating shard that lanced through him in accompaniment to the spirited music. He deserved all of the agony and more.

For the hundredth time that morning, he asked himself the same question.

How could he have let things go so far?

Contrary to his last conscious wish before passing out, he'd awakened to find himself still alive. The only consolation had been the belief that the indomitable Miss Elkheart had undoubtedly packed her clothes the night before and left the premises at the crack of dawn. He'd sat on the sofa in his study for nearly an hour, his head cradled in his hands, and wondered how any man could be such an unmitigated ass. Lyon was totally and thoroughly ashamed of himself.

Eventually, he had gathered enough intestinal fortitude to leave the safety of his sanctuary. He'd cringed at the thought of the reception he would receive from his horrified family. To his amazement, no one was waiting outside the locked door. Not a soul in the entire castle paid the least heed as he made his way to his suite of rooms on the third floor.

By the time he'd shaved, bathed, and dressed, he'd learned from the servants—always happy to gossip—that his brother and nephews had taken their lovely guest for an early morning ride. They'd then enjoyed a fine Scottish breakfast of buttered potato scones straight from the griddle and steaming bowls of oatmeal porridge. After a session spent in the library doing research with Lady Hester, Julie and Rob had retreated to the music room, where Lyon found them.

He watched her now, beside his handsome brother, and wondered if Rob was the reason she'd stayed. No surprise there. Although Julie was very young, the two were not all that far apart in age—four or five years at the most. And Rob had the dashing good looks females found so attractive. No one had ever broken Rob's nose for him. Or carved up his face with a dagger. Hell, there wasn't a woman in

Strathbardine between eight and eighty who wasn't half in love with Robbie MacLyon.

He only hoped Rob didn't feel the same way about her. He had no intention of allowing a match between his younger brother and the intrepid little Canadian. Not when The MacLyon, himself, couldn't accidentally brush up against her without turning into a slavering beast.

The chirping songbirds were interrupted for the second time that morning when two enormous gray deerhounds came gamboling into the music room, followed by Neil and Jamie.

Julie and Rob ceased their caroling and turned to watch the fun. The dogs barked in happy excitement as they tussled and rolled on the carpet with the two laughing boys.

"Ah, ye wee loons," Rob called to his nephews. "Are you trying to frighten our bonny guest with your overgrown rats?"

Neil paused in the midst of the rumpus to give her an encouraging smile. "Don't be afraid, Miss Elkheart," he said. "They're big, but they won't bite you."

"This is Tiree," Jamie told her proudly. He grabbed a handful of the dog's long, wiry fur and patted its head. "The other one's Dunbar."

Unlike most strangers who'd never before seen a large, sturdy deerhound up close, Julie didn't cringe or cry out in alarm. She scooted around the edge of the bench to face them, held out her hand, and called softly to the formidable animals in her native language.

The MacLyon males watched in amazement as the hunting hounds stopped their frenzied barking and went to her instantly. They touched their black noses to her outstretched fingers, sniffing and nuzzling in curiosity.

Giving another command in Cheyenne, she pointed to the floor. The dogs folded their long legs and laid down in front of her, muzzles resting on their paws. She praised the intelligent pair for their quick obedience, the strange words flowing over them like a mother's caress. Dunbar and Tiree looked up at her from beneath thick, shaggy brows, their dark eyes adoring, and didn't move a muscle.

"What did you tell them?" Neil questioned in awe.

"I told them they would have to mind their manners from now on," she replied with an entrancing smile.

Jamie walked over to Julie, sank down on his haunches, and peered at his pets. "Did they understand you?"

"Yes."

"What else did you say?"

"That I knew they were used to behaving like wild antelope in springtime, but they would have to change their uncivilized ways if they wanted to be around me."

Lyon sat forward in his chair. She wasn't talking about the deerhounds. She was giving him an ultimatum. He'd either change his brutish ways, or she'd have nothing more to do with him. His scowl of self-abnegation slowly turned into a reluctant grin. He looked from the chastened dogs to her magnificent almond eyes, glowing with a winsome charm.

The wee, brown-eyed lass had the audacity to issue a warning to the chief of Clan MacLyon, a decorated army officer, who towered more than a foot above her dainty head and outweighed her by a good hundred pounds.

Well, he had a warning of his own to issue. She'd soon learn that he'd be far harder to tame than the good-natured, affectionate deerhounds at her feet.

In the momentary quiet, Lady Hester entered the room. She paused in surprise, for by this time, Neil and Jamie had thrown themselves out full-length on the floor alongside their pets. "I see you've met the rest of the family," she said to her houseguest, "and with your usual bewitching effect."

Julie's soft, husky laughter floated across the room and poured into a hole in Lyon's heart. The unbearable ache he always carried inside eased, as if by a magic spell. "It was the Cheyenne commands that did the trick," she said.

Lady Hester looked at Rob, who, like his brother, had risen when she entered the room. She motioned for them to sit down. "If you hope to be back from Rothnamurchan in time for supper, you'd best get started. We'll be having *sole á la Hollandaise* along with *grillé aux vin de Champagne*. You won't want to miss it."

"Can we go to Rothnamurchan, too?" Neil asked, scrambling to his feet.

Black eyes alight in hopeful expectation, Jamie popped up from the rug to stand beside his brother. "Please let us go!"

Lady Hester came to sit in the chair next to Lyon. "Not today, lads," she said. "You need to do your lessons this afternoon with Mr. Dittmar." They hung their heads in disappointment, and she waggled a finger at them. "No fussing, now. Your schooling is very important."

"But we want to go with Uncle Robbie and Miss Elkheart," Neil protested. "Lessons are boring. We never get to do anything fun."

"No, nothing fun," Jamie concurred.

Lyon motioned to Neil, and the six-year-old came to stand between his uncle's knees. Jamie immediately bounded over and crawled onto the chair's soft arm, where he sat with his feet resting on Lyon's trousered thigh.

"You'll do exactly what Nana says," he told the youngsters firmly. "One of the most important lessons a man can learn in life is never to argue with the lady who's in charge of the menu."

Rob played a rolling trill on the keyboard, then accompanied his words with a children's bedtime melody. "Or you'll have creamed turnips for dessert every night for a week."

"Creamed turnips! Ugh!" Neil cried. He made a face of disgust, but his blue eyes sparkled with merriment.

"Ugh!" his brother echoed, breaking into ecstatic giggles.

Lyon put an arm around each one and gave them an

affectionate squeeze. "If you work very hard with Mr. Dittmar this afternoon, we'll ask Cook to serve pudding with cinnamon and sugar, instead."

"Hurrah!" they shouted, clapping their hands.

Lyon glanced over at Julie. She was reaching down to pat the deerhounds, her head bent, her face partially hidden. "So you're planning to ride to Rothnamurchan, then?" he asked his brother in an offhand manner.

Rob nodded, absently tinkling the black and white keys. "Julie would like to see the hand-looming of our local tartans."

"That's a good idea," Lyon said. "I think I'll ride along with you."

Julie's head flew up. She met his gaze for a startled moment, her dark eyes troubled, and then looked away.

Rob stared at Lyon in amazement. He opened his mouth, decided against whatever he'd been about to say, and struck a final, rousing chord, instead. "Great. Flora's coming too. We'll leave in twenty minutes."

"In that case," Julie said, "I had better change into my riding habit."

She stood, and the two men politely rose to their feet. Tiree and Dunbar jumped up and started to follow her to the door. At her brief order, given in Cheyenne, the hounds immediately sat down and watched her go.

Without thinking, Rob and Lyon did the same. Their gazes met, and the two brothers grinned sheepishly at the clear evidence of their mutual captivation.

The moment Julie disappeared into the hallway, Neil crawled up on Lyon's knee. "She uses magic words, Uncle Lyon," he said solemnly.

Still perched on the arm of the chair, Jamie leaned forward and spoke close to Lyon's ear. "Magic words."

"No, they're not magic," he said, trying not to laugh. "Miss Elkheart was using the language she first spoke as a child. That's why she pronounces English with such an unusual accent.''

Jamie slipped his arm around Lyon's neck and, with a knowing pat, confided in an undertone, ''We think she's a fairy.''

''What makes you think so?'' Lady Hester demanded in astonishment.

''Well, she talked to Dunbar and Tiree in her secret language,'' Neil said, ''and they understood her.''

''It's not a secret language,'' Lyon corrected. ''It only sounds secretive because we've never heard it before.''

Neil wasn't so sure. ''Then how did Dunbar and Tiree understand her? They've never heard it before, either.''

''I don't know,'' Lyon admitted.

''Besides, she always wears green,'' Jamie said with a happy smile.

Lyon shook his head in disagreement. ''Not always. She's dressed in yellow, today.''

''But she wore green yesterday,'' Neil said stubbornly. ''And she had a green cloak on the day she saved your life. You told us so.''

Lyon looked from one lad to the other in bafflement. ''What has green to do with it, anyway?''

Rob tickled the piano keys and grinned. ''Besides having a singular love of music, which they use in casting enchantments, fairies always wear green,'' he explained for his older brother's edification. ''It's their special color.''

''A mere coincidence,'' Lyon assured the two youngsters. He patted Jamie's smooth black locks. ''Miss Elkheart happens to like green, that's all.''

Neil wasn't impressed with his eldest uncle's logic. ''Fairies are wee, little people,'' he said, ''just like she is.''

''Some people are born that way,'' Lyon instructed patiently. ''Even as adults, they never get very tall. Miss Elkheart is little, but she's not incredibly tiny. She wouldn't fit into a bottle or anything like that.'' He glanced at his grandmother, hoping to enlist her support.

Lady Hester's eyes glowed with mirth. She shook her head, refusing to come to his aid.

"Uncle Robbie told us that fairies can disappear in the blink of an eye," Neil stated with absolute conviction.

"And change their size just as fast," Jamie added. He snapped his pudgy fingers in demonstration.

Grasping each boy under his arm like a sack of barley, Lyon stood up and jostled them playfully. "I'm telling you, lads, there are no such things as fairies. Now who are you going to believe? Me or your Uncle Robbie?"

"Uncle Robbie!" they shouted in glee.

At Lyon's whistle, the two deerhounds leapt up and began licking the children's faces. Imprisoned in their uncle's hold, Neil and Jamie could do nothing but try to push the dogs away and giggle hysterically.

"We believe you! We believe you!" they cried in surrender.

"And fairies are a foolish Highland superstition. Now say it," he commanded.

"Fairies are a foolish Highland superstition!" they chorused after him.

But as he set them on their feet and gently swatted their behinds, telling them to get to the schoolroom and their overdue lessons, he heard Neil whisper to Jamie.

"She really *is* a fairy."

Chapter 7

Juliette and MacLyon rode side by side, well in front of their two companions. With the laird's permission, she'd chosen a dainty white Arabian from the Strathlyon stables. Once he realized his guest from Canada was more than just a competent rider, MacLyon leaned forward in his saddle, gave his own mount a signal, and raced ahead. Juliette accepted the unspoken challenge. To her delight, the spirited mare matched the pace set by the laird's powerful thoroughbred stallion.

They left the road, galloping across an open pasture dotted with black-faced sheep, the woolly creatures watching them in stolid complacency as they flew past. When they reached a burn, they halted to rest their horses and wait for Rob and Flora.

MacLyon dismounted and lifted Juliette down from her sidesaddle. She rested her hands lightly on his broad shoulders, and their gazes met. At the smoldering hunger in his eyes, she flinched inwardly, as though he'd burned her with his touch. Breathless, she fought the urge to blurt out a warning. Her knife was strapped to her thigh beneath her skirt. But his hands tarried on her waist only a fraction of a second after setting her on her feet. Together, they turned and led their horses to the trickling stream.

She watched him cautiously from the corner of her eye, uncertain if he'd mention his outrageous behavior of the previous day. He wore a dark riding coat, buff breeches, and high black boots. With his usual informality, he had no hat or neck cloth. His white shirt collar stood open, revealing the hollow at the base of his throat.

If his purpose was to unsettle her, he was wide of the mark. She'd been raised in a culture where men wore breechcloths in warm weather—and precious little else. It would take more than a glimpse of crisp, russet chest hair to make her swoon in agitation.

MacLyon pulled two apples out of his jacket pockets and tossed one to her. The roan stallion snuffled his hand lovingly before chomping the treat with noisy greed.

"How is the research coming?" he asked without ceremony.

"Not very well," Juliette admitted, offering her horse the other apple. She released a pent-up breath, thankful he hadn't renewed his tirade of the day before. She felt as restless and edgy as a doe approached by an imperial stag in the rutting season. "We spent a good part of the morning searching the records for some mention of the Danielson clan, but to no avail. It's as though they never existed."

"Their name is rarely mentioned," he said. "They've been called the Clan of the Clouds for good reason. After they massacred the MacLyon Highlanders in Glen Kildunun, the Danielson men were executed and their womenfolk scattered. The entire clan seemed to disappear into the clouds."

MacLyon adjusted his saddle girth, then came over to check her stirrup straps. The white mare nickered and nudged his shoulder, and he patted her nose affectionately.

"Evidently all mention of the clan was expunged from local records, as well," she said. "We couldn't find the name of Danielson on a single deed or will. Not even on a record of rents or a bill of sale."

"They were probably removed to prevent any foes from tracing a person's ancestry back to the murderers—just as a measure of self-protection. Until you appeared at Strathlyon with your great-grandfather's plaid, no one, to my knowledge, had ever made an attempt to prove a connection with Clan Danielson. Quite the contrary. Until two days ago, I'd never laid eyes on a lavender and pink tartan. I recognized it from my grandmother's descriptions. And my father's stories.''

Biting her lip, Juliette looked up at MacLyon from beneath lowered lids. "Stories that were not very pleasant, I am sure.'' When he shrugged his shoulders with apparent indifference, she gathered her courage. "How far away is Glen Kildunun?''

He looked at her questioningly. "A half day's journey by paddle boat up Loch Linnhe. Why?''

"I would like to see the site,'' she replied evenly. "I cannot explain why. At least, not now.''

They heard the sound of hoofbeats and turned to watch Rob and Flora ride over the brow of the hill and down to the burn.

"Thank goodness you waited for us,'' Flora called gaily as they cantered up. "Otherwise, we never would have caught you. I'm not such a bruising rider as everyone else.''

Juliette stroked the Arab's sleek neck. "Voxpenonoma is as fast as the winter wind blowing a storm across the prairie,'' she said with pride.

Flora jerked on her reins, and her bay side-stepped nervously. "*What* is as fast as the wind?''

"White Thunder,'' Juliette translated.

"I thought . . .'' Flora's apprehensive gaze darted to MacLyon and then back to Juliette. "That is . . .''

"I had no idea Miss Elkheart had renamed my prize Arabian, if that's what you're wondering,'' the laird said. His mouth twitched suspiciously, but he continued in a matter-of-fact tone. "How could I? She always talks to animals in Cheyenne.''

Rob gave a soft snort of laughter. "And by some magic, they understand her.''

MacLyon sent a warning frown to his brother, but his

green eyes flashed with some mirthful secret. Before she had a chance to question him, he swung Juliette up to her sidesaddle, then remounted himself. "Rothnamurchan is just over the next hill, Miss Elkheart. Let's go see how they hand-loom tartans."

A cluster of white-washed cottages stood huddled together on the northern shore of Loch Etive. Smoke from their peat fires rose slowly above the thatched roofs. Flower gardens, now past midsummer's lush bloom, sprinkled petals over the ground.

The four riders left their mounts to graze in a stand of elms and walked down the narrow road that curved through the village.

"Rothnamurchan is on MacLyon land," the laird told Juliette. "The original foundations go back to the twelfth century. These homes have been restored under the direction of the Scottish Tartans Society. Much of the money for their preservation was donated by my father and grandfather. MacLyon clansmen, who know the old crafts and are willing to practice them as a trade, live here rent free. It's our way of protecting the ancient traditions."

Perplexed, Juliette hurried to keep up with his long, easy stride. "I thought you believed your ancestors were nothing more than sneaking cattle thieves."

"I didn't say I supported Rothnamurchan," he answered dryly. "I said my father and grandfather did. The glorification of a myth is hardly my idea of—"

"Lyon didn't always feel that way," Rob interjected. "Since he returned from the Sudan, my brother's been in a bloody foul mood." He leaned closer to Juliette and added in a theatrical whisper. "Till you arrived."

MacLyon glared at him and spoke through clenched teeth. "No one's interested in your asinine evaluation of my moods."

"But now he's a stark, raving lunatic," Rob finished

cheerfully, as though his brother hadn't spoken. "He'd start a fight in an empty house."

On the other side of Rob, Flora clapped her hand over her mouth, too late to cover a surreptitious giggle.

Fortunately a woman came out of the nearest cottage at that moment, forestalling any further conversation. Plump as a little prairie dog, she threw her hands up in delight when she saw her visitors. "Guidsakes! It's the laird, himself, comin' to see us." She bobbed up and down in a joyous curtsey, the edges of her black shawl flapping in the breeze like the wings of a crow.

MacLyon greeted her with a warm smile. "Good day, Grizel. We have a guest from the plains of Canada who'd like to learn about the looming of tartans." He turned to Juliette. "Miss Elkheart, this is Mrs. Conacher. She knows as much about clan tartans as Lady Hester knows about Highland genealogy."

When Juliette offered her hand, the woman clasped it in both her plump ones. "Ach, 'tis true, then," she said, her ruddy cheeks dimpling in welcome. Her alert blue eyes glistened with merriment. "We heard ye was as lovely as a princess in a fairy tale."

"You are very kind," Juliette replied. She could feel the intensity of MacLyon's gaze and struggled to hide her embarrassment.

"Come away in, then!" Grizel urged, slipping her hand into the crook of Juliette's elbow. "Come away in!" With a flutter of her work-roughened fingers, she bustled her four visitors into her tidy home.

Inside, a silver-haired woman, thin as a willow sapling, sat at a spinning wheel near the hearth. Turning its wheel with a foot treadle, she deftly twisted the fibers off the spindle and wound the yarn onto a bobbin in one fluid motion.

"Mither!" Grizel exclaimed. "Look who's come to see us!"

When Juliette was introduced, Goodwife Dowel looked

up from her work and smiled, all the while continuing to spin. "Ye maun call me Aggie," she said with a nod of greeting. "We're no' so fancy here, as up at the castle."

On one side of the room stood a large wooden loom, where a pattern of black and white threads was being formed. At Grizel's invitation, Juliette and Flora went to stand in front of it.

"The Balmoral tartan," Grizel explained. She pursed her lips and wrinkled her nose disparagingly. " 'Tisn't at all old, ye ken. The Prince Consort designed it. This cloth will be worn by Her Majesty's ghillies." She pressed her hands to her apple-red cheeks and shook her head, as though catching herself in a dreadful mistake. "Och, but 'tis an honor to be chosen for the weavin' of it, ye understand."

Stacked on a table were folded lengths of wool, woven in patterns of various colors. As she showed the tartans to her Canadian guest, Grizel pronounced the clan names in her rolling Scots accent. Stewart, MacLyon, MacDougall, MacGregor, Campbell, McCorquodale.

Running her hand lovingly over the material, she explained how the twill weave made a flexible but heavyweight cloth, ideal for a *feileadh-beag*—or little kilt. Her eyes glistened with pride. "It makes a hard tartan, ye ken, that'll ne'er wear out. And the kilt will be comfortable and have the proper swing."

At the faint sound of whimpering, Grizel left the table and scurried over to the stone hearth. For the first time, Juliette noticed a wooden crate on the floor. A sable and white collie lay inside the box on a pile of soft rags. The animal was panting heavily.

"Ah, puir thing," Grizel crooned. She stooped and comforted the dog, running her hand gently over its head and long, tapered muzzle. "Sweetie's havin' a verra hard time of it. I'm worrit to death for fear she'll no' be makin' it, but I dinna ken what else to do for her. She seems to be gettin' weaker and weaker by the minute."

Juliette crouched down beside the box. The collie bitch

thumped her long tail once, then twice, in melancholy greeting. The catch in her respiration and the glazed eyes told of the pain she was enduring. "May I check her?"

Grizel nodded emphatically. "Oh, aye, lass."

The mother-to-be was clearly in distress. She lay on her side, with her head perfectly still. Her ribs heaved with every breath, and her dark, troubled eyes seemed to plead for help. Juliette ran her hands carefully over the distended abdomen, feeling the larger bumps that meant heads, and the smaller ones that were paws. She couldn't tell how many puppies, but felt certain there were at least five.

"I think she needs a veterinarian," she told Grizel in concern.

"A veterinarian?" the woman gasped, as though she'd suggested an Edinburgh surgeon.

MacLyon came over and sank down on one knee beside Juliette. "This is the Highlands, Miss Elkheart. There isn't a vet for thirty miles. And his practice is for horses and cows."

Juliette rose, quickly removed her riding jacket, and rolled up the sleeves of her white blouse. "Then I will need some hot water and strong soap," she told Grizel. "And some clean cloths . . . or an old blanket will do."

From her stool in front of the spinning wheel, Aggie jumped to her feet with the speed of a woman twenty years her junior. "I'll fetch what ye need," she called. "We've a kettle o' water already boilin' for tea."

Grizel wrung her hands on her sparkling white apron as her mother bustled around the room. "Can ye help our puir Sweetie?" she asked. She appeared to be wavering between hope and despair. "She's been tryin' to birth since early this mornin'."

Juliette met the woman's worried eyes. "Sweetie is quickly reaching the point of exhaustion. I think one of the puppies must be badly positioned and blocking the delivery. I am not sure I can save her and the puppies as well, but I am willing to try if you will let me."

MacLyon put his hand on Juliette's arm, his low voice incredulous. "Do you know what you're doing?"

Before she could answer, Rob and Flora came to stand beside them. They looked down at the sheepdog and then at Juliette in wonder.

"Surely, you can't mean to . . ." Flora said in strangled voice. She put her hand to her throat, unable to go on.

"I was raised on a ranch," Juliette assured them. "There was no veterinarian within a hundred miles, nor a doctor or dentist within eighty. I have helped my father deliver colts, fillies, calves, and puppies. We never lost a mother or a baby." She smiled at Grizel and added briskly, "Now if I may borrow an apron, please?"

"God be thankit," Aggie said. She whisked her long, bib apron off her spare frame, slipped it over Juliette's skirt and blouse, and tied the strings in back.

In spite of her show of confidence, a small voice inside Juliette's head reminded her that she'd only *assisted* her father during the birthings. In times of crisis, Strong Elk Heart had made all the hard decisions and given the necessary orders, which she and Jennie carried out without question. But she knew that without help the collie might well die, and the unborn pups with her.

Juliette washed her hands in the strong yellow soap Aggie provided. When she learned there was no antiseptic in the cottage, she had Grizel add a generous splash of whisky to the water in the basin and rinsed her hands in that. Then she knelt down on the floor. Following her directions, MacLyon gently lifted the sheepdog out of the crate and placed her on the old, torn blanket.

Juliette spoke to the collie in Cheyenne, telling her not to be afraid. Sweetie lifted her head, as though to assure Juliette she understood, then lay back wearily.

Carefully, Juliette inserted the tips of two fingers, feeling for the confirmation of a small head or tiny tail. It was just as she feared. The first puppy lay nearly crosswise, obstructing the delivery. She waited for the pressure of a contraction to subside, then inched her fingers in further, careful not to scratch the vaginal wall. All the while, she comforted the suffering animal in soft Cheyenne words.

When Sweetie strained again with another contraction, Juliette waited patiently. She could feel the powerful squeeze against the joints of her fingers. The moment the vaginal muscles relaxed, she used her two fingers like a forceps and cautiously tried to move the pup, while pushing on the outside with her other hand. It was easier than she dared hope. Bit by bit, she turned the jammed body, smiling to herself when she felt the tiny nose.

"Sometimes it is a blessing to have small hands," she told the people hovering above her. "My father always said I was surprisingly strong for my size."

Not daring to pull, she gently guided the pup towards her with each succeeding contraction. "Come on, Sweetie," she coaxed. "I cannot do this without your help. Push for me, now. Push!"

The collie seemed to realize the worst was over. She strained and strained again, and Juliette eased the puppy free. With a sigh of joy, she cradled the newborn in her hands. The little fellow was breathing. He was alive. Laying him down on the blanket beside his tired mama, she looked up at the fascinated faces above her.

"We should wait for a while," she told Grizel and Aggie. "I think once Sweetie catches her breath, she may be able to deliver the rest of the puppies by herself." Juliette looked around in puzzlement. "Where are Rob and Flora?"

MacLyon grinned. His eyes shone with admiration and a burgeoning mirth. "He took her outside before she fainted and landed on top of you."

They had tea and hot buttered oatcakes while they waited. Seated in a circle of wooden chairs, Grizel and her mother explained to their guests about the variations of setts, ancient colors, native lichens used for making dyes, thread counts, and selvages, all the while keeping an eye on the collie and her pup.

"I can weave seven yards in a day," Grizel stated with understandable pride. "But Mither can make ten, for she ne'er has to look at a line of writin' to make any sett."

"Aweel, if it weren't for his lairdship's kindness," Aggie disclaimed, "the hand-loomin' of our local tartans would have nigh disappeared. And may do so yet, for there's no' a weaver in Rothnamurchan under the age of fifty."

At this piece of news, Juliette peeked at MacLyon from the corner of her eye. He studiously avoided her gaze. It seemed the Lion wasn't nearly as ferocious as he'd like her to believe.

Within the next hour, the rest of Sweetie's litter was born without incident. Six greedy puppies were soon feasting on their mother's milk, and the visitors prepared to leave.

The women stood in front of the cottage saying their good-byes, while the men went to fetch the horses. Using the excuse of checking on the new family one last time, Juliette asked Aggie to accompany her back inside.

"Would you be willing to make a special tartan for me?" she queried, once they were alone.

"Oh, aye," the elderly woman immediately agreed. "Is it a sett ye thought of yerself, then?"

Juliette hesitated. "No . . . no, it is an old clan tartan from this part of Scotland. I can draw the pattern for you and try to explain the colors. Or I can bring you a sample tomorrow."

"There's nae need for doin' either. If it's a local clan tartan, I have the sett right here." Aggie touched her forehead with the tip of one crooked finger. "And I can make any dye that was ever used in these parts of the Hielan's. What colors will I be needin'?"

"Lavender and pink."

The wizened old woman gazed at Juliette in silence for a moment, then spoke softly. "Lavender and pink are the

colors of the Danielson Fencibles. Why would ye be wantin' such a thing, girl?''

"Because I believe that my great-grandfather was a descendent of Clan Danielson. I have his plaid, now frayed
and worn. I would like a new one made.'' Unconsciously,
Juliette straightened her shoulders and lifted her chin.
''Will you do it?''

Aggie looked down at Sweetie and her hungry brood.
She pursed her lips in contemplation, then met Juliette's
gaze with quiet resolve. "I will," she agreed. " 'Twill take
a bit o' time to gather the right lichens for the dyes. Those
particular shades havena been used for many, many years,
ye ken.''

"Thank you," Juliette said in a near-whisper. She released a heartfelt sigh, only now aware of how tense she'd
been. ''Whatever your usual fee, I will gladly double it.''

"Na, na. There'll be no fee, child o' the clouds," Aggie
replied. "My mither's mither was a Danielson, though no
one hereabouts kens it. And I'd appreciate it, *mo chaileag*,
if ye kept that fact to yerself.''

The two women—so different in age and background,
yet somehow tied to each other in the distant past—walked
outside together.

MacLyon stood waiting with Grizel near the cottage
door, holding the reins of their mounts. "Flora and Rob
have already left," he said. "We'd better go now, or we'll
be late for supper.''

Juliette touched Aggie's arm. "May I talk to you about
this later?''

"Forbye, lass, some things are best left unspoken," she
demurred. "But come again soon, for anither visit.''

On the way back to the castle, Lyon made no attempt to
catch up with Rob and Flora. Julie's willingness to be alone
with him surprised him, at first. He suspected that she foolishly believed she could defend herself from any unwanted
attentions on his part. He'd warrant she was carrying the

knife carved with mystical totems on her person right now. Was she really so naive as to believe it was magic?

He led her to a rocky point and reined in his stallion. "The view is magnificent from here," he said, as Julie halted the white mare beside Thor.

Lyon helped her dismount, ignoring the dull ache in his injured arm, then watched in silence as she strode to the edge of the cliff and gazed about her in wonder.

A deep, narrow glen wound down to Loch Etive below them, with streams rushing down its steep, forested sides. The faint cry of whaups carried upward on a breeze laden with the crisp smell of Scots pine. To the east, snow-capped mountain peaks glistened in the late afternoon sun, their glory reflected in the still, cold waters of the loch. Across the western horizon stretched the Firth of Lorn and the purple-hued outline of the Island of Mull beyond.

"That's Ben Cruachan in the distance," he told her, motioning in a southeasterly direction.

Julie removed her felt bowler, tossed it on the ground, and turned in a slow circle, gazing in every direction. The skirt of her gray riding costume was stained with blood, despite the apron she'd worn earlier at the cottage. Her chignon had come loose and now fell down her back in a long, silken braid to her hips.

"*Hesc!*" she said softly. "It is amazing." A look of wonder lit her face, and her generous mouth turned upward in delight.

The glow of pure happiness that shone in her eyes beckoned to him like the siren song of a sea nymph. A song of illusion that threatened to break down his resistance, only to dash him against the hard rocks of reality, where he would break to pieces like a ship foundering on the shore.

Lyon walked over to stand beside her, careful to leave a safe distance between them. There wasn't going to be any repeat of yesterday's folly. This afternoon, he had himself firmly under control.

"The scenery is not nearly as amazing as watching you

deliver that puppy," he said, striving for a light-hearted tone. The truth of it was, he'd watched her in awe. The feelings she'd awakened in him now went far beyond sexual attraction, and the strength of those feelings scared the bloody hell out of Lyon.

Julie lowered her head and made a self-deprecating little shrug. "My parents would not think it amazing at all. Nor any of my family, for that matter. When I return home, I will be enrolling in the University of Pennsylvania with the goal of someday becoming a veterinarian."

He couldn't conceal his astonishment. "They allow women to study veterinary medicine in America?"

"It will take all my grandfather's influence to get me into the school in Philadelphia," she admitted. "Grandpapa is a United States senator. Right now, he is on a goodwill tour for the president. My sister, Jennie, is with him in London. From there, they will travel across Europe to Constantinople."

"And so you came to Edinburgh with your uncle, instead."

"Yes. Since Uncle Benjamin was going to study surgery at the university there, it was a wonderful chance for me to visit Scotland. It is something I have wanted to do for several years." Frowning, she plucked a leaf from a whortleberry bush and absently rolled the stem between her fingers. "But I worry that I should have gone with Jennie."

"Why is that?"

"This is the first time we have ever been separated. I have always been responsible for her—I am the older twin." She laughed softly and added, "If only by a few minutes."

"Why should one twin be responsible for the other?"

"Because Jennie is so impetuous. She does things without first weighing the consequences. Since we were children, my parents have expected me, as the prudent, practical one, to keep her out of trouble."

Wisely, he didn't bring up the fact that, since her arrival

in Scotland, Julie had killed a murderous assailant, thereby saving a man's life. Or that she now stood alone in an isolated spot with a large, aggressive male, whose throat she'd threatened to slit the previous day. Far from being prudent or practical, it was an astonishingly naive thing to do. Such potentially dangerous behavior brought out Lyon's protective instincts.

"How old are you, Miss Elkheart?" he growled. "All of seventeen?"

She tossed her head in an aggrieved movement. "I am eighteen."

"Barely, then."

"I turned eighteen in July."

"Oh, my mistake," he retorted with a grin. "Eighteen years and two months."

Shredding the leaf into pieces, she muttered crossly, "How old are you?"

"Old enough to be your father."

"Hardly!"

Lyon didn't bother to argue the point. He'd lost his virginity at fourteen, though to his knowledge he hadn't sired a child, then or later. At thirty-four, he was far too old and world-weary for an innocent lass like her. Julie was intelligent and idealistic and filled with lofty dreams. He was a crippled, guilt-racked degenerate, who didn't deserve anyone half so wonderful.

"I hope you get your wish, Miss Elkheart," he said, and he meant it sincerely. He was overjoyed at the news of her goal, however unlikely it might be to achieve. "I hope you get into that college of veterinary medicine in Philadelphia. From what I saw today, you'll make a wonderful vet."

What he didn't say was that *anything* was preferable to having her married to his younger brother. Lyon knew he couldn't endure that kind of torture—not for the rest of his life.

But if Rob wasn't the reason she'd stayed at Strathlyon in the face of his behavior yesterday, what was? Why would she be willing to ride with the man who'd forced his attentions upon her, in order to visit an insignificant cluster of cottages in the Highlands?

Lyon held out his hands, palms up, in apology. "I hope you can overlook my behavior, Miss Elkheart. I'd like us to begin again."

Juliette stared in surprise at his proffered hands. She hesitated, for they were larger than most men's, and therefore, conceivably more dangerous. The broad palms were hardened with calluses; the fingers long, with blunt tips. She remembered what Lady Hester had claimed: MacLyon was descended in the direct male line from Norse kings. His were the strong, conquering hands of a Viking.

Her pulse fluttering wildly, she looked up to find him watching her with fierce male pride.

He would apologize.

He wouldn't beg.

The western sky glowed with the setting sun, turning his reddish-gold hair to burnished copper. Beneath the fitted riding jacket, his wide shoulders and upper arms bulged with muscle. The tight buff breeches and high boots clearly outlined his powerful thighs and calves.

Juliette felt a belated ping of alarm. If MacLyon decided to attack her here, in this lonely spot, she'd need more than her knife and her Cheyenne courage to protect her.

"Very well," she said, her low voice sounding suffocated and faraway. "We shall start over." Gathering the resolution of a warrior-woman about her like a sacred buffalo robe, she placed her hands in his, palm to palm. He didn't make any attempt to clasp her fingers, just let them lie there, resting trustfully.

Then he turned her hands over, cradling them lightly, the same way she'd cradled the newborn puppy. A smile of rare tenderness touched his lips, and her heart leapt within her.

"Such wee, small hands," he murmured. "No bigger than a bairn's. And yet . . . so powerful."

To her astonishment, he lifted her cupped hands to his mouth, as though he were going to drink from them. She could feel his breath, warm and gentle, just before he touched his lips to her palms. A feeling of awe swept through her that this magnificent giant could be so heart-touchingly tender.

"MacLyon," she whispered. She slid her fingers along the unyielding jaw, feeling the rough stubble of his day-old beard. He remained absolutely still, his hands loosely encircling her wrists. She heard a quick, in-drawn breath catch in his throat as she traced the line of his upper lip with her fingertips.

Scarcely aware of her own movements, Juliette stepped closer. She inhaled the pungent smell of leather and pine that hovered about him. A sense of anticipation quivered inside her, as though she stood on the brink of some over-whelming discovery.

Lyon watched the feelings of wonder and expectancy that played across Julie's exotic features and cursed himself for a fool.

He should never have touched her.

Far, far worse, she should never have touched him.

The light, tentative exploration of her fingers sent the blood surging through his heart. His lungs collapsed, as the breath flew out of him in a whoosh. He closed his eyes, willing himself to remain passive while every fiber in his being twanged with delirious sexual energy. He was under the thrall of the evening star, his only desire to capture her shining rays in his hands.

"I thought about you last night," she confessed in her husky contralto.

"Did you?" His lips moved against the soft pads of her fingers. His manhood lurched against the snug crotch of his breeches.

"Yes, I wondered why . . . well, you know . . . yesterday, when you . . ."

The shy innocence of her words struck him with the

force of a battering ram. Guilt slammed against the iron wall of his need. No gentleman would take advantage of such incredible sweetness, such obvious inexperience. But damn! How much temptation could a battered old soldier resist?

Lyon bent his head and grazed the inside of her wrist with his tongue. When he heard her tiny sigh of pleasure, all lingering thoughts of restraint were consumed in the bonfire of lust. He cupped her bottom in one hand and lifted her up for his kiss. As he molded his mouth to hers, pressing and adjusting and tasting, Julie slipped her arms around his neck and leaned sweetly against him.

He swept his tongue across the seam of her lips, parting their dewy softness with the hard pressure of his own. When he entered her mouth, her eyes flew open and she stiffened in surprise. He held her head captured in his hand and explored the soft, moist cavern that awaited him. His tongue slid across her even teeth to trace the roof of her mouth. As her velvety tongue met his in startled discovery, Lyon caressed her, thrusting greedily in and out, showing her by example what he wanted to do to her adorable body.

When he broke the kiss at last, she made a low, hushed sound in the back of her throat, like the satisfied purr of a kitten.

Lyon pressed greedy kisses on her eyelids, her nose, her cheeks, her chin. She tasted like heaven. Like all the stars in the night sky, melted and swirled into a shimmering syrup on his tongue.

He could feel the response he sought in her languid movements as she slowly tipped her head back, exposing the graceful column of her neck above the demure white collar of her blouse. He bent his head and nipped the base of her throat, fighting the urge to suckle the delicate skin and leave his mark.

He wanted to mark her as his own.

He wanted to possess her forever.

He wanted to take her virginity as proof of his possession.

He was insane with need.

And he knew he had to stop.

Now.

Lyon spoke to her hoarsely in Gaelic, putting into words the desire that threatened to rage out of control. "I long to kiss you all over, little one . . . to taste every silken inch of your firm, ripe body. I want to lay you on the grass and feel you, naked and writhing, beneath me."

Through a haze of sensual pleasure, Juliette heard MacLyon speaking in the ancient Celtic language. It took several moments before the meaning of his words penetrated her befogged brain.

"Stop!" she insisted. "Stop it!" She yanked on his hair, then realized he was already setting her on her feet. She was trembling like a newborn fawn. Her legs were so weak her knees threatened to buckle beneath her.

Grim-faced, he released her and stepped away in one easy movement. Then he snatched her hat from the ground and handed it to her.

"We'd better get going, Miss Elkheart," he said with cool detachment. "Lady Hester would never forgive me if I brought you back late for supper."

Chapter 8

Hamish Macfie opened the door of the long gallery containing his collection of artifacts. Of all the memorabilia representing Scotland's glorious past displayed in his fine manor house, these were his prized possessions. With a sweep of his hand, he motioned the ladies into the high-ceilinged room.

"I'm sure I know less than you do about Clan Danielson, Lady Hester," he said with a regretful smile. "Not particularly surprising, of course, considering that my family didn't lose any lives in the atrocity."

He looked at the diminutive lass standing between the two MacLyon women and feigned sympathy. "You must realize, Miss Elkheart, that all the clans in the surrounding area aided the MacLyon chief in seeking out and punishing the Danielsons. The Macfies were only peripherally involved in the matter."

Juliette Elkheart returned his gaze, her feelings hidden behind a mien of cool detachment. Those insightful, cat-shaped eyes seemed to look right through him, and Hamish had to remind himself not to overdo the commiseration. No one would expect him to be more than moderately interested in her genealogical research.

"I appreciate your agreeing to see me, Laird Macfie," she said. "And I apologize for wasting your time."

Hamish's sister clucked her tongue with genuine concern. "Tch, tch, lass." Georgiana's long, narrow face puckered consolingly. "We're always glad to have company. Especially when it's a lovely young lady who's traveled all the way from Canada to see us. And we truly enjoy showing off our treasures."

Hamish guided his visitors to a circular shield prominently displayed on one wall. "Now, here's a very fine specimen, of which I'm justly proud. It still has its original spike. The concentric circles of iron nails which fasten the leather covering give the shield added strength. This targe belonged to a Macfie chieftain and was last carried into battle in the late seventeenth century."

As Miss Elkheart stepped closer to examine the targe, Hamish took the opportunity to examine her. She was a tiny thing, but perfectly proportioned, attractive in a small-busted sort of way. He preferred women with big, pendulous breasts and wide, ample hips. The kind who promised successful breeding. Well-endowed females like Flora, there, who'd given the MacLyons two potential male heirs.

Two boys in four years of marriage, and their father fighting in the Sudan for half of them. Christ! what fertility! Had James returned home alive, God alone knew how many more she'd have popped out in the years to follow.

Hamish's big-boned wife, Emma, had died barren through no fault of her own. He'd suffered a childhood disease late in adolescence that had left him sterile. No matter how many dairymaids or gardener's daughters he'd poked, he'd never sired a single bastard.

And Georgiana's two sickly bairns hadn't lived past their second winter. Pah! Her husband, paltry runt of a man, hadn't proven any heartier than his spawns, turning up his toes after only five short years of marriage.

Then Hamish's younger brother, Malcom—their last, best hope for producing the next Macfie chief—had gone and blown his own brains out, like the puling coward he was, before producing so much as a whey-faced daughter.

Every time Hamish thought of the braw, sturdy MacLyon lads, he nearly choked on his own bile.

His bitter reflections were interrupted when Georgiana turned from the battle shield and indicated an array of relics inside a glass-topped cabinet. "These flint arrowheads reputedly date back to the Stone Age. They're the oldest items in our collection."

Lady Hester accompanied Miss Elkheart to the display case. "They are known as *saighdean nan sìth*," she told her curious young friend, "which means fairy arrows in Gaelic. They're found in many parts of the Highlands and were probably used by Scotland's earliest inhabitants. Later peoples, who discovered them, were ignorant of their origin and so ascribed them to the fairies."

Miss Elkheart bent over the case and inspected the arrowheads with interest. "Yes," she said thoughtfully. "I can see where they were chipped into their triangular shapes with a heavy rock or some kind of crude tool."

"The Highlanders were—and in many cases still are—very superstitious," Hamish explained, assuming the air of a kindly university professor. "Our people continue to practice many customs that can be traced directly back to the old pagan culture. The lighting of bonfires on Samhuinn, or Halloween, has come down to us from the ancient Druids. If you're still here at the end of October, Miss Elkheart, you'll see forty or fifty fires burning on the hilltops. And if you venture close enough, you'll find people dancing around them like heathens."

Juliette smiled distractedly. There was something about the chief of Clan Macfie that had put her on guard from the moment she met him. He was an attractive, gray-haired man of average height. In his early fifties, he appeared to have a bull-like strength, with a thick chest and burly arms. She'd caught him watching her in cold appraisal, as though weighing her assets. His guarded gray eyes reminded her of a prowling wolf.

And something in Macfie's voice didn't quite ring true.

He wasn't sorry he couldn't assist her search for her Danielson forebears. Of that, she was certain. Strong Elk Heart had taught his daughters to watch a man's eyes when he talked, not listen to his words.

"I shall be gone long before Halloween," she told the clan chief. "But I shall certainly be sorry to miss it."

"Oh, you mustn't be in a hurry to leave us," Flora said in a rush. She clasped Juliette's hand and sent an imploring look to the elderly woman beside her. "Tell Julie she must stay with us for as long as possible."

"I absolutely insist upon it," Lady Hester stated in her imperious manner. "If we're going to help trace your Scottish ancestry, my girl, you must give us a little more time. Proper genealogical research isn't accomplished overnight."

"I appreciate everything you have done already," Juliette assured them. "But I mustn't leave my uncle alone in Edinburgh too long. I promised to act as his hostess during my stay in Scotland." She bent over the glass case once more, this time to examine a flintlock pistol that had caught her eye.

Hamish used the moment to draw closer to the quiet-spoken lass. "That is one of a pair carried by a Macfie in the Forty-five. You can see the interlaced M's on the butt."

She nodded, clearly intrigued by the weapon. Beside the pistol lay the Macfie clan badge, on which three wolves were attacking a hind. Inscribed on the silver badge were the same Gaelic words embossed on the targe's leather cover—the Macfie battle cry. *Mac Dubh-shidhe*. Son of the Black Elf.

"You may not know, Miss Elkheart," he continued smoothly, "that the Danielsons were reputed to be a clan of seers."

That got her attention. She jerked upright, her brown eyes alert. "I was not aware of that," she said. "What exactly does being a seer mean?"

Lady Hester smiled thoughtfully at the girl's odd reaction. "The Danielsons were rumored to have the second sight. Many of them could foresee events which would happen in the future. A famous prophet, the Oban Seer, belonged to their clan."

"If he was a prophet," Flora said, "why didn't he realize that his fellow clansmen would one day be put to the sword and their womenfolk scattered to the four winds?"

"Perhaps he did," Miss Elkheart answered softly. "Perhaps there was no way he could have altered events that were to come, and so he wisely said nothing."

"Well, if you believe that kind of rot, I guess it would have been possible," Hamish agreed. "At any rate, such blether isn't given much credence today."

"What about past events?" Juliette questioned. "Were the Danielsons known to see things that had already happened?"

Lady Hester shook her head and lifted her thin brows in speculation. "Not to my knowledge. But who's to say?"

"Why would anyone want to see something that had already happened?" asked Flora. "What good would it do?"

"For one thing, it would make writing history a whole lot easier." Georgiana smiled at her brother with doting regard. "And for another, Hamish wouldn't have to spend hours and hours poring over those dusty manuscripts of his."

"Speaking of which," he said expansively, "I'd be happy to let you examine them, Miss Elkheart. You may have free run of my entire collection. But I can already guarantee, you won't find a single word written about Clan Danielson. I'm quite familiar with every document in my collection."

"That will not be necessary," she replied. "It was only a hope, no more, that there might be something—a will or deed—that mentioned them."

Lady Hester patted the young woman's hand fondly. "Why don't we go to Stirling? The archives in the Tolbooth might be your best chance of tracing your Scottish ancestry. We'll plan a holiday for the whole family. The lads would love to take a ride on the train.''

''Oh, yes!'' Flora exclaimed with girlish enthusiasm. She slipped her arm around Juliette's waist and gave her an affectionate hug. ''There are wonderful shops in Stirling. We can spend several days and visit the dressmakers and the milliners while we're there.''

Hamish studied Miss Elkheart with renewed interest. The possibility that there was a match in the offing with either of the MacLyon brothers brought a sense of disgruntlement. However, nothing in her manner suggested the coy bashfulness of a bride-to-be. She seemed far more interested in historical research than flirtations with the opposite sex.

Yet Robbie MacLyon was a dashing buck, whose smile attracted all the unmarried lassies. And just because The MacLyon hadn't littered the countryside with bastards was no guarantee he couldn't sire an heir in the blink of an eye.

The Scots weren't nearly so fastidious as the Sassenachs when it came to bairns born out of wedlock. A laird could legitimize his offspring by subsequent marriage to the woman who bore them. More than one member of the Standing Council of Scottish Chiefs had succeeded to the chiefship through a parental nomination accepted by the Crown.

Hamish was well aware of MacLyon's current preference for the voluptuous tarts available for a hefty sum at the Golden Dirk. But with a fresh little trifle like Miss Juliette Elkheart staying at Strathlyon Castle, that could change far too quickly.

''Here is a fine selection of Highland weapons,'' Georgiana called from across the room. The women joined her in front of the cabinet, where a dirk lay on a cloth of velvet, alongside its sheath, bye-knife, and fork. ''These were used by Captain Duncan Macfie, who died in the battle of Prestonpans. One of our family's illustrious heroes,'' she added.

''Julie is a heroine,'' Flora told her hosts proudly. ''And

she has a knife of her own, too. Her father made it for her, when she was a young girl. She used it to save Lyon's life.''

As Hamish and his sister listened to the incredible tale, he struggled to conceal his displeasure. So this was the mysterious woman who'd saved MacLyon's life that morning in Edinburgh.

Lady Hester planned a family picnic for the morning of Juliette's knife-throwing demonstration. Neil and Jamie raced around the Strathlyon stables like a pair of rambunctious prairie dogs, while they waited for the adults to be ready to leave. With Dunbar and Tiree in gleeful pursuit, the boys zipped up and down ladders leading to the loft, scampered in and out of the open victoria that'd been pulled from the coach house by a team of matched bays, and crawled over stacks of hay.

''Boys! Boys!'' Flora cried. She held her parasol over her head and twirled in a circle, trying to follow their antics. ''You shouldn't be running around like that. You're liable to fall and hurt yourselves.''

The youngsters scarcely slowed at their mother's shrill warning.

With an unperturbed air, Lady Hester supervised the footman who was loading three bulging straw baskets onto the floor of the small carriage. Three horses and two Welsh ponies stood saddled and ready in the yard, two grooms patiently holding their reins. Flora had chosen to keep Lady Hester company. Riding in the victoria gave the pretty widow the opportunity to wear a stylish violet and white creation that had just arrived from the dressmaker in Strathbardine.

Attired in a cocoa-colored riding habit, Juliette stood beside Rob and surveyed the bustling scene with pleasure.

''Ah, the wee loons are a tad whipped-up this morning,'' Rob said. His smile was as carefree as the children's. ''I hope their mad capering doesn't annoy you. It tends to drive their mother to tooth-gnashing distraction.''

"Not at all," she replied with a happy laugh. "This morning's hectic activities remind me of my childhood. Every summer, my family would take packhorses and ride into the Rockies, where we would hunt and fish for nearly three months. It wasn't a mere lark like today's excursion, but the very serious business of gathering provisions for the harsh Canadian winter.''

Lyon strode into the stable yard, finished at last with the meeting with his factor. The moment he appeared, Flora hurried over. "You have to do something about Neil and Jamie," she complained. "If they continue to behave like savages, I'll come down with one of my ghastly headaches. And then I'll be forced to spend the next two days in bed.''

"They're just high-spirited," he said, trying to be patient. "James wouldn't have wanted them any other way.''

"James!" Flora pressed one hand to her tucked bodice. Her voice rose to a hysterical pitch. "What about what I want? You never pay the least attention to my wishes.''

Lyon ignored her histrionics. He whistled sharply and the youngsters stopped in their tracks. A flick of his finger brought them running. "Get on your ponies," he told them. "We're ready to leave.''

With eager whoops, the boys dashed toward their mounts, and the footman helped Lady Hester and Flora into the carriage.

Lyon smiled at the sound of their joyous cries as he walked over to Rob and Julie. He liked to see the lads act like wild savages. James would have been damn proud of his sons.

"Take Neil and Jamie for a gallop," he said to his brother, "and let them work off some of that excess energy. I'll accompany Miss Elkheart.''

"Aye, and what else is new?" Rob murmured under his breath. But he was grinning to himself as he walked away.

If Julie heard the ill-timed comment, she didn't let on. Lyon swung her up to the sidesaddle, thankful she was as light as thistledown. His bad arm ached like the devil that morning, but there was no way in hell he was going to let any other man put his sweaty hands on her. Not a footman, not a groom, and especially not his personable young brother. Then Lyon mounted Thor, and they cantered out of the stable yard together.

The entourage, which included the deerhounds, rode to a wooded glen not far from Strathbardine, where Dr. MacDougall and his fiancée joined them. Juliette took an instant liking to Annie Buchanan.

"I could hardly wait to meet you," Annie said, when they were introduced. She had a wide, friendly smile, a riot of light brown curls, and laughing hazel eyes. "Keir has told me so much about you and Dr. Robinson. Well, your whole family, really."

"And I have been looking forward to meeting you," Juliette replied. "Your future husband spent the entire train ride from Edinburgh extolling your praises."

Keir beamed at their words. He took his fiancée's hand with a proprietary air and tucked it in the crook of his elbow. "Why shouldn't I be proud? Annie will make the best doctor's wife in the Highlands."

"Flatterer!" she scoffed. But the corners of her eyes crinkled with merriment.

Neil and Jamie came over to join them, the hounds frolicking at their heels.

"Miss Elkheart is going to show us how she throws her knife," Neil said. He tossed a stick for the dogs to fetch, then skipped around the grownups in a lopsided circle, too excited to stand still.

"But Uncle Lyon has to be there to watch," Jamie confided before executing a perfect cartwheel.

"A wise decision, I'm sure." Annie stooped to meet the boys on their own level. "I've never known you lads to listen to anyone but your Uncle Lyon."

Neil's expression grew serious. "We listen to Miss Elk-heart, too. But we have to listen real hard."

Jamie moved closer and lowered his voice to speak in Annie's ear. "She talks with magic words."

"Wheesht! You don't say!" Annie looked up to meet Juliette's gaze, her eyes sparkling with hilarity. "How very exciting."

While the coachman and footman spread out the blankets beneath the oaks and unloaded the picnic baskets, the family walked down to the stream bank. Earlier, a servant had set up a round wooden target marked in circular colored bands, for the morning's exhibition.

Kneeling on the grass, Juliette showed the youngsters the intricately beaded sheath her father had made to encase the double-edged steel blade. She explained how Strong Elk Heart had carved the knife handle from antler bone and made it especially to fit her small hand.

"Do not ever try to throw a knife like this without an adult watching you," she cautioned. "It is a dangerous weapon, not a plaything."

"We won't," they agreed. From their solemn faces, she knew they were sincere.

"Good." She rose to her feet. "While I throw, I want you to stand behind me, right next to Uncle Rob."

"We will," they promised in unison.

The boys hurried to stand beside their tall uncle. Keir and Annie walked over to join them. Lady Hester and Flora decided to stay in the shade and watch from the blanket. The pair of deerhounds weren't so cooperative. Barking loudly, Dunbar and Tiree bounded to the target and back.

Lyon decided the dogs would have to be tied up for their own safety. He was about to whistle to them, when Julie called out.

"Voxpenako, Maxenako," she said, and the huge animals gamboled over and sat down in front of her. At her soft-spoken command in Cheyenne they stretched out close to her feet, their tongues lolling in happy satisfaction.

"See what I mean?" Jamie asked Annie.

"I do, indeed," she replied. "What did Miss Elkheart call them?"

"Gray Bear and Big Bear," Neil explained. "That's what she named them, because she thinks they look like shaggy grizzlies."

"Grizzlies?"

Jamie turned a somersault and landed at Annie's feet. "Bears in Canada, Miss Buchanan," he cheerfully explained.

Everyone watched in hushed excitement as Julie hurled her knife. She struck the inner circle time after time, while Lyon stood by to retrieve the weapon for her. Next, Rob and Keir attempted the feat, with far less accurate results. Lyon wisely declined to try. Then they moved closer to the target, and Julie helped Neil and Jamie throw.

When the demonstration was over, Lyon replaced the blade in its colorful sheath. "That was very impressive, Miss Elkheart," he said. Although he'd seen the results of her talent that morning in Edinburgh, he still found it hard to believe a young lady could be so accurate and so deadly with a knife.

Julie lifted one shoulder, as though to dismiss her accomplishment. "It is not really all that remarkable," she said. "My sister Jennie has amazing skill with a bow and arrow. And I am far more accurate with a gun than a blade."

He knew she must be exaggerating. "Care to show us?"

At her casual nod of agreement, he called to the coachman. The man immediately brought a pistol from its holster in the victoria. The small repeater, made especially for traveling, had belonged to Lyon's father.

She took the gun and examined it closely. "Is it loaded?"

"Of course."

"Is it accurate?"

"It shoots a trace high and to the left."

Without another word, she raised her arm and put two bullets squarely in the center of the target.

Applause broke out from the others, who'd retired to the picnic blankets. Dunbar and Tiree howled their ecstatic approval.

Lyon stared at the target in disbelief. "That was incredible."

A self-satisfied smile flirted around the corners of her adorable mouth. "Not really. There is not much of a challenge in hitting a stationery target."

This time he wasn't so positive she was exaggerating. "You can hit a moving one?"

"Do you have a coin in your pocket?"

"How's this?" He pulled out a shilling and held it between his thumb and forefinger.

"That will do fine. Now go stand near the target, and when you are ready, toss it into the air."

Lyon frowned, not anxious to take the chance of her missing the coin and hitting him by mistake. "You're certain you know what you're doing, Miss Elkheart?"

"That is exactly what you asked me the afternoon I helped Sweetie deliver her puppies," she reminded him. Her eyes twinkled a challenge.

Lyon went to stand near the bullet-pocked target. By now, the rest of the party had clambered to their feet. They watched in mesmerized silence as he turned and gazed at Julie. She held the pistol down at her side, her stance relaxed, her lovely countenance serene.

"Are you ready?" he called.

"At your pleasure, MacLyon."

Lyon tossed the coin, sending it sailing high over his head. The sharp bark of the pistol reverberated through the trees, and Flora gave a piercing squeal of surprise. Dunbar and Tiree howled their admiration. When the shilling fell to the earth, Neil and Jamie tore across the trampled grass to find it.

"She hit it!" Jamie shouted.

"The bullet notched the coin!" Neil verified. The boys raced to the blankets to show everyone the proof.

Lyon walked back to Julie, and she calmly handed him the repeater. "You were right," she acknowledged. "A little high and to the left. But more accurate than most British-made pistols."

"Miss Elkheart," he said, "I'm bowled over. Had anyone told me a female could shoot like that, I'd never have believed him."

Shouting huzzahs, Neil and Jamie gave Lyon the coin to inspect, then danced a wild jig around her.

Damned if it wasn't true.

She'd notched the shilling.

"That was nothing, really," she said. Her exotic features glowed with impudence. "It is fairly easy to hit a moving target when you are standing still. It is a little more difficult while galloping on horseback."

Lyon shook his head in wonder. "I'm speechless."

"Will you do some more tricks?" Neil begged.

"Not this morning." She tempered her refusal with a smile. "It is time to enjoy our lunch, and I, for one, am starving."

"When?" Jamie insisted. "When will you do more tricks?"

She took each boy by the hand and led them toward the blankets. "I understand that one of you will be celebrating his birthday soon."

"Me!" Neil shouted. "I'm going to be seven years old."

"On your seventh birthday, I will put on a shooting exhibition," she promised. "You may invite all your friends to see."

Jamie did a little hop-skip of joy. "Will you shoot holes in more coins?"

Julie peeked over at Lyon, and the deviltry in her flashing eyes set his pulse racing. "If your uncle will provide the coins," she agreed with her husky little laugh, "I will be happy to shoot holes in them."

*   *   *

After everyone had their fill of warm mutton pie and glasses of cool, fresh milk, the picnickers broke into small groups. The boys went down to the stream to skip rocks with their Uncle Rob. Flora and Lady Hester sat visiting in lazy contentment, while Annie and Keir slipped away for a quiet walk.

At Lyon's invitation, Julie agreed to do likewise, and he purposely guided her in the opposite direction from the engaged couple. He took advantage of a slight incline to clasp her elbow and offer his help, as they followed a path through the trees.

"I'm sorry your visit with Macfie proved so disappointing," Lyon said. "I know how much you were counting on finding information about Clan Danielson in his manuscripts."

"It was frustrating to learn he had no record of them in his library," she admitted with an unhappy sigh. "Lady Hester suggested that I try the archives at Stirling Castle. Perhaps I should have started there to begin with."

She allowed Lyon to hold her arm, her thoughts apparently more involved with the failure of yesterday's excursion than their kiss on the way home from Rothnamurchan. He wasn't sure he was relieved or irritated by her preoccupation with Macfie.

Lyon had lain awake half the night thinking about Julie. He'd decided to embark on a light flirtation—just enough to prevent her attention from fastening upon his younger brother, while at the same time keeping a firm rein on his own lusty inclinations. It shouldn't be difficult to enjoy an innocent dalliance with a green girl without turning into a bloody lecher. He had been brought up as a gentleman, even if he didn't always behave like one.

"Nana is already planning the trip," he told her. "She met with me first thing this morning and issued orders like a general. I'm to have Thomas Gairdner, my steward, see that the MacLyon rail coach is scrubbed inside and out and pulled off the siding. And Davie Grierson has already been sent to the Thistle and Crown in Stirling to ready our private suite.''

Her delicately arched brows drew together in concern. ''I am sorry to put everyone to so much trouble.''

''No one considers a visit to Stirling any trouble,'' he assured her. ''The entire family is looking forward to the holiday. The boys are ecstatic, Flora's practically turning cartwheels, and Robbie's busy making a list of outings. Museums, art galleries, and, naturally, the great castle itself. Just be sure to bring along a pair of comfortable walking shoes. You'll need them.''

They came to a spot overlooking a waterfall. The full-throated song of a mavis could be heard above the rush of the burn cascading over the rocks. Julie left Lyon to stand beside a tall silver birch near the edge of the cliff. She leaned back against its trunk and gazed out at the view.

He drew in a long, labored breath at the mouthwatering sight of her. Earlier, she'd removed the jacket of her brown riding outfit and left it at the picnic site. The pristine whiteness of her blouse highlighted her chestnut hair and honey-gold skin. Sunlight filtered through the leaves overhead, dappling her slender form in shifting patterns of light and dark.

Lyon watched her, fighting the slow heat that spread insidiously through his groin. His blood stirred in his veins, thick and hot, pulsing to every part of his taut frame.

''I understand you received a letter from London yesterday,'' he said. ''I hope your sister is doing fine without you. I know you worry about her.''

She turned her head to meet his gaze, and the untrammeled purity in those velvet eyes awakened the Viking slumbering inside him. He took a step closer, the heat bursting into flame.

''Mohehya is fine,'' she replied with a smile, oblivious to the danger spiraling around her. The mermaid was about to be caught in the sea raider's net. ''She is staying with friends that we made during the crossing. She sent the letter to Edinburgh, and my uncle forwarded it on to me.''

''Mohehya?''

''That is my father's pet name for Jennie,'' she answered. ''It means Magpie. As a child, she never stopped chattering.''

''And what is his special name for you?''

Unaware of the pagan instincts spurring him on, she lowered her eyes. The lush ebony lashes fluttered against her smooth cheek. ''Vehona,'' she said shyly.

Lyon moved to stand directly in front of her. The rapacious need to take at will, to keep without qualm, to conquer by force and bend to his every carnal desire flooded his body. He braced one hand on the pale bark above her head and bent closer.

''Vehona,'' he said in a hushed tone. ''That's very pretty. What does it mean?''

Her long lashes fanned upward as she peeked at him. A blush stained her cheeks. ''Princess.''

''Princess?''

''*Nihoe* said that I always behaved like a princess, even when I was just a little girl.''

''Vehona,'' he murmured huskily. ''It suits you.'' His lips curved upward in a teasing smile. ''You still *are* a wee lass.''

Lyon traced the line of her high cheekbone with the tip of his finger, and the sheer pleasure of touching her sent shock waves of desire reverberating through him. He sucked in a quick breath of surprise at the utter bliss of catching a falling star.

Juliette met MacLyon's brilliant green eyes and prayed she could conceal her feelings. The sound of her special name spoken in his rich baritone called to the deepest yearnings of her soul.

The tall Scotsman stood so close, she could feel his body heat pour over her. He was so alive, so pulsing with fierce male energy, a line of sparks seemed to follow the path of his fingertip. Her heartbeat quickened. Her lungs compressed. Her nerve endings triggered an explosion of conflicting sensations. Something within her had responded to this formidable giant from the moment they'd met. Was it the warrior-woman inside who hungered for a mate of such rampant ferocity?

Inhaling the marvelous scent of the forest that clung to him, she ran her tongue over her suddenly dry lips. "You . . . you think the name suits me?" she asked, hoping to divert his attention.

He immediately touched her lower lip with his finger. "Mm," he said, his gaze fastened on her mouth as though he'd like to take a bite of her. "Serene, graceful, regal . . . a princess."

Juliette pressed back against the tree trunk till she could feel the rough bark through her cotton blouse. An image of their mating, wild and impassioned, flashed before her. Bodies naked, limbs straining, mouths seeking. His animal heat seared her lungs.

"I . . . I am not always serene," she whispered in denial.

"I'm going to kiss you, Vehona," MacLyon said, "and you're going to kiss me in return." He came closer still, till their lips were scant inches apart.

Juliette quivered like the feathers of an arrow ruffled by the wind. The Lion seemed to sense the effect the Cheyenne syllables, spoken in his beguiling Scots accent, had upon her. Though he spoke softly and with unimaginable tenderness, his words conveyed absolute conviction. "Do it now, Vehona," he murmured. "Kiss me now."

The erotic invitation in his shuttered gaze would not be denied. Juliette's breath caught high in her chest, and she made a tiny whimper of acquiescence. She stretched up on her tiptoes, wrapped her arms around his neck, and kissed him passionately.

Using the knowledge he'd imparted so freely, she touched her tongue to his lips, and he instantly opened his mouth and welcomed her in. She tasted him, just as he had tasted her. The freshness of evergreens and cool mountain lakes rolled across her tongue, as seductive and inviting as a bubbling stream on a hot summer day. His lips molded against hers, taking possession of her senses, sending ripples of delight coursing through her.

When Juliette pulled back in startled awareness of what she'd done, of what she'd allowed him to do, her breath came in quick, little pants.

Lyon kept his hands planted firmly on the tree trunk above her head. For just as she'd put her arms around his neck, he'd caught the flash of a blue shirt in the undergrowth. His nephews were hiding beneath a bush.

"We have company," he told her softly.

"Who?" she asked, her low voice cracking with mortification.

"Neil and Jamie."

"*Hesc!*" she exclaimed with an overbright smile. "I think it is time to rejoin the others."

"You go ahead, Miss Elkheart," he said. "Tell them I'll be there in a minute."

Julie ducked under his arm and hurried down the path.

Before the boys had a chance to creep away, Lyon swooped down on them. He lifted them up by their shirt collars and shook them. "What the devil are you two doing?" he demanded. "Haven't you been taught better than to spy on grownups?"

Their eyes were round with excitement. "She's a fairy princess, Uncle Lyon," Neil said. "I heard her say it!"

"A fairy princess," Jamie echoed.

He set them both on their feet. "Her father *calls* her Princess," he corrected. "That doesn't mean she is one. And it certainly doesn't mean she's a fairy. Now, I've never taken a belt to either one of you, but if I catch you lads spying on me or Miss Elkheart again, I'm going to get my razor strap and flay the hide off your little butts."

At that moment, Rob came loping up the path. "There you are!" he called to the youngsters. "How did you two disappear so fast? I turned my back, and you were gone.''

Lyon turned to his brother with a scowl. ''When you're with these boys, you don't take your eyes off them. Not for a moment. They could have fallen on the rocks or into the burn.''

Rob stared at him in surprise. ''Aye,'' he said quietly. ''I'll take care they come to no harm.''

''See that you do.''

Without another word, Lyon strode past him and down the path.

Rob dropped to one knee and surveyed his nephews. ''Just what did you two blethering gowks do to get Uncle Lyon so angry?'' he asked sternly.

They looked at one another with guilty expressions.

''Let's have it,'' he insisted. ''Tell me the worst and get it over with.''

''She kissed him, Uncle Robbie,'' Jamie said in an accusing tone. ''We saw it from over there.'' He pointed a pudgy finger at a nearby bush.

''Uncle Lyon told her to kiss him, and . . . and she did,'' Neil offered, the disbelief in his voice unmistakable.

''I see,'' Rob said. ''So Uncle Lyon caught you peeking at him. No wonder he was angry. I'd be angry, too.''

''She's a fairy princess,'' Jamie said. ''She told him so. We heard her say it.''

Neil nodded emphatically. His coppery locks glistened in the ray of sunshine streaming through the leaves overhead. ''Miss Elkheart put a spell on Uncle Lyon, and then she kissed him.''

''What makes you think she put a spell on him?''

''Why else would he let her kiss him?'' Neil demanded. The censure in his eyes said he'd brook no other consideration.

''You don't have to fret about your uncle,'' Rob assured the two worried youngsters. ''Uncle Lyon's a big man.

Why, Miss Elkheart doesn't even come up to his shoulder. He can take care of himself.''

"Kissing a fairy puts a man under her power until the enchantment is broken,'' Neil said in an awed voice. "And she can change his size with a snap of her fingers.''

"Cook told us so,'' Jamie chimed in. "Cook said a fairy can make a grown man so small he'd fit right in our hand.'' He cupped his palm and held it out in illustration. The thought of his huge uncle sitting docilely in his palm brought a look of pure exhilaration.

"We know Miss Elkheart's enchanted Uncle Lyon,'' Neil declared. "Since she came to the castle, he's been smiling again. We shouldn't leave him alone with her anymore.''

Rob shook his head, unable to keep from grinning. "Ye wee, daft loons,'' he said. "What else makes you think she's a fairy? Come on, I can see you're fairly spitting with clever ideas.''

"Well, Miss Elkheart gave Dunbar and Tiree magic names,'' Neil said. He glanced at his younger brother for support.

Jamie patted Rob's shoulder for emphasis. "And . . . and we heard her call Uncle Lyon's Arabian mare a magic name, too. Cook told us fairies always ride prancing white steeds. And they use magic names to enchant you.''

Neil moved closer to Rob and spoke in a hushed voice, as though afraid they'd be overheard and enchanted themselves. "Miss Elkheart said her sister shoots with a bow even better than she throws a knife. Everyone knows that fairies charm people with their invisible arrows.''

Rob rubbed his chin thoughtfully. "I can see you've got your minds made up, so I won't bother trying to argue you out of it.''

"One thing's for sure,'' Neil announced with a stubborn lift of his chin. "Miss Elkheart's got Uncle Lyon under her spell.''

Rob rose to his feet and stared in the direction his brother had taken. "Damn, if I don't think you're right about that," he admitted with a grin. "She *has* got him under her spell."

He chuckled softly to himself as he headed down the path with his nephews.

Chapter 9

Stirling Castle sat high on a basalt crag like an eagle perched on a mountain aerie. From the castle's ramparts could be seen the passage northward between the Gargunnock Hills and the steep Ochils, with the fertile lands bordering the Firth of Forth spreading out below. Through the divide in the hills, the southern rim of the Highlands rose up in a vast panorama. For centuries, the fortress had commanded the roads and rivers leading into the very heart of Scotland.

Earlier that afternoon, MacLyon and Juliette had visited the Renaissance palace, with its courtyard, chapel, great hall, and private royal suites contained within the castle walls. Now the couple stood on a parapet and gazed out over the Stirling Plain.

"This spot has witnessed the heroism of William Wallace, the triumph of Robert Bruce, and the residency of the Stewart kings," MacLyon told her. "Today the castle is still used for the training of Highland regiments which will be sacrificed for the glory of the British Empire. The Argylls, the Sutherlands, and the Cameronians have all completed their training here and gone forth to pour their blood on the desert sands of the Middle East and North Africa."

Juliette cocked her head, peering at him sideways. The bitterness in his voice was unmistakable. She assumed that his brother's death in the Sudan and his own lasting injury

123

were at the root of his enmity. "You think their deaths were wasted?"

His rugged features grew somber. He surveyed the landscape below them through narrowed eyes, their corners crinkled from the Egyptian sun. "I think, Miss Elkheart, that the fabled empire—on which the sun never sets—has been built at an enormous cost of Scottish blood. The Highlands, especially, have provided a nursery for fresh young lads, eager and willing to be slaughtered in the name of duty and honor."

She turned to him, searching his guarded expression. "Rob said you refused to take part in planning the Strathshire Gathering."

His mouth quirked in a sardonic smile as he met her inquisitive gaze. "Does it surprise you that I don't choose to fan the flames of Scottish nationalism?"

"Quite honestly? Yes, it does."

"Flag-waving is idiotic nonsense, whether it's done by Scottish or English patriots. And people who dress up in their clan plaids and carry antique weapons in a misbegotten attempt to relive the glorious past are the worst type of idiots. They have no notion what the sight of fallen soldiers, wrapped in kilts so soaked with blood the tartans are unrecognizable, can do to a man's guts. Or how the sound of bagpipes can bring back—" He stopped abruptly, his jaw clenched.

Juliette waited, afraid she might say the wrong thing and unwittingly cause more heartache. She believed his caustic words were an attempt to conceal a deep inner pain, his cynicism masking an abiding love of his country and people.

The anguish he suffered because of James's death made MacLyon short-tempered and irascible. But this virulent rancor wasn't his real nature, or he wouldn't be surrounded by such a smiling, happy family. Whenever he stomped and roared and swore a blue streak, they gave his temper-tantrum a passing glance and continued on their merry way.

Even Flora, though she'd complained that he kept her at Strathlyon against her will, never seemed to be afraid of him. If anything, she resented his lack of attention.

That afternoon, the others had gladly left Juliette and her tedious research in MacLyon's hands while they scattered in various directions. Rob and the boys planned to wander about the gates, wynds, and closes of the city, while Lady Hester and Flora visited the shops.

To Juliette's relief, MacLyon broke the uneasy silence between them. "I'm glad you were able to find the name of Danielson in the museum archives."

"At least now I know the last chief was Ninian Danielson," she replied with a smile, "and that he died with his wife, Catriona, and their youngest son, Iain, when his castle was destroyed after the massacre at Kildunun. What happened to the rest of his people, or how my own great-great-grandfather came to America, will probably remain forever a mystery."

The laird's gaze softened with compassion. He realized how disappointed she'd been with the meager facts they'd gleaned.

"It's not very likely the thirteen-year-old lad survived the destruction of his father's island stronghold," Lyon said. "But if Iain Danielson made it to the seacoast alive and caught a ship for America, he'd almost certainly have changed his name. Iain is Gaelic for John. And the MacDougalls were his family's nearest neighbors. So the Americanized name of John McDougall would have been a logical choice."

Juliette turned away, trying to hide the extent of her disappointment. "I guess I will never know for sure."

She rested one hand on the stone guardrail and stared out at the horizon with unseeing eyes. Nothing she'd learned that day had brought her any closer to resolving the true purpose behind her vision. Yet she remained convinced the Maiyun—the Great Powers Above—had sent it to her.

MacLyon stepped behind her, and the force of his physical presence immediately intruded on Juliette's disheartened thoughts. Sensitive to his every move, his every breath, she felt her heart shimmy with joy at his nearness. Her nerves vibrated like a bow's string at the release of the arrow.

"What's most surprising to me," he said with quiet bemusement, "is that the Danielson lands were forfeited and the titles transferred by the Crown to Clan Macfie. I'd never heard that part of the story before."

Juliette attempted to follow the conversation, while making a mental note of the physiological changes in her anatomy. Heartbeat . . . stuttering. Respiration . . . shallow. Pulse rate . . . unbelievable. Diagnosis . . . dangerous to the point of being lethal.

"I do not think that Hamish Macfie is aware of it, either," she replied. She prayed he couldn't detect the breathless rasp in her voice. "He told me that his clansmen had very little to do with the entire episode. But considering that his forebears were awarded the Danielson estates, that seems rather unlikely, doesn't it?"

"It does," Lyon agreed. "I remember my grandfather telling me as a lad that the Macfie chief and his clansmen came to the area near Loch Etive shortly after the Battle of Culloden. They were originally from the eastern part of Scotland and were forced to leave because they'd supported the Jacobite cause. Strange that their acquisition of the forfeited estates of the Danielsons remained such a tightly kept secret."

Juliette could feel MacLyon trace a line with his fingertip along the nape of her neck just below her braided chignon, as he added thoughtfully, "Until you discovered the information in the archives today."

His light, lingering touch sent a current of sensations flooding through her. She knew this powerful man was capable of tremendous passion, but his display of tenderness caught her unprepared, trapping her in its silken web. Her body refused to move away from him. She struggled to keep from betraying the ache of longing inside her.

"Not so strange," she said. "Not when the name of Danielson was obliterated from all the local records in the area around Strathbardine." She glanced over her shoulder at him. "Do you know the whereabouts of the ruins?"

Lyon's hope that Julie had given up her genealogical research plummeted. He didn't need to ask which ruins she meant. The fact that the nineteenth chief of Clan MacLyon had destroyed Castle Danielson and its inhabitants after Kildunun was well known in Strathbardine. She had only to inquire to learn its whereabouts.

Taking her to the site where her ancestors had been annihilated by his held all the appeal of being hanged, drawn, and quartered. Still, if he didn't tell her the truth, someone else would.

"Yes," he admitted reluctantly.

"Will you take me there?" The eagerness in her voice brought a sense of cold dread.

"There's nothing to see," he hedged. "It's just a pile of old stones."

Her back stiffened, and she squared her shoulders combatively. "Still, I would like to visit what remains of the castle. Is it far from Strathlyon?"

"No, it's not far."

She batted aside an ostrich plume that a gust of air blew into her eyes. She retied the blue satin bow of her straw bonnet under her chin with an air of crisp determination, which only made her appear even younger than her eighteen years.

"I will ask Rob to guide me there," she stated unequivocally.

"I'll take you," he said in defeat, knowing he'd regret it.

Julie whirled to face him, and her look of bright expectation left him paralyzed with desire. Her nutmeg eyes flashed like starshine, and the brilliance of her sudden smile reminded him of the first day they'd met, when he'd had the fantastic notion that she carried a ray of sunlight in her pocket. Whenever he was with her, he felt that beguiling warmth, that unconscious yet inescapable allure. In this country of continual mist and rain, to possess Miss Juliette Elkheart would be to possess endless sunny days and cloudless starry nights.

"I'll take you there," he repeated hoarsely. He stepped closer, till he could feel the soft folds of her skirt bump gently against his trousers. "But it will cost you."

"A fee?" She gave a startled, little laugh. "Very well, MacLyon, what will it cost me?" The smug satisfaction in her gaze told him she had no idea what he intended to exact as payment.

They were alone on the parapet. They'd spent most of the day in the cellar of the Tolbooth, poring over a mountain of documents together. Since the legal records were written in Latin and Gaelic, he'd read and translated them for her.

Working so close beside Julie had proven to be heavenly torture. He'd been in a state of sexual arousal the entire time, determined to fight her allure with the iron strength of his will. Yet in the end, his traitorous body had resisted every effort of his principled mind. He ached with the sweetest, most insistent carnal need he'd ever known.

Lyon met Julie's confident gaze. A wayward lock, tugged loose by a puff of wind from her thick braid, dangled in front of her ear. He rubbed the silken wisp between his thumb and forefinger, releasing the delectable scent of her hair, then touched the amethyst that sparkled on her earlobe.

"The fee is one kiss, here and now—"

"A kiss?" she interrupted. Her brows drew together in a frown. "You have kissed me twice already."

He put two fingers against her lips to shush her, as he continued with ruthless determination. "—and another kiss after we've seen the castle ruins."

That part of the agreement had to be irrevocable.

Lyon dreaded her reaction to the scene of carnage, fearing she'd blame him, as the present chief of Clan MacLyon, for the unspeakable desolation that continued to linger about the ruins. He wanted a chance to wipe away the stigma of being the direct descendent of the man who'd wreaked such merciless havoc on his neighbor.

Julie pulled back from his touch, her laughter bubbling up. "I do not have to make a bargain with you, MacLyon," she scoffed. "I will simply ask Rob to take me there, instead."

"He may not know the way," Lyon warned her. "It's not exactly a spot mentioned in the guidebooks." At her pucker of disbelief, he quickly added, "You know yourself that few people have any real knowledge of the Clan of the Clouds."

She lifted one shoulder in vexation. "*Haxc!* If I find that Rob does not know, I will think about your offer and make my decision then."

"But then, it'll be too late," he stated coolly. "Either you accept my terms now or not at all."

"I believe this is called extortion," she retorted.

He grinned at her easy capitulation. "I believe you're right."

Lyon moved so close their bodies almost touched. He could feel her enticing warmth beckon him. This overpowering reaction to a female was without precedent. He'd always enjoyed wenching, and the ladies had never been hard to attract. Truth was, from the age of fourteen, they'd been too bloody easy.

But this time was different.

God Almighty, how it was different.

His heart hammered against his ribs in a painful tattoo. His groin muscles clenched with a hard, fierce need. The anticipation of kissing her—just kissing her, for he knew he dared not do more and expect to retain his sanity—sent a thrill coursing through his veins.

Juliette could almost feel MacLyon's gaze move over her, and her bones seemed to melt beneath its scorching heat. The stirrings of desire welled up inside her, until there was nothing she wanted more than to have his lips pressed against hers.

"Only one kiss," she stipulated, "right now."

He spoke with absolute confidence. "And one after we visit the ruins." He spanned her waist with his long fingers and turned her, so her back was to the castle wall. Should anyone come upon them unaware, his much larger frame would hide her from view.

As MacLyon lifted her up, Juliette slid her arms around his neck. She could feel his cool breath fan over her, and with a sigh of acceptance, she lowered her eyelids, tilted her head to give him access, and graciously awaited his kiss.

"This one, you give me," he directed in a husky whisper. "The next kiss, I'll give you."

She laughed softly and brushed her lips across his, thinking that was all the kiss he would get for his trouble. But the touch of his mouth felt so wonderful, she did it again. And then, once more for good measure.

He gave a low murmur of encouragement, and Juliette smashed her lips against his. She clung to him, as she swept her tongue inside his inviting mouth. Her heart pounded so wildly, she was afraid he could feel its frantic thump-thump-thumping against his chest. She cupped his cheeks in her palms, drew his face nearer still, and proceeded to kiss him hungrily.

Lyon bracketed Julie's sides with his hands and discovered that, once again, she wore no corset. He brushed his thumbs against the curves of her breasts. The feel of her slight young body made his throat constrict with a knot of unbearable tenderness.

He could literally count her ribs beneath the play of his much stronger fingers. He flicked the pads of his thumbs across the uptilted tips of her breasts and realized, with a start of incredulity, that his hands were shaking. Damn! It happened every bloody time he touched her. His sex pushed against the crotch of his trousers, so engorged and hardened, the muscles of his thighs tightened in anticipation.

Lyon felt as though he were a fourteen-year-old lad again, scarcely moments away from a premature, but glorious, ending to his virginity during a wild romp in the hay.

"*Nanoseham*," she whispered thickly, "*nihoatovaz*." Framing his unsightly, battle-scarred face in her delicate hands, she kissed the marred cleft of his chin, the bridge of his broken nose, his cheeks, his eyelids.

His instincts told him she was whispering Cheyenne love words, and the thought of such unalloyed sweetness being offered to a demoralized, crippled ex-soldier like himself was enough to drive Lyon mad.

"*Vehona* . . . little princess," he murmured.

The force of his need battered him like a siege-engine smashing down a fortress gate.

From the far end of the parapet, the faint sound of footsteps intruded. He instantly set her down. He braced his hands on the rough wall behind her, keeping her safely hidden from curious eyes, while he took a moment for his ragged breathing to calm. Then he glanced up the stone rampart. Two guardsmen in the green tartan of the Argylls, their gazes politely averted, waited for him to recoup.

"Damn it to hell," he muttered under his breath.

Then he slipped his arm around Julie's slender shoulders and whisked her down the nearby stairs and out of their sight.

Eilean Danielson was once an island stronghold at the western end of Loch Etive. Seated in the prow of the rowboat, Juliette strained to see the ruins as they approached. The heavy growth of woods screened the castle from view.

MacLyon pulled rhythmically on the oars, and the soft slush of water was the only sound to disturb the uncanny stillness that hung over the island.

"Does anyone ever come here?" she asked softly.

"Not often."

"Have you been here before?"

"Oh, aye, several times. Youthful curiosity brought me to the island when I was a lad of nine or ten. James and I came twice more after that."

"Have you returned since you were a boy?"

She could hear the aversion in his clipped response. "Aye."

When he offered nothing further, Juliette glanced back at MacLyon. He'd stopped rowing. He held the oars flat over the water and stared ahead at the dense wall of trees and undergrowth. His eyes bespoke an unbearable sorrow, and she turned to survey Eilean Danielson once more, searching in vain for the cause.

She'd known from the outset that he hadn't wanted to bring her here. But she wasn't prepared for the disturbing effect which the very sight of the island had upon him.

Lyon couldn't bring himself to tell Julie about the last time he'd wandered through the deserted ruins. He'd come to Eilean Danielson the previous April. After returning home from the military tribunal in Cairo, he'd laid James to rest in the MacLyon burial grounds. Needing to get away from inquisitive eyes, he rowed to the island following the memorial service. As he sat in silent contemplation of the wreckage, Lyon was overwhelmed with grief and guilt. The place's utter desolation had crept into his soul.

Over and over, he'd asked himself why he had hesitated to disobey orders and start off immediately for the garrison at El Durman. The wasted twenty-four hours had meant the difference between life and death for the besieged Highland regiment. He should have risked everything, including a court-martial and execution by firing squad, rather than arrive too late.

Lyon pushed the dark recollections aside. He began rowing once more, the repetitive movements soothing despite the dull ache in his elbow. Just in front of him, Julie sat watching the island grow nearer, her posture elegant. He found her innate grace a continuing source of delight.

She wore a plum-colored walking suit trimmed with black velvet, its coquettish pouf of draperies accentuating her little bum. A black bowler sat at a cocky angle on her head, and the veil's gossamer netting sailed out behind her in the breeze.

He smiled at the memory of her generous offer to help with the oars, when he'd removed his jacket and laid it on the seat beside him.

"I am stronger than I look," she'd told him, her dark almond eyes serious. "You should not have to do all the work, while I sit idle."

He'd known she was thinking of his injured arm. "Princess, I could carry you over my shoulder on a forced march and never feel your weight," he'd replied with a chuckle.

With a regal toss of her head, she'd hopped into the boat and motioned for him to commence rowing, as though she were queen of the Nile and he a lowly galley slave. Now, that fantasy had possibilities . . .

The evening before, Julie had blithely announced at the supper table that Lyon was taking her to Eilean Danielson so she could view the ruins. There'd been a momentary pause, as the adults exchanged silent glances over the china and crystal. He'd fully expected both Rob and Flora to immediately offer their company. A young unmarried female didn't venture off sightseeing without a chaperone. But neither said a word.

More amazing still, not even Lady Hester quibbled at the notion. Neil and Jamie looked around expectantly, hoping they'd be included in the excursion. Lyon had sent them a ferocious scowl, and they'd wisely held their eager tongues.

His family's behavior had perplexed him. It seemed they were willing to forego the proprieties where Miss Elkheart was concerned. He realized, then, they wanted desperately to keep her at Strathlyon, each for his or her own reason. And they were hoping Lyon would be the reason she'd stay.

That left only the mystery of Julie's willingness to go alone with him. He sensed that although she'd been taught British society's strict rules of decorum, her own culture's attitude toward courtship and marriage was far more open and natural. And always, there remained her unshaken belief that she could protect herself from any male's unwanted attention. That mistaken notion would have to be rectified for her own safety. The thought of another man purposely hurting her turned the blood to ice in his veins.

The moment the boat touched shore, he jumped into the shallow waves and pulled the prow up onto the sloping bank. Then he lifted Julie out, grabbed his jacket, and guided her up the narrow path that led through the nearly impenetrable underbrush. Dreading what was to come and unwilling to sever the contact between them, he kept his hand firmly on her elbow.

Juliette drew a deep, fortifying breath as they left the stand of birch and willow. At one time, the citadel of deep-umber sandstone had loomed high above the trees. Now the gaping shards of its blackened outer walls rose no taller than the humblest croft. Not a tower had been left standing.

They crossed a wide, dry ditch that once served as a moat, the drawbridge now a mass of jumbled stones, and climbed the knoll on which the castle stood. She realized, then, that MacLyon had purposely approached the island from its low-lying wooded side, so she wouldn't see the dark, jagged skeleton of Danielson Castle etched across the cloudless blue sky. The fortification had been built on a slab of solid rock that rose straight up from the northwest shore.

Ironically, a gentle current of air from the sea loch swept over the tumbled stones, carrying the perfume of blossoms. Yellow wildflowers grew along the once massive foundations, and honeysuckle climbed the remnants of the thick curtain-walls. Most striking, however, was the cheerful warble and chatter of birds that broke the oppressive stillness.

She'd prepared herself for a frightening, possibly devastating, ordeal. If her vision had been a call from her murdered ancestors for vengeance against their foes, she would know the moment she set foot within the rubble.

Juliette could feel the tension in MacLyon's fingers as he clasped her arm. He, too, had foreseen an unnerving experience. She touched his hand lightly, signaling her desire to proceed alone.

"Julie," he said, his deep baritone harsh, "I don't think you should explore the ruins without me."

"This is something I must do alone," she replied.

After a moment's hesitation, he released her.

Juliette took a calming breath. Prepared to shrink back in horror from the keening of ghosts, she closed her eyes for a moment and sent a prayer to Maxemaheo for strength of purpose. The Cheyenne people believed that what occurred at a certain place was always happening there. Her heart thumping with dread, she walked slowly through the large, overturned stones scattered randomly across the grass surrounding the remnants of the castle.

What had once been a massive gateway was destroyed nearly beyond recognition, although the outline of the bailey and its four flanking towers remained. The intensity of hatred that had resulted in such complete obliteration was plainly evident. Long after the last Danielson had been put to the sword, the besiegers had continued to pull the stronghold down on top of their lifeless bodies.

Trembling with apprehension, Juliette entered what remained of the great hall, its walls now only waist-high. She tried to picture the enormous fireplace, the tapestries, the gleaming candelabra, the stone-vaulted roof.

The conflagration had taken place only a few years before the American Revolution. The castle's inhabitants must have been wearing white powdered wigs, the women in hooped skirts, the men armed with swords, muskets, and flintlock pistols.

She fought the dizziness that swirled inside her, threatening to demolish her calm, inner center. From childhood, she had practiced a warrior's mastery of unflinching self-control, even in the face of pain and death. She would not surrender to the whirlwind of fear that rose up in a coward's heart to wreak his own destruction.

Juliette gazed about the ruins and waited in dreadful expectation for the spirits of her fallen ancestors to call out to her.

Chapter 10

Nothing extraordinary happened.

Only the sweet notes of a thrush pierced the quiet afternoon.

Juliette suffered no sense of anguish or mental disturbance, though she experienced no particular feeling of peace either. She pressed her hands to her chest, whispering a prayer of thanksgiving.

Moving more surely now, she wandered through the site of the former kitchen, which contained the still recognizable hearth of a huge oven. Open, moss-covered stairs ran down to what had once been cellars or dungeons, but were now open pits. She discovered a small, narrow room that must have served as a chapel or parlor, then returned to the great hall.

At the sound of footsteps, she looked over to find MacLyon standing at the gaping entryway, his folded jacket draped carelessly over one shoulder. He watched her with haunted eyes.

"Tell me about it," she pleaded.

He ran his fingers through his hair and looked around the burnt shell in distraction before meeting her gaze once again.

"Only if you agree to come away from here," he said brusquely. "There's a meadow a short distance from the ruins, where we can sit on some fallen stones and talk."

Juliette nodded in agreement.

As they crossed the open bailey, he took her arm in his firm clasp. The tension in his strong fingers and the stiff purpose of his gait conveyed MacLyon's uneasiness.

Together, they descended the hillock and entered the sheltering trees. A small clearing opened up, and Juliette sank down on a large block of stone.

The tall Scotsman strode restlessly back and forth through the high grass, then braced his shoulders against a sturdy tree trunk and folded his arms across his chest. His sun-weathered features hardened into an inscrutable mask.

Juliette could feel his suffering. She yearned to smooth her hand over his tortured brow and free him from pain with her touch. An ache of compassion welled up inside her for this brave, lost warrior, who couldn't find his way back from the battlefield. But she knew he had something he desperately needed to say. Something about her ancestors. And his.

She folded her hands, took a deep breath, and told herself to remain composed, no matter what. Using the technique her father had taught her, Juliette concentrated on the scene around her, alert to its smallest detail, while she marshaled her inner resources of courage and strength.

The cream-colored blooms of the meadow-sweet filled the air with a delightful fragrance, and the drone of honeybees brought an unexpected sense of tranquillity. Through the stand of trees the charred husk of Danielson Castle could barely be seen.

Lyon looked up at the spreading branches of an oak that formed a shifting canopy of green over their heads. Before long, the leaves would turn a deep bronze and drift to the ground, leaving behind the stark outline of brittle, dry twigs. Long before that, the gorgeous creature before him, who waited patiently for him to begin his gory tale, would be gone from the Highlands.

He expected Julie to leave Strathlyon once he'd finished his story, for there was nothing more she could learn about her ancestors—and nothing more she'd want to know about his. The emptiness of life without her stretched endlessly before him like a doomed trek across the blistering Sahara.

He closed his eyes, welcoming that emptiness, that unending loneliness he so well deserved. It was the torment of her presence that he couldn't endure. Once she was gone, he'd be able to cope with his self-inflicted alienation. *Until* she was gone, he had to hold firm against the sniveling coward inside, who wanted to beg her to stay.

"I am waiting," she reminded him softly.

His lids flew open, and he met her brilliant eyes. A shaft of pain shot straight through his chest as though he'd been struck by a fairy's dart. He longed for the solace of her gentle caress, for the sweet kindness glowing from within like a magic lamp. She was the evening star, shining in the night sky, guiding him to a place of peace . . . of forgiveness . . . of love. A place he could never reach, not even in his dreams.

Lyon's throat tightened with an unbearable ache of regret for what could never be. He released a rusty breath, scarcely able to begin. "My great-grandfather's name was Aeanas MacLyon," he said, his words labored. "He had two sons, of whom he was, no doubt, justly proud. Though his younger brother had died, the chief had three fine nephews as well. The MacLyons were longtime allies of their nearest neighbors. . . ." He halted, dreading the thought of going on.

"Who were Clan Danielson," she added quietly. She removed her jaunty bowler, set it on top of his jacket, and nodded for him to continue.

"Aye," he said. "The MacLyons have been known as intrepid fighters since the first Norse invaders came ashore. In the years following the Jacobite uprising of forty-five, Highland chiefs continued to form their own regiments, such as the Frasers, the Argylls, and the Sutherlands. The MacLyon Highlanders played an important part in defeating the French in Canada during the Seven Years' War."

She smiled encouragingly. "Jennie and I studied that war from another perspective, when we attended the French embassy school in Washington, D.C."

Unable to return her smile, Lyon ignored his misgivings and forced himself to go on. "For some unknown reason, the Danielsons turned against us in a callous act of betrayal. Their chief, Ninian Danielson, sent word to the MacLyon regiment garrisoned at Fort William, that he and his family were being held hostage by an outraged crowd in a place near Glen Kildunun not far from the fort. Every MacLyon clansmen in the regiment rode to his rescue."

Stepping away from the gnarled oak, Lyon moved to where she sat. He braced his foot on the edge of the sandstone block and rested an elbow on his bent knee.

"The reason behind the treachery," he said, "was never discovered. But the fact remains that the Danielsons trapped the MacLyons in a steep, narrow glen." He paused and met her somber gaze. "The MacLyons were outnumbered more than five to one. Caught completely by surprise, they were cut down without mercy by men they had always believed were their trusted friends. The wounded were brutally murdered, their throats slit as they lay helpless on the blood-soaked ground."

Her misty eyes sparkled with tears. "I know," she said simply. "I do not doubt the accuracy of your words."

"Every male heir of the old chief was slain. His sons and nephews were brought down in their prime. Not a single MacLyon was spared." He stopped, not wanting to continue.

Julie turned her head and gazed through the trees to the blackened debris beyond. Tendrils of hair blew gently against her cheek. The rays of light streaming through the leaves overhead shimmered across the chestnut strands, sparking glints of cinnabar and claret. Her hands, encased in black kid gloves, lay loosely in her lap.

As the silence lengthened, she tipped her head back to meet his eyes. "Go on," she urged in her throaty contralto, and the faint, breathless trepidation in her words squeezed his heart in a painful vice.

"When the news was brought to Aeneas MacLyon, his fury was unparalleled. He sent the Fiery Cross round to all the local clans, asking for their help in punishing the Danielsons. Together, MacDougalls, Macintyres, McCorquodales, and Campbells stormed this island, with the seventy-year-old chief of Clan MacLyon leading them.

"They executed every male over twelve found within the castle walls. Except for Ninian's immediate family, who were hanged alongside him, the women and children were rowed across the loch and scattered into exile. The remaining Danielson clansmen were hunted with dogs throughout the Highlands, till every last one of them had been found and slain. The clan was forever outlawed. From that time onward, anyone bearing the surname of Danielson or caught wearing their tartan was put to death. They were called the Clan of the Clouds, for like a race of fairies, they disappeared from the face of the earth."

Her words were little more than a whisper. "And the Danielsons never confessed why they'd betrayed the MacLyons?"

Lyon straightened and massaged the cramped muscles of his arm. "They protested their innocence to the end. Not a single Danielson, man, woman, or child, would say why they'd turned on us."

"I see." Julie's disappointment was tragically apparent in her bowed head and slumped shoulders.

Lyon thanked God she hadn't tried to run away from him or attempt to deny her forebears' perfidy. He crouched on one knee in front of her and took her small gloved hand in his. "Believe me, Juliette Evening Star, they were guilty as sin. Crofters in Glen Kildunun hid behind rocks and witnessed the massacre. They swore the atrocity was committed by the Danielson Fencibles. Their distinctive lavender and pink tartan could be seen from the hillsides."

"I believe you," she said, unable to meet his gaze. Teardrops splashed on his hand.

Relief washed over Lyon. When he could bring himself to speak, his voice was a harsh croak. "Then you don't blame me for what happened on this island?"

She raised her long, dark lashes, their tips spiked with crystals. Her lips trembled as she made a valiant attempt to smile. "How could I blame you, Lyon, when Ninian Danielson, the man who could be my ancestor, was the cause of it?"

At that moment, a bolt of lightning, followed by an ear-splitting boom of thunder, made them look up. While they'd been engrossed in the past, a bank of storm clouds had blown over the island. Julie's mouth fell open in amazement, for the clear cerulean sky had suddenly grown black, and raindrops splattered around them.

Lyon snatched up his jacket and held it over her head. She reached up to clasp its edges, using it as a makeshift umbrella.

"There's an abandoned croft not far from here," he shouted over another roll of thunder. "We can take shelter there."

With Lyon leading the way, they raced through the trees in the pouring rain.

The little stone house had only one window, but the thatched roof was still intact. The lintel over the door was so low, MacLyon had to stoop to enter the building. They found it swept clean of dust, with fresh rushes scattered over the packed dirt floor. A crude wooden table and chairs and a bed in the corner were the only furnishings, but someone had left a folded blanket on a low chest that stood at the foot of the bed.

Astonished, Juliette took in the air of tidy simplicity. "Are you certain this home is abandoned?"

The amazement on MacLyon's face told her he was equally baffled by its snug appearance. "This croft has stood empty for years," he said. "An occasional fisherman might use it for shelter in a storm, but no one's made a permanent home on this island since I was a lad."

She hung his drenched jacket over one of the rough wooden chairs to dry and dropped her ruined hat, along with her gloves, on the seat. Her upswept hair had come loose, and stray damp locks lay on her shoulders and tumbled down her back.

"Who do you think has been here?" she asked, trying without success to restore her damaged coiffure.

His lips twitched suspiciously, as he sat on the chest and pulled off his boots. "There's a superstition in the Highlands, that the *sìth* will sneak into your home and do your work for you in secret. There's no other plausible explanation."

She stared at him, scarcely able to believe her ears. "Do you believe in fairies?"

"I didn't used to," he said with maddening nonchalance. He shrugged out of his wet shirt and tossed it over the other chair. Then he found a box of matches, bent over the slate hearth, and lit a stack of peat in the fireplace.

"And now you do?"

"I don't know what I believe now," he answered. As he coaxed the fire to life, the pungent aroma of burning peat filled the cottage.

Unable to keep from shivering, Juliette stepped closer to the low flames and peeked at MacLyon from the corner of her eye. She gulped back a lump that rose in her throat at the sight of him.

The broad expanse of his back was ridged with muscles. His upper arms bulged with an imposing display of male strength. The soaked riding breeches plastered against his legs revealed massive thighs of undeniable power. When he'd said he could carry her on a forced march and never feel her weight, he hadn't been boasting. It'd been the plain truth.

The Cheyenne were tall, strong, handsome people. She'd

seen stalwart men, including her own father, wearing little more than a breechclout and moccasins. But nothing had prepared her for the sight of this magnificent giant, stripped to the waist.

Juliette caught her breath, tensing for flight. The quickened rise and fall of her breasts revealed her awakened sense of vulnerability. She crossed her arms tightly over her chest to keep from shaking.

MacLyon rose from the fire, and his six and a half foot frame seemed to fill the shrinking croft. His head grazed the ceiling at its highest point.

Juliette took a quick, involuntary step back, painfully aware of how insignificant she appeared in comparison. She touched the lump on her thigh, where her knife was hidden beneath her petticoat, and reminded herself to breathe in a smooth, even rhythm, so he wouldn't suspect how nervous she suddenly felt.

His eyes sparkled, as though he were reading her thoughts. For the first time, she caught a glow of playful mischief in their leaf-green depths. He propped his hands on his hips, and his mouth quirked in a devilish, sideways grin.

His rich baritone reverberated in the small enclosure like the low, resonant thrumming of a war chant. "Do you realize that Neil and Jamie think you're a fairy princess?"

Juliette shook her head, unable to keep her eyes off his muscular chest. Over the marvelously contoured pectorals, he had a thick mat of rust-colored hair in the shape of an inverted triangle, from his collarbone down to the waistband of his riding breeches. His flat nipples were tight and erect from the rain. She tore her gaze away and blinked repeatedly at the streaked windowpane, where the storm beat insistently.

"You are a grown man, MacLyon, not a child," she scolded, channeling her confusion into a display of scorn. "How could you possibly believe I am any such thing?"

"One thing I do know is that you're soaked to the skin."

He placed his hand on her shoulder, and she knew he could feel her quiver beneath his touch. But his words were detached and unemotional as he continued. "There's a warm blanket on the bed, Julie. Slip your outer clothing off, and you can wrap it around you."

She realized it'd be foolish to balk at the practical suggestion. Her wet clothes clung to her uncomfortably. She'd never get warm if she didn't remove her walking suit and hang it by the fire to dry.

"Very well," she agreed, adopting his matter-of-fact manner.

Juliette plopped down in front of the hearth and took off her shoes, stockings, and garters. Regaining her feet, she removed her jacket and handed it to him. Next came her skirt. She waited for MacLyon to turn his back as he placed them over wooden pegs near the fire, then unbuttoned her lilac blouse and slipped it off. He took it without a word and hung it beside the rest of her clothing, not seeming the least surprised over the lack of a corset beneath.

Clad only in a damp chemise, petticoat, and drawers, she gratefully accepted the red and green plaid he draped over her shoulders. She pulled the soft wool around her and sank back down in front of the flames, drawing her knees up to her chin. With a heartfelt sigh, she snuggled into the blanket's cozy warmth.

"I found a clean towel in the chest by the bed," he said. "Let me dry your hair."

Before she could refuse, he knelt behind her and sank back on his haunches. The clean, refreshing scent of him reminded her of branches of balsam fir brought inside on a cold, wintry day.

MacLyon gently removed the few pins that hadn't fallen out during their race to the croft and carefully laid them on the hearth. He caught her disordered locks in the linen toweling and rubbed the damp hair as dry as possible. Then he smoothed out the tangled mass, letting it fall down her back.

"Better now?" he asked softly.

"Much, much better," she confessed. She crossed her arms and rested them on her bent knees, gazing into the fireplace. "I feel like a lizard sunning itself on a rock in the middle of July."

A chuckle rumbled deep in his chest, and she smiled to herself, thinking she'd never heard such an entrancing sound.

"The blanket happens to be woven in the MacDougall tartan," he commented wryly. "I wondered if you'd recognized it."

She clucked her tongue. "You sound disappointed."

Drawing Julie close, Lyon cuddled her between his thighs. Her thick, straight hair tumbled past her waist in a luxuriant waterfall of satin. He carefully arranged the damp tresses so they weren't caught between their bodies.

Lyon silently thanked whichever member of his family had sent a servant earlier that day to clean and ready the croft. Someone, God bless his well-meaning heart, had hoped he'd make good use of it, should the opportunity arise. He hadn't planned on such a blissful opportunity—hadn't even dreamed of it—but he bloody hell didn't intend to let it slip by.

"I'd much rather be wrapping you in the MacLyon tartan," he told her. He kissed the top of her head, then bent and grazed her temple with his lips. "Better still, I'd rather be wrapped in it with you."

"Are you cold?" she asked with sincere concern.

Lyon squeezed his eyes shut.

Why did she have to be so damn innocent?

"No."

With a deep exhalation of contentment, she sank back against him. "It *is* getting warmer in here," she agreed.

"Princess," he said hoarsely, "I'm burning up."

Lyon caressed her throat, following the delicate curve with his fingertips to dip into the hollow of her clavicle. Bending his head, he traced the shell of her ear with the tip of his tongue, and the gratifying sound of her in-drawn breath brought a smile to his lips.

"That tickles," Julie complained with a throaty laugh. But she didn't pull away. She tilted her head to one side, allowing him to delve deeper.

He spoke in her ear, his words a soft buzz. "I'm going to sip your sweet nectar like a greedy bumblebee."

Her entire body quivered beneath the touch of his probing tongue. She started to turn her head toward him, as though to offer her mouth for a kiss.

"Hold still," he warned her, "or I'll sting." He caught her ear lobe between his teeth, exerting just enough pressure to make her tighten with expectation.

"Surely not," she breathed.

Lyon pushed the strands of her long hair aside. He kissed her smooth neck with his open mouth, twirling his tongue over the sensitive spot behind her ear. "You taste like heaven, Miss Juliette Evening Star," he said with a low growl of pleasure. He nipped her playfully. "I could eat you alive."

"Mm," Julie murmured. Her head fell back to rest on his naked chest, and she relaxed against him.

He slipped his fingers beneath the edge of the blanket to feel the swell of her breast, then nudged the red and green wool out of the way. His rough jaw grazed her cheek, as he placed a kiss beside the lacy strap of her chemise on her exposed shoulder.

The delicious floral scent that clung to her moist skin vied with the sharp smell of the peat fire. For an instant, a streak of lightning lit the dim interior, and the following crash of thunder shook the ground. But the croft remained cozy and dry.

"*A ghaolaich,*" Lyon whispered, calling her his darling in the Gaelic. He slipped his hand beneath her damp underclothing and cupped her breast. He could feel the velvety nipple tighten into a bud against the callused palm of his hand.

The youthful firmness of her small, round breast brought a surge of guilt. He had no right to fondle such fresh innocence, such untouched, silken purity. Years of voluptuous carnal pleasure with high-priced courtesans from London to Cairo had left him a debauched, empty shell.

Lyon ruthlessly suppressed the carping voice inside that reminded him he didn't deserve to know this happiness.

Dammit, he had himself firmly under control.

He would touch her no more than was necessary to bring her to fulfillment. He didn't dare turn her around in his arms, for he couldn't trust himself to kiss her, to suckle her, to lick her, and not yield to his own sexual desires. But this much he could do, without risking the loss of her virtue. Or his mental faculties.

As he lightly rubbed the palm of his hand in a circle, barely skimming the puckered coral crest, he spoke to her in Gaelic. Just being able to put his graphic thoughts into words gave Lyon some relief from the driving need that spurred him onward. He thanked God she didn't understand a syllable he uttered.

"I long to know you in every way possible, little princess," he said huskily. "I want to stroke your sweet femininity with my tongue."

Juliette frantically translated the unfamiliar phrases in her mind. *Sweet femininity* . . . surely he didn't mean . . . he couldn't mean . . .

What she knew about the physical mating of a man and a woman was limited and sketchy. Although her mother had explained the basic concept, the action to which Lyon alluded came as a titillating shock. She could feel her breasts swell and tighten beneath his gentle manipulation. He scarcely touched her. Yet the light, gliding motion tantalized and enticed, making her wild for more.

As though he'd heard her ardent thoughts, he pulled the blanket down to her hips and slipped the straps of her camisole over her shoulders. With a swift, easy movement, he shoved the cotton garment to her waist, freeing her arms.

Then he cupped both breasts in his palms to continue the tender ministrations.

Without conscious awareness, Juliette raised her arms and rested the backs of her hands on his broad shoulders. She arched against him, as she lifted herself higher for his touch.

"I want to feel your slick petals unfold for me," he told her in Gaelic. The soft, strange vowels rumbled around her, their meaning slowly penetrating her dazed mind. "Just let me caress you, my darling lass."

He drew her petticoat up, then slid his large hand inside the wide opening of her loose-fitting drawers. If he noticed the *nihpihist* tied at her waist and thighs, he gave no sign. The presence of a Cheyenne chastity rope would be no more daunting to a man of his size and determination than the knife strapped to her leg.

She should tell him. She should explain that he couldn't touch her while she wore it. That it was forbidden. But somehow, the words refused to be formed.

As his fingertips smoothed their way across her stomach, Juliette gave a tiny sob of anticipation. She drew a deep, ragged breath.

"Ah, yes, sweet princess, yes," he crooned in Gaelic. "I've dreamed of caressing you like this. Of exploring your secret place with my lips and my tongue. Of memorizing each fragile tissue that quivered beneath my ravenous mouth. Night after night, I've lain awake, aching for you."

Lyon moved one hand lightly back and forth across her exposed breasts, as he sought her center-most jewel with his other hand. His fingers eased into a fluff of down, then parted her velvet folds. She was swollen with desire and dewy moist. He smiled at the irrefutable proof of her response to his touch. Placing a finger on either side of her sensitive nub, he gently, slowly massaged her.

"Lyon . . ." she gasped. "Oh, no! I cannot! We must not!" She pushed back against him, her legs bent, her knees apart, her bare feet flat on the floor.

''Shh,'' he murmured in her ear, this time speaking in English, so she'd understand. ''It's all right, lass. Don't fight it. And don't hurry it. Let the feelings surge over you and through you, till the sensations go deep, deep down into your very core. Forget everything, but the feel of my touch. Let go of everything, but how very, very good it feels. At this moment, I am your slave, Evening Star, and you are my queen. Give in to the pleasure I've been longing to give you.''

Juliette heard his whispered words as her body stiffened and trembled beneath his hands. All sense of time became suspended as tremor after tremor of pure enjoyment pulsated through her. She clutched his forearms, as though she had the physical strength to stop him if she'd wanted to.

He barely moved his fingers, only enough to continue the pressure, building up a spiraling ache, an irresistible yearning, slowly and steadily inside her. She started to whimper, to plead for something she didn't understand, but wanted desperately.

Lyon could feel her exquisite response to his slightest touch. Julie lifted herself up against his hands, her breasts as tight and swollen as her silken core.

He had no intention of hurrying.

This was the only intimacy they'd ever share.

He would never take her virginity. Never feel her delicate fingers stroking him. Never bury himself in her warm, caressing flesh. But he *would* know the rare joy of bringing her to a climax, while he held her in his arms.

As he edged her lingeringly, inevitably, to a shattering culmination, Lyon knew in his heart exactly what he was doing. He could never possess her, never keep her as his own. But he was making damn sure she'd remember him in the years to come. No matter what braw young lad claimed her as his bride, she'd always remember this first experience and the Scotsman who'd shared it with her.

Juliette was sobbing now.

The intense sensations, coming close to pain, were nearly

unbearable. She dug her fingernails into the muscles of his arms. She could feel her own wetness slicken her folds beneath his fingers. Her entire body tautened like a spring. And then she was catapulted into convulsions of pleasure, the feeling driving itself deep, deep inside her, just as he'd predicted, as her sobs became one long, impassioned cry of fulfillment.

Gradually her heartbeat and breathing returned to normal, and with that came consciousness of her surroundings. She rested against him, languid and dreamy, and slowly became aware that he had readjusted her clothing.

"Lyon," she whispered. She tried to turn around and look at him, but he held her fast.

"No," he said, "don't move. Stay as you are a little while longer. And then we'll have to go."

"Go?"

"The rain has stopped."

Juliette cocked her head and listened. The quiet was almost unnerving after the chaos of the storm. She waited for Lyon to say something about what had just happened between them. Some soft words of reassurance. When he continued to hold her in his arms without uttering a sound, the heat of a flush spread over her. She'd reacted so unrestrainedly, she wondered if he'd been shocked or repulsed. *Hesc!* She was more than a little astounded herself. What had happened to the prudent, cautious Juliette Elkheart everyone relied upon?

She bit her lower lip, desperate to say something to break the mortifying silence. "Will it be safe to cross the loch in the rowboat?" she asked at last, her low contralto sounding deeper and huskier than ever.

He bent his head and pressed his face against her hair, as though considering the notion. "Thunderstorms aren't common in the western Highlands. It sounds as if the squall has completely blown over. We should be safely back at Strathlyon before supper time."

"I am sure everyone is worried about us," she said lamely.

"They'll be sorry to see you leave," he replied. "My family has grown quite fond of you."

At his cool, impersonal tone, she stiffened and tried to sit up straight. With one heavy arm draped casually across her waist, he held her against him with ludicrous ease.

"I am not leaving right away," Juliette informed him. She tugged on his wrist in a useless attempt to pry his hold loose.

He spoke with infuriating calm. "You must return to Edinburgh, Julie. Now that you've found out what you came to learn, I'd like you to leave as soon as possible."

Juliette swallowed back the humiliation that burned her throat and stung her eyes. *Ahahe!* she thought woefully. She didn't have to wonder if he'd been repulsed by her uninhibited behavior. The answer was plain. But she wasn't going to leave, no matter what he thought about her. Not before she tried everything possible to resolve the puzzle of her vision. "I promised Neil I would give a shooting exhibition on his birthday," she stated cheerfully. "So I cannot possibly leave before that."

MacLyon released her and stood up. She immediately rose and turned to face him. He glowered at her, his eyes as cold and hard as a Canadian blizzard. "I'm telling you, Miss Elkheart, that you must leave now. I want you on the train to Edinburgh in the morning."

Tears sprang to her eyes. Tears of anger and hurt pride. Nothing more. She *refused* to feel anything more.

Juliette straightened to her full five feet, two inches, determined not to be coerced by his towering height or his daunting size. "I will decide when I leave the Highlands, MacLyon. And I will not go back to Edinburgh until I am ready."

He clasped her shoulders, pulled her to him, and spoke through clenched teeth. "God dammit, Julie, if you stay at Strathlyon, I won't be responsible for what happens."

He released her with a vile oath in Gaelic and stalked out, slamming the door. The whole croft shuddered beneath the force of his anger.

Juliette wanted to burst into tears, to plead for him to come back and hold her in his arms again. She wanted to keen like a Cheyenne widow bewailing the death of her courageous warrior husband. She wanted to run back to Edinburgh and never see the chief of Clan MacLyon again. Not for as long as she lived.

But she refused to give in to her foolish emotions. The spirits of her Scottish ancestors had called her to the Highlands for a reason. And she would stay until she discovered it.

Chapter 11

Lady Hester used the celebration of Neil's seventh birthday as an opportunity to invite all her friends and neighbors to meet her Canadian guest. Most of the village of Strathbardine was in attendance that afternoon, as well as the local gentry from the surrounding countryside. Everyone flocked to Strathlyon Castle with unabashed curiosity, since Miss Juliette Elkheart was reputed to be a survivor of the infamous Clan of the Clouds.

Laird Hamish Macfie spotted the young woman standing momentarily alone. He was anxious to learn if she'd uncovered the fact that his forebears had been far more involved in the slaying of the Danielsons and the razing of their island castle than he'd implied. It was imperative that nothing link the Macfies to the butchery at Kildunun.

He threaded his way through the crowd to her side and presented his most engaging smile. "Was your trip to Stirling successful, Miss Elkheart?"

"No, I would not consider it a success," she said. "Although I did learn the name of the last chief of Clan Danielson, I could find no proof that he was my direct ancestor. And since the records of that clan ended with his death, I am stymied as to how to go on. All I know for certain is that my great-great-grandfather, who went by the name of John McDougall, brought a Danielson tartan with him to America."

Hamish hid his relief at her straightforward reply. "It's unfortunate that you couldn't trace him."

"Yes, but thank you for inquiring." She met his eyes with an unwavering gaze, giving no indication that she might be deceiving him. Either she was as ignorant as she professed or an extremely clever young lady.

"If you'll excuse me, Miss Elkheart," he said with a polite nod, "I'll see if Georgiana needs anything."

Juliette watched in speculation as the husky man joined his widowed sister. She wasn't quite sure why she hadn't mentioned the forfeiture of the Danielson lands to the Macfies.

Her intuition told her Hamish already knew and wanted desperately to keep it a secret. His crafty gray eyes betrayed his outward guise of friendliness. Macfie watched and waited from afar, the way a pack of wolves trails a herd of deer throughout the snowy winter.

The sun kept peeking in and out of the fluffy clouds overhead, but patches of cornflower blue promised a fine day for the festive event.

Juliette caught a glimpse of the chief of Clan MacLyon, visiting with several gentlemen attired in jackets and kilts. It wasn't hard to spot the Lion's reddish-gold mane, even in a throng of fair, long-legged Scotsmen. *Nanoseham* was a good head taller than every other male present, except for Robbie, who almost matched his older brother's height.

Unlike many of his neighbors, who'd donned magnificent clan plaids and Scottish bonnets decorated with sprigs of heather, holly, or juniper for the special occasion, The MacLyon wore a severely tailored black suit. Lady Hester had succeeded in her insistence that he wear a vest and neckscarf, as well. With his blunt-hewn features and massive physique, he was so unapologetically masculine that Juliette felt dazed and short of breath when she looked at him.

Following their visit to the ruins on Eilean Danielson two days ago, MacLyon's inexplicable anger had continued unabated. There was no need for Juliette, in her mortification, to try to avoid him.

He'd avoided her with a vengeance.

The laird of Strathlyon appeared to be biding his time, until his nephew's birthday celebration was over, before approaching her again with his ultimatum that she leave his home immediately or suffer the consequences.

The memory of the erotic Gaelic words he'd murmured to her in the abandoned croft brought a scalding flush to her cheeks. *Haxc!* She should have told him the first day she'd arrived at the castle that she could speak the Highlanders' tongue. It was too late now to warn him never to say such shockingly intimate things to her again. If she confessed the truth, he'd be even more horrified at her shameless behavior than he was already.

Juliette had tried both days to compose a letter to Jennie. Although she'd written her only once since arriving in Scotland, she couldn't bring herself to send a letter filled with false cheer. It would be impossible to fool her twin. Jennifer Morning Rose would read between the lines and know just how confused and miserable Juliette really was. She wouldn't worry her sister needlessly. She'd tell Jennie all about the brooding, headstrong Scotsman when she saw her in November.

Juliette did scribble a note to Uncle Benjamin, assuring him that she was making progress in her genealogical research, but wasn't ready to leave Strathlyon Castle yet. And she set no date for her return to Edinburgh.

In her misery, the notion occurred to Juliette that she might be falling in love with MacLyon, a notion she immediately rejected. The man was gruff, short-tempered, and cynical, with a tendency to erupt into violence at the least provocation. His size alone made him formidable and—for any female except a Cheyenne warrior-woman—a trace frightening.

Hesc! She had no intention of giving up her dreams. She was going to return to America, enroll at the university in

Pennsylvania, and one day study to be a veterinarian. She hoped to eventually set up practice in Medicine Hat, where she'd be close to her family. No, her place was definitely not here in these rugged, majestic Highlands with a fierce Scottish laird.

Determined to shake off the unhappiness that dogged her, Juliette had thrown herself wholeheartedly into the plans for Neil's birthday. She intended to ignore the laird of Strathlyon and enjoy the day's festivities. When Dr. Keir MacDougall and his fiancée came up to join her, she smiled a warm welcome.

"Jock Ogilvie told me you stitched up a gash on Big Blue's flank," Keir said, beaming with admiration. "It takes courage to work on a huge draft horse, even for a man. The old crofter claimed to be frightened to death that the laird would strip his wrinkled hide off his bones and nail it to the stable door, if you got kicked."

Annie Buchanan leaned toward Juliette, and the edges of their parasols bumped gently. Her hazel eyes sparkled with a whimsical humor. "Jock said the moment Blue heard the soothing sound of your magical language, he behaved like a well-mannered Welsh pony."

Juliette laughed. "I would make a very poor veterinarian if I were afraid of large animals. Especially on the Alberta plains."

After she'd sewn up the gelding's wound, the stooped, wizened crofter had confided to Juliette that his father's mother had been a Danielson. When she'd informed Jock Ogilvie that someone was weaving a lavender and pink tartan for her, his pale blue eyes flashed with excitement. He didn't ask the weaver's name, but she was certain he'd surmised it.

"How was your trip to Stirling?" Annie asked. That afternoon, she had pulled her riotous curls into a loose, upswept style. Light brown tendrils floated around her heart-shaped face, refusing to be tamed, and giving her the look of an irrepressible pixie.

"Overall, it proved rather uninformative," Juliette said. "But I did learn a great deal more about your country's history. I am presently reading a book about William Wallace, which Lady Hester gave me."

"Annie and I belong to the Scottish National Society," Keir reminded her. "Our goal is to preserve our Highland heritage." The genial doctor wore a plaid over his jacket shoulder, pinned with a silver brooch. His *feile-beag*, or little kilt, of MacDougall red and green tartan, fell to just above his knees. A Scots bonnet, pinned with a silver clan badge, was perched on his sandy head.

Intrigued, Juliette folded her parasol and rested the tip on the ground. "Rob has been teaching me some of the old ballads and folk tales. He is working on a play about Bonny Prince Charlie, which he hopes someday to have performed on the London stage."

"If you're interested in Scottish customs," Annie suggested enthusiastically, "why don't you come to our meeting next Monday? We'd love to show you the traditional dances we've been practicing for the Strathshire Gathering. Rob often attends. He plays the pipes for us sometimes and joins in the dancing, too. You won't lack for a partner, I promise you."

"I would like that," Juliette replied.

MacLyon's head snapped around at her answer. The scowl on his face made it plain he wasn't at all pleased about Annie's invitation.

"Lyon used to enjoy folk dances and music, too," Annie said. She gave The MacLyon a friendly wave, undismayed by his thunderous expression. "In fact, he used to read and discuss Scottish poetry with us. The laird was especially fond of Robert Burns."

"And if you learn some country dances, you could participate in the festivities at our clan gathering," Keir added.

"Unfortunately, Miss Elkheart won't be here for the gathering," MacLyon announced. He'd left his cronies and now stood at Juliette's side. "She promised to act as her uncle's hostess, and Dr. Robinson is anxious for her to return. She'll be leaving for Edinburgh almost immediately.''

"Oh, that's too bad!" Annie exclaimed. "We've hardly gotten a chance to know you."

Juliette met MacLyon's frigid eyes. He smiled with smug self-assurance, challenging her to call him a liar in front of his friends.

"You must come to visit me in Edinburgh," she told Annie in a choked voice. "We can further our acquaintance there." Looking down at the smooth courtyard stones at her feet, she fidgeted with the handle of her parasol to conceal her embarrassment.

Keir stared at his childhood friend in mystification, as though unable to believe MacLyon's blatant display of bad manners. Then he turned to Juliette. "At least say you'll come to our wedding," the kind-hearted doctor insisted.

"I received your invitation," Juliette replied, smiling wanly at the engaged couple. "And I want to thank you for including me among your guests, but—"

"We're all devastated that Miss Elkheart can't attend," MacLyon drawled, before Juliette could complete her apology. "She really must leave at once for Edinburgh. Her uncle's depending upon her." He clasped her elbow in his large hand and squeezed a warning.

"Tut, tut," Lady Hester scolded, as she waded into the middle of the group. "Of course Julie will be able to attend Keir and Annie's wedding. I wrote Dr. Robinson last week, asking his permission for her to stay a while longer than originally planned. Only this morning I received his gracious reply."

"You did?" Annie said hopefully.

The dowager marchioness patted Juliette's cheek. "You may stay as long as you wish, *a chiall mo chridhe*," she said, calling her "my dearest dear" in Gaelic. She took Juliette's hand and drew her out of MacLyon's hold. "Now come with me. There are more guests I wish you to meet."

Juliette glanced back over her shoulder at MacLyon in triumph. "I will ask Rob to bring me to the Scottish National Society's meeting next week," she called to Annie and Keir. "And I would love to learn your country dances."

MacLyon's large frame was stiff with fury, and the look he shot her carried the promise of swift retribution. But short of picking her up and throwing her bodily off his property, there wasn't anything he could do to get rid of her now.

Not until after the wedding.

The guests mingled together in the courtyard. While liveried servants, carrying trays loaded with delicacies, weaved their way through the maze of fashionably clad people, a piper in MacLyon plaid filled the air with sprightly music.

Gradually, everyone drifted down through the terraced gardens to the bottom of the glen, where white garden chairs had been set up in the magnificent natural amphitheater. Gossip and rumors circulated through the curious assemblage about the shooting exhibition to be given by Miss Juliette Evening Star Elkheart, a young lady who'd been raised on the plains of Alberta.

Rob sat beside Lyon in the front row, waiting with eager anticipation for Julie to appear. Like his brother, Rob was attired in jacket and trousers with a starched white shirt and silk neck cloth. He'd helped plan the demonstration and knew exactly what was about to take place. Lyon, bless his surly, battered phiz, didn't have a clue.

Rob watched his brother from the corner of his eye. With his arms folded across his chest, his granite jaw locked in displeasure, Lyon scowled at anyone who came near. Next to him perched Neil and Jamie, with their mother and great-grandmother completing the row. The deerhounds settled themselves at the lads' feet, tongues lolling contentedly.

For the last two days, every member of the family had

given the laird a wide berth. The quaking staff pussyfooted around him. Whatever had happened on Eilean Danielson had turned Lyon into a raging maniac. He stomped, he stormed, he swore, he threw things. Luckily, his valet was a master at the art of dodging flying missiles. And the wee fellow was clever enough not to mention the name of a certain bonny lass within the laird's hearing.

The one thing Lyon hadn't done in the last two days was go anywhere near their beautiful houseguest.

Rob brushed aside the niggling guilt that assailed him. He'd sent a servant over to the island to clean the abandoned croft and leave a few essentials for a comfortable dalliance. He'd hoped Lyon would follow his natural inclinations—the inclinations he'd been trying so hard to resist—and succumb to the charms of Miss Elkheart.

Rob knew his brother would never force himself on an unwilling female. But a few kisses, a few pats on the bum, and Julie would have soon been the future Lady Mac-Lyon—which was exactly what everyone in the castle was praying for. But instead of bundling in front of a cozy fire, the couple had apparently engaged in a terrible row. They hadn't spoken to each other since.

"When's this circus going to begin?" Lyon demanded, interrupting Rob's musings. "I've got better things to do than sit on my ass all afternoon."

"Just wait, Uncle Lyon," Neil assured him joyfully. The lad bounced up and down on his chair, setting it rocking to and fro on the grass. "Just wait till you see Miss Elkheart shoot your guns."

"Just wait," Jamie chirped. "Just wait till she shoots."

Grabbing the back of Neil's chair to keep him from taking a spill, Lyon leaned forward in his own. He took a closer look through narrowed eyes at the weapons on the table some distance in front of them. *"My guns?"*

"I loaned them to her," Rob explained with a grin. "Obviously, Miss Elkheart can't tote her own weapons along when she travels."

"Obv'usly," Jamie parroted. "Can't tote her guns."

"Bloody hell," Lyon muttered as he sank back in his seat.

Rob leaned closer to his brother and spoke in a secretive tone. "The rest of the family talked about taking up a contribution yesterday."

Lyon shot him a look of surprise. "To buy Miss Elkheart a rifle?"

Rob pitched his answer low, so only his brother could hear him. "Nay. We thought we'd collect enough sillers to buy you a train ticket to Edinburgh. We hoped a *business trip* might put you in a better frame of mind."

"The only reason I don't break your neck here and now," Lyon grated, "is that people will think I acted out of sibling rivalry and not righteous anger."

"Forbye!" Rob retorted in his best Scots burr. "And how could a gowk be jealous of his own brother over a wee, braw lassie he wilna even speak to?"

But Lyon refused to be baited. He settled back in the white garden chair, propped an ankle on one knee, and stared straight in front of him.

By that time all of the guests had found seats, and an air of expectation descended over the glen. A table, with an impressive array of firearms laid across its cloth-covered top, stood on the grass in front of them. At the other end of the natural arena, a second table supported several large boxes, holding items to be used in the exhibition. Farther away, shooting traps had been set out in a line along the edge of the woods.

With a skirl of fanfare from the bagpipes, a horse and rider burst out of the stand of trees and galloped across the grass. There was a collective gasp of astonishment as they recognized Miss Elkheart. Dressed in western riding attire, she stood balanced gracefully on the dainty Arabian's bare back. One long, thick braid flew out behind her.

Lyon leaned forward in captivation, unable to take his eyes off the small, slender figure. Julie rode so effortlessly, it looked as though she were floating on the horse's back.

As she raced White Thunder along the length of the glen, servants released the traps one at a time. She fired Lyon's double-barreled Lancaster shotgun from a distance of twenty yards or more, bringing down every clay pigeon. Then reloading, she turned and headed back. This time the traps were released in pairs, the next, in triplets, and on the fourth dash across the glen, four birds at a time. In a blur of motion, Julie never missed a shot.

Everyone burst into stunned applause. Trapshooting, along with game hunting, was one of the most revered sports in the British Isles. That a diminutive female—from the wilderness of Canada, no less—could grass every bird, while standing on a galloping mount, was truly phenomenal. The words *Cheyenne princess* buzzed up and down the rows.

Miss Elkheart dropped to a seated position on White Thunder, both legs dangling primly over one side, and guided the mare to the center of the grassy field. At her signal, the intelligent animal drew up its forefoot and knelt on one knee in a bow.

"Hurrah! Hurrah!" Neil and Jamie shouted over and over, beside themselves with excitement, while the two deerhounds barked in chorus.

Lithe and agile, Julie slipped down from the horse's back and smiled shyly at her audience from beneath the stiff, wide brim of her western hat. She wore an embroidered vest over a loose-fitting bodice. Her gored denim skirt came to her calves, the fringed hem swinging gracefully above high, beaded, doeskin moccasins. Her dark eyes aglow, she radiated a joyous vibrancy.

Lyon could feel the need tugging in his gut. Hunger spread through his thighs and up into his chest. The intense longing, the savage, insatiable yearning, threatened to choke off his breath. Unfulfilled desire pushed down on his lungs, compressing every bit of air out till the long, sharp stabs of pain nearly drove him to his feet.

It was all he could do not to rush over, toss her across his shoulder, and ride off with her—to hold her captive in some secret place and ravish her, like his Highland forebears of old, till this insane, primal urge was spent.

As a stableman came to lead White Thunder away, Rob jumped up from his seat and hurried to stand beside Julie.

He held up one hand to quiet the animated, chattering guests. "Friends and family," he announced, "Miss Elkheart has asked me to be her assistant this afternoon. So if you'll be kind enough to bear with me, we'll proceed with this dazzling display of marksmanship. Prepare yourselves to be amazed, for you have never seen anything like what you're about to see now."

He bowed formally to Julie, who bobbed a curtsey in return. Then he strode to the farthest table, while she went to stand in front of the nearer one, her back to the firearms.

As Rob started tossing golf balls high into the air, Julie turned to snatch up a Remington rifle and whirled around. The balls exploded in a shower of gutta percha splinters.

Next came empty vials, smashed to bits with Lyon's pair of gold-plated, pearl-handled Smith and Wesson pistols, fired simultaneously. Whisky glasses, hard-boiled eggs, coins, it didn't matter how many Rob launched at one time. As fast as he could hurl the items into the air, Julie brought them down, using the various firearms available.

Rob smiled in triumph at his audience. "Next, we're going to include the family pets." He whistled shrilly, and Dunbar and Tiree bounded up from the grass. At his signal the huge deerhounds leapt onto the table, where they promptly sat at attention. Rob carefully placed an apple on each of their heads and stepped aside.

To her audience's amazement, Julie held out two fingers to the animals and spoke to them soothingly in Cheyenne. Then she turned her back on the dogs. By this time, every guest was on his feet. With a rifle propped backward across her shoulder, she sighted in a mirror held in one hand, and shot the apples off their heads.

When the applause faded at last, Rob addressed his guests. "Now Miss Elkheart has one more feat she'd like to perform for you this afternoon. But we'll need a courageous volunteer to help." He grinned wickedly at Lyon, extending his hand in invitation. "If the laird of Strathlyon will be so kind as to indulge us?"

Lyon looked at Julie. A mischievous smile danced across her kissable lips. Her twinkling eyes dared him to stand up in front of his friends and put his life in her hands. He'd humiliated her in front of Keir and Annie only a short time ago. If he refused now, he'd look like a veritable coward.

Hell, he'd *be* a veritable coward.

Lyon rose to his feet, his chin tilted upward in cool defiance, and strode over to Robbie. "What do I have to do?" he asked in a bored tone he was far from feeling. "Hold an apple on my head and bark?"

"Not quite," Rob said. He pulled a cigar out of his jacket pocket and offered it to Lyon. "If you'll allow me, I'll light it for you."

Lyon stuck the cigar in his mouth, and Rob struck a match. Drawing on the fragrant tobacco leaf, Lyon tipped his head back and blew smoke rings into the air. "Now what?"

"All you have to do is hold the cigar in your mouth. But for God's sake, stand still."

Incredulous, Lyon turned his head to stare at Julie. She waited in front of her table, her back to him and her head bowed as she studied the guns lying before her.

For the past two days he'd ignored her as though what had happened between them on Eilean Danielson was no more important than a casual tumble in the hay. For the past three nights he'd paced the floor unable to sleep, the need burning in his veins so hot, he'd considered ordering a servant to lock him in his study. Or chain him to his bed. Anything to keep him from going to Julie's room, taking her in his arms, and making love to her again and again, until they both were so sated and drained neither of them could speak or move.

Rob leaned closer, his low words filled with a goading mockery. "I told Julie she ought to go ahead and shoot you and put you out of your misery, but she wouldn't agree to it. So don't worry. You're safe—from her bullets, anyway." With a chuckle, he left Lyon standing alone.

Lyon jammed the Havana between his teeth and turned sideways to present the cigar, feeling like the ill-fated party in a duel. In the awed silence that followed, he knew Julie was using her mirror to sight the target. He hoped to hell she was using his .32-caliber Stevens. It was the most accurate gun he owned. He held his breath and stood perfectly still, waiting in suspense for the rifle's report.

The explosion came like the crack of doom.

She'd shot the ash off the end of his cigar.

The gentlemen cheered and whistled. The ladies screamed. Several females in overtight corsets, Flora included, swooned dead away.

Lyon puffed on the expensive Havana as he turned to face Julie. His anger at her stubborn refusal to leave Strathlyon Castle faded at the sight of her shining eyes.

She shook her head slowly, as though reproaching a fractious child. "I told you before, Scotsman, that you were in no danger from me. I never miss a target at this close range."

Tossing the cigar away, he strode across the grass, took the rifle from her hands, and laid it on the table. Then he slipped his arm around her waist and kissed her. The guests applauded in the mistaken belief the buss was her reward for the fantastic performance.

Aye, it was a reward, all right.

Lyon's reward, for having gone two whole days without taking her in his arms and kissing her.

"Hurrah for Uncle Lyon!" Neil shouted.

"Hurrah for Miss Elkheart!" hollered Jamie.

The two lads danced around them like sprites round a Maypole, while Dunbar and Tiree barked in jubilant approval.

Chapter 12

Lyon pulled off his riding gloves and lounged against the doorjamb of the abandoned lighthouse's topmost room. "You have everyone at the castle worried about you, Miss Elkheart," he said quietly.

She whirled around at the sound of his voice. Her dark eyes appeared enormous in her pale, drawn face. Although the day was cool and blustery, beads of perspiration dotted her upper lip.

Alarm gripped his vitals at her haunted expression. He took an immediate step toward her, realizing she was frightened.

"You . . . you startled me," Julie replied in a creaky voice. "I did not hear you come up the stairs."

Lyon strode across the planking to stand beside her. When he'd first found her, she'd been staring out one of the high, wooden-paned windows, completely lost to the world.

"I'm sorry," he said. "I didn't mean to scare you."

He looked suspiciously about the dusty lantern room. From an iron pedestal in its center hung the circle of whale oil lamps that had once shone their guiding light out across Ardmucknish Bay. The austere furnishings included a crude wooden cabinet and a tall, three-legged stool. A narrow metal box stood near the open doorway.

There wasn't a sign of another person.

Not so much as a footprint, other than hers, on the dust-covered floor. If she'd come to meet a beau, the bastard hadn't arrived yet.

Rage at the thought boiled inside him, spewing its scalding brew through him. Lyon clenched his fists in automatic reaction to the rush of fierce male aggression flooding his nervous system. He'd beat the sonofabitch to death with his bare hands, the moment he showed his face.

"What in bloody hell are you doing here, anyway?" he growled.

She ignored his question and asked one of her own. "How . . . how did you find me?"

"It wasn't all that hard," he said brusquely. "When Lady Hester and Flora told me you were missing, I went to the last place you'd been seen. You left a book lying open on the library table with a sketch of the old Ard-mucknish Bay Lighthouse in plain view. When I found White Thunder hobbled in the trees outside, I knew my deductions had been right."

"I did not mean to upset anyone," she said, her lovely features contrite. "Please forgive me for leaving the castle without telling anyone where I was going. I had something on my mind this morning."

He walked over to one of the glass panes and gazed out, wondering what she'd found so terrifying. The Firth of Lorn stretched southward, a deep cobalt blue above a cloudy sky. Steamboats churned up whitecaps as they made their way past the sandy bays of the Island of Mull toward Loch Linnhe. Sailboats and fishing skiffs scooted across the waves, northbound toward Lismore Island and beyond. To the south, the entire island of Kerrera could be seen from the lighthouse's panoramic vista.

"It is a spectacular view, isn't it?" he said.

She drew a deep, shuddering breath and nodded.

"Nothing really frightening out there, though," he added thoughtfully.

"Nothing frightening at all," she agreed.

The high, sturdy stool, once used by the lighthouse keeper to maintain a watch with his telescope during storms, stood near the window. With a swipe of his leather gloves, Lyon sat down and stretched his legs out in front of him. "Would you care to tell me why you came here alone, without telling a soul of your destination?"

Julie clasped her hands in front of her. Lyon could almost see her mind clicking over the possible explanations she could offer, trying to decide which one he'd most likely believe.

Little by little, he'd begun to see through her facade of limitless calm. The vital, ardent sensuality he'd discovered beneath her cool exterior on that rainy afternoon at Eilean Danielson had shaken him to his core . . . and delighted him beyond measure. There was far more to Juliette Evening Star then she wanted people to believe.

At the moment, she was hiding something from him. He suspected that she'd been hiding something from him since the day she'd first arrived at Strathlyon Castle. What other secrets besides her passionate nature did she keep locked in her mystical heart?

"As you pointed out," she answered smoothly, "the scenery from here is marvelous. When I read about the lighthouse being so near, I wanted to see it for myself."

"Near? A two-hour ride?"

She foolishly attempted a smile, then bit her lower lip when she realized it was trembling. She cleared her throat and started again. "I . . . ah . . . I did not mention coming here to anyone simply because I did not wish to be a bother. I have been too much of a nuisance already."

He made no attempt to hide his disbelief. "And so you rode to a desolate lighthouse all by yourself, smashed the bolt on the door with a rock, and strolled on in. How cavalier of you."

"I am sorry about that . . . about the broken lock, I mean." She averted her gaze, but not before he saw the telltale gleam in her eyes. Hell, she wasn't sorry about anything—except for the fact that he'd found her. "Does the lighthouse belong to you?" she asked penitently.

"No, it belongs to Keir. This whole area was once MacDougall territory."

"Well," she said with forced cheerfulness, "I will have to apologize to Keir for trespassing."

Lyon laced his words with irony. "Not to mention breaking and entering."

She jerked her head in agreement. "That too." She turned toward the stairwell, as though dismissing the entire matter.

His harsh voice echoed against the lamproom's glass walls. "Why did you come here, Julie? I want an answer, and I want it now."

She stopped in her tracks at his ominous tone. Glancing back at him over her shoulder, she sighed in exasperation. "I saw this lighthouse in a dream last night."

"In a dream?"

"Yes."

"This particular lighthouse."

She turned to face him with a grimace of irritation. "I did not know it was the Ardmucknish Bay Lighthouse, until I found the sketch in the book. Naturally, I wanted to see it."

He waited, saying nothing, giving her time to realize he was determined to have more of an explanation.

She moved to stand in front of him "If you must know, MacLyon," she said in an aggrieved tone, "I sometimes have dreams in which I see things."

"Most people do."

"But my dreams are more like . . ." she paused and stared down at her gloved hands before continuing, ". . . like visions."

The roiling jealousy and anger churning inside him dissipated like fairy lights at the coming of dawn. He smiled as a surge of tenderness washed over him. Reaching out, he caught her hand and pulled her between his outstretched legs. "I know just what you mean, lass," he said softly. "Whenever I dream of you, I swear it's a heavenly vision sent to torment me."

Her luxuriant lashes flew up, and she glared at him. "That is not what I meant, and you know it."

Lyon tugged at the fingers of her glove, slowly peeling the gray kid off her hand. "Very well, what did you see in your dream?" He brought her bare fingers to his mouth and kissed their oval tips. "I take it, it wasn't me?"

She smoothed her fingers across the lapel of his jacket, making no protest as he removed the other glove and shoved it into his pocket with the first. "I dreamt that a boy of about thirteen came to this lighthouse. It was storming, and he was wet and cold and terribly frightened."

Lyon raised Julie's hand and gently kissed the inside of her wrist. The scent of wild roses and violets drifted around him. Her sweetness poured over him, drenching him with moonbeams and starlight in the middle of the day. As she trembled and leaned toward him, his already bruised heart smashed against his ribcage with a painful thud.

"Then what happened?" he questioned huskily.

"A woman lived in this lighthouse." Julie glanced around the sky-lit room. She seemed scarcely aware that he'd pulled her closer and now held her hips wedged between his thighs. Her voice sounded faint and faraway, as though she were seeing it all again. "The woman was here at the top of this tower, trimming the wicks, cleaning the sooty lamps, and putting more oil in them. Then she lit each lamp carefully, until the room glowed like a giant beacon.

"When the boy appeared at the doorway, she recognized him at once. He was so terrified, he couldn't speak. But she took him down to the bottom floor, where there was a fireplace, and she fed and sheltered him. When he wrapped himself up in his plaid and fell into an exhausted sleep, she came back up the stairs and signaled from that windowpane over there. Late that night, she rowed the boy out to a sailing ship in the pouring rain. She embraced him and called him by name when she bade him farewell.''

Lyon's hands bracketed Julie's waist. He could feel her quaking, as though caught in the throes of a horrible nightmare. ''What did this woman call the lad?''

''Iain,'' she whispered. ''She called him Iain Danielson.''

Lyon kissed Julie's forehead and the tip of her nose. ''It was a dream, lass,'' he soothed, his lips brushing her cheek. ''Just a dream, brought on by your wish to find your Scottish ancestors. Don't fash yourself so with imaginings.''

She braced her hands on his shoulders and leaned away from him. ''It is not my imagination, MacLyon. These things happened just as I saw them. That is why I came here today.''

Lyon took her hands and lifted them up, placing her arms about his neck. She slid her fingers into his hair and stared at his mouth, slowly becoming aware of their close proximity. He could read the awakening desire in her expressive eyes.

Her hips brushed the insides of his thighs, and his entire body responded in delirious anticipation. Heat radiated from him as his heart pumped the blood like a high-pressure steam engine, dangerously close to exploding.

''You should have left for Edinburgh when I told you to, princess,'' he said huskily.

He smoothed his hands over the shoulders of her blue riding habit, his thumbs coming to rest at the base of her throat, just above the silk scarf. Her pulse raced beneath his touch, but her accelerated heart rate couldn't come close to matching his own.

Her words were breathless. ''There are reasons why I cannot leave yet.''

''I suppose there are,'' he said, wondering absently if those reasons had anything to do with her superstitious belief in visions.

Lyon unfastened the swath of veiling that had been

looped under her chin and lifted it up to the brim of her gray top hat. He bent his head and gently nipped the soft flesh of her earlobe. Her golden skin tasted like honey. Like manna in the desert.

She shivered as he traced the delicate shell of her ear, then dipped his tongue inside. He breathed in the intoxicating scent of her like a drowning man gasping for air. His body had become addicted to the taste and feel and smell of Juliette Evening Star, craving more and more each time.

"Did you know that sailing ships were once lured to the rocks below this lighthouse by the siren call of the sea maidens?" he murmured in her ear.

"I have never heard of a sea maiden," she confessed on the sweetest sigh imaginable. "I think you are making it up just to tease me."

"Ah, nay," Lyon said, as he slipped his hands behind her slender form and cupped her little rump. He brought her up against the bulging crotch of his riding breeches, thankful he wasn't wearing his kilt.

No man alive would have the willpower to resist that much temptation.

"A *muir-òigh* is half fish and half beautiful woman," he continued. "On a moonlit night, a mermaid will sit on a large rock by the shore and comb out the long, flowing tresses of her splendid hair."

"Naturally," Julie interjected, "she would be beautiful and have long, splendid hair."

"Naturally," he agreed. "A sea maiden can shed the scaly covering over her long, shapely legs and walk about on land, like you and me. If a man finds the covering and hides it, he can keep her from ever returning to the sea."

Her lips twitched in beguilement. "Why would he want to?"

Lyon smiled at her unconscious naiveté. "Perhaps to make her give him a magical wish."

"What would you wish for?"

The afternoon light from the surrounding windows played across Julie's clear-cut features, revealing a flawless complexion that seemed to glow from within. The vivid coloring of her dark eyebrows and ebony lashes enhanced the breathtaking beauty of her deep brown eyes. His gaze drifted over the high cheekbones, classic nose, and sensual mouth, and the longing to protect and cherish her for the rest of his life set his heart thundering.

Lyon's throat clogged with a tenderness he'd never known before, and his words came on a harsh, ragged breath. "If I told you, *a ghaolaich*, would you grant me my wish?"

"What do you wish, Lyon?" she whispered unsteadily. Her gaze entangled with his, and he could read the yearning in the depths of her magnificent almond eyes.

A shudder went through his large body. The ache was so deep, so intense, sexual hunger invaded every muscle, fiber, and nerve in his being. The knowledge that she wanted him burned like a fuse through his carefully built defenses, threatening to ignite the passion he'd fought so hard to contain and smother.

Lyon wouldn't, he *couldn't* take this guileless young woman. To use his vast carnal knowledge to plunder her sweet innocence would be the act of an irredeemable libertine. He would give all he possessed to be a fresh, green lad again, to come to her with a heart that was whole and a mind that was pure. But he couldn't change the past, any more than he could stop the tide.

By sheer force of will, he dragged his hands from her hips and gently clasped her upper arms. He tried to speak lightly, with a wry, self-deprecating humor. The words torn from his throat came out rough and harsh, instead. "I wish, to God . . . I was as good a marksman as you, Vehona."

Caught by surprise, she gave a trill of laughter. "All it takes is practice, Scotsman."

He ignored the reflexive clench of desire at the spellbinding sound and managed an awkward grin. "You were marvelous at yesterday's celebration. Neil and Jamie can't stop talking about it—nor anyone else, for that matter. How did you ever learn to shoot like that?''

''*Nihoe* taught me.''

''You mean your father?''

''Yes.''

''Any chap would be a fool to make you angry,'' he said. He traced her upper lip with his forefinger, then tapped her lightly on the forehead. ''You could put a bullet neatly between his eyes before he had a chance to make a dignified retreat.''

He could hear the smothered chuckle in her reply. ''Does my skill with weapons frighten you, *veho*?''

''*Veho*?''

''It means white man,'' she explained, her eyes twinkling.

''Miss Elkheart,'' he said with quiet gravity, ''I've never been afraid of anyone in my life, until I met a wee, spry lass with velvety brown eyes that promised a trip to heaven—and a razor-sharp knife that threatened to send me to hell.''

He bent his head to kiss her, then stopped short.

The acrid stench of smoke drifted through the open doorway and filled his nostrils.

Julie turned in his arms, looking toward the stairs. ''Something is burning,'' she said.

Lyon gently set her aside and strode to the door. A dense black cloud billowed upward, filling the stairwell. He could hear the crackle of a blaze in the deserted living quarters on the ground floor, and quickly shut the door.

Juliette hurried to MacLyon's side. His hardened features betrayed his apprehension. ''Can we make it down the stairs?''

''No. We'd suffocate before we reached the bottom.''

''What about the fog bell? Could we ring it to attract help?''

"The bell was moved to the new lighthouse when this one was closed eight years ago."

He hurried to the small door that led to the gallery circling the outside of the lantern room. It was bolted with a huge lock. He looked around, searching for a tool to break it.

Juliette fought back the fear that threatened to engulf her. This wasn't the time to behave like some foolish *vehoka*, wringing her hands and wailing helplessly.

"Can we stay here?" she suggested. "The tower is made of stone. It will not burn."

MacLyon shook his head. "Too risky. The smoke and heat will continue to rise, turning the tower into a chimney. We'd be roasted alive before anyone noticed the fire."

He opened the low cabinet that stood beside the stairway door and hastily rummaged through it.

A prickle of fear tightened the skin at the nape of her neck. "Is there anything helpful?" she asked.

"Just broken lamps," he said in disgust. "And crockery used for holding whale oil. Nothing of use, dammit."

He raised the lid of the narrow metal box beside the cabinet and smiled in triumph. "Just what I was hoping for," he said. He lifted out a large coil of rope. "It was probably used to rescue people tossed overboard in a storm. Lighthouse keepers often had to row to the scene of a shipwreck."

Juliette prayed he wasn't thinking what it sounded like.

"Now, if this is just strong enough and long enough . . ." he muttered abstractedly, as he sank down on his haunches and examined the thick hemp cordage he'd piled on the floor.

Her heart started to pound in earnest. She laid a hand on his shoulder, her fingers trembling. "How . . . how far up are we?"

"Well over a hundred feet. Probably closer to a hundred and thirty."

He heard her sharp inhalation of air and glanced up.

"Don't be afraid," he said, sounding far more confident than he had a right to feel. "I want you to stand over by the door. Go on."

A numbing sensation curled in her belly like a poisonous viper. But without questioning his instructions, she quickly did exactly as she was told.

"Now, turn around," he said, "and cover your face with your hands."

As she crouched against the wall, her head down, she heard him lift the metal box and hurl it through the window. The old glass panes shattered, sending splinters through the room like a crystal shower. By the time she looked around, MacLyon had wrapped his jacket over his hand and was breaking out the remaining shards along the bottom sill. He had a gash on his cheek and one above his eyebrow.

Carefully picking her way through the broken glass, she went to stand beside him. "Lyon, your face is bleeding." She slipped off her neckscarf and tried to dab at his wounds.

He shook his head, motioning for her to quit fussing. "I'm all right," he said gruffly. "A couple more scars won't make any difference."

Juliette moved away to the windowsill. Far below them, the waves of the firth crashed against the jagged boulders.

"Can we go down the other side of the tower?" she asked, offering a silent prayer to Maxemaheo that Lyon would agree. It would be far easier to drop to the grassy bank that led up to the lighthouse than go down the sheer side of the cliff.

"No," he said. "If the fire was deliberately set, the bastard who did it will be watching in that direction, just in case we try to escape from the ground floor."

"You think the fire was started on purpose?"

"It's a possibility."

He climbed through the broken window and onto the narrow gallery that circled the lantern room. "Come on," he said, "out you go." He lifted her over the sill and set her on the wooden planking beside him.

Juliette's insides froze into a solid ball of ice. She didn't realize she was clutching Lyon's shirt sleeve until she felt him gently pry her clammy fingers loose. Ashamed of her childish behavior, she lifted her wobbly chin, bit her lip to stifle a whimper, and met his steady, reassuring gaze.

She could hear the waves slapping against the crags directly below them. An image of their broken, twisted bodies lying on those sharp rocks flashed before her, and everything her father had ever taught her catapulted over the edge of the platform and took a nose dive straight into oblivion. What an appalling time to learn she was terrified of heights.

Juliette clamped her lips shut to keep from betraying the panic rising within her. She watched in horror as Lyon tied the rope to the gallery handrail that circled the top of the tower, tested its strength, and then threw the line down.

By now, she was shaking with fright. "Are you going first or am I?" she croaked, giving up all pretense of composure. Nothing in her life had prepared her for such an insane feat.

"We're going down together," he replied. "I'm going to carry you over my shoulder."

Juliette gasped at the thought. "What about your injured arm?" Horrified, she backed up against the tower wall. "You might drop me."

"Don't worry, lassie," he said, his Scots burr soft and soothing. "I could carry you and another hundred pounds with ease."

She shook her head, flattening her body against the rough stones. The wind blew strands of hair into her eyes, and she shoved them away with a shaky hand. "You go first, and I will follow you," she promised.

"No," he answered, his deep baritone implacable. He caught her trembling hand in his steady one. "I can't let you go down by yourself, Julie. You're not strong enough.

And if your hold should slip, I might not be able to catch you in time.''

"Please, do not try to carry me with your injured arm," she begged. A paralyzing fear crept insidiously through her limbs.

His rugged features were grim. Behind them, the lamproom slowly filled with the thick smoke that seeped under the door.

"Carrying you down is not a problem," he rasped. "But I'll need to lower our combined weight with my good arm. Now are you going to do as I tell you, or do I take you down unconscious?"

She reached out and gripped the metal handrail with tenacious fingers. "What are you talking about?" she shouted over a gust of wind. "Do you intend to whack me over the head?"

He gave her a sideways smile as he touched her lightly at the base of her neck. "I wouldn't have to, princess. All I'd need to do is touch this pressure point right here, and you wouldn't remember a thing."

Nothing seemed more terrifying than descending the hundred-foot tower in a state of unconsciousness. *"Ahahe!"* she wailed in defeat. "I will do as you say."

"Good lass. Then up you go," he said and tossed her across his shoulder. She grunted as the air left her lungs. "Whatever you do," he warned, "don't scream. We don't want any unexpected company as we make this drop."

Juliette didn't even try to answer. She was so petrified, she couldn't have made a sound if she'd wanted to.

With Juliette slung over his left shoulder like a sack of oats, Lyon stepped over the gallery railing with the surefooted grace of a mountain lion. He caught the rope in his right hand and dropped, swinging to and fro, until he could brace the soles of his boots against the stone wall. Then he slowly and carefully lowered himself down the side of the tower.

Juliette clutched the back of Lyon's shirt and watched

her hat fall to the rocky shore, where it was snatched by a wave and washed away. Buffeted by the wind from the firth, she squeezed her tearing eyes shut and silently chanted a strong-heart song her great-grandmother, Porcupine Quills, had taught her as a child.

The giant who carried her gave no sign of tiring. His breathing continued smooth and even as he lowered their heavy weight, letting the lifeline slowly slide through one hand. His physical stamina was awe-inspiring. She could feel the powerful muscles of his shoulders and back shift and bunch as he dropped steadily down the rope's length. His injured left arm pressed against the back of her thighs, holding her firmly and securely in place.

He had the nerve to whistle under his breath! She caught the tune of a Scottish martial air and realized he wasn't showing off; he was trying to keep her calm and still. He didn't want his burden to start wiggling and bucking in panic.

When his boots crunched on the rocky shore Lyon released the rope, and for the space of moment, he cupped her fanny in his large hand and patted her as though she were a frightened child.

"That wasn't so bad, now, was it?" he asked, amusement deepening his rich baritone.

He lifted her down, but kept his hands on her waist as she stood wobbling on shaky legs. Her entire body shook in delayed reaction to their death-defying drop.

"Since you were having so much fun, Scotsman, it is a shame we cannot do it again," she said through chattering teeth. "Only next time I will carry you, and we will see how much fun you have then."

He grinned like Wihio, the wily trickster spirit, and without thinking she threw her arms around him. She blinked back tears of fright. What would her parents say, if they could see their warrior-woman daughter behaving like a baby?

Lyon's arms closed around her in a comforting embrace.

Then he spoke quietly. "We can't stay here, lass. Not until we know for sure that no one's lying in wait for us."

They moved stealthily across the boulder-strewn shore and scrambled up the bank of the cliff. Following his orders, Juliette waited as Lyon moved carefully around to the front of the lighthouse.

He soon returned. "If there was anyone here," he said, "the bastard's gone now. White Thunder and Thor are right where we left them."

They looked up to see flames billowing out of the lantern room at the top of the tower.

"People have already seen the smoke and are coming from the fishing village nearby," he told her. "They'll do what they can to save the lighthouse. I'm going to ride back with you to Strathlyon and then return here with Rob to investigate."

She caught his sleeve. "There is no need to escort me back. I can return to the castle alone, while you do what needs to be done here."

"You will *not* ride back alone," he replied. His features grew stern, and his r's rolled like the low rumble of thunder. "If you ever leave the castle by yourself again, Julie, I'll thrash your bare bum like the stubborn, willful lassie you are."

"Do not be absurd," she said sharply. "I can take care of myself."

He clasped her arms, ensnaring Juliette in his unforgiving grip. The determination in his tense fingers demanded her complete attention. "You *think* you can take care of yourself, but your skill with a knife and a gun gives you false confidence. What would have happened to you today, if I had not been here?"

Juliette looked at the burning tower. "The fire was a freak accident."

"Not necessarily."

"Why would anyone try to kill me?"

He cupped her cheek in his palm, attempting to reassure

her, but she could detect the concern in his guarded gaze. The blood on his face had congealed, but the gash above his eyebrow would probably need stitches. He was fortunate not to have lost the sight of an eye.

"If the fire was set intentionally, you weren't the target, lass—just an innocent bystander who got caught up in the foul deed."

"Like that morning in Edinburgh?"

MacLyon scowled, not at all happy at her astute guess. Without deigning to reply, he caught her elbow and guided her toward the stand of trees and the waiting horses.

Chapter 13

Dr. Keir MacDougall and Miss Anne Buchanan were married in the Kirk of St. Columba in Strathbardine on the eleventh of October. Though it rained that morning, neither the wedding couple nor their guests thought to complain. A fine Scottish mist couldn't diminish their happiness.

It was a braw Highland wedding. Bagpipes skirled; plaids swirled. Firearms were discharged by the groom's party, the pistol reports echoing back from the steep hillsides. And pure Glen Livet whisky passed among the gentlemen before the ceremony even commenced.

The groom and groomsmen were resplendent in the dress uniforms of the Royal Scots. Radiant in her bridal gown and wreath of orange blossoms, Annie smiled in bliss as she and her husband walked beneath the officers' arched swords on the way down the kirk steps.

After the ceremony the celebration continued at the home of the bride's bachelor uncle, Mr. Absalon Buchanan. Long tables stood at one end of the ballroom, ready for the wedding supper. Bunting, roses, and swaths of the MacDougall and Buchanan tartans decorated the manor house. True to Highland tradition, the bridesmaid and best man broke an oat cake over Annie's head as she crossed her uncle's threshold, to insure good fortune for the couple in the years to come.

It had been over a week since the lighthouse fire. Lyon hadn't been able to determine if the cause had been arson, or if the suspicious blaze was merely an ill-timed accident. But since that day, he went everywhere armed with a pistol. Everywhere, except to participate in a marriage ceremony.

He stood near the table that held the towering wedding cake and watched his debonair brother dance a strathspey with Miss Elkheart. In honor of the occasion, their guest from Canada had donned her finest apparel. And the chief of Clan MacLyon couldn't take his fascinated gaze off her.

Julie wore a creamy-white doeskin dress trimmed with blue and white beading. Deep fringes graced the sleeves and hem, swaying gently when she moved. Her straight hair spilled down to her hips like a lush, tropical waterfall. As she dipped and twirled to the lilting strains of "The Flowers o' Edinburgh," two long, narrow sidebraids, tied with bands of fluffy white fur, swung to and fro over the tantalizing curves of her breasts.

From the moment he'd seen her that morning, when the family had met in the Strathlyon drawing room prior to departing for the kirk, Lyon had moved in a daze of lust. It'd been a miracle he'd made it through the ceremony without making an ass of himself. He couldn't even remember fishing the bride's ring out of his sporran and handing it to Keir at the proper time.

Damn!

Lyon *knew* Julie should never have stayed for the wedding.

His unhappy ruminations were interrupted by the sound of his nephews' voices. They were speaking to each other in Gaelic, which meant they were probably up to no good. He looked around the crowded room, but was unable to spot either Neil or Jamie.

The lads had been warned to be on their best behavior. No leaving sticky fingerprints on the sparkling white tablecloths, no spilling juice on a chair's velvet upholstery, no wrestling with each other in Mr. Buchanan's formal drawing room. And absolutely, positively, no fighting with the other loons present—no matter what the provocation. For the entire duration of the wedding festivities, they were to refrain from leaving the usual path of destruction in their wake.

When Lyon heard them speak again, he realized they were under the table, hidden by its abundant white covering.

"How do you know she's very, very rich?" Jamie asked his brother.

"Cook said all fairies possess untold wealth," Neil informed him in a tone that brooked no questioning. "You heard Miss Elkheart tell Uncle Lyon she's a princess. That means her father is *king of the fairies*. One day, she'll be queen. She'll have lots and lots of gold. And we'll get it all."

His younger brother sounded doubtful. "Will she really give us her gold?"

"Aye, but first, we have to capture her."

"We do?" squeaked Jamie.

Neil's voice lowered, and Lyon strained to hear. "We have to sneak up on her, when she's in her tiniest size. No bigger than a butterfly."

"What we'll do with her then?"

"Keep her!" Neil declared boldly, bringing a smile to his uncle's lips. "We'll keep her hidden at the castle until she's a queen. Then we'll make her give us all she owns in exchange for her freedom. We'll have a *fortune* in jewels and gold!"

"What if she gets angry and puts a spell on us?" a dubious Jamie questioned. "She put a spell on Uncle Lyon."

Scowling, Lyon stared down at the lacy tablecloth. What the bloody hell were they talking about now?

"Cook says fairies use magic riddles to enchant people," Neil explained. "If we can ask a fairy a riddle she can't answer, we can cast a charm on her. We can make Miss Elkheart fall sound asleep."

"How long will she sleep?"

"Till I'm old enough to marry her," Neil stated in exultation.

Lyon cocked his head, incredulous.

"But I'd like to marry Miss Elkheart," Jamie complained.

There was a thump and a grunt, as one of the boys pounded his sibling on the shoulder or chest.

"I'm oldest," Neil insisted angrily. "I should be the one to marry her."

"But I think she likes me better."

"She does not!"

"Does, too!"

As the lads began to scuffle, Lyon bent down to drag them out from under the table. In the ensuing turmoil one of them kicked the table leg, causing forks and spoons to rattle ominously.

They were fighting in earnest now.

Before Lyon could reach them, Jamie grabbed hold of the white lace cloth, trying to find his way out from under their hiding place, while his brother tugged with singleminded determination on his ankle. Silverware, china, and the lofty, three-tiered wedding cake started to slide toward the edge of the table.

"Dammit! Get out from under there, ye blasted halflins!" Lyon roared, as he grabbed for the tottering cake.

The ballroom grew deathly still. Even the pealing of the bagpipes faded as everyone turned to see who in God's name was causing the commotion.

Rob hurried over and snatched the two boys out from under the table. "What in blazes are you lads fighting about?" he demanded.

Jamie was blinking back angry tears. Neil's lower lip jutted out, and he scowled mutinously.

"I want to marry Miss Elkheart," Jamie announced in Gaelic, his youthful, high-pitched voice carrying through the silent room. "But Neil says *he* gets to marry her, because he's oldest."

Approximately half the guests present understood what had been said and started to laugh uproariously. The other half leaned toward their Gaelic-speaking neighbors in hopes of a hasty translation. On the dance floor, the good-natured bride and groom joined in the mirth.

Rob straightened, a devilish grin flashing across his fair face. He looked at Lyon, who stood holding the shivering cake in both hands, then back at their two unhappy nephews.

"Ye twa daft loons!" Rob scolded. "No wonder your Uncle Lyon's so angry. He thinks because he saw the bonny lassie first, no one else should have a go at her. But it looks as if she's got you both under her spell."

Lyon eased the cake carefully down on the table, his eyes glued to the topmost tier. He lifted a wee, fallen lovebird and set it back under the heart-shaped trellis beside its partner, cursing the size of his big, clumsy hands under his breath. As the second bird started to wobble, Julie's dainty fingers reached past him and straightened the miniature pair.

"That was close," she said with her usual composure. "I thought for a moment that we would be scooping wedding cake up from the floor."

The scent of wildflowers drifted around him, more besotting than fine Scotch whisky. His juices salivated at the thought of her scrumptious lips and candy-sweet tongue. A picture of her coral-tipped breasts, just made for a man to devour in greedy, gulping mouthfuls, flashed before his eyes.

Julie was so close, he could see each individual bead on the choker necklace encircling her throat. Her soft ivory dress molded itself to her supple curves, and a wide beaded belt encircled her slender waist. Tiny silver bells attached to the skirt tinkled enchantingly as she moved.

Beneath his kilt, Lyon's muscles clenched as his manhood leapt to attention. *Ah, there she is*! it seemed to say, as though charged with a life of its own.

Damn! and bloody hell!

Flora hurried over, fluttering her hands. "Neil! Jamie! Look what you almost did! I'm going to die of mortification." She turned to Lyon, her eyes awash with tears. "You must make them behave or I'll be in bed for a week with a megrim."

At moments like these, he wondered what James could have found so attractive in this hare-brained brunette. "You go dance with Rob," he instructed his sister-in-law. "I'll deal with the lads."

Lyon caught Julie's hand before she could slip away and turned to Neil and Jamie. Simultaneously, the youngsters' gazes moved to the exotic beauty at their uncle's side and then dropped to their polished shoes.

The guilt on their faces made their thoughts transparent. They were wondering just how much of the conversation he'd overheard. He had to bite the inside of his lip to keep from grinning, when he thought of their cockamamie plan to capture Miss Elkheart and hold her for ransom and marriage. Though actually, that might not be such bad idea . . .

"Lads," he said sternly. They straightened their shoulders and raised their wide, stricken eyes to meet his. "I'm going to dance with Miss Elkheart now. While we're dancing, you're going to sit next to Nana and Mr. Buchanan and not move a muscle. Not so much as a little finger. Understood?"

"Aye, Uncle Lyon," Neil answered.

"Aye, sir," piped Jamie. "Not a finger."

"Good. Now go." He pointed to two empty chairs and they trooped off single file, heads bowed and shoulders slumped as though marching to their own execution.

"What were they arguing about?" Julie asked, the soft laughter in her husky contralto ensnaring Lyon's heart in its bewitching web.

"They were fighting over a prize."

"What prize?"

Without answering her question Lyon drew Julie onto the floor, where they joined the double line of dancers for a reel, the men on one side and the women on the other. The blue glass beads dangling from the ornament of hammered silver in her hair sparkled like precious jewels beneath the glow of the chandeliers. The sight of her in the exquisite native costume enthralled him.

Captivated, Juliette looked across at her long-limbed partner. The Lion wore a red military jacket, his massive chest decorated with medals and ribbons. A kilt of red and black tartan stopped just above his knees, displaying the sinewy legs of a born athlete.

The MacLyon clan badge fastened the Royal Scots plaid draped over his broad shoulder. Its single Gaelic word, *Duinealachd*, curved over the top of the lyon rampant embossed in silver.

Manliness.

She couldn't think of a clearer distillation of Lyon's complex, multifaceted characteristics.

When the bagpipes and fiddles started to play, she was so mesmerized by the sight of him she almost forgot to move. She tore her gaze away from MacLyon and concentrated on the lively tempo of the "Highland Laddie." Watching the other ladies from the corner of her eye, Juliette followed the steps she'd learned at the meeting of the Scottish National Society.

MacLyon smiled at Juliette when they met in the center. He circled around her with the smooth-muscled suppleness of a mountain lion stalking its prey. "I'm impressed," he said, with a bow to her curtsey. "You've excelled at your lessons."

She laughed, pleased at the compliment. "I am part Scot, after all," she reminded him. "But Cheyenne dances are not so very different. You just move your feet to the rhythm of the drums . . . or the bagpipes. Someday, I will teach you the Red Shield buffalo dance. It is done only by our bravest warriors."

"I'd like that," he said, his eyes lighting up at her obvious praise.

The laird of Strathlyon danced with agile grace, despite his great size. He guided her easily, helping her through the spirited steps of the Scottish reel. His arm was there to turn her and send her off to meet another gentleman, and waiting for her when she returned.

"I thought you disliked wearing a tartan," she said, her gaze sweeping over the red and black plaid on his shoulder.

He arched an eyebrow ironically. "Being a groomsman has its responsibilities. Keir and Annie insisted we wear our uniforms. I could hardly say no to the bride and groom."

"You look very beautiful in your kilt," she told him shyly, as they glided down the lines together.

He laughed out loud. Around the dance floor, people turned their heads and smiled at the seldom-heard sound. "No one in their right mind would call me beautiful," he chided. "Not with this mauled visage."

"I would," she said simply.

She'd been staggered by the sight of *nanoseham* in his Highland garb. During the ceremony, she'd had eyes only for him. The three eagle feathers pinned to his Scots bonnet proclaimed his status as the chief of Clan MacLyon. And the marks of battle on his rugged features only enhanced his attractiveness, for they proclaimed his valor on the field.

"May we talk for a few moments alone," she asked, "when the dance is over?"

"Only if you'll continue to flatter me so outrageously," he said with a teasing smile.

She tried to conceal her apprehension. Immediately after the ceremony, Flora had once again begged Juliette to speak to MacLyon for her. Reluctantly, she'd promised the young mother she'd plead her cause as soon as possible. The teary-eyed widow had sent Juliette a heartbroken glance before leaving MacLyon and the boys to dance with Rob.

Juliette suspected that Flora's frequent headaches were brought on by homesickness, for her disposition was naturally sunny. She only became overanxious and depressed when the boys were too rowdy and she felt unable to discipline them properly.

After the dance ended, Lyon stopped to speak briefly to Neil and Jamie, who solemnly promised to remain on their best behavior before slipping down from their chairs and scampering away. Then he led Julie through a side door and out of the ballroom. They descended a back staircase, and he guided her down a narrow corridor and into a deserted parlor. Motioning her inside, he closed the door behind them.

He watched her cross the carpet, her slender hips swaying beneath the marvelous dress. Bustles, poufs, and ruffles were no match for the clinging doeskin. Julie was the essence of feminine grace. She made Lyon feel big and awkward and gauche, like a lad in his early teens struggling to master the sudden changes in his body.

"What was it you wanted to talk to me about?" he inquired from his spot just inside the door. He had no intention of going closer until he had a firmer grip on his ravenous sexual appetite.

"Flora asked me to plead her case," Julie said, sinking down on a sofa.

"What case?" he asked curtly, although he was certain he already knew. He could read the uneasiness in Julie's gaze from across the room.

"Flora wants to take the boys and move to Glasgow. She wants to live with her parents."

Lyon leaned his shoulders against the closed door, his feet spread wide, his thumbs hooked on the leather belt above his sporran. "You've seen Flora with Neil and Jamie. She has no control over them whatsoever. They're strong willed and stubborn, like all MacLyon males. What would happen to the lads if they were allowed to grow up without discipline?''

''Flora finds it difficult to govern them,'' Julie admitted. ''But although the boys are strong willed, they are good hearted. And they love their mother very much.''

Frowning, Lyon rubbed his elbow in pensive abstraction. Flora's disposition had improved enormously since Julie had arrived at the castle. There'd been no more bouts of melancholia or pouting to get her own way. Still, the thought of her taking the children to Glasgow was completely unacceptable.

''You have no difficulty making the lads obey,'' he said. ''They follow you around like a pair of puppies. And you never seem upset by their obstreperous behavior. Rob told me the day they tried to scare you with their pet rats, you put one animal on each shoulder and took them in to tea.''

She laughed, her eyes glowing at the memory. ''Yes, and Lady Hester merely peered over her tea cup at me, too polite to mention the fact that I was wearing a matching set of white rodents with little pink noses and long wiggling whiskers.''

He grinned and shook his head. ''The point I'm making, Julie, is that Flora loathes the wee buggers . . . the rats, I mean, not the lads.''

She nodded in sympathy at his obvious exasperation. ''I am Cheyenne,'' she said. ''We believe in guiding children by example, not physical punishment. Unlike the *veho*, we do not try to break their spirit. We use gentle words of encouragement and praise and tell interesting stories to demonstrate the virtues of bravery, honesty, and generosity to those less fortunate. Like all youngsters, Neil and Jamie respond to a kind word and a light touch.''

''Blast it, is that what I've been doing wrong all this time?'' he asked with a rueful grin. He left the door and strode restlessly back and forth across the room. ''It seems I have to shake the rafters from the roof before I can be sure they're listening. And the moment I give them permission to leave, after a tongue-lashing that'd do justice to a drill sergeant, they bounce out the door as though they haven't a care in the world.''

Juliette knew the boys were never upset by their uncle's irascible moods. When she'd first arrived at the castle, they'd explained to her that he'd been cross and grouchy since coming back last spring from fighting in the Sudan.

"Uncle Lyon tried to save Papa,'' Neil had told her in a somber tone. ''He's still sad about his death.''

"Mama's afraid of Uncle Lyon,'' Jamie confided. He'd patted Juliette's arm consolingly. ''But he only roars like a lion when he's angry. He never bites.''

Juliette watched Lyon pace across the carpet and recalled what Grizel Conacher had told her about the looming of tartans. The twill weave made a heavyweight cloth with just the right amount of swing. His kilt swayed about his corded thighs, and she wondered what kind of *veho* drawers he wore underneath. Perhaps he wore a breechclout, like her father.

Returning to the problem at hand, she dropped her gaze and studied the beaded toes of her high moccasins. She knew how much MacLyon loved his nephews. She could see how miserable the mere thought of their leaving made him.

"The boys adore you,'' she said with sincerity. ''They are very happy at Strathlyon.''

He turned and held out his hand in a display of quiet authority. ''The lads *belong* at Strathlyon, where they'll get the discipline and guidance they need. If James were still alive, he'd never consider moving to Glasgow.''

"But your brother is not alive,'' she reminded him gently. ''And Flora is lonely.''

"Lonely?'' MacLyon stared at Juliette as though the idea had never occurred to him. ''She has Nana and the two lads to keep her company, not to mention Rob and myself and a castle filled with servants.''

"She misses a gentleman's company,'' Juliette expounded, treading lightly. "Flora is a beautiful young woman. She needs someone to . . . cherish her and . . . make her feel special . . . and loved."

His words came sharp and staccato. "James has only been dead a year."

"It has been a year and four months since your brother died," Juliette said. She met his wrathful gaze and braced herself to continue. "And he left Strathlyon Castle to fight in the Sudan seven months before that. Flora's period of deep mourning has been over for some time now. You cannot expect her never to marry again."

"If Flora wants another husband," he replied with mulish determination, "I'll find her one when the time is right. There are several honorable men of property in Strathshire, who'd make the lads a fine stepfather."

"But Flora does not want to marry a Highlander."

"What the devil is wrong with marrying a Highlander?" he growled.

"For one thing," Juliette replied in a placating tone, "you frighten her. You are too loud and argumentative and aggressive."

"Bloody hell!" he shouted, "I never laid a hand on the brainless twit. Why in God's name should she be afraid of me?"

Juliette looked at the giant warrior, bristling with indignation, and smiled in spite of herself. "This may come as a shock to you, MacLyon, but a defenseless woman can find you a trifle overpowering."

His hands clenched at his sides, he stopped directly in front of Juliette and glared down at her.

"Do I frighten you?"

Chapter 14

Juliette ignored the thudding of her heart, folded her hands in her lap, and met Lyon's furious gaze. *"Na-zestae,"* she said quietly. "I am Cheyenne. I have been trained since childhood to be fearless in the face of an enemy."

His flinty features softened at her words. He sank to his haunches in front of her and took her hand. "Am I your enemy, Juliette Evening Star?" The reverberation of his rich baritone set her heart thrumming like the flight of wild geese across the autumn sky.

She gazed into his searching eyes and felt her heart stumble. Despite all her plans, she was falling in love with this hard-headed Scotsman. She'd seen how tender and caring he could be with his loved ones . . . and with her. Nothing meant more to him than his family.

"No," she whispered unsteadily, "you are not my enemy. I know you would never hurt me. You saved my life."

"As you did mine."

"I am not so certain that is true," she confessed. "I believe you would have survived the attack in Edinburgh, even if I had not happened along that morning."

His mouth twisted in an ironic smile. "You think I could have fought off three men with cudgels by myself, in spite of my game arm?"

"Now that I know you? Yes."

They gazed into each other's eyes, the longing between them a tangible presence. It was as if each stood at the edge of a precipice with a chasm between. One false step, one hasty, thoughtless act could lead to lasting ruin. And prudent, cautious Juliette Elkheart, who'd spent her young lifetime guarding her impulsive twin from danger, was about to take that foolhardy step.

She drew a ragged breath. "I have a favor to ask, MacLyon."

He caught her long hair in his hands and eased it over her shoulders, so the loose tresses spilled across her breasts and fell to her waist. Then he raised her hand to his lips, kissed her palm, and released it. "Anything," he said.

With the tip of her trembling finger, she traced the snarling lion on the silver badge that pinned his plaid. "I . . . I want to go to Glen Kildunun. Will you take me there?"

He placed his large hands on either side of her body, stroking the butter-soft dress. "You're not wearing your knife today," he replied.

"It is inside my moccasin."

"And the thin cord?"

Juliette looked down at her lap in mortification. So he had noticed on that rainy afternoon. "Yes, I am wearing it. I always wear it."

His long fingers found the cord's outline through the doeskin and traced its path around each thigh.

"Why?"

"It is called a *nihpihist*. In my culture, it is worn to protect a young woman's honor. No Cheyenne man would ever violate the chastity rope. If he took a maiden against her will, her relatives would have the right to kill him." She raised her eyes and met the Lion's steady gaze. "It is a great taboo for one Cheyenne to kill another, but in such a case it is allowed, for the purity of our women is known throughout the high plains. Will you take me there?"

Lyon realized the narrow cord was all the undergarment

she wore beneath the supple, form-fitting dress. The knowledge struck him with the force of an exploding cannon. He felt as though he'd just been thrown against a wall of uncontrollable, undeniable passion. Buffeted and tossed, bruised and battered, his tormented soul slid to the carpet at her feet.

He smoothed his hands over her hips and thighs, his gaze never leaving hers. "To Kildunun?"

"Yes."

"And then you will return to Edinburgh?"

"If you want me to."

Holding her flanks between his forearms, he cupped her little bottom and inched her closer to the edge of the sofa. He answered in the Gaelic, his words a low, hoarse rasp. "I want to bury myself in your soft womanhood, Juliette Evening Star, and worship you with my body."

Never taking his gaze from her eyes, Lyon slid his hand beneath the fringed hem of her dress, following the delicate curve of her calf above the tall moccasin and passing over the fragile cord on her thigh.

His high-minded resolutions lay on the floor, expiring alongside his wicked, accursed soul. As she spread her bare legs to give him access, his greedy fingers found the nest of fluff he sought and parted her moist folds. The sexual hunger that gripped him in its claws demanded to be fed on this sugared sustenance, this delectable morsel.

Her nutmeg eyes shimmered with sweet acquiescence, the radiant eyes of a virgin going willingly to the sacrificial altar. An innocent priestess, who had no concept of the sacrifice required by a pagan god.

Easing his finger slowly and carefully inside her, he brushed her precious nub with his thumb. She was so tiny, so tight, the pressure of her soft warmth robbed him of his breath. Beneath his kilt, his massive sex rose turgid and insistent, wanting . . . yearning . . . *demanding* entrance into her dainty temple.

Lyon watched in awe as the response he sought swept

across Julie's vibrant features. Her heavy eyelids drifted shut, her face softened with passion, her lips parted, revealing the edge of even white teeth. His finger probed deeper, caressing and compelling, till he came to the barrier he'd expected. Her lashes flew upward, and the exquisite pleasure she felt was mirrored in her expressive eyes. She made no attempt to hide her feelings or the breathless reaction he created inside her.

His other hand curved along her slim neck, as Lyon leaned forward to capture her mouth with his. Their tongues danced to the rhythm he set, till her breath came in broken gasps. He brought her to the pinnacle and then nudged her over, smothering her sob of release with his open mouth. Then he drew his hand away and smoothed down her rumpled dress.

Neither said a word.

The stillness that surrounded them quivered like a plucked string on a fairy's harp.

Lyon buried his face in her lap, breathing in the enchanting, female scent of her. He kissed her through the soft fabric, his hands bracketing her willowy form, while he fought, with every ounce of his willpower, the voracious need that wracked him . . . that held him imprisoned and refused to set him free.

He could feel her fingers gently lace through his hair. She bent and kissed his head, and the incredible sweetness of her touch made his doomed soul ache with remorse.

Ah, Julie, sweet Julie, how shall I ever let you go?

Lyon cursed himself for a fool.

He had used his acid tongue and violent moods in an effort to make her leave, for the longing she evoked in him was far more dangerous than mere sexual desire. The fathomless serenity he found in her unblemished spirit called to him like the siren song of a sea maiden, luring them both to destruction.

Only a bloody fool hungered for what he could never have.

He should have left for Edinburgh that first day she'd come to Strathlyon, and buried his misery in smooth whisky and raw sex.

Now it was too late.

Now he couldn't bring himself to go.

And the conflict inside was tearing him apart.

The pealing of the bagpipes playing "The Bonnie Banks o' Loch Lomond" floated down from the ballroom. Lyon rose to his feet and offered Julie his hand.

"We'd best rejoin the dancers," he said solemnly. "Someone may have noticed our absence."

He didn't promise to take her to Kildunun, though he knew he would. He would never, however, allow Flora to take James's sons away from Strathlyon Castle.

"Do not stand at the doorway," Juliette said with a smile of invitation. "Come in and join me."

The two boys peeked around her bedroom door, which they'd opened a crack, the carroty head above, an ebony one below.

"Did you hear the thunder?" Neil asked.

"Did you see the lightning?" queried Jamie.

"Yes."

Jamie pushed the door farther ajar and stepped into the room. His older brother followed right behind. They were wearing nightshirts with long, cuffed sleeves and collars buttoned at their throats. The white flannel fell to their ankles, revealing bare pink toes. Eyes shining with excitement, they looked like angelic imps, up to no good.

Juliette was sitting in bed, brushing her hair. She'd left the heavy drapes open so she could watch the stormy night sky. Rain slashed against the windowpanes. A jolt of lightning lit the dim room for an instant, followed by a deafening crash of thunder.

"We came to see if you were scared," Neil stated generously. "We don't have thunder and lightning very often."

Without waiting for a further invitation, the boys came over and leaned against the soft feather mattress to stare at her in fascination.

"What's that?" Jamie asked, pointing to the object that dangled from the canopy over her head.

Juliette set her brush on the night table, beside her unfinished letter to Jennie, and lifted the hoop down. "This is a dreamcatcher," she explained, holding it closer for them to see.

Neil touched it curiously with his finger. "What's a dreamcatcher?"

"See the net?" she said, pointing to the fine buffalo sinew strung in the center.

They nodded and propped their elbows on the comforter to take a better look.

"The hoop's web catches all the bad dreams and holds them until daybreak, when they fade in the light of the sun. The good dreams slip through the tiny hole in the center and bring the sleeper thoughts of happiness and contentment."

Neil's tousled head bent over the object. "What are the shells and blue feathers for?"

"They are for decoration, Maevess. The feathers of the mountain bluebird were chosen because blue represents the serenity of a cloudless sky. Strong Elk Heart, my father, made this dreamcatcher for me. Everything he makes is magical. Since the day he gave it to me, when I was only fourteen, I have slept with it above my head."

"What did you just call me?" Neil demanded with a suspicious frown.

"It means Redbird," she told him with a smile. "All Cheyenne children are given special names when they are no longer babies."

"I'm not a bairn anymore," Jamie declared, his bright eyes flashing. "What's my special name?"

"You are Hehen." At his quizzical look, she ruffled his thick straight hair. "That means Blackbird."

Jamie's face lit up. "Can we stay with you for a while?" he pleaded.

"Were you frightened by the storm?"

They exchanged conspiratorial glances, then looked at her and nodded. Juliette realized it was only an excuse to come to her room, but she was willing to go along with their game. Though she'd pretended differently at the wedding supper, she knew what they'd been arguing about beneath the table.

"When I was a little girl," she said, "my great-grandmother, Porcupine Quills, would tell my sister and me stories on stormy nights like this. We can build a tipi, and I will tell you some Cheyenne stories. Would you like that?"

"Aye!" Neil agreed.

"What's a tipi?" asked Jamie.

"I will show you."

Juliette climbed out of bed. She was wearing a voluminous cotton nightdress that covered her from her neck to the tips of her toes. A cheery blaze burned in the fireplace, so there was no need to put on a dressing gown.

Shoving the heavy yellow comforter aside, she stripped the sheets from the mattress. Then she hung the swaths of white linen from the brass rings on the unlit chandelier, creating a snug tipi in front of the fire. She added fir cones to the pine logs and the crackling blaze brightened the room, filling it with the wonderful smell of the forest.

With the boys' help, she placed the down quilt on the lodge floor and piled soft pillows on top of it to form comfortable backrests. Then she hung the dreamcatcher from one of the brass rings on the chandelier, so it dangled inside the tipi. The light from the flickering flames wavered over the draped sheets, casting shadows around them in the darkened bedroom.

Together with Neil and Jamie, Juliette crawled into the tipi.

Jamie's eyes were enormous in his small face as he

looked around the lodge. "Is this a fairy house?"

"It seems magical to me," she answered with a happy laugh. "My family spent our summers in a lodge like this, only it was made of animal skins. We would go up into the Rocky Mountains to fish and hunt."

"Did you hunt with a knife or a gun?" asked Neil.

"Both." She looked at them fondly. "Now, what kind of story would you like to hear?"

"Any kind!" Jamie said with unqualified enthusiasm.

"Any kind at all," Neil eagerly agreed.

So Juliette told them about a pair of naughty gray squirrels, who were always getting into trouble because they were too busy playing to listen to their parents and grandparents. The moral was obvious, even to five- and seven-year-olds.

"That's a good story," Neil said. "Will you tell us another?"

"Please?" Jamie pleaded.

A deep masculine voice interrupted their cozy bedtime party. "So this is where you two lads disappeared to." MacLyon crouched down to peer inside the tipi. Barechested and barefooted, he wore only a pair of trousers. "I went to check on you," he told the boys, "to be sure the thunder hadn't awakened you. I was just going to see if you were with your mother or Nana, when I heard you talking as I passed by the door."

"Miss Elkheart's built us a *sìthein*," Neil explained, using the Gaelic word that meant the dwelling place of the fairies.

"And she's telling us stories," added Jamie.

Without invitation, Lyon started to crawl through the opening to join them.

"I don't think you'll fit, Uncle Lyon," his eldest nephew protested.

"This fairy house is for little people," Jamie stated.

"I'll fit," their uncle grumbled, "if I have to boot the two of you out to make room."

Neither offered another complaint.

In the glow of the firelight, Lyon met Julie's gaze. "Go on with your tale, Miss Elkheart."

"I will tell you the story of Wihio," she said. She looked at the boys and smiled puckishly. "Wihio is a clever trickster, who lives in the land of my birth. He can change his form whenever he wishes. He is deceitful and greedy, which you both know is not a very good thing to be."

The brothers exchanged sheepish glances and then nodded their heads in mutual agreement.

Lyon watched Julie spin her effortless enchantment around the two lads, like the fairy princess they were convinced she was. Her satiny hair flowed over her shoulders, spilling in dark, lavish waves against her pristine white gown. Her winsome humor and easy way with the children entranced and beguiled her three listeners, and he was reminded of the tale of Scheherazade. He felt like the man who'd discovered the magic lamp. The riches of the sultans lay before him, sparkling and winking in the light glowing in her eyes. Only he'd forgotten the enchanted word and couldn't find his way out of the secret cave.

After he'd returned Julie to the ballroom yesterday, Lyon had spent the rest of the wedding celebration playing billiards with several other gentlemen. He'd downed the free flowing whisky in the hope of drowning his carnal frustration.

By the time the closed landau was brought round for the MacLyon family, he had the satisfaction of knowing he'd succeeded in concealing not only his desire for the lovely Miss Elkheart from curious gazes, but also his advanced state of inebriation.

From everyone except Robbie, of course. One look into his older brother's tormented eyes, and Rob had instantly taken charge of their return to the castle.

Lyon pushed his troubled thoughts aside to listen to Julie's bedtime story.

"One day," she continued, "Wihio changed himself into

the shape of a woman. He carried his friend, Coyote, enfolded in a blanket like a baby, so they would be welcomed into people's lodges and given food.''

Neil leaned toward her in rapt attention. ''Did people give them some?''

''Yes,'' she said, ''they gave Wihio roasted buffalo tongue, which is a great delicacy.''

Engrossed, Jamie placed his small hand on her knee. ''Did Wihio get caught?''

Her eyes gleamed with amusement. ''When the trickster refused to give some of the meat to Coyote, the make-believe baby tipped back his head, bared his sharp, canine teeth, and howled to the moon. Then everyone in the camp knew the truth!''

''What did the people do?'' Neil asked.

''*Hesc!* They could not catch Wihio. He was too nimble and quick.'' She snapped her fingers under the lads' noses. ''He jumped up and ran out of the lodge, faster than even Coyote. Faster than even the two of you.''

Neil and Jamie giggled in delight.

''Now, it's time for you lads to get to bed,'' Lyon said.

''Before we go,'' Neil begged, ''we want to ask Miss Elkheart a riddle.''

Julie was clearly intrigued. ''What kind of riddle?''

His nephews met Lyon's gaze, pleading for permission to stay a while longer. ''All right,'' he conceded. ''One riddle. Then, off you go.''

''One riddle each,'' Neil bargained.

Lyon nodded his consent. He suspected the boys were going to ask enchantment riddles from an old Celtic ballad about the *sìth*, the fairy people. By asking her a riddle she couldn't answer, they hoped to trick her into shrinking in size.

Neil gazed at Julie with a seraphic smile, certain he could best her. ''What is whiter than milk?''

''My turn,'' said Jamie, before she had a chance to consider.

"Go on," Julie urged, "what is yours?"

He wrinkled his nose and flashed a sly grin. "What is softer than silk?"

Julie propped her chin on her hand and looked up at the roof of the tipi. "Mm," she mused, "now let me see. "Whiter than milk . . ." She beamed in triumph as she met Neil's glowing eyes. "I have it," she claimed. "Snow is whiter than milk."

Neil's jaw dropped in astonishment.

She tipped her head to one side, returning Jamie's hopeful gaze. "Now for yours," she said softly. "Let me think. Softer than silk . . ." She tapped her finger against her pursed lips, than leaned forward and bussed his forehead. "Goose down is softer than silk."

"Wow!" Jamie cried, scrambling to his feet and bumping his head against the draped sheeting.

Lyon stared at Julie in amazement. The riddles the lads had given her were from an ancient ballad written in Gaelic. To his knowledge, they'd never been translated into English. It was *possible*—though highly improbable—that she'd figured out both answers on her own; more likely Rob may have read and explained them to her.

"Tell Miss Elkheart goodnight," he ordered his nephews.

"Goodnight," they chorused together. They threw their arms around her and hugged her tightly.

"Goodnight, Maevess," she said, kissing Neil's cheek. She kissed Jamie in turn. "Goodnight, little Hehen."

The lads grinned in delight as they met Lyon's quizzical gaze. "That's our magic names," Neil explained happily.

"Magic," Jamie echoed, his black eyes shining.

"Get right to bed," he instructed, giving each one a hug. "If I hear a peep from either of you, there'll be dire consequences in the morning."

Lyon stood at the doorway, watching his nephews scurry down the hall and into their bedroom. After waiting a moment to be sure they were going to stay put, he stepped back into Julie's room.

His gaze lit on the night stand that stood near her canopied bed. Her knife, in its beaded leather sheath, lay next to her comb and brush. Beside them, a thin, white cord lay coiled on the gleaming cherry top.

He closed the door behind him and turned the lock.

Chapter 15

Juliette waited inside the makeshift tipi, praying Lyon would return to her. It seemed as though not a moment had passed since he'd touched her so intimately the previous day. She ached for him. For his touch. For his voice. For his lips. But it was more than physical longing that had become a part of her every breath, her every thought.

This stalwart, tormented Scotsman combined a warrior's bravery and strength with the tenderness of a loving husband and father. He was everything she'd been taught to admire and respect. The chief of Clan MacLyon would never desert his home, his family, or his people to seek his own fulfillment. Responsibility to his loved ones and those placed in his care was as natural to him as breathing. She knew that ghosts from his past continued to haunt him, and she longed to heal his inner pain with soft words and gentle hands.

Her goal of returning to America and enrolling in the university no longer seemed of primary importance. And with that startling realization came the admission she'd been refusing to make . . . even to herself.

She had fallen in love with Lyon.

She heard the sound of his bare feet padding softly across the rug, and then he crouched in front of the lodge's opening.

''I prayed to Maheo that you would come to my room

this evening," she said quietly, "as I prayed for you to come last night."

Even in the shadows of the dimly lit bedroom, his eyes revealed a terrible anguish, though he spoke in a dry, ironic tone. "By the time I'd consumed enough whisky to get myself under control, I was in no condition to go anywhere last night. Least of all to your room. My brother listened to my incoherent babbling as he undressed me and put me to bed."

"The white man's fire water is a very potent brew," she replied with a tiny smile. She motioned for Lyon to enter the tipi and join her.

After a moment's hesitation, he ducked beneath the draped sheeting and sank down on the quilted blanket. He crossed his long legs in the fashion of a Cheyenne male. The sight of him sitting in the lodge, clothed only in the white man's trousers, brought a warm glow of nostalgia. She could almost imagine them in the Canadian forests, with the fresh scent of pine needles cleansed by the rain swirling about them.

"In Gaelic, whisky is called *uisge-beatha*," he said, "which means the water of life. Your name for it is more appropriate, but there's a saying in Latin, *in vino veritas*." He smiled lopsidedly. "In wine there is truth."

"And when you told your brother the truth, did he offer you any advice?"

"Oh, aye. Rob was full of clever ideas."

"What did he advise?"

"He suggested I do one of two things. Either I put a pistol to my head and blow my brains out, or I surrender to my innate, God-given instincts and let nature take its course."

Juliette stopped breathing. "And which alternative have you chosen?"

His jaw clenched. "Neither," he replied with a forced smile. "I don't have the guts to execute the former, and too much conscience to indulge in the latter. I came here this evening looking for Neil and Jamie.''

The air she breathed became the icy draft of a howling blizzard, freezing her lungs. The cold numbness spread through her entire chest cavity. She struggled hopelessly to keep the hollow sound of her frozen heart from her hushed voice. ''They are safely asleep in their beds now.''

''Where we all should be.''

Although the worst of the storm had abated, rain continued to splash against the windows. Inside, the firelight filtering through the lodge's triangular entrance wrapped them in its lambent glow.

Lyon reached up and touched the dreamcatcher, running his fingertip idly along the downy feathers of the bluebird.

''Do you want some help dismantling the fairy house and remaking your bed?'' he asked, his deep baritone permeating every inch of the small space. ''I'll be happy to restore your room to its former condition before I go.''

Juliette patted the silken cushion at her elbow. ''No, I will sleep here in the lodge tonight. I will pretend I am back in the Rocky Mountains, listening to the raindrops beating against the lodge skin.''

There was a long moment of silence. The Lion looked around the improvised tipi, wondering, no doubt, what it must be like to actually live in one. To a white man, the comparison to Strathlyon Castle would seem incomprehensible.

He stirred, his hands clenching and unclenching on his folded knees. ''I watched the lads' faces as you told them the bedtime story. You have a marvelous way with children.''

Juliette smiled, pleased at the compliment. ''Neil and Jamie are delightful companions.''

''I hope your plan to become a veterinarian doesn't mean you don't want to have a family of your own some day.'' His eyes narrowed thoughtfully. ''It'd be a shame if you didn't . . . have children of your own, that is.''

Juliette stared at Lyon, dismayed that such a thought would even occur to him. *"Hesc!* All Cheyenne love children. The *veho* gathers material things around him. Furniture. Paintings. Sculptures. Castles." He quirked a brow at the direct hit, and she smiled to soften her words. "My people prefer the blue sky for a roof and the warm earth as a floor. Our children are our treasures." She paused and proudly lifted her chin. "Yes, I hope one day to be a wife and mother."

Lyon's steady gaze never left her face. "Your husband will be a very lucky man."

Juliette's teetering hopes came crashing down like lodgepole pines in a fierce gale. Her lips trembled, but she smiled bravely. "And your wife will be a most fortunate woman."

His entire body flinched, as though she'd inflicted a lethal blow. The hoarse words were torn from deep inside him. "Do you think, Julie, that I could ever marry anyone but . . . ?" He caught himself and gave a harsh, bitter laugh. "Why should I inflict my mangled carcass on some poor, innocent female?"

Juliette reached out and reverently traced the rugged lines of his face. She followed the weathered creases at the corners of his eyes, drew her fingertips along the bridge of his broken nose, and pressed the pad of her thumb against his scarred chin.

"My people cherish the marks of a warrior," she told him. "No Cheyenne maiden would ever consider accepting a man who had not proven himself in battle as a suitor. I have to smile, sometimes, at the foolish white girls who sigh over the pretty looks of the untried and untested young boys. We honor the experienced soldier, who has risked his life for his people."

"You don't know what you're saying," he answered sharply.

Juliette leaned toward him, laid her hand on his arm, and lightly caressed the puckered scar on his injured elbow.

"You place too little value on yourself, Lyon. You blame yourself for things which I am sure could not have been done differently."

He cupped her face in his hand, his thumb tracing the line of her cheekbone. His mouth twisted in self-derision. "It's you, Juliette Evening Star, who place too little value on yourself."

She turned her head, kissing the hard palm, then rose to her knees in front of him. She placed her hands on his solid shoulders. "I am not wearing my knife this evening, Scotsman."

"I know."

"Nor the *nihpihist.*"

His hissed reply came on an anguished rush of air. "Why?"

She leaned closer and brushed his forehead with her lips. "I have no need for them. I knew that only one man might come to my room tonight. And that one man is here."

He caught her waist in his long fingers, grasping her so tightly her breath stalled in her lungs. "Juliette," he said on a broken, bitter laugh, "don't you know that you're torturing me?"

"Then surrender to the pain," she pleaded. "For I am tortured, too. And only you can release us from our suffering."

Juliette bent her head and her long hair fell forward to brush his cheeks as she kissed him—a gentle, healing kiss. She traced the seam of his closed lips with the tip of her tongue, using all the knowledge he'd given so freely, turning that knowledge against the force of his stubborn will.

A shudder went through his powerful body. His fingers gripped her firmly, and she braced herself, afraid that he was about to push her away.

She knew the exact instant he surrendered. He groaned as he caught her in his arms and crushed her to him.

"Julie, Julie," he whispered, his mouth moving against hers. "God help me . . ."

Lyon kissed her passionately, his hands roving freely over the billowing cotton nightdress, seeking the supple feminine curves hidden beneath. He eased her back against the pile of thick pillows. Leaning over her, he kissed her eyelids, her brow, her nose, her chin, the corners of her mouth. The sweet perfume of her hair drifted around them, bringing back every indelible memory of their few brief times together.

Never enough time.

Never enough.

If he held her in his arms for the rest of his life, there wouldn't be time enough to show her how much he loved her.

His carping, acrimonious conscience kicked vainly against the bastion of his black soul, the door slammed and bolted by his need. Every muscle in his body tensed as burgeoning excitement spread through his veins. Consumed with desire, he released the buttons at the base of her throat and dipped his tongue into the silken hollow there.

"I tried," he murmured, nuzzling the graceful curve of her neck. "God forgive me, I tried . . ."

"Shh," she breathed. "We both tried." She buried her fingers in his hair and brought him closer as he suckled her through the fine cotton cloth. She arched her lithesome form, lifting herself to him, giving herself freely. "I dreamt of you last night, *nanoseham.*"

"Tell me what the word means," he demanded gruffly. "You've called me that before."

She smoothed her hands over his bare shoulders and upper arms, and a current of white-hot sparks seemed to follow her touch.

"*Nanoseham* means mountain lion. With your red-gold hair and your eyes the color of spring leaves, you remind me of the great wild cat that roams our forests and plains. Cunning . . . predatory . . . dangerous."

He chuckled as he brushed his cheek against the enticing mounds of her breasts. "I thought you were whispering love words, and here you were hurling insults at me. What other names did you call me that afternoon at Stirling Castle?''

She countered his question with a pert complaint. ''You speak Gaelic to me and seldom explain your words.''

''What I say when I'm sexually aroused isn't fit for your delicate ears,'' he grumbled. He caught her hands and pinned them on either side of her head. ''Now tell me what else you called me that day.''

Boldly meeting his gaze, she ignored his demand. ''I dreamt that you came into my room last night. You had taken the shape of *nanoseham*.''

He grinned at the thought of the practical Miss Elkheart indulging in erotic fantasy. ''Did I roar and frighten you?''

''You leapt up on the bed, where I was sleeping,'' she said huskily, ''and stood above me, with your great forepaws on my shoulders so that I could not get up and run away.''

''Like this?'' He came over her on all fours, his large hands pressing her body down into the soft comforter, his knees on either side of her hips. He kissed her, his tongue darting inside to savor her sugary mouth. ''What else did I do?''

''You split my nightdress apart with one swipe of your sharp claws,'' she answered in a quiet, somber tone.

Leaning back, Lyon grasped the unbuttoned placket at her throat in both hands. ''Like this?'' He ripped the gown straight down the middle, tearing the thin fabric all the way through the hem.

Julie jumped in surprise, her eyes wide. She licked her lips and swallowed, but her gaze never wavered. Nor did she attempt to cover her bared breasts with her hands. The velvet nipples tightened into coral buds beneath his heated gaze.

Lyon unfastened the pearl buttons on her cuffs and eased the rent garment off her shoulders and arms, then he drew back and feasted on the sight of her.

Her glorious tresses spilled over the pillows. In the flickering light that streamed through the lodge's opening, her skin glowed from within, a golden shimmer of warmth.

In that moment of heart-stopping awareness, he realized fully how different she was from every other woman he'd been with. Except for the scanty silken down at the juncture of her thighs, her lissome body glistened as smooth as a marble statue.

She smiled at his look of astonishment. "My father's people do not have hairy bodies," she said softly. She stroked her fingernails across the rough stubble on his jaw. "The women have none at all, and the men do not grow beards and mustaches like the *veho*. What few chin hairs sprout are plucked, for hairiness is considered unattractive."

In addition to the thick mat of hair that grew on Lyon's chest and under his arms, his thighs and forearms had a light covering of russet. Not to mention the dark wiry patch on his groin. He scowled at the thought of how he must appear to her—like some lumbering caveman.

"Do you find me repulsive?"

Her sloe eyes glittered with amusement. "No, Scotsman, I do not find you repulsive. The first time I saw you barechested, I wanted to run my fingers through your rusty pelt. It reminded me so much of the mountain lion's thick fur, I wanted to feel its warmth and softness beneath my touch."

"Do it," he urged. "Pet me."

She hesitated for a moment. Then with trembling fingers, she touched his naked chest. Her hand glided over his pectorals, and the muscles bunched reflexively. She buried her fingers in his chest hair and traced the nipples that tightened and pebbled beneath the pads of her exploring fingers.

The need to possess this marvelous woman raked through him, scoring him with razor-edged rowels of lust. The blood pulsed, hard and fierce, in his veins. Lyon would be satisfied with nothing less than her total capitulation. He wanted all of her. Her body. Her soul. Her indomitable Cheyenne spirit.

He rumbled deep in his chest, the sound reminiscent of a great, predatory cat. "I dream of you every night, Vehona," he admitted, "but never one in which I take the shape of a mountain lion. Tell me more about your flight of fancy. Did I devour you with my sharp fangs?"

Her breath came out in a rush. "You nipped me with your teeth, *nanoseham*, but it did not hurt. It was as though you were marking me as your own."

Lyon crouched over her, his fingers buried in the chestnut locks cascading over the pillows in ribbons of satin. He bit her shoulder, then her breast—light lover's nips that left small red smudges on her honeyed skin. "What did I do next, *a ghaolaich*?"

She answered in a thready whisper. "Then you bathed me with your tongue."

He bent his head and laved her. Like a lion grooming its young, he washed her with slow, steady strokes. He traced a moist path from her wrist to her elbow. He licked the inside of her arm, the round curves of her breasts, the bumps of her ribs, the plane of her stomach, the delicate lines of her hip and thigh. She tasted like sugar and cinnamon and honey.

"You are so perfect in every way," he crooned to her, "how you look . . . how you speak . . . how you move. Did you know, I couldn't take my eyes off you, little princess? Not from the first day I saw you."

Her only answer was a long, drawn-out hum of pleasure.

He suckled her, the feel of her tight buds against his tongue sending his engorged shaft lurching toward her beneath the confines of his clothing.

"Lyon," she whispered. "Please . . ." She fumbled with the waistband of his trousers.

He withdrew only long enough to peel them off, then knelt over her once again. He'd worn nothing beneath them. As he crouched above her like the predatory beast she'd envisioned, his heavy arousal was rampantly apparent.

Lyon heard her shocked intake of air. He leaned back on his haunches and met her startled eyes.

Christ, he'd never felt so damn big.

"I'm not going to make you do anything you don't want to do, Julie," he promised, stroking his hands down her arms in a comforting gesture. "I may look like a great, clumsy brute, but I'd never force you against your will, lass, I swear it."

Juliette had never felt so small . . . or so overwhelmed with awe. Her Highland warrior was magnificent. His massive body loomed above her, the long, hard contours of his bones outlined beneath the firm, vibrant flesh. An aggressive, physical vitality emanated from him in waves of heat and musky male scent.

Virile.

Primal.

Conquering.

"*Nihoatovaz,*" she said softly.

"Tell me so I can understand," he insisted with a muffled laugh. "If you're going to call me names, I should at least know what you're saying."

"I want you," she replied. "*Nihoatovaz, nanoseham.* I want you, mountain lion."

She reached up and stroked his furry chest, following the tapering line of rust down to the abdomen ridged with muscle. Then she paused and searched his eyes.

"Go on," he urged in a strangled voice. "Pet me, darling. Tame me with your touch."

With his knees braced on either side of her hips, his powerful thighs corded and tense, he rose to soar above her. The muscles tautened over his flat stomach. His erection sprang from a mat of crisp russet curls, as though yearning for her caress.

Juliette took the hard length of him in her hand, the feel of his flesh warm and inviting. His lids drooped, till his thick lashes shadowed his cheeks and his face darkened with passion. Completely, utterly still, he allowed her to explore him, to cup him and stroke him. His fierce male body, rising above her, yielded to her gentle power.

The Lion watched Juliette through shuttered eyes. "I can't take much more, *a ghràidh shìth*," he rasped, "or . . ."

He'd called her his fairy sweetheart, and the endearment sent shivers of delight spinning though her like a magical rainbow of lights.

"Or what?" she whispered.

"Or I'll start to purr like a damn house cat."

"Go ahead," Juliette encouraged with a shy smile. "I want to hear you rumble and growl like *nanoseham* on the scent of a helpless doe."

"Not yet," he told her with a shake of his wavy mane.

He gently removed her curved fingers from his engorged manhood. Lifting one of her knees and then the other, he repositioned himself between her bent legs. He clasped both her wrists in his hands and bent over her. A tender smile teased the corners of his mouth, and his soft Scots burr was the rolling purr of seduction itself.

"Right now, lass, I'm going to finish what I started."

Chapter 16

⌒◯◯⌒

Juliette lifted her brows in wonder, feeling as vulnerable and skittish as a newborn fawn as Lyon brushed his rough cheek against the sensitive skin of her inner thigh. She flinched in surprise. Her breath caught in her throat.

"Lyon?" she gasped. "What are you going to do?"

"Bathe you with my tongue."

He spread her bent legs wider, then scooped her bottom up in his large palms and raised her toward him. She could feel his reddish-gold waves brush against the insides of her thighs, as he leaned over and lapped her with unbelievable tenderness. A thrill of ecstasy reverberated through every nerve in Juliette's body. His soft, rhythmic strokes were like nothing she'd ever imagined, spreading convulsions of pleasure through her. With a long, joyful sigh of submission, she closed her eyes and gave herself up to the unfolding rapture of sweet fulfillment.

When the quivers of her culmination began to subside, Lyon eased his finger inside her slick, moist warmth, readying Julie for his entrance. His heart thundered against his ribcage. He'd never lain with a woman so small. Never lain with a virgin.

"I'm going to come into you now, *a ghaolaich*," he told her. "Try to stay as relaxed as you are at this moment. Lay back on the pillows, and let me do all the work."

219

Her lush ebony lashes flickered. At the moment, she seemed barely aware of his presence.

So much for an appreciation of his expert foreplay.

"Work?" Her voice sounded faint and faraway.

He kissed her just above the sparse line of silken chestnut down. His fingers sought the pliant aureoles of her breasts and tugged gently on their buds, then smiled as her body writhed beneath his lingering caresses.

"Aye, lass, work. But it'll be the most rewarding work I've ever done."

He gently inserted two fingers, to stretch her as much as he dared. Then he eased out and began to push his thickened sex carefully inside her narrow passage.

Jesus, she was tight.

It was like trying to fit a cannonball into the barrel of his Lancaster rifle.

His back and shoulders grew slick with the effort of maintaining control over his rampaging lust. The ache in his bad arm became a dull throb, and his entire body shook as he braced himself on his forearms to keep his crushing weight off her. Lyon could feel Julie grow tense and attempt to retreat.

"Are all your father's people this tiny?" he asked lightly, continuing to edge himself inside her, bit by bit.

"No," she replied in a strained voice. "The Cheyenne are a tall, strong race. I inherited my stature from my mother. She is the one with Scottish blood."

"Then the Danielsons must have been the runts of Scotland," he grated.

She laughed, just as he hoped she would, and the resulting relaxation allowed him further access.

His tranquil princess started to chatter nervously. "My sister and I were so tiny when we were born, *nihoe* was afraid we'd never survive. He built a log cabin that summer to protect us from the Canadian blizzards."

Lyon bumped against her maidenhead. Clasping her

shoulders in his hands, he nuzzled the curve of her neck and held her captive.

"We have just a little more to go, darling," he murmured in her ear. "And I'm going to make it quick and clean." Before she could brace against him, he thrust deep inside her.

"Ahahe!" she cried softly.

She made a fluttering little sound in the back of her throat, part gasp, part whimper, as he drove deeper. He'd known from the first he couldn't bury himself to the hilt in her tiny body.

"I know, sweetheart, I know," he soothed. "I'm too damn big, aren't I?" He started to withdraw.

She shook her head, her hands clasping him to her, her nails digging into the muscles across his shoulder blades. "No," she whispered. "Do not stop now, *nanoseham*. My heart would collapse in disappointment and regret."

He covered her mouth with his own, pouring all the love he felt into his kiss. She buried her fingers in his hair, returning the kiss, her tongue seeking his for comfort and reassurance.

As the breathless moments ticked by, her small, feminine form accepted his massive invasion. For the first time in his adult life, Lyon blinked back tears. Then slowly, and with ultimate care, he began to worship her with his body.

Juliette could feel the weight of him pressing her down into the thick comforter, even though he braced most of his large frame on his arms. She ran her tongue over his shoulder and tasted the salt of perspiration.

"Your injury," she murmured, as the pleasure gradually built within her. "I forgot about your elbow. Are you all right?"

"I've never been more all right in my life," he groaned.

Breathing in the wonderful male scent of him, she sucked on his upper arm, barely resisting the urge to bite him. Then she tipped her head back on the pillow and met his gaze.

"Namehota, nanoseham," she whispered.

"Tell me in English," he urged thickly, as he continued his rhythmic thrust and withdrawal.

"I love you, mountain lion."

He halted, his face harsh and stern. "I forbid you to love me, Julie," he rasped.

His manhood moved deep inside her, and he scowled, as though he resented his own lack of control. Then once again he plunged and retreated, this time faster and harder.

She couldn't conceal the hurt in her voice. "You do not feel any affection for me?"

The exquisite delight he was bringing to her body battled with the agonizing disappointment in her soul. She struggled to draw away from him, and he growled in warning.

"What I feel is irrelevant," he gritted in her ear. "The only thing that matters between us . . . is you . . . and your life . . . and what you do with it. Do you understand that, princess? You are not allowed to feel anything for me . . . except desire . . . and . . . pity."

Juliette strained to follow his words, while her body continued to respond to his every movement with quivers of irresistible pleasure.

"Pity?" she gasped, trying to fight the sweet convulsions radiating through her. "Why should I feel pity for you?"

"Because . . . when you leave here . . . and you will leave, Juliette Elkheart . . . I promise you . . . I don't . . . I can't . . ."

The throbbing, driving excitement he was building inside her increased inexorably, till wave after wave of shimmering ecstasy spread through Juliette and she lost all sense of what he was saying. She wrapped her arms and legs around Lyon, every nerve, every fiber straining to get closer to him. Her breasts crushed against his chest, her breath coming in shallow pants, she sobbed his name. And then she yielded to the undulating spasms that racked her, as her very being seemed to meld with his.

Lyon waited till the throes of Julie's climax waned. The pressure of her tight sheath on his sex was unimaginable.

With three more quick strokes, he brought himself to a shuddering conclusion. He withdrew at the last moment, catching his spilled seed in his cupped palm.

Her eyes closed, Julie lay sprawled against the pillows in a state of sweet oblivion. He pulled a handkerchief from his discarded trousers to wipe his hand and his still tumescent sex. Blood stained the clean linen cloth. The vivid proof of her lost virginity brought an overwhelming sense of guilt.

Damn! What he'd done couldn't be undone, but he would make bloody sure the lass he loved so deeply wouldn't be the one to suffer for it.

Lying down beside her, he took Julie in his arms and cuddled her close against his naked body. With a languorous sigh, she flung her arms about his neck and buried her face in his hairy chest.

"Mm," she sighed, her breath cool against his overheated skin. "So . . . unbelievably . . . wonderful."

"Aye, my fairy sweetheart," he said tenderly in the Gaelic. He brushed aside the long chestnut strands that had fallen across her face and kissed her temple. "Now go to sleep, my bonny, wee love, while I hold you against my heart."

For tonight, he would push back the harsh realities of life. He'd kiss her and tell her how beautiful she was, how very, very special. For tonight, he would hold Julie close and watch her drift into sleep.

He'd stay with her for a while longer.

And then he'd *never* allow this to happen again.

"You're in a foul bitch of a mood," Rob said pleasantly. "Do you have to act like a miserable bastard all the time? It gets dammed hard living with you."

"I wouldn't be such a miserable bastard to live with, if it weren't for my braw younger brother," Lyon replied. "So save your blasted complaints about my sour mood." He took another puff on his Havana, met Rob's skeptical gaze, and added sardonically, "I'd have retreated safely to Edinburgh three weeks ago. But I was afraid if I left Strathlyon, I'd come back to find Miss Elkheart my future sister-in-law."

Rolling a fat cigar between his fingers, Rob leaned against the steamboat's railing with his usual sangfroid. "Well, hell, there's just no accounting for taste, is there? Given the choice between the two of us, any other lass with a lick of sense would have picked me."

The two MacLyon men stood on the *Elfin Queen's* promenade deck, enjoying a smoke. Clustered together several yards away at the prow's curved railing, Julie, Nana, Flora, and the lads were pointing at passing boats and chattering with animation.

The velvet ribbons on the ladies' hats whipped gaily in the breeze. With her usual lack of foresight, Flora had chosen to wear a wide-brimmed straw boater that kept flapping into her face with every gust. Laughing gaily, Julie reached out and caught the monstrosity as it lifted and threatened to sail out over the waves like some tipsy yellow sea bird. Neil and Jamie cheered her quick agility with loud hurrahs.

"Aye," Lyon agreed, "all the petticoats of Strathbardine gladly dance to your tune. But I should have realized that any female intelligent enough to study veterinary medicine wouldn't be taken in by a bonny face and a tinker's charm like yours."

Rob laughed. "Julie's a lass o' parts, all right. She'll make a fantastic vet. Word of her gift for healing animals has already spread throughout Strathshire."

The news didn't make Lyon any happier. "Has it, now?"

"Yesterday morning, Tommy MacGugan came to the castle asking for her. He wanted Miss Elkheart to go to his farm and take a look at his daughter's lame pony. Julie drained the pus and packed the crack in the pony's hoof with medicine she'd brewed herself."

"How the devil did she brew her own medicine?"

Rob ran his fingers through his windblown hair, shoving

it back off his forehead. "Every time we've gone for a morning gallop, she's collected some wild plant for what she calls her Cheyenne medicine kit."

Lyon nodded, his gaze riveted to her slender form. Energetic and nimble as the lads, she was leaning out over the white wooden railing, watching an osprey splash into the loch to snatch a fish in its claws and soar away.

"Julie has an innate compassion for all living things," he said quietly. "Especially the suffering and injured."

"Which explains her preference for a battered old soldier like you over a suave, dashing blade like me," Rob retorted with a grin. "So when's the wedding?"

Lyon glared at his brother. "There'll be no wedding. After this jaunt to Kildunun, Julie's returning to Edinburgh and her uncle. I have her word on it."

"Ye poor, thrawn fool," Rob said softly. His eyes blazed with scorn. "I can't believe you're actually going to let the lassie go."

Lyon took a long pull on his cigar and slowly exhaled. "Miss Elkheart is only eighteen years old."

"What the hell difference does that make?" his brother demanded. "Plenty of men far older than you marry debutantes barely out of the schoolroom. Especially rich, titled men intent on producing an heir."

"I'm not going to use my wealth and power to buy a young, fertile bride just so you won't have to accept the responsibility of being the next chief of Clan MacLyon."

"*Buy* her!" Rob snorted in disgust. "Julie's in love with you, and you damn well know it."

"It's a passing fancy, nothing more. Juliette Elkheart has a wonderful and fulfilling life ahead of her. She's been accepted at a university in Philadelphia for the spring semester. There's nothing here in the Highlands to offer someone with her unique talents."

"Not to mention her incredible beauty or her courageous spirit." Rob swore, but didn't waste time trying to argue.

Thin ribbons of smoke curled from the steamboat's twin

stacks as the *Elfin Queen* chugged smoothly up Loch Linnhe toward Fort William. They'd passed the mouth of Loch Leven, and now the towering peak of Ben Nevis rose in the distance. The rainstorm of two days before had been followed by brilliant sunshine. That morning the weather continued mild and clear, making it a perfect day for a family outing.

Rob braced his elbows on the promenade rail and gazed distractedly at the snowy mountain top. "Why do you think Julie is so determined to visit Glen Kildunun?"

"Damned if I can figure it out," Lyon answered with a shrug. "Why would anyone want to go the site of their own forebears' treachery? It doesn't make sense to me."

He had to admit, there was a lot about Miss Juliette Elkheart that baffled him. The intense passion that burned beneath her cool exterior had rocked him with the force of an artillery bombardment.

Her lovemaking, though inexperienced, had been generous and uninhibited, filled with playfulness and a lively sense of humor. Although she'd compared him to a ferocious mountain lion, she'd shown no fear at the sight of his big, naked body. She'd acted out an erotic fantasy with him, yet there was no doubt of her virginity. Or of her infatuation with an older man she considered some kind of ridiculous war hero.

At that moment, the gifted, lovely lass under discussion came to join them. Lyon met Julie's somber gaze. Every time she looked at him, her eyes bespoke a baffled vulnerability. The pain inside him increased tenfold, like a scalpel wielded with the brutal precision of a sadistic army doctor carving up his insides.

He steeled himself, refusing to be swayed by the hushed entreaty in their fathomless brown depths. He'd avoided being alone with her since the night they'd lain in each other's arms.

"You gentlemen look very serious," Juliette said. Despite her cheerful tone, her heart ached at the uncompromising cast of Lyon's stony features. "I came to see if I could interrupt your chat and coax you to enjoy the beautiful scenery with me, instead."

Rob welcomed her with a ready smile. "I was telling my brother how you treated Meggie MacGugan's pony."

"It was only an infected hoof," she replied. "Nothing serious at all. And Shananikins was a wonderful patient."

After she'd cared for the sweet-mannered pony, Tommy MacGugan had confided that, he, too, was a descendent in the female line of Clan Danielson. When Juliette explained that she was having a plaid woven in the lavender and pink tartan, Tommy had flashed a puckish grin. He put a work-gnarled finger to his lips, gave her a conspiratorial wink, and said no more.

"MacGugan's family was pretty impressed," Rob declared. His sky-blue eyes twinkled with amusement. "Especially when I explained to them that you were talking to the pony in a magical language only the two of you understood."

She shook her head at his teasing, then addressed Lyon with a questioning look. "When I mentioned my surprise that we were the only passengers on board today, Neil and Jamie informed me that the *Elfin Queen* belongs to you."

"Aye," he said, his austere gaze fastened on her lips. "The first steam engine was invented by a Scot and the first workable steamboat by another countryman. My grandfather was fascinated by the possibilities of steam. Along with oceangoing vessels, Angus invested heavily in locomotives and paddle wheelers. Ordinarily, the *Queen* takes paying passengers up and down Loch Linnhe. But I reserved her solely for our use this trip. I thought it'd be more comfortable without a crowd."

"It is very pleasant to have it all to ourselves," she agreed in amazement.

Flora and the boys had taken Juliette on a tour of the floating palace when they'd first come aboard. They'd visited the ladies' saloon with its thick Brussels carpet, peeked into the gentlemen's social area, where they'd glimpsed a carved oak bar and tables for cards, and wandered past the fifty staterooms on the promenade deck.

Neil and Jamie had gladly explored the library and post office on the second deck with their fascinated guest. Later, Lady Hester had shown her the spacious dining hall. They were to enjoy their evening meal, served by white-coated stewards, beneath gilded chandeliers and stained glass sky-lights set afire by the setting sun.

Julie's astonishment brought a reluctant smile to Lyon's lips. Evidently it had never occurred to her that the MacLyons had accumulated anything more than an ancient castle stuffed with relics from the past.

Rob chuckled. "My brother must have forgotten to men-tion he owns an entire fleet of paddle steamers, which ply the waters of the Inner Hebrides taking families on holiday excursions."

"I suppose it is not something one would just drop into a conversation," she said gaily. Then her cheeks reddened, and she bit her lower lip as though regretting the innocent remark.

Lyon suspected Julie was thinking about their last, very private conversation. At the erotic image it conjured up, a sudden, fierce need gripped him and his groin muscles tightened involuntarily. Two days. Two frigging days, and he burned with sexual desire. He could swear the heat was oozing out of every pore.

Rob looked from one to the other, a wide grin spreading across his chiseled features. "Well, Miss Elkheart," he said amiably, "since we came on this outing to enjoy ourselves, let's do just that. If you look over to the right, I'll point out any spots of historic interest on the way."

The three turned to admire the view. The only sound was the rhythmic slapping of the paddles and the panting hiss of the high-pressure engines. Herring gulls wheeled in the near-cloudless sky. Off the prow, a gannet spotted a fish and dove at its prey, its black-tipped wings folded tight as it sliced into the water.

Wisps of smoke floated above piles of burning seaweed in the fishing hamlets dotting the shore. Farther off, the towering bluffs, hostile escarpments, and endless pine forests of the eastern mountains glided by.

Juliette was achingly conscious of Lyon's nearness. From the corner of her eye, she could see the outline of his grim profile. He stood like a fierce Highland chief, obstinate and tyrannical. Cold dread wrapped itself around her heart. He had every intention of sending her away.

Yesterday afternoon, she'd found a package on her bed. Inside the layers of tissue lay a nightdress of delicate Chantilly lace and soft, shimmering white satin. In place of a note, a single white rose accompanied the exquisite creation.

The closer the boat drew to their destination, the more anxious and unhappy she became. Lyon had made it painfully clear he didn't want to listen to another girlish confession of love. Though he'd often been near her in the past two days, they'd never once been alone. And her pride hadn't allowed her to seek him. What was the use? She knew he'd refuse to listen to anything she had to say.

She'd given herself to a man before marriage, something Cheyenne girls never did. But when she'd dreamt of Lyon coming to her in the shape of *nanoseham*, she'd believed it had been a vision sent by the Maiyun. Now she wasn't so sure.

Juliette was stunned by the overpowering desire Lyon had aroused in her, and even more shocked by her own impetuous behavior. For the first time in her life, she'd tossed aside her inborn caution and followed where her emotions led. And now only Lyon's rejection would keep her out of his arms.

She still hadn't finished her letter to Jennie, even though she'd had time in the past few days. She couldn't write about her visit to the Highlands—not in her present frame of mind. Jennie would sense something was wrong and worry needlessly over what couldn't be changed.

Almost as troubling was the fact that, since returning from Stirling, she'd not once had the recurring dream that had brought her to Scotland in the first place. Had the Great Powers lost faith in her? If her visit to Kildunun proved pointless, she'd have to accept the fact that she'd misinterpreted the vision. And she would have to honor her pledge to leave Strathlyon once they returned to the castle.

Her anxious thoughts were dispelled by the appearance of Neil and Jamie, who wiggled their way in between her and Lyon.

"Miss Elkheart, we have another riddle," Neil announced brightly.

"Another riddle," Jamie said with a happy giggle.

Juliette stooped down to their level and met their clear, open gazes. "I am waiting, little redbird," she said to Neil.

"What is higher than a tree?" he asked.

She nodded for Jamie to take his turn. "Now you, little blackbird."

"And what is deeper than the sea?"

Lyon puffed on his cigar, waiting curiously to see if Julie could do it again. He'd questioned Rob about the riddles, demanding to know if his brother had translated the ancient riddlecraft ballad for her. But Rob had interpreted so many old songs and poems for Julie, he honestly couldn't remember.

She rose and moved to the railing to rest her hands on the smooth wood. Gazing out across the white caps, she repeated the riddles softly to herself. Then she snapped her fingers in triumph. "I have it!"

The lads looked up at her with confident grins, certain she'd never be so lucky twice.

"Heaven is higher than a tree," she said, pointing a finger upward. "And hell is deeper than the sea," motioning down below.

"Wow!" Jamie cried. His eyes glowed with admiration.

Disappointed, Neil frowned. "You're right," he admitted glumly.

Over their heads, the two brothers' gazes met in mutual disbelief. Rob shrugged, indicating he was as baffled as Lyon.

Incredulous, Lyon met Julie's sparkling eyes. She awarded him a beatific smile, then turned to the lads.

"And now may I have my dreamcatcher back?" she queried with a teasing lift of her brows.

"Honestly, Miss Elkheart," Neil replied in total sincerity, "we don't have it."

"If you do find it," she said, "please return it, and I will make you each one of your own." She gave the lads an encouraging pat on their shoulders and rejoined the other ladies.

"Haven't you loons been able to locate Miss Elkheart's dreamcatcher yet?" Rob asked his nephews with a frown.

They shook their heads.

"No, Uncle Robbie," Neil answered. "We looked all over our bedroom, but we couldn't find it."

"Couldn't find it," echoed Jamie.

Their tall red-haired uncle eyed them dubiously. "Well, keep searching. I'm sure it will turn up eventually." He suspected the two lads had filched Julie's feathered hoop the night she'd told them bedtime stories in the *sìthein*.

But the laird of Strathlyon knew differently. The dreamcatcher was hidden beneath Lyon's pillow each night and tucked safely away in a drawer the next morning. And he had no intention of returning it.

The pretty trinket was the one thing of Julie's he planned to keep, long after she'd boarded the ship for America. Not that he needed anything to remember her by. The night they'd spent together in the fairy house would remain etched in his memory forever.

But since confiscating the dreamcatcher, he hadn't had one bloody nightmare about the Sudan. In fact, for the past

three nights his dreams had had an almost mystical quality
about them. And they were always of Julie.

Hell, he didn't believe in visions or second sight. That
was just another foolish Highland superstition. But if he
was going to spend the rest of his life without her, he'd
need something to get him through the lonely, endless
nights to come.

Chapter 17

❦ ❦

"**G**len Kildunun is one of the loveliest spots in Scotland," Lady Hester explained, as the two hired carriages came to a halt beside a stand of oaks.

"Rather sad that it's also the site of one of our country's bloodiest massacres," Rob added, with a sympathetic glance at Juliette. "But our history is filled with tragic events. The Highland clans butchered one another with appalling regularity."

"Oh, it *is* very pretty!" Flora exclaimed. "What a pleasant surprise." Her enjoyment in the outing was reflected in her radiant smile. She folded her burgundy parasol and shielded her eyes with a gloved hand as she watched a flock of wild geese fly over.

They'd driven through a narrow rocky pass beneath a high bleak mountain to a scene of magnificent beauty. On one side of the glen rose great, rugged peaks split by craggy ravines. On the other, steep slopes, with forests of pine at the higher elevations, soared to the brilliant blue sky. The floor of the glen was flat and grassy, with a small loch fed by streams and cascading waterfalls. A dirt road wound past the gray-blue waters of the loch. Oak and birch woods covered the nearer hillsides.

As Juliette looked out across the tranquil glen, her pulse began to race. She clutched her bouquet of roses and Queen

Anne's lace tighter, till her hands grew damp inside her lavender kid gloves.

The pastoral scene was so wretchedly familiar.

Lyon and the two boys jumped out of the barouche which had stopped just ahead. "We'll have the drivers pull up under the oaks," he said, coming over to the open landau. He looked at Juliette, and his stern features softened. "If you'd like, I'll walk to the monument with you."

"Yes," she said gratefully. "I would appreciate that."

"Can we come too, Uncle Lyon?" Neil asked.

In spite of his kilt, Jamie clambered up the side of the carriage. "Can we come?"

Lyon's gaze remained on Juliette. "I'll take you lads up to the memorial later," he told them. "I think this time Miss Elkheart would prefer to have some peace and quiet for reflection. She's been wanting to visit Kildunun for quite awhile now."

"You two loons come with me," Rob said with an inviting grin. In honor of their visit to his ancestors' graves that morning, he wore a kilt of the blue and black MacLyon tartan. With his coppery hair, lapis lazuli eyes, and imposing height, he cut a figure that would have turned any lassie's head. "We'll see if we can tickle some trout in the stream," he suggested. "Then we'll sneak down to the loch, and try to spot a black-throated diver in its nest. But you'll have to be very quiet to do that."

"We'll be quiet!" they shouted.

"While you lads explore, Flora and I will direct the coachmen," Lady Hester announced. "There's a lovely burn that cuts through the woods. We'll set our picnic baskets alongside it. After that, we'll bring our floral tributes to the marker."

Lyon lifted Juliette down from the landau, his hands lingering for a moment at her waist. His closeness brought her a renewed awareness of his physical size and strength. He seemed larger than life. His fierce, dominating nature was as inborn as his green eyes and red-amber hair. The big Scotsman combined an intimidating presence with an unconscious assurance that he was meant to be in command.

Shivery vibrations, part fear, part yearning, twanged up and down Juliette's spine. She trembled like a little brown prairie rabbit caught in the thrall of a ferocious mountain lion. When it came to pitting her will against his, she didn't stand a chance. And he knew it.

They walked in silence across the meadow dotted with autumn wildflowers. The tall granite marker, its tapered column piercing the clear sky, stood on the top of a high knoll.

Lyon took her elbow, guiding her up the steep incline. Unlike the other MacLyon males that day, he wore a dark coat and trousers.

"My Grandfather Angus had this memorial erected," he told her. "I've only been here a few times myself. My father brought the three of us to see the gravestone when Rob was scarcely old enough to understand what it was all about."

Juliette tried to conceal the dejection in her voice and failed miserably. "Then your father wanted to be sure you would never forget the treachery of the Danielsons?"

Lyon stopped and turned her to face him. His brows pulled together in displeasure. "You have to realize, Julie, that hatred between warring clans is an integral part of the Highland past. Belligerence and a stubbornness to the death and beyond are deeply embedded in our character. Bitter rivalries lasted for centuries. Innocent people were slaughtered. Women abducted and raped. Children kidnapped and held for ransom. Even now, some clansmen have nothing good to say about their old enemies. No one is more thrawn—more stubborn—than a Highlander."

Juliette turned her head and gazed up at the monument. A terrible sadness pressed on her chest like a weight, making her breathing labored and uneven. "Why was this particular mass slaying considered so unforgivable?"

"Because the MacLyons and the Danielsons had been

allies for as long as anyone could remember. Their betrayal was against all concepts of Highland honor and decency. The massacre had been deliberately planned by the very people whom the MacLyons believed to be their greatest friends. It was considered a crime of murder under trust and regarded by law as an aggravated form of murder, carrying with it the same penalties as treason.''

Juliette longed to have the bitterness of the past reconciled, at least between the two of them. The way it had been on Eilean Danielson. She wished that Lyon would hold her in his arms and comfort her as he had that day. She wanted to ask him why he'd avoided her since the night they'd spent together, why he'd been so cold and aloof. But her Cheyenne pride wouldn't let her.

Lyon took her arm once again, and they continued up the grassy slope to the towering pillar.

A Celtic cross of ancient design decorated the top. At the foot was a bronze plaque, the words inscribed in both Gaelic and English.

> *In memory of the forty-three valiant*
> *MacLyon Highlanders, who, on the sixteenth*
> *of October, 1771, were lured to this glen,*
> *entrapped, and murdered by the Danielson*
> *Fencibles. May the infamous name of*
> *Danielson be forever proscribed.*

Juliette clutched her bouquet, fighting back tears. They'd arrived on the one-hundred-fifteenth anniversary of the massacre. "And so," she said softly, "the Danielsons were hunted down with dogs."

"Aye, bloodhounds. *Coin dhubha*, they're called in Gaelic. Black dogs. Though the Danielsons protested their innocence, eighty-two were hanged, forty-three shot, and another twenty-one died of wounds while being captured. The killing didn't stop until the entire clan had been wiped off the face of the earth." Lyon stared up at the cross, his

features contorted with disgust. "Is it any wonder I'm cynical about our glorious past? There was nothing romantic
about the old Highland way of life, Julie. For centuries, the
virulent feuding soaked this country's soil in blood."

Juliette stooped and laid the flowers at the bottom of the
stone marker. The cool morning breeze ruffled the pink and
white petals, and their sweet perfume swirled around them.
She bowed her head, her words soft and filled with a profound grief. "I am sorry for what my ancestors did in this
place. I hope you can find it in your heart to forgive them."

She wasn't certain whether she spoke to Lyon or to the
men who lay in eternal silence beneath the knoll.

Lyon drew Juliette to her feet. "What was done in this
place has nothing to do with you, lass," he said. "My God,
if there's anyone free of all blame, it's you."

She gazed into his stormy eyes. Her lips trembled, as a
feeling of emptiness washed over her. Tears trickled slowly
down her cheeks, and she wiped them away with her gloved
fingers. Scalding mortification clogged her throat, making
it nearly impossible to speak. Where was her vaunted sto-
icism when she needed it?

"I thought, perhaps, that was why . . . why you didn't
. . . why you can't . . . love me . . ."

He made a low, anguished sound as he drew her closer.
"Don't ever think, Julie, that this place has anything to do
with—"

The distant rumble of horses thundering into the steep
glen cut off his words. Hoofbeats pounded along the narrow
dirt road that wound along the loch, as a group of kilted
horsemen came into view.

Without a word of explanation, Juliette broke free of
Lyon's grasp and started to run down the sloping bank.
Grotesque images flashed through her mind. The fearsome,
ghastly knowledge of what was to be scoured her senses,
knocking the breath from her lungs.

They were coming!

She raced across the meadow, stumbling in the tall grass

and tripping over the hem of her walking skirt. She landed on all fours, and the impact sent pain jolting through her wrists and knees.

"Wait!" Juliette cried. She scrambled to her feet. "Wait! Do not go any farther!"

The soldiers continued to gallop up the road. They wore the blue and black tartan of the MacLyon Highlanders. Their kilts flew about their bare thighs. The plaids on their shoulders sailed out behind them in the wind.

Gasping for air, Juliette reached the side of the dusty roadway. She waved her arms, signaling them to halt. This time, she remembered to call out in Gaelic. "Stop! Please, stop!"

They were completely unaware of her existence. The horsemen never slowed as they raced toward her—and certain death.

From the opposite end of the valley a second group of riders appeared, coming at breakneck speed. Their distinctive regimentals were unmistakable, even from a distance. They wore the lavender and pink tartan of the Danielson Fencibles.

Juliette turned to find the Highlanders almost on top of her. She could see clearly their silver clan badges, with the MacLyon motto, *Duinealachd*, above the lyon rampant, on their blue bonnets. They slowed their pace at the sight of the clansmen they believed to be their friends—relieved, no doubt, to find the crisis over and their help not needed after all.

Not one Highlander readied a musket. Their cartridge pouches dangled unheeded beside their leather sporrans. Pistols stayed holstered in their shoulder-belts. Broadswords and dirks remained sheathed.

Tragically, they greeted the newcomers with shouts of "*Failte!*"

Welcome.

Their leader's long, clubbed hair flew out behind him in a rusty-gold blur. Juliette caught sight of his rough-hewn features, and her lungs constricted in fear. Her hand flew to her throat, as the breath caught high in her chest. For a second, she thought it was Lyon. Then she realized the officer must be Colonel Gilbride MacLyon, heir to the then chief of the clan, Aeneas. She grabbed vainly at the reins as he drew near.

He never looked down.

"It is a trap!" she shouted. "Wait! It is a trap!"

No one paid her the least attention.

The second group of horsemen never slowed. They reached the MacLyon Highlanders charging at full gallop. At the last possible second, their shrill, Gaelic battle-cry pierced the beautiful morning.

"Mac Dubh-shidhe!"

Frantically, Juliette translated the words.

Son of the Black Elf.

The Macfie battle cry!

"Treacherous dogs!" Gilbride MacLyon roared. "What foul trick is this?"

Belatedly, the stunned Highlanders reached for their weapons.

"Stand fast!" they shouted.

Without warning, the Macfies fired their muskets and charged through them with fixed bayonets. Once in close quarters, they stabbed and hacked with broadswords and dirks.

Despite their valorous efforts, the MacLyons were quickly surrounded by the much larger force.

Terrified, Juliette found herself caught in the middle of the battle. All around her, powerful warriors fought at close range.

Horses screamed, reared, and plunged.

Pistol shots rang out.

Men shouted and swore in rage and pain.

The paralyzing din of hand-to-hand combat echoed through the glen.

The two leaders came together with a clang and scrape

of swords. Blood spattered over Juliette. She lunged aside, shaking with fright. A nauseating dizziness assailed her, and the bitter taste of bile choked her. She was so close to the combatants, she could have reached out and touched them.

Fighting desperately, Colonel MacLyon slashed at his foe with his basket-hilted broadsword. He fought valiantly, though the end was inevitable. His opponents enclosed him, cutting him off from his fellow clansmen. They rushed at him from every side with swords and dirks. Hands reached out to pull him from the saddle.

To Juliette's horror, three men in lavender and pink tartan, bound, gagged, and tied to their saddles, were led into the midst of the carnage. She heard the Macfie leader's order to kill them, and the helpless Danielson hostages, eyes huge with terror, were murdered in cold blood. Their executioners cut the ropes and shoved the savaged bodies to the ground to be trampled under the hooves of the frightened horses.

Then the victors methodically slit the throats of the wounded and dying. Sickened at the sight, Juliette staggered and fell. Her stomach heaved. Her breath came in raw, painful gulps. As the jubilant Macfies milled about her, she stared up in horror at the figures depicted on the clan badges pinned to the their bonnets.

A hind being attacked by three wolves.

Juliette looked down in horrified bewilderment at her walking suit. The soft lavender wool was stained with splashes of brilliant crimson. Beside her in the trampled grass lay Colonel Gilbride MacLyon, his throat cut, his body slashed, his leaf-green eyes staring up at the cloudless blue sky.

Juliette screamed and screamed and screamed.

Then blessed darkness overcame her.

"Julie," Lyon called softly. "Julie, wake up." Seated on the grassy bank beside the road, he held her limp form in his arms. His family crowded around them, their eyes wide with concern.

"Is she going to be okay, Uncle Lyon?" Neil asked. He crouched down at her stockinged feet and touched the hem of her skirt, as though to reassure himself she'd soon wake up.

"Forbye," Lady Hester said, patting the lad's tousled hair. "Miss Elkheart is going to be just fine. She may have gotten a wee too much sun, that's all."

Julie's lovely face was drained of color. Her palms were moist and clammy. They'd stripped off her gloves and removed her kid button boots, then eased off the short jacket of her walking suit and opened the ruffled collar of her blouse.

Thinking she may have become overheated, Flora had dipped a silk scarf in the cold burn. For the third time, Lyon smoothed the wet cloth gently over Julie's cheeks and forehead. None of their ministrations had revived her. With each minute she remained unconscious his pulse rate increased, till his heart felt like it would burst from the strain.

Rob knelt on one knee beside his brother, holding Jamie close to keep him calm. "Give her another whiff of the smelling salts," he suggested.

Lyon waved the vial beneath Julie's nose. "Come on, lass," he urged briskly. "Time to wake up."

Relief swept through him as she jerked her head away from the fumes and grimaced in distaste. Her lashes fluttered, and she pushed the vial away with a grumble of contempt. Disoriented, she looked around at the five MacLyons staring at her, then lifted her lids to meet Lyon's worried gaze.

"What happened?" she asked in a croak.

"You fainted, that's all," he told her in a soothing tone. When she tried to sit up, he held her securely in place. "Stay right where you are for a few more minutes," he ordered, "till you get your bearings."

"Oh, Julie," Flora said softly, her eyes filled with compassion. "You frightened us. You cried out and then collapsed. We couldn't bring you round for the longest time."

Lady Hester reached down and patted Julie's hand. "We'll forget about the picnic, my dear, and go back to the boat. We can have our luncheon after you've rested in bed for a bit."

"No, please," Julie said weakly. "I do not want to spoil the morning's outing. I will be fine in a moment." Once again, she tried to rise. Lyon held her tightly in his arms. She gazed up at him entreatingly and placed a trembling hand on his shoulder. "Please do not insist on going back immediately."

"We can stay," he said with a frown, "if you promise to sit in the shade and take it very easy for the rest of the morning. I think you may have been more affected by the visit to the monument than you realize."

"I promise," she said with a wan smile.

They rose to their feet, and Lyon felt her wobble unsteadily beside him. She reached out, catching his sleeve to keep her balance. He swept her up in his arms. As he carried her to one of the blankets that had been spread beneath the oaks, Julie's head drooped against his shoulder, and the wave of protective tenderness that overtook him nearly made him stumble.

"How long was I out?" she asked, when he'd set her on the blanket and crouched down beside her.

Lyon searched her face. She was still pale and drawn. Beads of perspiration dotted her upper lip. Her eyes had a faraway look, the pupils enlarged.

"About eight minutes," he said. "Long enough to scare the bloody hell out of us."

Damn! His heartbeat still hadn't returned to normal.

Julie ran a shaky hand over her forehead and exhaled a long, ragged breath. She stared down at the front of her skirt with a look of horror. Smoothing her shaky fingers over the wool fabric, she inspected the folds as though looking for a stain of grass or a smudge of dirt.

"I don't think you did any permanent damage to your pretty outfit," he said. "Fortunately, you landed in the soft grass rather than on the packed dirt of the roadway."

He studied her, as an unsettling feeling nudged him. It wasn't like Julie to fuss over her clothes. And why had she run away from him in the first place? She'd torn down that slope like she was being chased by demons.

"What was Clan Danielson's war cry?" she asked in a distant tone.

Her odd question sent a chill snaking through him. He thrust his hand in front of her face. "Julie, how many fingers am I holding up."

"Naha."

"How many?" he asked, more loudly than he'd intended.

She waved a hand to calm him. "I meant to say three. I guess I am a little more confused than I thought."

"That's it. We're going back to the boat." He glanced over his shoulder, ready to call Rob and the drivers.

She clutched his hand in both of hers. "Wait. Please. I need to talk to you about what just happened to me. But I need to talk to you alone." Tears welled up in her beautiful eyes. The sight of them ripped a hole in his heart.

"Very well," he agreed. "I'll speak to the others. The lads are hungry, so they can eat lunch while you and I talk. But if I'm not satisfied that you're coherent, princess, we're going back to the boat at once, and I'm having a doctor look at you. Period."

Chapter 18

Lyon glanced around the glen, so idyllic in its magnificent setting. He'd always hated the damn place.

After he explained to the family that Julie needed some quiet time alone, he returned with a cup of tea and a pastry.

She sipped the hot liquid gratefully, then nibbled on the mutton pie. She looked at him in expectation. "Will you have something to eat?"

He shook his head, too worried to even consider it. He waited impatiently for her to finish, then propped a coach pillow against the tree trunk and helped her sit back. The tea had revived her. Her vivid coloring had returned, and her eyes were clear, the pupils normal.

"Well," he said abruptly, as he sank down beside her, "I'm waiting."

Juliette pleated and repleated a fold of her skirt as she glanced at the large Scotsman seated beside her. His rugged features emanated a fierce determination. Was there ever such a strong-willed man? Thrawn, he'd called it. *Hesc!* He was thrawn to the bone.

"I did not come to Scotland solely to trace my forebears," she began.

He cleared his throat and folded his arms across his chest, but he didn't interrupt.

"That was one of the reasons," she hastened to explain, "but not the most important."

"I see. Go on."

She steepled her hands and brought her fingertips to her lips, searching for the right words. In order to fully describe what had just happened to her, she might have to admit that she understood Gaelic. He'd be furious at her for keeping it secret, especially considering the shockingly erotic things he'd said to her in that tongue. But there might be no other way to convince him.

"I am what your people call fey," she said at last. "I have the second sight." She looked down at her lap, unable to meet his incredulous gaze. "My people consider them visions and believe they are sent to a favored few by the Maiyun—the Great Powers above, who guide us on our journey through life. My visions often come in the form of dreams. Both my father and my sister share with me the ability to interpret them."

He made a scoffing sound, part snort and part cough.

Juliette pursed her lips. A nervous tremor skittered across her flushed skin. She cautiously raised her lids and met his wintry eyes. "I knew this would not be easy. That was why I avoided discussing the topic with you."

"So you had a dream about the Highlands and thought it'd be a pretty place to visit," he drawled. "That's really not such an unusual thing."

Juliette scrambled to her feet, and Lyon rose to tower over her. Bracing her hand on the tree, she gazed out across the glen. She lifted her shoulders and released a long, apprehensive sigh. She wanted him to believe her with a heartbreaking desperation that was all the more wretched for its sheer unlikelihood. She could tell by his rigid posture, by the muscle twitching in his clenched jaw, that Lyon would never accept what she was about to tell him.

"The Cheyenne believe that what happens in a place is always happening there," she said. "Time and space are irrelevant. I saw Glen Kildunun long before I ever left my homeland. I saw the battle between the MacLyon Highlanders and the men in the lavender and pink plaids, exactly the way it occurred. But in my vision, I saw it all from the hillside over there.

"Today," she continued in a quavering voice, "I was there in the midst of the battle. I saw it up close, as it was happening."

"Bloody hell! I don't believe this!" He glared down at her with a ferocious scowl, his gaze incredulous.

She turned to him and clutched his arm, and the sinewy muscles tightened beneath her grasp. "Believe it," she implored. Tears burned her eyes, and she quickly brushed them away with a shaky hand. "The spirits of my ancestors are calling out to me. And now I understand why. I did not know before, but now I realize why they brought me to Scotland."

Lyon clasped her shoulders, trying to calm her, trying to calm himself. "Julie, I'm sure you believe what you're saying, because I know you couldn't lie. What you experienced was nothing more than a vivid dream while you were unconscious. There's no way in hell you'll ever convince me there's such a thing as a vision. Or the second sight."

"Then you will not help me?"

"Help you what?"

"Prove what really happened that day. Prove that the Danielsons, as well as the MacLyons, were innocent victims of that terrible slaughter."

Lyon stared at Julie in dismay. Tears streamed down her cheeks. Her eyes were wide and beseeching. His heart skidded to a halt.

He took her in his arms and kissed the top of her head. He understood her heartache. She was so abjectly ashamed of her forebears that she wanted, somehow, to clear their names. An impossible task, for the truth, whatever it was, lay buried deep in the past. He'd give anything to lift the burden of disillusionment from her shoulders. But he couldn't pretend to believe her fairy tale of visions, or battles which continued to happen again and again, regardless of time and space.

He drew back and chucked her lightly under the chin, then wiped the tears from her cheeks with his thumbs. "Forget this damn place," he said softly. "Forget we ever came here. No one, absolutely no one, blames you, Julie. If you don't believe anything else I've ever said, believe that."

Juliette threw back her shoulders and met his gaze with steadfast resolve. "I can never forget what happened here," she stated in a low, firm tone. "And I am sorry to have to tell you this, MacLyon, but I must break my promise. I will not be leaving immediately upon our return to Strathlyon. If I cannot remain at the castle, I will stay with Keir and Annie in Strathbardine."

"The hell you will."

He stepped back as though her touch burned him. He swore in Gaelic, a prolific string of oaths that brought a flush to her cheeks.

From the other picnic blanket, his family looked up in shock. Neil and Jamie clambered to their feet, looks of profound awe on their cherubic faces.

Lyon pivoted on his heel and stalked away. "Hurry up," he snapped at the coachmen, lounging beside the brougham. "Get this damn stuff picked up and packed in the baskets. We're leaving."

Lady Hester hurried over to Juliette, her eyes filled with concern. "What is the trouble, child?"

"May I stay with you at Strathlyon a while longer?" Juliette pleaded, taking the dowager's outstretched hands.

"Of course," Lady Hester immediately replied. She leaned closer and bussed Juliette's cheek. "You may stay all winter, *a chiall mo chridhe*," she said with a soft chuckle. "In fact, why not remain with us for the rest of your life?"

Juliette smiled through her tears. Her lower lip trembled, and she pressed her fingertips to her mouth.

"Thank you," she said on a broken laugh. "But I think that might be pushing my luck a wee bit."

At that moment the brilliant blue sky grew dark, as sudden storm clouds swept over the glen. Before they could get the baskets packed, rain poured down on the picnickers, drenching them. Lightning struck the loch, the thunder booming against the hillsides. The earth shook beneath their feet.

"What's happening to the weather?" Rob shouted to his brother, as they struggled to raise the landau's top. "This is the third thunderstorm in three weeks."

Lyon glanced across the glen. A giant bolt struck the ground near the base of the monument, bathing the gray stone column in an eerie glow.

"How the hell should I know?" he snarled. "Maybe Miss Elkheart brought the thunder and lightning with her from Canada."

The *Elfin Queen* chugged southward, leaving the rain behind. The late afternoon sun, a great orange globe in a red-streaked sky, was sinking behind the islands of the Outer Hebrides.

On the main deck, Juliette stood at the railing with Neil and Jamie, keeping watch for seals. Rob and Lyon were in the gentlemen's social hall on the promenade deck, smoking cigars, drinking whisky, and playing cards. And swearing brilliantly in Gaelic, too, no doubt. Lady Hester and Flora had retired to the library on the second deck to read the magazines on ladies' fashions.

Like the boys, Juliette was too restless to go inside and sit down. The cool breeze wafting against her face soothed her raw nerves, and the chattering youngsters demanded her constant attention, keeping her from dwelling on the unhappiness that perched on her shoulder like a great horned owl.

At supper in the luxurious dining room, Lyon had barely spoken. The rest of the family tried to make up for his icy demeanor with sparkling conversation. By then, Juliette had regained her composure. Though dying inside by inches, she returned Rob's lively repartee, answered Neil and Jamie's endless questions, and gossiped amiably with the two other ladies. Not for a thousand-elk-tooth dress would a Cheyenne warrior-woman quail in the face of such blatant hostility.

"You like music, don't you, Miss Elkheart?" Neil asked, putting an end to her pensive reverie.

"Very much."

"And you like to dance," added Jamie with all the confidence of a five-year-old.

"I do, Hehen." She knew the reason for their curiosity. Dancing was a favorite pastime of fairies.

"We saw you dancing with Uncle Lyon at Dr. Mac-Dougall's wedding," Neil said. "He laughed right out loud."

His feet braced on the bottom rail, Jamie clutched the top one in both small hands and bounced up and down in carefree abandon.

"Uncle Lyon hasn't danced in a long, long time," he confided. "And he's hardly laughed at all, since he came back from the Sudan."

Not knowing how to answer, Juliette waited for the next unpredictable comment.

"Don't worry that he's so angry at you now." Neil moved closer, brushing against her arm like a friendly puppy. "Uncle Lyon watches you when you're not looking, and I can tell he still likes you a lot."

"Thank you for your encouragement, Maevess," she replied with a chuckle.

Neil cocked his head to one side, considering her thoughtfully. "If you got mad at us, you wouldn't try to take Uncle Lyon back home with you, would you, Miss Elkheart?"

Juliette burst into laughter. "I do not know how I could do that! Unless I put him in my pocket."

The two boys stared at her in solemn contemplation. It

was clear from their worried gazes that they'd taken her literally.

Jamie's shoulders slumped. "Then we'd never get to see him again."

She put her arms around the boys' shoulders and drew them close. "I promise I would never—"

Her words were cut off by a mighty explosion. The steamboat rocked and shuddered, and the force of the blast lifted the three of them off their feet and hurled them into the frigid water.

Juliette automatically reached for the boys as she was propelled beneath the surface. She caught Jamie's collar and kicked her way back up to the top, where she frantically looked around for Neil.

His head popped up nearby. He sputtered and tossed his thick red mane like a dog shaking off water.

"Can you swim?" she called over the slapping of the waves.

"Aye! So can Jamie."

But the little boy hung limp in her grasp. "He's unconscious," she cried. "Stay close beside me, Redbird. They'll find us easier if we're all together."

She struggled to tread water with one arm. Her petticoats clung in a heavy mass around her legs. Unable to discard her shoes while holding onto Jamie, she fought desperately to stay afloat.

"Whatever happens," she told Neil between gasps of air, "do not try to help me or your brother. Just keep kicking. And shout for help, if you have the strength."

The ear-splitting boom echoed through the trembling paddle wheeler. Windows had burst, sending shards of glass flying everywhere, and pieces of wood shot through the air like shrapnel. The whistle screamed, notifying nearby ships of the disaster.

Lyon jumped up from the card table. *One of the boilers had exploded.*

Ice flowed through his veins, freezing his soul. Juliette and the lads had been near the prow the last time he'd seen them. He raced out of the hall to the promenade railing, Rob following right behind.

Smoke billowed up from below. The captain hurried from the pilothouse above, shouting orders. Pounding feet crisscrossed the deck as the crew fought to bring the calamity under control. The side-wheeler glided soundlessly, no longer under power, while the frantic shouts of the engineers fighting the blaze in the boiler room carried through the stricken vessel.

"Man overboard!" a crewman hollered.

Lyon jerked off his coat as his gaze swept over the dark water. The reflection of the setting sun made it almost impossible to discern anything on the moving surface. Together, he and Rob ran the entire length of the port side, searching for a bobbing head or a piece of clothing. Then they started down the starboard side.

From the second deck, Flora screamed in terror. "My babies! Where are my babies!"

Lyon clenched the rail with both hands as he searched the water. He forced himself to stay calm and ignore the heart-jolting fear that pumped through him, making him want to spring instantly into action, any action. It'd be foolish to leap in the water and end up on the wrong side of the boat, too far away to be of any help.

God in Heaven, where were they?

With a thrill of joy he spotted the three of them, holding onto a piece of the main deck's white railing. "There!" he called to Rob, as he pointed. "Over there!"

The two brothers dove from the promenade deck, slicing the surface of the loch side by side. In moments, Rob had Neil safely in his grip. Lyon closed his arm around Julie, who was holding tightly to Jamie's limp body.

The crew tossed ring buoys attached to lifelines and pulled them safely to the side of the paddle wheeler, where they lifted them aboard. Julie, still clutching Jamie, sank to the deck in a sprawl of heavy, water-logged clothing.

"They're freezing," Rob said, holding a shivering, white-faced Neil in his arms.

Lyon shouted for blankets as he pried Jamie's shirt from Julie's stiff blue fingers. She was so cold, she could barely let go of the wet material. And far too exhausted to speak.

He bared his teeth in sheer rage. If the accident had been caused by some crew member's carelessness, he'd rip the bloody bastard's heart out.

A crew hand scooped Jamie's unconscious form up in his brawny, tattooed arms, looking to Lyon for further instructions. Blood trickled from a cut on the lad's forehead, and his small, still face was ashen. But his breathing was steady and true.

"Take them to the ladies' saloon," Lyon ordered. "And get a fire started in there immediately."

Rob carried Neil, the burly seaman carried Jamie, while Lyon lifted Julie up in his arms. Other hands tossed blankets over the three still forms, and they moved quickly down the passageway.

Once inside, Lady Hester, with Lyon's help, removed Julie's soaked clothing in the privacy of the saloon's dressing room. Julie was too dazed to protest, and his grandmother was far too practical to quibble at Lyon seeing their guest's bare, shivering body. They slipped a robe on her, wrapped a thick towel around her wet hair, and then enveloped her in a warm comforter.

Lyon placed Julie on a settee near the blazing iron stove in the center of the saloon, then checked on his nephews. The lads had been stripped, right where they lay on the sofas by the fire, and bundled snugly in thick quilted blankets. Flora hovered over them, but though she was pale with fright, she remained in control of her volatile emotions. Lyon nodded to her in reassurance, and she offered a wobbly smile in return.

By now, Jamie was conscious. He'd apparently been struck by the broken railing as he flew over it. Lyon inspected the cut, then sank back on his haunches and grinned at his nephew. "Nice work, sailor. You're not even going to need stitches."

Lifting his heavy lids, Jamie smiled weakly. "I know."

"Miss Elkheart s-saved us," Neil announced with total conviction. His teeth chattered as he talked. "While we were . . . h-hanging onto the r-railing, she . . . s-sang us a strong-heart song in her m-magic language. She . . . p-promised it would w-work and it did."

Tears flooded Flora's distraught eyes. "What would have happened to them without her?" she whispered in horror.

A steward brought hot tea on a silver tray, along with jam and buns for the accident victims.

Lyon rose to his feet and moved to his brother's side. "I need to check with the captain and see how badly the crew-men in the boiler room were injured. They took the worst of it. And I must assess the extent of the damage. You get out of those wet clothes and take charge in here."

Rob jerked his head, signaling agreement.

Lyon turned to Julie. Delayed shock at what might have happened tightened his throat. His closed his eyes for an instant and swallowed painfully, then met her gaze. Co-cooned in the enormous down quilt, she watched him with solemn eyes.

"Thank God you knew how to swim," he said, his voice harsh with suppressed emotion.

There was so much more he wanted to tell her. But he was afraid if he tried, it would all come out in a mangled, humiliating rush. He clenched his teeth instead.

A faint smile skipped across her pale lips. "All Chey-enne girls swim like beavers," she said wearily, "but usu-ally we do not jump into the water wearing petticoats and button shoes. Thank Maheo, you came to our rescue when you did. We could not have lasted much longer."

Lyon turned with a scowl and left the saloon.

Dammit. This was the second time he'd had to blink back tears.

What the hell was happening to him?

Chapter 19

"I didn't put out good money for a string of failures, you ignorant bastards." Hamish Macfie glared at the pair of imbeciles. "You told me the plan was foolproof. The whole damn family was supposed to go up in a blaze of pyrotechnics that'd be seen all the way to Inverness!"

Archie Syme kicked a stone across the dirt floor of the abandoned broch. "Dinna blame me," he said with a sullen glance at his swarthy cohort. "Brodie, here, claimed he kent all about steam engines."

Grig Brodie shoved his stringy black hair out of his eyes and fingered the bandage that covered his cheek. "Dammit, man, I canna figure out what went bad. The force of them two high-pressure beauties explodin' at the same time should've blown 'em halfway to kingdom come. It's the devil's own luck, that's what I call it. I nearly froze my balls off, swimmin' to the rowboat. And with half my damn face skinned off, too."

"Whatever you did, you did it wrong," Hamish snarled.

He had taken a huge chance, meeting the two Glasgow men so close to Strathbardine. He'd pulled his horse inside the gloom of the circular stone tower. Windowless, it rose nearly fifty feet in height. Stone stairs led up to what had once been wooden galleries. The ancient fortress was a relic from Scotland's past, when sea raiders were the scourge of the coastal waters.

Ironically, Dubhgall Broch stood on MacLyon land. Though no one ever came here as a rule, there was always a chance someone would see them coming or going. In the western Highlands, strangers would always be noticed and talked about.

"What do ye want us to do now, laird?" Syme asked. He jammed his hands in his pockets and hunched his bony shoulders. His eyes were the color of brackish water, his brows and hair the hue of moldy straw. In the gloom, his long, pock-marked face resembled a goblin's mask.

"I want you to kill them," Hamish said. "Every last bloody one of them."

"Christ! The old lady, too?" Syme frowned uneasily. "I never killed a woman before. I mean not with me own twa hands." He held up his thin fingers and stared in alarm, as though seeing them for the first time.

"Who gives a bloody damn about the women?" Hamish shouted. "I don't care if they live or die. But I want every last MacLyon male planted in his grave."

"Whatever ye say, Macfie." The puckered scar below Brodie's bristly left brow stood out in grisly detail. He fisted his hands and confidently flexed his muscles beneath his shirt. It was clear he thought Hamish was bonkers, but he'd do it. For enough money, Grig Brodie would garrote his own granny.

"Howanever, I dinna think we should try to get them all at the same time," Syme said with a dissatisfied grimace. "Too risky."

"Don't think," Hamish told him. "I'll do the thinking. Now, I want you two to go back to Glasgow and hire a couple more men."

"We dinna need more men just yet," Brodie said. "And we dinna need to get all the MacLyons at once. We'll start with the wee laddies first. They'll make easy pickings. Then we'll kill the younger brother next."

Hamish smiled as he met Brodie's deep-set black eyes. "I'd like that. I'd like The MacLyon to know, at the moment of his death, that his line dies out with him.'' He put up a hand to caution them. ''But it has to look like an accident. Otherwise, he'll never rest until he finds the killers. And once he's on to what's happening, he'll be impossible to catch unawares.''

Brodie touched his forehead with a dirty finger in mock salute. ''Leave it to me, laird,'' he said. ''I'll take care of the halflins, while Syme goes to Glasgow for more men.''

''This time, don't fail.'' Hamish jerked his head toward the open doorway. ''You two go first. And make damn sure nobody sees you.''

After they'd left, Hamish stood at the arched stone entrance and waited to be certain it was safe. The broch had been built on a bluff overlooking the sea loch. Below, the sleepy fishing village of Strathbardine lay nestled, protected by the calm bay.

His hatred for the chief of Clan MacLyon seethed and boiled inside him. Hamish couldn't remember a time when he'd not disliked the pompous ass. With his royal lineage and his unbelievable wealth, MacLyon had always thought himself better than anyone else.

When Hamish had discovered the old letters in his collection of documents and learned how close his own great-grandfather had come to erasing the MacLyon chiefship from the world, he'd nearly laughed himself silly. But the idea of murdering MacLyon hadn't occurred until his brother Malcolm had killed himself in Cairo, and their mother died of the shock.

Hamish didn't have to ask whose fault that was. The military tribunal had scarcely convened when his brother took the craven's way out. He'd written to Hamish the night before he shot himself, whining that it wasn't his fault an entire battalion—including Major James MacLyon—had been lost to the Mahdi. But he knew Colonel Lord Lyon MacLyon blamed him and would offer scathing testimony against him in the inquiry. Malcom feared he'd be forced to resign in disgrace, or at the very least his future career in the army would be irrevocably blighted.

What actually happened in that hellhole in the Sudan, Hamish didn't know. And he didn't care. All he knew was that the Macfie chiefship would die with him. There wouldn't even be an heir in the female line, for Georgiana had refused every possible suitor Hamish had suggested. Though she'd never admit it, he knew she was too humiliated by her brother's suicide to face the prospect of having a gentleman reject her.

Since Malcolm's death, Hamish had concealed his loathing for MacLyon, even from his sister. But the galling shame heaped upon the entire clan by the revelation that General Malcom Macfie had died at his own hands, a weak, vacillating coward, would never be forgiven or forgotten.

Hamish led his horse through the small doorway and climbed into the saddle. He couldn't bring his mother or his brother back. He couldn't force Georgiana to marry again, let alone produce an heir at her age. But he could have his revenge on the man responsible.

Juliette rode slowly back from Ned Gibb's croft, deep in thought. It had been four days since the steamboat accident. She'd received a new vision from the Maiyun last night. At least, she thought it was a vision. She dreamed of seeing two lambs lying dead beside a tiny lochan. In her dream, she'd come upon their small bodies and wept in anger and frustration. Their shepherd had put his arm around her shoulder and told her sadly that they'd been poisoned.

Upon rising, she'd immediately taken Voxpenonoma and galloped to Ned's croft, nestled in the hills near Strathlyon Castle. She'd often visited the old shepherd on her morning rides with Rob and the boys.

When she told the small, wizened man that she had the second sight, he never doubted her for a moment. "Och, lassie, if ye think something might be wrong with my sheep, let's have a wee look."

They'd checked every one of the woolly animals in his care. As a precaution, Ned even tasted the water in the nearby burn.

"I guess I must have been mistaken," she admitted in bewilderment.

Ned shoved his knitted tam back and scratched his bald head. "The flock's healthy, God be thankit. Ye can see, lass, the lambs born last spring are strong and bonny."

They'd smiled as they watched the young sheep frisking and bounding through the heather. There had been nothing about the peaceful scene that seemed to relate to her strange, sad dream.

She wondered if her failure to correctly interpret the vision was because of her missing dreamcatcher. She'd helped Neil and Jamie search every inch of their bedroom, with no results. The boys seemed so sincere, she couldn't believe they were purposely concealing it from her.

As she returned to the castle, she smiled at the memory of their asking her the fairy riddles. She knew the answers because she'd studied the ancient riddlecraft ballad while learning Gaelic. Like the boys, she also knew fairies were reputed to have magic combs, which they used to groom their unbelievably long hair. Now her comb and brush were missing, too. In her sweet-natured way, Flora had presented her houseguest with a new set to replace them.

When Juliette reached Strathlyon Glen she dismounted and walked White Thunder slowly through the birch woods, remembering the afternoon of the shooting exhibition there. The dry autumn leaves crunched beneath her feet, a reminder of how quickly the days had passed since she'd first arrived.

Since the explosion on the *Elfin Queen*, there'd been no mention of her leaving the castle. Lyon's anger had seemed to evaporate. In its place came a brooding watchfulness. He never sought her out in private, never came to her bedroom, as she hoped and prayed he would. And he avoided all mention of Glen Kildunun and her vision of the battle.

She longed to talk to him about what she'd experienced that day. The events seemed to indicate that the men who'd slaughtered the MacLyon Highlanders were not Danielsons. But Lyon's steadfast refusal to believe in the second sight kept her from discussing it with him.

She stopped beside a stream while the sweet, well-behaved mare took a drink of the cold water that rippled over the stones. Since returning from Kildunun, Juliette had searched the library at the castle for any mention of Clan Macfie.

The Macfies had arrived in the Strathshire area shortly after the uprising for Bonny Prince Charlie in the middle of the last century. Only after the Kildunun massacre and the forfeiture of the Danielson lands had their chief become a wealthy, propertied laird. Had Lyon's great-grandfather not sired a son in his old age, the MacLyon chiefship would have died out. In one fell swoop, the two most powerful clans in Strathshire, the MacLyons and the Danielsons, would have been leaderless—leaving the Macfies to fill the vacuum. But that didn't prove they'd planned and perpetrated the mass murder.

Juliette thought about visiting Hamish Macfie's manor house again and asking if she could look through his collection of papers. If he did possess incriminating evidence against his own ancestors, though, he'd never willingly show it to her. And the documents must surely be kept under lock and key.

Hamish was inordinately proud of his heritage. At the Scottish National Society meetings she'd attended, he'd claimed he wanted to reestablish the former glory of the Highland clans. She suspected it was his own clan he was thinking of.

The sound of voices interrupted her meandering thoughts. At the far end of the grassy glen, a tinker had pulled up his cart to rest. The bucolic sight had become familiar since her arrival in the Highlands. Tinkers, some with their families, wandered the country roads, selling everything from bootlaces to brooms. They called at the crofts along the way, offering combs, pots and pans, boxes of matches, and small tins of tea.

Neil and Jamie, along with Dunbar and Tiree, had discovered the fellow's wagon. They crowded close to him, pestering the thick-set stranger with eager questions. When the black-haired tinker looked up and saw her watching them, he hastily climbed up on his rackety cart and drove off, disappearing in the dense stand of trees. Afraid to be accused of trespassing, no doubt.

Juliette smiled at the youngsters' boundless energy. The boys and dogs frisked about, jumping and playing like Ned's sturdy young sheep.

Lambs.

A horrible suspicion brought a mind-numbing dread.

An icy ribbon of panic curled through her belly.

Two little lambs.

Juliette mounted White Thunder and urged the dainty Arabian into a gallop. The moment she reached the boys, she slid out of the saddle.

"Jamie! Neil!" she called. "Did that man give you anything to eat?"

They nodded happily.

"Sweets," Jamie said with a bright smile.

"Did you eat any of it?"

"Not yet," he replied. He looked at the bag of candy in his hand and wrinkled his nose. "I'm still full of porridge from breakfast."

"Do not eat any, Jamie!" she cried. "Do not even put your hands near your mouth."

She looked at Neil, and he lifted his shoulders in perplexed confirmation. "I had a piece."

"Come here quickly, Maevess." She put her arm around his shoulders, drew him tight against her side, and took his chin in her hand. "You may have been poisoned," she warned him. "I have to make you throw up the candy."

She didn't give him a chance to argue or tighten his jaw

in resistance. Inserting her finger down his throat, she forced him to gag reflexively. Neil vomited onto the grass at their feet.

He blinked as tears streamed down his cheeks. "I didn't eat all that much," he said in fright. "But I gave some to Dunbar and Tiree."

"Ahahe!"

She couldn't take time for the deerhounds now. Once again she made Neil gag and vomit, until she was sure there was nothing more he could regurgitate. "We have to get you home," she said. "Right away."

She quickly mounted, pulled Neil up in front of her, and helped Jamie scramble up behind. Then she raced up the slope, through the terraced gardens to the castle, with the two large deerhounds loping behind.

Juliette came into the children's room in the middle of the night. Lyon sat in a chair by Neil's bed, his chin propped on his hand, watching his nephew. The other bed was empty. Jamie was sleeping with his mother in the big, canopied four-poster in her suite.

The Lion rose to his feet, rumpled and disheveled. His shirt collar lay open, partially revealing the mat of rusty-gold chest hair that matched the stubble on his jaw. He'd rolled his sleeves up and removed his boots.

"You should be sound asleep," he told her with quiet gravity. "You must be exhausted."

She crossed the rug to stand beside him, keeping her words low so as not to disturb the slumbering child. "I could not fall asleep, even if I tried. Flora needs to stay with Jamie, in case he wakes up and is frightened. But I should be here."

She leaned down and placed a hand on Neil's forehead. He was cool to the touch and appeared to be resting peacefully, but the ravages of the poisoning had left their mark. His small face was chalk white, with purplish circles under his sunken eyes. The thick red hair, soaked and darkened with perspiration, lay plastered against his head.

"Rob and Nana left not long ago," Lyon said softly. "I told them to get some rest. Keir assured us we've done everything that can be done. All we can do now is wait."

Juliette sank wearily on the edge of the mattress beside Neil. "Yes, it is in the hands of Maxemaheo, the All-father," she whispered.

Lyon sat back down in the chair. The anxiety and dread on his haggard face made her spirit weep. She'd never imagined she could love anyone so much. This strong, abrupt, cynical man had shown such tenderness, such immeasurable compassion in the last twelve hours that her heart ached at the thought.

It had been a harrowing day.

Lyon and Rob had both been gone when she and the boys arrived back at the castle. It was harvest time, and they were supervising the farm hands bringing in the crops.

Lady Hester had sent a servant to fetch Dr. MacDougall and another to find her grandsons in the hay fields. While waiting for Keir, Juliette gave Neil a mixture of mustard and water as an emetic, hoping to flush out his stomach completely.

Despite her terror, Flora had remained calm and helpful throughout the crisis. She'd comforted Jamie, holding him in her arms as she watched Juliette and Nana minister to Neil.

When Keir arrived, he'd examined the bags of sweets. "The mint balls and jujubes appear to have been dusted with arsenious acid," he told them in a shocked voice. His bluff, amiable features grew dark with wrath. "Arsenic is a white, tasteless powder resembling confectionery sugar. It's the commonest poison used for a homicide."

He'd washed out his small patient's stomach by means of a funnel and tube. Through the morning, Neil suffered from diarrhea and agonizing abdominal cramps. With Juliette's assistance, the doctor had cleansed the colon with a warm saline solution and administered an injection of morphia for the pain.

Before noon, Lyon and Rob, dressed in dusty work clothes, rushed into the youngsters' bedroom. From that moment, neither uncle left their nephew's side.

The family, not the servants, attended to the boy's every need. With the help of Juliette and Lady Hester, the men changed soiled bed linens, emptied chamber pots, and filled water basins. They took turns washing Neil down and giving him water for his terrible thirst.

And they'd prayed.

In the quiet room, the only sound was the crackle of logs in the fireplace. Lyon studied Julie in the flickering light. A flowing ivory dressing robe, with ruffles at neck and wrists, covered her all the way to the toes of her satin slippers. Her lustrous hair flowed free to her waist. She looked like a sloe-eyed angel as she bent over Neil and pushed the heavy lock of damp hair from his ashen forehead.

A very weary angel.

The loving concern etched on her tired features touched Lyon more deeply than her ethereal beauty. She'd been a pillar of strength during the entire day, never leaving Neil's bedside, never showing fear, never once losing her composure. Her quiet fortitude had acted like a balm on the child's mother, keeping Flora quiet and rational.

For the first time, Lyon realized fully the extent of the change in his flighty sister-in-law since Julie had arrived at Strathlyon. Flora's newfound confidence and poise seemed a small miracle.

There was no doubt Neil had been poisoned. Dunbar and Tiree had both died in agonizing pain in less than three hours, despite all attempts of the stable hands to save them. The two lads would be heartbroken when they learned of the tragedy.

"How did you know?" he asked Julie softly.

She turned from the sleeping child. For what seemed like

an eternity, she met Lyon's gaze with unblinking calm. "I saw it in a vision," she answered at last.

He didn't know what to say. Awe shivered through him, as though the heavens had suddenly opened up and bathed her in a circle of iridescent light. She glowed like a candle flame before his eyes, pure and radiant.

His practical mind denied the possibility of visions.

Yet how could she have known otherwise?

His words came hoarse and thick with incredulity. "You saw Neil being poisoned in a dream?"

She folded her hands in her lap in that serene, other-worldly way of hers. "No, I saw two little lambs. I rode out to Ned Gibb's croft early this morning, thinking his sheep were in danger. But that proved to be wrong. On my return, I saw the tinker talking with the children. At the sight of Neil and Jamie, I realized the meaning of my vision. My visions are often symbolic. Sometimes it is difficult to be sure I have interpreted the dream correctly."

Lyon leaned forward in his chair and took her hands. He studied the delicate bones, the tapering fingers, the small oval nails. Next to hers, his own looked like the big, rough hands of a blacksmith.

She seemed so tiny beside him, and yet her courage and generosity were boundless. Before he'd met her, his bitter heart had devoured itself. Her goodness, her sensitivity, her gentleness now filled his empty, hollowed-out heart with hope. If she believed in the second sight, maybe . . . just maybe, it was possible.

"I sent men to look for the missing drummer and his wagon," he said. "So far, neither has been found."

Juliette realized what Lyon had purposely left unsaid. He didn't put any credence in her gift of prophecy, but he was willing to go along with the idea at the moment, rather than upset her. They were both emotionally and physically exhausted by the day's ordeal. And they had the long night ahead of them before Neil was completely out of danger. Everything would depend on how much arsenic had re-

mained in the child's system. Both boys had eaten a sub-
stantial breakfast that morning. That, thankfully, was why
they hadn't gorged on the treats immediately. Dr. Mac-
Dougall explained that the presence of food in Neil's stomach would also delay the action of the poison. With
Juliette's quick intervention, it was possible that all he'd
suffer was the irritant effect on his stomach and intestines.
There was a good chance the heart, kidneys, and other or-
gans would not be affected.

They would know in the hours to come.

"There was something strangely familiar about the tinker," she said pensively, "although I was too far away to
see his face. I cannot recall when or where, but I am sure
I have seen the man before."

Lyon squeezed her fingers. "In Strathbardine?"

"I do not think so."

"On the *Elfin Queen*?" he suggested. "We lost a crewman in the boiler explosion. A new hand, who'd hired on
just the day before. He was blown overboard and never
found. We assumed he'd been drowned."

She bowed her head, frustrated that she couldn't remember. "I am not sure. It is possible."

"From now on," Lyon said, "I don't want any member
of my family left alone. And that includes you, lass. First
the fire at the lighthouse, then the explosion on the paddle
wheeler, and now this. They can't be explained away as
just a series of unlucky accidents."

"I will be very careful," she promised, keeping her gaze
fastened on his strong, steady hands. She didn't promise,
however, not to go anywhere alone.

This was not the time to tell Lyon of her suspicions about
Clan Macfie. Compared to the life of a small boy, the cause
of a hundred-year-old battle seemed very unimportant. But
once she was certain that Neil was completely recovered,
she intended to do a little snooping in the manor home of
Laird Hamish Macfie.

Lyon brought her fingers to his lips and kissed them tenderly. "Thank you, Juliette Evening Star," he said, the timbre of his deep, quiet voice enveloping her. "Once again, I am in your debt. A debt far greater than I could ever repay."

She raised her lids and met his gaze. His eyes shimmered with a naked yearning that mirrored her own. She felt the need within him reach out and caress her, enfolding her in its warmth like the rays of the sun on the prairie grass.

"Do not be foolish," she replied in a husky whisper. "You must know how much I love Neil and Jamie."

Chapter 20

❧◦◦❧

Lyon stooped to put another log on the fire just as Rob came into the room shortly before dawn. Julie had fallen asleep at the foot of Neil's bed, and Lyon had covered her with Jamie's quilted comforter.

"How's Neil?" Rob asked.

"He's fine," Lyon said, getting to his feet. "His breathing has been steady and even all night. He's going to make it."

"Thank God," Rob said hoarsely. "That was a close one."

The two brothers put their arms around each other in relief and thanksgiving. Then Rob turned to look down at the lad's still figure. "Who'd do such a black-hearted thing to an innocent child?"

"I wish to God I knew." Lyon rubbed the stiff muscles in his left arm in an abstracted attempt to ease the pain. "I've spent the entire night trying to figure it out. Hell, I've made enemies in my life. What man doesn't? But who would hate me enough to try to harm my family?"

"Only a maniac would be capable of it."

"Julie thought there was something familiar about the tinker, but she couldn't recall where she'd seen him. We'll find him, though. You can't hide a cart that size for long." Lyon clenched his fists, white-hot rage burning inside him.

"When we do find that cold-blooded bastard, I'm going to tear him to pieces with my bare hands."

"You go on to bed now," Rob said, clasping Lyon's shoulder in brotherly affection. "Get some sleep. You look like hell."

"Thanks," Lyon replied with a wry grin. He pushed the comforter aside and scooped Julie up in his arms. She stirred, laid her head in the curve of his neck, and muttered something in Cheyenne.

Rob met Lyon's gaze and shook his head in amazement. "You know," he said in a hushed tone, "I'm beginning to think the lads are right. She is a fairy princess."

"I don't think there's any doubt of it."

Lyon smiled down at Julie, making no attempt to conceal his emotions from his brother. Rob knew how he felt about this small bundle of beauty, brains, and pluck. She was everything a man could want, all rolled into one delightful package.

He carried Julie into her room and placed her in her own bed. Her lashes drifted upward, though she was only half awake.

"Is Neil all right?" she asked, as he tucked the blankets around her.

"He's doing well." He bent and kissed her brow.

"*Namehota*," she murmured, closing her eyes once again.

"Tell me in English."

"I can't. You told me I wasn't allowed to say it," she grumbled as she drifted off.

But he hadn't forgotten what it meant.

"Go to sleep, my fairy sweetheart," he whispered in the Gaelic.

I love you, too.

Holding White Thunder's reins in one hand, Juliette stood on a hillside and looked down at the rambling brick manor. She'd had no trouble finding Hamish Macfie's home, wending her way through hay fields and shadowy pine woods in the evening dusk. She hadn't told a soul at Strathlyon where she was going or why. No one would have allowed her to leave had they known. Besides, she didn't want to involve any of the MacLyons in something illegal.

With the resilience of youth, Neil had quickly recovered from the effects of his battle with arsenic poisoning. But the loss of Dunbar and Tiree had been a terrible ordeal for both children. They'd sobbed brokenheartedly as they laid bouquets of flowers on the deerhounds' graves that afternoon. Afterward, Lyon had considered canceling the family's excursion to Strathbardine planned for the next day, but missing the gathering of the clans—coming so soon after the death of their beloved pets—would have seemed almost unbearable to the two little boys.

As daylight slowly faded, Juliette watched the twinkling of lamps appear in the windows. She'd wait until dark, then leave her mare tied behind an outbuilding and slip into the manor house.

There was really nothing to worry about, she assured herself. Strong Elk Heart had taught his daughter how to move with silent stealth. She'd be in and out of Macfie's home in less than twenty minutes, with no one the wiser.

"Find what you're looking for, Miss Elkheart?"

Juliette whirled around. Hamish Macfie stood at the door of the gallery. He held a derringer aimed at her heart.

"A trifle late to come calling, don't you think?" he asked in an unctuous tone. "And usually our visitors ring the bell and come in through the front entrance." He stepped inside the long, high-ceilinged room that contained his priceless collection and shoved the door closed with his heel.

"I . . . I did not want to disturb you," she said. She glanced at the open casement window, wondering how quickly she could reach it.

Hamish sauntered up to the writing table. His secret documents were scattered across the green malachite top, illumined by the small paraffin lamp she'd lit. Nearby, the inlaid walnut door of his carved Empire secretary hung open. She'd broken the lock with tools she'd brought for that very purpose.

Considering the damage she'd done to his elegant furniture, his voice was amazingly calm. "Doing some late night research, I see."

She boldly attempted a bluff. "Yes, you said I could have free run of your collection. At the time, I was hoping to find information at Stirling." She shrugged philosophically. "But as you know, there was nothing of importance in the Tolbooth there. So I decided to take advantage of your generous offer."

His oily gaze slithered down her body and back to her face. "And why, may I ask, did you come dressed as a boy? So you could climb in and out of the window without snagging one of your lovely riding habits?"

Juliette took a wary step back. She'd donned the breeches and shirt she always wore on her family's ranch in Alberta to give her the freedom she needed to enter undetected.

She cleared her tightening throat. "If . . . ah, if you will excuse me, Laird Macfie, I should get back to Strathlyon now."

Pinning her in place with the canny eyes of a wolf, he waved the gun beneath her nose. "I could shoot you quite easily, my dear. It'd be a tragic error, of course. But finding you dressed like a man is a most unfortunate happenstance, don't you agree? Who wouldn't believe that I mistook you for a burglar and shot before I realized your identity?"

Juliette touched her waist, reaching instinctively for her knife. It wasn't there. She'd purposely left her weapon behind, knowing if she should get caught breaking and entering, it would be far better to surrender and take the consequences, than injure an innocent person.

"You would kill me over a few old pieces of paper?"

"Come, come, Miss Elkheart. We both know what those letters say. They're written in Scots English."

He stood right beside her now and deftly grabbed the long braid that fell down her back. He yanked viciously, jerking her head back.

"I did not have the chance to read them," she lied. Tears burned her eyes at the searing pain in her scalp. Her words were calm and deliberate, despite the frantic drumming of her heart. "I only just found them. Why not let me leave, and we will pretend this never happened?"

He ran the muzzle of his derringer along her jawbone, as light as a mother's caress. "I have a better idea. Why don't I find out what it's like to poke my cock in a redskin?"

A chill of apprehension lifted the hairs on the back of her neck. When she'd planned to break into the house, she'd thought the worst that could happen would be her arrest by an officer of the law if one of the servants discovered her.

"I am sorry if I have made you angry," she said in a placating tone. "But do not do something that you will regret."

He set the small pistol on the table and shoved it across the glassy top, well out of her reach. One hand still clutching her braid, he covered her breast with the other and squeezed painfully. As he shoved her back against the edge of the table with his hips, she could feel his burly strength and the hard bulge of his erection. Short, solid, deep-chested, he was built like a rutting bull.

"I'm not going to regret this," Hamish assured her with a chuckle. He pressed his meaty leg between her thighs, forcing her backwards and off balance. "And you won't tell anyone about it, either. You'd have to admit you broke into my home dressed in this scandalous costume. I'd claim your intent was to seduce me. What sanctimonious Scots jury would find me guilty?"

Juliette knew it was true. He could rape her with impunity, then kill her, if he wanted. She stared into his cold gray eyes, trying to read his intent. She wasn't sure if he was merely trying to frighten her or meant what he said. His breath smelled of liquor, but he wasn't drunk. He was dangerously, unpredictably sober.

He let go of her hair and clasped the back of her neck in a brutal hold. She shoved against him, not budging him an inch.

"Do not, *veho*," she warned. "Or I promise you will be sorry."

Hamish bent her over the table, one hand groping between her legs, and ripped open the front of her shirt. She fought back with all her strength, attempting to gouge his eyes. He caught her wrists in both hands and slammed them on the hard malachite top. Stunned by the pain, she bit her lip to keep from crying out.

His entire bulk pinned her to the table—then, suddenly, Hamish flew backwards and crashed against the cabinet behind him.

"You filthy sonofabitch," Lyon growled. He lifted Hamish up, caught him by the throat, and slammed him against the wall. With one hand, he squeezed the man's trachea in a merciless grip.

Juliette scrambled off the table. Her wrists throbbed, and her legs threatened to crumple beneath her.

"Stop!" she cried.

Lyon ignored her as he cut off Macfie's air supply with the inexorable pressure of his thumb. The man's disbelieving face turned red, then purple in the faint lamplight.

Hamish tried desperately to break the relentless hold on his throat, clawing in panic with both hands. His eyes bulged. He gurgled deep in his cinched throat. Then his arms fell limp at his sides as he started to lose consciousness.

Juliette panted breathlessly. "Do not . . . kill him! Not

... in his own home. You will be charged ... with murder.''

She yanked wildly on Lyon's coat sleeve. He seemed completely unaware of her existence. She beat on his broad, muscular back with her fists, then threw her arms around his neck and hung on with all her weight.

"Lyon, please!" she begged. "Stop it!"

Lyon released Macfie, and the inert body slid down the wall to the floor.

"Is he dead?" she whimpered in horror.

"No."

He stepped back from the senseless man and turned to Juliette, his eyes blazing with fury. His features had hardened into the murderous mask of a stranger. He grabbed her arm and started for the open window. "Let's go."

"Wait," she pleaded. "My cloak is on the table."

Without a word, he paused to snatch it up. She used that precious moment to scoop up the papers and press them to her chest.

Lyon tossed her cloak through the window, then lifted her up and over the casement.

Rob was waiting with their horses. The two brothers had found her little mare tethered behind the stables.

"Lyon," she said in exhilaration, as she tried to keep up with his long stride. "I have the proof I need!"

His determined jaw locked tighter. He led her to the horses, took Thor's reins from Rob, and handed his brother her cloak.

"Lyon, listen—"

"Not now, Julie," Rob cautioned in a low voice. He lifted her cloak over her shoulders and pulled it around to cover her torn shirt. "Lyon doesn't like being scared. It makes him real mean. And you don't ever want to annoy Lyon when he's feeling mean."

Shouts of alarm came from inside the home. Someone had already discovered the brutalized laird on his gallery floor.

Rob tossed Juliette up on White Thunder's back, and the three galloped away from the manor house.

No one said a word on the ride back to Strathlyon.

Lady Hester and Flora met them in the castle's main hall. One look at Lyon's face, and the two ladies held their tongues.

Ignoring their presence, Lyon clasped Juliette's elbow, marched her into his study, and slammed the door. Then he released her arm and stalked over to his desk. His riding crop crashed down on the polished desktop with an ear-splitting bang.

Juliette jumped in surprise.

"Never!" he roared. "Never again!"

"Let me explain," she said. "Read these letters, and you'll understand why I went there. I have proof that the Danielsons did not murder the MacLyons!"

"I don't give a *damn* about those bloody papers. I don't give a damn about visions. I don't give a damn about some blasted battle that took place a hundred years ago!" he shouted. "The only thing I care about is you!"

Juliette's mouth dropped open. She pressed the sheaf of pages against her breast in exultation. "Does that mean you love me?"

Lyon leaned against the edge of the desk, folded his arms across his chest, and glared at her. He spoke through clenched teeth. "I didn't say that."

No, but he'd meant it!

Joy sprang up inside her, puffing out its ruff, fluttering its wings, and displaying its fan of tail feathers in the spectacular nuptial dance of the prairie's sage grouse. A smile turned up the corners of her mouth as she lifted her brows in feigned nonchalance.

"Then there is nothing to be upset about, is there?"

Still clutching the riding crop, he rose to his feet, picked up a porcelain paperweight, and hurled it against the far wall. The gilded egg smashed with a thud, the pieces scattering across the carpet like snowflakes.

"Frigging bloody hell!" he bellowed. "I learn you've been missing for hours and no one's seen you since twilight, I track you down to another man's home—which you've broken into—and find you about to be raped, and I'm not supposed to be *upset*?"

"How did you know where to find me?"

"A vision," he snarled.

"A vision?"

He sent her a withering glance. "Nana said you'd been reading everything you could find in the library about Clan Macfie in the last four days. It didn't take a genius to figure out where you'd gone."

"Can I tell you why I went there?"

Smacking the crop against his leg, the Lion prowled back and forth in front of his desk. "No, you cannot. Nothing you found there could be worth risking your life for."

She sniffed righteously and lifted one shoulder. She could be just as intractable as the mule-headed laird of Strathlyon. "Very well. I will keep them to myself."

With a glare, Lyon crossed the room and yanked open the door. His family stood just outside, their worried gazes glued to the portal. He jerked his head for them to enter, and they trooped inside in silence.

Flora's eyes were round with pity as she met Juliette's gaze. Lady Hester and Rob glanced at their house guest sympathetically, then turned their attention to the large, angry Scotsman in the center of the rug.

"I told everyone this morning that no member of our family was to go anywhere alone," Lyon stated in a biting tone. "I made it clear that included Miss Elkheart. But she chose to ignore my orders. If it happens again, I will hold every person in this room responsible. You are to see that our guest goes nowhere without one of you accompanying her." He smacked the crop against the palm of his gloved hand. "I trust I've made myself plain?"

No one dared to argue.

"For the next two days, while we're in Strathbardine for the gathering," he continued, "I want everyone to be especially alert. The village will be filled with strangers from the outlying districts. If you see anyone who resembles that damn tinker, don't approach him. Find me or Rob."

His family nodded their understanding.

Lyon rounded on Juliette. "As for you, Miss Elkheart." He took a step closer, and she edged a step back. "Since you are residing in my home, I am responsible to your uncle for your safety and well-being. If you persist in ignoring my orders, I will treat you like the willful, disobedient lass you are."

Juliette eyed the crop in his hand. She jerked her chin up and returned his threatening gaze with the steadfast resolution of a warrior-woman.

"The Cheyenne people do not believe in beating their children," she said with tenacious conviction. "No one has ever laid a hand on me in anger."

A ghost of a smile played about his lips, and his eyes glinted with irony. "But then, Miss Elkheart, I'm not Cheyenne, am I? And the Scots believe in thrashing their unruly children within an inch of their life."

Flora gasped in shock, and Lyon's attention moved back to his mesmerized family. "It's late. We'll all have a busy day tomorrow. Good night."

Juliette made sure she was the first one out the door, the purloined documents still clutched in her hand.

Chapter 21

❝**H**esc!❞ It is beautiful. How can I ever thank you?❞

Juliette pushed the tissue paper aside and lifted the lavender and pink wool from the package. The sett was an exact replica of the pattern on the blanket she'd brought with her from Canada; the muted colors were the same as those of the tartan worn by the Danielson Fencibles. Only this plaid wasn't frayed and tattered from years of use.

Goodwife Dowel and her daughter, Grizel Conacher, were in Juliette's room with her at the Dalriada Inn. The MacLyon family planned to remain in Strathbardine that night after the gathering of the clans.

Aggie beamed with pride at Juliette's heartfelt praise. ❝There's nae need to be thankin' me, child o' the clouds. And you're no' the only member of Clan Danielson to ask me to weave this verra same tartan.❞

Juliette looked up from the plaid in surprise. ❝Who else besides me asked for it?❞

❝Jock Ogilvie and Tommy MacGugan both secretly ordered the tartan. Most likely, they willna be wearin' it at the gatherin'. With years of hatred toward the name o' Danielson, they'd risk mockery and scorn by appearin' in it in public.❞

Grizel smiled, her blue eyes shining with excitement. ❝But Mither and me will both be wearin' a lavender and

277

pink plaid today, just like yours. For too many years, we've hidden our true heritage. If a visitor from across the ocean has the gumption to wear the Danielson tartan, we willna let her face the bletherin' folk o' Strathshire alone.''

"Thank you," Juliette said. She returned the beautiful plaid to its package on the bed and took their hands. ''I appreciate your support, but it is you who are brave. You will be here long after I have returned to my home.''

Aggie patted Juliette's arm. "Dinna fash yerself about us, lass. People from all over the British Isles place orders for our tartan cloth. The clishmaclaver o' clackin' tongues in Strathshire willna harm us.'' She paused, a frown deepening the creases in her wrinkled forehead, then continued in a serious tone. "We heard about the poisonin' up at the castle. We'll offer prayers o' thanksgivin' at the kirk on Sunday that the wee lad wasna hurt.''

"We're sorry about the deerhounds, too," her daughter added. "We're goin' to send twa o' Sweetie's litter for the halflins, soon as the puppies are weaned.'' She reached into her handbag and retrieved a small box. "This is for you, lassie. Mither gave it to me years ago, and it's been hidden away all this time. I want ye to have it.''

Curious, Juliette took the box and opened the lid. A silver brooch lay inside. Two intersecting hearts were engraved with intricate Celtic designs. She picked it up with an exclamation of delight and wonder.

"Nakoe!" she cried softly. "This is too precious for me to accept.''

"Na, na," Grizel replied. "Only someone with your pluck deserves to be wearin' it. My great-grandmither found it in the wreckage after the razing of the castle on Eilean Danielson. 'Tis a betrothal token, given by the last chief to his promised bride. Their names are on the back.''

Juliette turned the pin over and read the inscription. *Ninian* and *Catriona 1741*.

Tears sprang to her eyes. "This brooch must have belonged to my great-great-grandfather's parents.''

"If that's so, *mo chaileag*," Aggie said, "then your mither is the chief of Clan Danielson."

"My mother will crow with delight when she hears it," Juliette said with a chuckle. "For my father is one of the head chiefs of the Cheyenne nation. Now I have something to show you." She hurried over to the bureau. Setting the brooch on top, she pulled out the bottom drawer and withdrew the hidden papers. "Read these," she urged.

Mother and daughter read the letters in growing astonishment.

"Guidsakes!" Aggie exclaimed. "Are these genuine?"

"Yes. I discovered them in Laird Macfie's collection of documents. To tell you the truth," Juliette admitted, "I stole them."

"Och, 'tis nigh unbelievable." Grizel pressed her dimpled hands to her rosy cheeks and shook her head. "To think that all these many years, the Clan o' the Clouds has been wrongly blamed for the slaughter at Glen Kildunun."

Juliette steepled her fingers beneath her chin. "The question is, what shall I do with the proof, now that I have it?"

"Will ye trust me with these letters, lass?" Aggie asked. "I believe I ken who best to give them to."

"Certainly, I will."

There was a tap at the door, and Flora peeked in. "Hurry up, Julie," she called gaily. "The family's waiting for you downstairs." Her lovely face glowed with anticipation.

"Tell them I will be right there," she replied.

As Flora disappeared down the passageway, Juliette hugged each of the elderly women in turn. "Thank you for everything," she said. "I shall never forget your kindness."

Barouches, gigs, pony traps, dog-carts, and farm wagons crowded the normally quiet streets of the fishing village, their iron-bound wheels squeaking and scraping noisily. Every inn was full. The Dalriada, a three-story stone building with gables and turreted towers, looked out over the waterfront. Sailboats, excursion steamers, and fishing craft jammed the sheltered bay, where fresh prawns, crabs, mussels, halibut, and herring were displayed in wooden barrels along the sandy shore.

The jingle of bells hanging on the shop doors rang out as the MacLyon family strolled down the main thoroughfare. Window fronts were decorated with swaths of tartan cloth and evergreen branches, enticing the customers inside.

Lyon walked beside Juliette, while Neil and Jamie skipped along just ahead of them. Directly behind, Rob followed with Lady Hester and Flora.

"What is a wapenschaw?" Juliette asked her companion.

Everyone had always referred to the event as a gathering of the clans. Lyon was the first person to use the unfamiliar term in her hearing.

"A wapenschaw is a show of weapons," he explained. "Originally the clan gatherings were held for the inspection of men and weaponry by the chief, who was responsible for the defense of his territory. His armed clansmen arrived to demonstrate their loyalty and their readiness to wage war on his behalf, and ultimately for the defense of Scotland. While they were all gathered together, it was only natural for the men to take part in games that tested their strength and prowess."

Neil turned to walk backward, so he could see the grown-ups. He was his usual hardy self, his bright blue eyes sparkling with the joy of life.

"Before he went to the Sudan, Uncle Lyon tossed the caber the straightest of all," he told Juliette proudly.

"The caber?" she asked with a laugh. "What is that?"

Jamie joined his brother walking backwards. "It's a great big tree trunk, Miss Elkheart." He lifted his hands high above his head to indicate its tremendous height, then looked up at his tall uncle with boyish adoration. "Will you toss it today, Uncle Lyon?"

"From now on, I'll leave the feats of strength to your Uncle Robbie," he said. "And I want both you lads to remember what I told you earlier. You're to stay within an arm's length of one of us at all times. If you wander off for so much as a minute, I'll pack up the whole family and we'll return to the castle.''

''We'll remember,'' they promised in unison.

They spun around and charged ahead, eager to avoid any further mention of their leaving early. They intended to take no chance of spoiling the outing. Juliette met Lyon's gaze and smiled. The excitement of the Strathshire Gathering had lifted them out of their doldrums this morning.

Like his nephews and brother, Lyon wore his clan's blue and black kilt. A matching plaid was draped over his broad shoulder and pinned with the MacLyon badge. His blue Scottish bonnet was adorned with a sprig of heather like theirs, but Lyon also sported the three eagle feathers of a chief. Contrasting with the azure cloth, his eyes were the rich green of pine needles washed by the rain. In the magnificent attire, he was every inch the fierce Highland warrior.

At first sight of him that morning, Juliette's heart had fluttered against her ribcage like the sudden, startled flight of wild geese at the approach of a hunter. She trembled now as the warmth of remembered pleasures radiated through her. His nearness brought back the bittersweet ache his touch had inspired. She fought to conceal the delicious quiver of longing that twanged through her and concentrate, instead, on the colorful panoply surrounding them.

Both Lyon and Rob wore shoulder belts with holstered pistols over their short jackets. These weren't ancient weapons for display in the wapenschaw like the dirks at their sides, but powerful Lancaster repeaters chambered for army cartridges.

Thankfully, Lyon's anger of the night before had disappeared. Juliette realized it had been born of fear for her safety. Seeing her about to be ravished had enraged him nearly to the point of committing cold-blooded murder. There'd been no more whacking of riding crops or threatening to thrash unruly children. She wondered if he regretted his violent outburst. She doubted it, but she had no intention of going anywhere alone to find out.

The realization that he still intended to send her away sliced through her happiness like a fine-honed bowie knife. Her gentle persuasion was no match for the strength of his indomitable will. She'd hurled herself against it too many times not to know she'd only end up bruised and battered. Lyon's decision stood as impregnable as the thick-walled fortress he lived in. Granite hard, unshakable, the force of his relentless determination would destroy her in the end, unless she surrendered to his wishes.

And his deepest wish, at the moment, was that she disappear from his life.

The sooner the better.

But Juliette was resolved to set the pain of his rejection aside and share in the children's and Flora's excitement and wonder that day.

They came to a meadow on the edge of the village, where stalls had been set up. Harvest produce of potatoes, turnips, squash, and apples were piled high in baskets. Booths, decorated with sprigs of juniper, holly, yew, mistletoe, and heather, were devoted to tartan cloth, silk-lined plaids, and ready-made kilts. Other counters were piled high with minced pies, little iced cakes, boxes of chocolate, and crystallized fruits.

The wonderful aroma of hot potato scones swirled in the cool morning air, along with the sharp scent of larch and pine.

That day, almost every man wore a kilt and sporran. The crofters had put aside their corduroy breeks and coarse striped cotton shirts, the shopkeepers their trousers and aprons. Heavy work boots shod with steel had been traded for polished brogues with shiny buckles. The women were attired in their loveliest gowns, many with a finely woven plaid draped daintily across the shoulders and fastened with an heirloom brooch. It was a day of tremendous Highland pride.

At the lads' suggestion, Lyon stopped to buy spiced buns for his family. Neil bounced up to Julie, holding his warm, raisin-filled pastry in a brown paper wrapper. His eyes gleamed with mischief.

"I have another riddle, Miss Elkheart."

"Aye, another riddle," Jamie agreed.

"*Hesc!*" she exclaimed. "More riddles!"

This time she looked doubtful, and Lyon met his brother's gaze with smug satisfaction. There was no plausible way she could continue her incredible string of luck. This time the lads would defeat her, and the niggling doubt at the back of his mind would be laid to rest.

Lyon fought the compelling urge to reach out and touch her, as an inescapable wave of sexual longing flooded every network of nerves and veins in his big, lustful body.

Julie looked exquisite in an ivory dress adorned with the lavender and pink tartan. She wore the Danielson plaid fastened to her right shoulder and loosely caught in the crook of her left arm. The antique betrothal brooch gleamed in the autumn sunlight.

When she'd entered the Dalriada's public room that morning, the MacLyon family had stared at her in amazement. With her lustrous hair pulled back in a smooth, braided chignon, Julie stood proud and graceful at the foot of the central staircase. She seemed to be daring anyone to cast aspersions on the Clan of the Clouds or her right to wear their tartan.

For a breathless moment, no one said a word. Then Lady Hester had moved swiftly forward and taken Julie's hand. "*A chiall mo chridhe,*" she said, "you look stunning."

Julie's regal serenity and fathomless courage had devastated Lyon's defenses. The carefully constructed bastion protecting his heart crumpled like the walls of a fort beneath a relentless barrage of artillery. The pain was so intense, he'd looked down to see if he'd been ripped wide open.

Now, the lads waited expectantly for their fairy princess to try to solve their riddles. She lifted her sloe eyes heavenward and sighed dramatically.

"I do not know if I should take the chance," she said. "I have already answered four of them. These new ones may be too hard."

Flora beamed at her two sons with motherly pride. "How do you lads know so many clever riddles?"

"Uncle Lyon taught us these two," Neil confided.

Julie's gaze swung to Lyon, and she lifted her brows inquiringly. He refused to offer a word in his own defense. He had every right to teach his nephews fairy-enchanting riddles. It was part of their Celtic heritage.

She tapped one fingernail against her teeth in indecision, then shrugged her shoulders and crouched down to their level. "All right, I will try. This time, Hehen may go first."

Thrilled, Jamie executed a little hop-step-jump. "What is sharper than a thorn?"

She looked at Neil. "And what is your riddle, Maevess?"

He leaned toward her, the certainty of success bringing a blush of happiness to his fair skin. "What is louder than a horn?"

She pressed three fingertips against her soft lips, and Lyon wished to God it was his mouth pressed there instead. His body's automatic response to her presence had become one continuous ache of need. The slightest whiff of her sweet scent, the most casual brush of her soft hand, and a rush of heated blood surged through his heart.

No doubt about it.

This would prove to be one of the longest days of his life.

"*Ahahe*," she said woefully. "These are hard ones. I think you may have stumped me this time."

She rose and stared intently at Lyon, as though she could

read the answers in his eyes. Laughter sparkled in her own. He had the uncanny feeling she knew some marvelous secret of the universe.

Her intrinsic tenderness towards anyone or anything in pain seemed to swirl around him, wrapping him in its silken embrace. The promise of infinite love and sweet forgiveness in her velvety eyes enticed as no skilled voluptuary ever could. Beneath his kilt, his groin muscles clenched, the hot, hard jolt of desire spreading through his thighs and abdomen. He wanted what he could not have with an intensity that seared his soul, leaving it a charred, smoking ruin.

Bloody hell, would this torment never end?

"Do you give up?" asked Neil.

"Give up?" Jamie parroted.

"I must, at least, take a guess," she replied in a scandalized tone.

"I'm sure I don't know the answers," Flora said. "Do you, Nana?"

A shrewd smile creased the dowager's face. She nodded her white head knowingly. "I taught the riddles to Lyon when he was a lad. But I won't give the answers away. It wouldn't be fair."

They waited patiently while Julie nibbled on her spiced bun and pondered. "Something sharper than a thorn," she muttered with a frown. "Something louder than a horn."

"We can't wait all morning, Miss Elkheart," Lyon goaded. The carnal frustration he'd tried vainly to smother made his tone harsh and abrupt. "The March of the Clans is about to begin."

"Very well," she said cheerfully. "I shall take a guess." She held out one hand palm up, as though offering her answers on an imaginary platter. "Hunger is sharper than a thorn, and shame is louder than a horn."

"You're right!" Jamie cried with a squeal of elation. "You're right, Miss Elkheart."

Neil dropped to his knees on the grass, covered his head with his hands, and groaned in defeat.

"I can't believe it," Rob said with sincere admiration. "You have to be the best riddle solver I've ever known."

Julie tossed her head with a pleased, self-satisfied air. "It must be a Cheyenne gift."

"Unless you already knew the answer," Lyon stated curtly.

Flora leapt to her defense. "How could she? I've never heard those riddles, and I'm Scottish."

Everyone stared at the curvaceous widow in befuddlement.

"Well, I am," she insisted. She put her hands on her hips and glared at them. "Glasgow's in Scotland."

"Oh, Mama," Neil said with a happy laugh. "These are Celtic fairy riddles. They're not written in English. You wouldn't know the answers, unless Jamie and I told them to you."

Lyon searched Julie's exotic eyes as he tried to recall all the graphically erotic words he'd spoken to her in the Gaelic. He sure as hell remembered the last thing he'd told her in that ancient tongue.

Go to sleep, my fairy sweetheart.

But the absolute innocence that shone on her clear features would have convinced the devil himself. She couldn't possibly understand the Celtic language, any more than he could understand her magical, mystical Cheyenne. Rob must have read and interpreted the riddlecraft ballad to her when she'd first come to Strathlyon.

Her memory, however, was certainly phenomenal—something he needed to keep in mind, for she may have picked up more Gaelic phrases during her short visit than he'd considered possible.

Then the skirling of the pipes caught their attention. It was time for the March of the Clans.

*   *   *

Several large pavilions had been erected along the side of the meadow, with seats provided for the spectators. Above the gaily striped tents, clan banners snapped in the breeze. Juliette sat between Lady Hester and Flora. Behind them several older people gaped at her, craning their necks to see the colors of her plaid. The younger set paid no attention, oblivious to the significance of the lavender and pink tartan.

"There'll be a piping competition this morning," Lady Hester told Juliette, "and an exhibition of Highland dancing by the men. You'll see the ancient dance of victory, in which the victorious clansmen danced over the swords of their foes, their own swords laid atop. Then the games will be held this afternoon."

"Later this evening, there'll be country dances for the young men and women," Flora added happily. "We'll be sure to attend."

The sound of massed bagpipes filled the air with the strains of "Highland Laddie." Each of the local clans marched around the grassy arena behind their standard-bearer and their own band of pipers. The MacLyons, the MacDougalls, the Campbells, the Macfies, the MacGregors, and the McCorquodales. With banners flying over their heads, they carried pistols, halberds, lances, dirks, two-handed claymores, Lochaber axes, pikes, and targes. The fearsome array of ancient weaponry inspired a feeling of awe.

The appearance of Lyon, Rob, Neil, and Jamie, along with their fellow clansmen, brought Juliette to the edge of her seat. The blue and black tartans, the wail of the piping, the banner with its gold lyon rampant on the deep blue background, sent a thrill of admiration through her.

In addition to their holstered pistols and sheathed dirks, the two men carried basket-hilted broadswords. Their nephews each held a leather-covered targe embossed with the MacLyon clan slogan. *Duinealachd*—manliness.

She'd wondered, at first, if Lyon would participate in the

opening march. But though pragmatic about politics and Scottish nationalism, the laird of Strathlyon felt a deep pride for his country and people.

Juliette clenched her hands in her lap as she watched Hamish Macfie march by with his clan. The evil-maker stared at her with such hatred, she drew back. Would he accuse her of theft in front of a crowd of strangers? She wondered where the letters incriminating Clan Macfie in the diabolical crime were now—the crime that had been hidden by Hamish and his forebears for more than a hundred years.

After the procession of the clans, the women joined their menfolk on the field to chat with each other. Gradually, a stir of excitement rippled through the crowd. The agitation started slowly, then seemed to gather momentum as it spread. People called to one another, motioning with their hands for their friends to come quickly. Others streamed in and out of the largest pavilion, which stood at the farthest end of the meadow.

Annie and Keir, attired in the MacDougall red and green tartan, came to join the MacLyons. With a radiant smile, the young bride put her arms around Juliette and kissed her cheek. "Keir told me how you saved Neil's life. We're both so proud of you."

"Your husband also had a lot to do with Neil's recovery," Juliette replied, returning Annie's warm hug. "And Neil's family was with him every minute."

"What's happening?" Flora asked the couple, motioning to the noisy throng milling about at the far end of the meadow. "Why are so many people hurrying into that pavilion?"

Keir put his arm around his wife's shoulder and pulled her close. The gratification on his bluff features was unmistakable. "That tent holds an exhibition of historical artifacts sponsored by the Scottish National Society."

Lady Hester cocked her snowy head to one side thoughtfully. "Why is everyone so excited?"

"Come and see," Keir suggested amiably. He met Annie's impish gaze, and the couple grinned in mutual satisfaction. Strangely, neither mentioned the Danielson tartan on Juliette's shoulder.

The MacLyon family and Juliette accompanied the MacDougalls across the grass and entered the gold and white striped pavilion. The moment they stepped inside, a hush descended and the crowd opened to make way for them.

The canvas walls were arrayed with clan targes. A vast collection of weaponry lay on tables set along the sides. The swords, lances, claymores, and halberds that had been carried in the March of the Clans invited closer inspection.

Juliette had expected people to glare at her for daring to appear in the tartan that had belonged to the Clan of the Clouds. But everywhere she looked, complete strangers were beaming and smiling at her. The MacLyons appeared to be as confounded as she, but Annie and Keir exchanged knowing glances.

"As president of the Strathshire branch of the Scottish National Society," Dr. MacDougall said, "I authorized a very special exhibition today."

They approached a cloth-covered table that stood in the center. Two documents, protected by glass, were displayed in ornate frames. On each side of the table hovered a man attired in the Clan Danielson kilt and plaid. Holding Lochaber axes, Tommy MacGugan and Jock Ogilvie stood guard over the priceless papers, their heads held high, their faces glowing with pride. Beside her father, little Meggie MacGugan wore the same lavender and pink tartan. Aggie Dowel and her daughter Grizel, with Danielson plaids on their shoulders, waited behind the table, ready to answer the questions of the curious onlookers.

The Clan of the Clouds had suddenly and mysteriously reappeared, as though they were indeed a race of fairies.

Mystified, Lyon picked up the shiny brass frames and read each of the letters in turn. The first, dated September,

1771, was from the then-chief of Clan Macfie to his younger brother in Strathbogie, detailing his plan for his clansmen to impersonate the Danielson Fencibles and murder the MacLyon Highlanders in Glen Kildunun.

The second letter, dated November, 1771, was from Chief Macfie to the duke of Argyll at Inveraray Castle, asking him to intercede with the Crown in the acquisition of the forfeited Danielson lands, as repayment for the previous Macfie chief's help in quelling the Jacobite rebellion.

Lyon realized in stupefaction that the preposterous tale Julie had told him at Kildunun was true. Clan Danielson had been innocent victims. Every one of them.

How, in God's name, could she have guessed the truth?

Stunned, he turned to her, guilt churning in his gut. He'd refused to even listen when she'd tried to explain. Instead, he'd threatened to whip her in front of his whole family.

"Were these the letters you tried to tell me about last night?" he asked, his throat aching in remorse.

With a look of apprehension, she leaned closer and whispered so only he could hear. "Yes, I took them from Macfie's home."

As if conjured up by his name, Laird Hamish Macfie entered the tent. He ignored the hostile silence that greeted him, strode up to the center table, and glanced at the documents. Then, his face livid and contorted with rage, he turned to glower at Julie.

She slipped her arm through Lyon's and edged closer. He could feel her slender form tremble, and he patted her hand in reassurance. Then he grasped the handle of his broadsword in an openly insolent challenge. "If you have anything to say about these papers, Macfie, say it now. And say it to me. I was there in your home last night, and I accept full responsibility for anything that happened."

Macfie nearly choked on his wrath. "I've never seen these bloody letters before in my life. They're nothing but damned forgeries."

Someone hooted with scorn. "They couldna be as bogus

as you are, Macfie. Ye claimed yer clan supported Prince Charlie in the Forty-five. Seems yer pawky clansmen knew all about dressin' up and pretendin' to be who they weren't.''

Part of the crowd started to laugh in derision, and the tent echoed with wisecracks and taunts. But others glared at Hamish and muttered that he should be punished for keeping the Danielsons' innocence a secret.

With a vile oath, the chief of Clan Macfie spun on his heel and left.

The games were held in the afternoon. There were foot races, putting the weight, and throwing the hammer. Rob excelled in all of them. The bonny lassies of Strathbardine watched with adoring eyes as two men raised the caber to a perpendicular position, and Robbie MacLyon lifted it off the ground. The massive tree trunk soared above him. He staggered slightly as he steadied its enormous weight for a moment, then threw it. The judging was done not on how far he tossed the caber, but how straight. The prize went to Rob, naturally.

Lyon didn't enter the contests. He knew he'd never win anything but jeers and catcalls with his crippled arm. The thought of humiliating himself in front of Julie kept his feet planted firmly on the sidelines.

For their protection, he stayed close to his family and their guest all that day. It seemed a diabolical form of torture, even for someone as foredoomed as he. Julie's unaffected ways, her tempting lips, her guileless brown eyes kept him in a state of arousal that could only have been hidden by his badger-skin sporran and the yards of tartan wool that made up his kilt.

He made damn sure he never touched her.

As frequently as possible, he kept another person between them, afraid that the slightest brush against her arm or the accidental meeting of their hands would lead to the betrayal of his feverish ardor.

Her somber gaze told him she realized he was purposely keeping his distance. And she was hurt by his aloof demeanor. But better her pride suffer for a few fleeting hours, than her entire life be ruined by the selfishness of one man.

To make matters worse, he knew his entire family wanted him to marry Julie and keep her with them at Strathlyon Castle. From the oldest to the youngest, they were all watching him that day with hopeful expectancy.

For supper they feasted on potato scones, cloutie dumplings with currants and orange peel, and honey ale. The family sat on the grass while they ate and chatted about the day's events. Although they'd all searched the faces in the crowd, no one had seen a man resembling the black-haired tinker.

Neil and Jamie insisted on knowing why their uncle hadn't entered the caber-tossing event and were openly dissatisfied when he told them the sport wasn't for old men like him.

Not missing an opportunity when she saw it, Lady Hester needled Lyon about seeking medical help for his injured arm. "Talk to him, my dear," she said to Julie. "Maybe he'll listen to you. He could go to Edinburgh and have your uncle examine his elbow. Dr. Robinson is studying surgery; perhaps he could remove that bullet fragment."

Julie reached across Jamie to touch Lyon's arm, and a current of erotic sensations flowed through his sex-starved body. The frantic primal beast inside him threatened to break its leash and destroy his hard-won control.

Her sensuous contralto was low and husky with concern. "It is true, Lyon. My uncle might be able to help you."

"No one's examining this old injury," he replied curtly. "Now let's just leave well enough alone and drop the subject."

When the country dances began in one of the pavilions, Lyon left the young women with Rob and the MacDougalls and returned to the inn with Lady Hester, Neil, and Jamie. It was bedtime for the lads. The dowager marchioness planned to sleep in the same room with the children as an extra precaution.

He saw the lads safely tucked beneath the covers, and wished his nephews and his grandmother sweet dreams. Then he went downstairs to the taproom.

Lyon lounged in a comfortable chair, where he could watch the central staircase that led to the second floor and his family's suite of rooms. He didn't have the luxury of downing enough smooth Glen Livet to blur the image of Juliette Elkheart in the ivory gown and lavender and pink plaid as she'd stood in front of those very stairs. He needed to remain alert and ready for possible trouble. But he could imbibe enough to ease the unbearable tension of being so damn close to her all day and not touching her, not kissing her—not dragging her off somewhere and slaking his hunger in her warm, welcoming arms.

Three hours later, Rob brought the rest of the family back to the inn. Flora's brilliant eyes shone with happiness as she chattered about the handsome swains who'd flirted with her.

Lyon realized with a pang of guilt how lonely for male companionship the pretty young widow was. He'd begin sorting through possible suitors as soon as Miss Elkheart was safely on her way back to Edinburgh. After today, Julie would have no excuse to remain at Strathlyon Castle.

Lyon rose and sauntered into the spacious public room, where he wished the ladies good evening with feigned nonchalance. Julie turned to him, searching his eyes and assessing, no doubt, the extent of his inebriation. He had the extraordinary notion she was looking into his black soul and finding him the unworthy coward that he was.

In spite of the Scotch whisky he'd poured down his throat, there was nothing he wanted to do more at that moment than take her in his arms and kiss her, to hold her close and tell her he was never going to let her go.

Instead, he watched in dour silence as she climbed the

stairs. Flora slipped her arm around Julie's waist, still giggling about something that had happened earlier that evening, and they disappeared down the hallway.

"Come on, ye damn fool," Rob said, his hand on Lyon's shoulder. "Let's go see if we can drown your sorrows."

After returning to the pub, where they discussed the plans for the morning's departure over another dram, the two brothers said goodnight and retired.

Lyon entered his room and paused just inside the threshold for the space of a heartbeat.

Illumined by the soft glow of the fire, Miss Juliette Evening Star Elkheart sat perched on the edge of his bed. She looked like a goddamned angel in her lovely ivory dress. Her spine straight, her hands folded primly in her lap, she gazed at him in tranquil silence.

Lyon closed the door behind him with a soft click of the lock.

Chapter 22

The laird of Strathlyon crossed the carpet with feline grace. He slowly and methodically removed his shoulder belt, holster, and sporran and hung them over the back of a chair. Then he turned to face Juliette.

His tone was cool, matter-of-fact, as though she were the maid waiting politely to turn down the covers and light the lamps. "You came, no doubt, to say good-bye."

If he saw her flinch at the cruel words, he didn't acknowledge it. In the flickering glow of the flames, his hardened features proclaimed his indifference. His red-gold hair, burnished to copper in the firelight, shone like a Viking's helmet. The towering specter of a ruthless sea raider rippled through the room like the waves of impending disaster.

Juliette's stomach knotted in fear and disillusionment. She'd made a terrible mistake by coming.

"Not exactly," she answered in a pitiful croak. "I mean, not yet. I will not say good-bye to you yet." She gathered her courage and met his unreadable gaze.

I refuse to let you send me away without telling me why.

Lyon moved to the fireplace, where he unbuckled his dirk and placed it with careful precision on the mantelpiece. Then he braced one arm on the carved marble slab and stared at the burning logs. The light wavered behind him, revealing no more than his shadowy outline in the dark room. He waited with oppressive civility for her to explain her presence.

The pop and crackle of the fire roared in Juliette's ears. The taste of inevitable defeat burned her tongue and scorched her throat. She closed her eyes for a heartsick moment.

Why did he have to make it so hard?

She used the only excuse she had. "Your grandmother wanted me to speak with you further about having my uncle examine your arm."

His disembodied voice floated around her, flat and emotionless, the syllables just the tiniest bit slurred. "I see. And you felt the discussion couldn't wait until morning."

Juliette looked down in despair at her hands. Her fingers were interlaced so tightly, the knuckles appeared translucent in the faint glow.

She forced herself to go on, praying he wouldn't notice the telltale catch in her throat. "Now that I have proven my ancestors were not responsible for the terrible slaughter at Glen Kildunun, I have no reason to stay in the Highlands any longer . . . unless . . ."

Lyon looked up, but didn't make a sound. His silence tore at her, shredding her pride, ripping her resolve into pieces. She wanted to jump up and dash out the door. To pretend she'd never come to his room, would never dream of doing such a pathetic, mortifying thing.

But she knew if she did, he'd have won. He would send her back to Edinburgh without a word of explanation. And he owed her the truth, at least. The thought of facing life without him was far more painful than the humiliation she was suffering now. If he believed he could make her run away by simply willing it, he greatly underestimated her determination.

She took a deep breath and began again. "Lady Hester said there is an excellent school of veterinary medicine in Edinburgh."

His head jerked back, as though she'd just delivered a

vicious blow. He stiffened, fists clenched at his side. Then he turned to her, his large frame relaxed in a casual stance, his hands propped on his kilted hips.

"She probably told you I own a home there, as well."

Her words broke and staggered with hurt and hopelessness. "She ... mentioned it. She said ... with your influence ... any qualified student ... would be accepted ... even a female."

Lyon moved to the chair in the corner and sank down. Deep in the shadows, he sat and looked at her. His silent, brooding contemplation paralyzed Juliette. Her mind scarcely functioned. She had the horrible feeling he was memorizing each feature, each braided strand of hair, each curve and plane of her body. That he was locking the sight of her now, at that moment—as she sat on the edge of his bed attired in her dress and tartan—into the deepest recesses of his brain.

The thought of his gaze moving over her, slow and shockingly intimate, set her skin on fire. Heat, desire, despair entwined themselves around her breaking heart.

Her mouth dry, her pulse racing, Juliette swallowed nervously. She wasn't going to quit, not now that she'd begun. If she had to humble herself, if she had to beg, she'd do it.

Tears stung the corners of her eyes, but she managed to utter lightly, with a hint of playfulness, "It is not as though Philadelphia is the *only* place one can become a veterinarian."

"Julie ... don't," he said hoarsely.

She started up, then dropped back down on the soft coverlet.

"If you would just tell me why," she whispered. Teardrops scalded her cheeks and plopped on her trembling fingers.

Their pain was a palpable, living force in the room. How could he sit there so quietly, while their lives were being shattered like brittle glass upon the anvil of his pride?

Head bowed and shoulders slumped, Juliette wiped her

wet cheeks with the backs of her hands. She waited, refusing to allow him this last, final evasion.

"I am not the hero you think I am," he said at last, the harsh, guttural words torn from some empty place deep inside him. "If I were, James would be alive today."

She turned her face toward the darkness that concealed him. "And because you failed to save your brother's life, you think you are not worthy to ever know happiness? Warriors die in battle. It does not mean that every survivor must spend his life singing a death chant because he was not the one killed. You are wrong to blame yourself."

"No, Julie." He lurched to his feet and came out of the shadows, self-hatred apparent in his contorted features and the tautness of his long limbs. "I *am* to blame. I should have been there in time to save him. I *would* have been there, if I'd left Dongola when I first wanted to."

She willed him desperately to go on. Truth was the only bridge that could cross the chasm he'd dug between them.

Lyon placed one hand against the window frame and stared out at the night sky as though looking into the past.

Remote and faraway, his dispassionate words resonated in the still room. "The situation in the Sudan deteriorated rapidly after the fall of Khartoum. By then, I'd spent enough time in the desert to know that the Mahdi's followers were religious fanatics and wouldn't be satisfied merely with the annihilation of General Gordon and his men. They'd continue their campaign of atrocities up and down the Nile, until the last British soldier was killed.

"At Dongola, we received orders from Cairo in the north to evacuate all outposts. But the rebel tribes had already cut the telegraph wire between our post and El Durman to the south, and there was no way to communicate with my brother's battalion. My commanding officer refused to listen to my warning that time was against us—that we had to send a rescue party at once or it would be too late."

The Lion paced back and forth, the imprisoned memories exploding within him in a rush of words. "General Macfie didn't want to risk sending a relief expedition to El Durman. His weak, vacillating mind spun a web of possibilities, contingencies, and subtle distinctions. No news wasn't necessarily bad news, he claimed. Maybe the garrison was in no serious danger. The men could probably hold out for months if they were surrounded. Or the line of retreat was still open, and they were already on their way to Dongola.''

Juliette could feel Lyon's pain, a pain so piercing she wanted to cry out for him to stop. She should never have insisted upon this. Never pushed him to reenter this pit of horrors, where his spirit remained transfixed on the spikes of self-reproach and self-accusation. But she couldn't have halted his disclosures now, if she had the power of the Maiyun.

She did the only thing she could do.

She listened.

''I wasted an entire day trying to persuade him. A whole goddamned day. In the end, the decision was taken out of Macfie's hands. Just as I was about to defy orders and go with a company of picked volunteers, the directives came from headquarters at Cairo. We were to march an entire regiment to El Durman and assist their orderly retreat.'' His soft cry of desperation slashed across Juliette's heart. ''God! I should never have waited for those orders.''

Her reply was scarcely above a whisper. ''You would have been shot if you had disobeyed your commander.''

''Macfie threatened a court-martial if I didn't comply.'' Lyon turned and stared at her, his low words razor-sharp with unforgiving bitterness. ''It would have been better had I been executed by a firing squad, than lived to see what had befallen the soldiers at El Durman.''

Juliette blinked beneath Lyon's searing gaze and waited in heartsick apprehension for him to go on.

''We were one day late. *One day.*'' Head bowed, he leaned his arm against the mantelpiece and pounded his fist impotently on the gray marble. ''We saw the desert hawks circling above the fortress as we approached. El Durman had been overrun by the overwhelming forces of the Mahdi. An entire battalion of Royal Scots had been wiped out in an orgy of blood lust and slaughter. Every officer was beheaded. Their heads were placed atop the spears of their murderers and set along the road that led to the fort.''

Lyon's deep baritone turned strangely calm and detached, as though the carnage he'd witnessed defied understanding or explanation or even belief. ''The blood-soaked bodies were so hacked and mutilated, we couldn't match them with the severed heads. I'm not certain whose torso lies in James's grave in the MacLyon burial ground. Or whose hands and feet and private parts.''

A tiny moan escaped before Juliette could stop it. Nausea roiled in her stomach, and she fought the dizziness that spiraled inside her.

Lyon came to stand directly in front of her. The cold determination in his gaze froze her soul.

''I *am* to blame. My blind adherence to duty, to the chain of command, to the belief in honor and patriotism, cost my brother his life as surely as if I'd been the one to stick his head on that pike.''

Juliette's despairing tears flowed unheeded, washing away the last vestige of hope. ''And you cannot find it in your heart to forgive yourself?''

''*Never.*'' He turned from her, his words raw and thick with pain. ''Now, please go.''

She sobbed openly. ''If you want me . . . to leave this room . . . you will have to pick me up . . . and put me out.''

He whirled around.

Clasping her by the waist, he yanked her off the bed, and Juliette knew that she'd lost everything in that last, final, desperate bid.

Lyon held Julie high above his head. Her eyes overflowed with love. Her soft mouth promised sweet oblivion, if only for this one, blessed night. Wracked with guilt, driven by a wild sexual hunger, tortured by a love he could never profess, he gazed up at his beautiful, enchanting fairy princess.

And nothing else mattered but her.

A feverish desire rushed through his veins. His hands burned where he touched her. His hard body quaked in response to her dewy softness and his thundering heart.

He would seize the night, this night, and let the devil take the hindmost.

Lyon brought Julie down to his very human level and covered her mouth with his, possessive and demanding. He lowered her to the bed and covered her completely with his body. He pressed her fiercely into the feather mattress, imprisoning her beneath his much greater weight. She was so small, and he was so large, and he wanted her to feel that. To feel his heaviness pressed against her and know that at this moment she belonged to him. And that this night, he would do whatever he wanted with her and to her.

"Lyon . . ." she whispered.

"Don't talk," he murmured, tasting the salt of her tears. He covered her face with kisses, sweeping the wetness away with his tongue. "I want this dress off."

He rose and brought her up with him. Unbuttoning the back of her gown, he swiftly pulled it, tartan and all, down to her waist and over her hips. Petticoat, chemise, knife, drawers, shoes, garter, stockings. He didn't give her a moment to think or protest or question.

Then he laid her back down on the bed, her naked softness pliant and cool beneath his questing fingers. He covered her breasts with his hands, the firm, silken mounds rising to his touch. He'd been right from the very beginning. She was a perfect little mouthful.

He lowered his head to suckle her.

"Wait," she gasped in surprise. "What about you? You have not removed a thing."

"Forget about me." The need for her raged inside him, frenzied and insistent. White-hot sparks seemed to follow wherever he touched her, and the sharp relish of anticipation speared through his tightened groin like a fiery lance. His sex stirred reflexively beneath his kilt, thick and heavy with lust.

All day long, he'd craved her.

All day long.

Nothing on God's earth could stop him now.

"I'm going to devour you," he promised, "inch by sweet, delicious inch. And then I'm going to impale you on my hard, hot flesh, the flesh that's howled and begged for your warm softness, till I thought I'd go out of my mind." He growled deep in his throat and nipped her honey-gold skin. "While you were busy solving riddles, princess, I was undressing you in my thoughts and putting my hands and my mouth here—and here—and here."

Julie shivered and quaked beneath his caresses. Lyon took her breast in his mouth, teasing her nipple with his tongue. He inhaled the glorious perfume of wildflowers and woman, and his swollen shaft lifted and twitched beneath his kilt as though scenting its prey.

She reached toward the front of his jacket, fumbling with the brass buttons, and he caught her wrists. Holding them captured in one hand, he raised her arms above her head.

"Keep your hands off my clothes," he warned her, "or I'll have to tie them to the head rail behind you."

Instinctively Julie grasped the brass railing, her luscious nude figure stretched out beneath his lecherous gaze.

"*Nanoseham*," she murmured. She bent her spread legs, inviting him with sultry eyes. Her lashes drifted lower, shadowing her flushed cheeks. Her mouth was swollen from his kisses. "*Nihoatovaz*. I want you."

"I can't wait much longer, either, princess," he said thickly. "My God, how I've wanted you."

He scooped her little bum into his big palms and lifted her to him. He taught her the sweet joy of eroticism with his tongue, bringing her ever higher toward fulfillment.

But not all the way there.

He wanted her to be as crazed and frantic with desire as he'd been all day.

When he retreated and laid her gently back down on the coverlet, she whimpered and tossed her head in confusion.

Lyon hitched up his kilt and entered her, more forcefully than he'd intended. She was still unbelievably tight. He gritted his teeth, stifling a groan of exquisite enjoyment. Oh, God in heaven, she was tight.

He bent over her, his weight braced on his forearms. Julie's ragged breath came in short huffs, her body tensed beneath the massive invasion.

"Relax and let me in, my wee lassie," he coaxed. "I've been there before; I know I can fit."

She laughed softly as she opened herself to him, giving him fuller access. "If you roll your r's over me like that, Scotsman, I will give you anything you want."

He smiled and kissed her. "Then you like my burr, do you?"

"It drives me mad." She slid her arms around his neck and returned his kiss with joyous intensity.

Lyon rolled onto his back, bringing her with him. Julie sighed with pleasure, settling over him, her small passageway gradually accommodating his huge, hardened muscle.

"Wrap your legs around me," he said, as he sat up. "And hold on tight."

Lyon rose from the bed, her weight as light in his arms as the fairy princess she was, and moved to stand in front of the room's tall dressing mirror. He cupped her bottom and allowed her to set the rhythm as he held her in place.

Juliette buried her fingers in his hair and kissed him deeply. Her tongue stroked wildly against his, and she tasted the mellow, smoky flavor of Highland whisky. "Mm, you taste intoxicating."

"It's yourself you're tasting," he said with a sidewise smile.

She ducked her head, embarrassed.

Lyon chuckled at her girlish reaction. He lifted her

slowly upward, then drew her back down on his rigid manhood, building the heat in her sensuous core.

"I did have a few drams of Glen Livet this evening," he admitted, "before retiring upstairs."

"I know." Juliette met his eyes, smiling shyly. She traced his mouth with her fingertip. "That is why I had the courage to come to your room."

"Oh, aye," he said with a devastating grin, "come to take advantage of the poor, drunken fool."

He rocked her gently against him, the soft sensations sending waves of delight through her.

"You are not poor," she said breathlessly. She fought to keep her mind on their conversation. He was going to drive her insane. "You are as rich as any king of England."

"Richer."

"And you do not act as though you are drunk."

"Now that is a matter of some doubt, lass. But I'll make every effort to satisfy you properly, regardless of the state of my inebriation."

The weave of his wool jacket and plaid scraped gently against her sensitive nipples, bringing deep, radiating jolts of pleasure. The front of his kilt bunched against her stomach, while the sides brushed lightly over her hips. Everywhere her body touched his, her skin vibrated with marvelous, tingling sensations.

"This is not at all proper," she gasped, "and you are definitely not a fool."

"Nay, no fool would ever be this lucky. Now hush, *a ghaolaich*, and look in the mirror."

Juliette turned her head. In the glass's reflection, a fully dressed Highlander in jacket, plaid, and kilt, still wearing his checkered stockings and buckled brogues, held a shamelessly naked woman in his strong hands, her arms and legs wrapped around him. Her cheeks were flushed with passion, her full lips pouty and sensual.

The sight was riveting in its blatant sexuality.

"Oh, Lyon," she moaned, "I cannot wait any longer."

"Aye, lass, you can," he said. "I waited all day. You can wait a few moments more. Now take down your hair."

"What?"

"Do it," he insisted.

"All right," she agreed, "but do not move me against you, or I will never be able to manage the pins."

"I'll move you how and when I choose, Juliette Evening Star."

He demonstrated, just to be certain there'd be no mistaking his effortless dominance. The pleasure was so intense, her muscles reacted automatically, pulling him deeper inside her, tightening around him.

"*Nakoe!*" she cried in surprise. She met his gaze, wondering if he'd felt it, too.

His marvelous green eyes were alight with the knowledge.

"Take your hair down," he said.

Dazed with passion, Juliette lifted her hands, withdrew the pins that held her braided chignon, and dropped them on the rug. She released the thick strands of the braid, combing through the tangled mass with her fingers, and then shook her head so it tumbled over her bare shoulders.

"Ah, God, lass, you're bonny," Lyon said. He turned part way, so she could see herself more clearly in the mirror. "Watch while I worship you, *a ghràidh shìth.*"

He lifted her slightly, then let her slide back down the hard length of him in a primitive, rhythmic tempo. The cadence of the beat increased steadily, matching the frantic pumping of her heart. With a tiny sigh of submission, she gave herself over to his total control.

In the looking glass, the incredible pleasure she felt was reflected on her face. Her lids grew heavy, her features softened, her mouth opened slightly as she drew in tiny gasps of air. Her bare, trembling thighs pressed against the folds of his kilt. Her nails dug into the thick wool of his plaid.

"*Nanoseham, nanoseham,*" she chanted to the primal

rhythm of his movements as the undulating ripples of orgasm spiraled through her. "*Namehota, namehota.*"

Lyon moved to the bed and eased Julie down, his big body quaking with an urgency past enduring. Her still quivering tissues clutched him, and he felt every delicate tremor against his heated, oversensitive flesh.

He spoke to her in the Gaelic, the words wrenched from him as unparalleled need drove him deeper and deeper inside her. "I love you, little fairy princess. Oh God, oh God, how I love you."

"I wondered what you wore beneath your kilt," Julie said. Her throaty laughter shimmered across Lyon's heart like a silvery sprinkle of moonbeams.

His naked body curved tightly against hers, his turgid sex pressed against her silken thigh. They hadn't slept all night, and it would soon be dawn.

"Now you know the truth about a Scotsman's underwear," Lyon answered with a grin. He took her hand and placed it on his thickened shaft. "All you had to do, princess, was reach underneath my kilt and feel for yourself. Whenever you were near, he stood at attention like this and saluted your beauty."

"Shame on you!" she cried softly.

Her brilliant eyes sparkled with delight at his boldness. Her fingers curled around him, caressing and gentle. The sweetness of her touch left him breathless.

Lyon took a handful of her luxuriant tresses and wrapped them around his wrist. "Your hair is so gorgeous," he said, smoothing the locks against his stubbled cheek and inhaling her delectable perfume. "Like strands of mahogany satin. I can't keep from touching it. I can't keep from touching you."

He bent his head and laved her nipples tenderly.

"Are you too sore?" he asked, as he raised his head and met her gaze. "Your wee buds are red and swollen."

She shook her head. "No. Yes. I do not care."

"Ah, lass, we shouldn't do this again so soon. I've lost track of how many times already tonight."

Lyon knew he was like a lost soul in the desert, parched with thirst. He couldn't get enough.

Julie ran her hands down his back, her fingers playing lightly along the bumps of his spine. "But it feels so good," she urged, her husky contralto slumberous with desire.

"Just one last time then, lass."

"Dinna fash yerself, my braw Hielan laddie," she said, imitating his burr. "I promise I will be verra, verra gentle."

The Strathshire Gathering was over. The booths were being dismantled, and the produce and goods not sold had been packed. A few people wandered up and down the trampled meadow, unwilling to say good-bye.

Lady Hester had already started out in the victoria with an armed coachman and outriders. Most of the family were in their saddles, ready to begin the trip back to the castle. Rob and Lyon still retained their shoulder holsters and dirks. They and the lads wore their jackets and kilts from the previous day.

A village lad ran up to Lyon, just as he placed a foot in the stirrup. "Here's a message, laird," the youth said, tugging politely on his cap.

Lyon tossed him a coin and opened the folded paper. "It's from Keir," he told the others. "He wants me to stop at the Scottish National Society's pavilion and get the letters Miss Elkheart discovered. Since they involve the massacre of the MacLyon Highlanders, they're going to be given to Nana for safekeeping with her genealogical documents." He looked up at Julie, seated sidesaddle on White Thunder. "It that's acceptable to you."

"That is where the papers belong," she replied.

The soft glow in her trusting gaze charred his wretched soul to a cinder. Their night of passion had left her tranquil and dreamy-eyed, as though her thoughts remained centered upon the pleasures they'd shared in his room at the inn.

Lyon knew no such peace.

They hadn't spoken of the future. He'd avoided all mention of her leaving or staying, but he hadn't changed his mind. Even though he'd succumbed to his devastating need for her, the brutal facts remained the same. He wouldn't snatch her dreams away and saddle her with a blighted shell of a man for a husband. Of all the sins he'd committed and all the mistakes he'd made, he refused to be responsible for this one.

While the grownups talked, Neil and Jamie rode their ponies around in circles, eager to get started.

"Do you want to race?" Neil called to his brother.

With a carefree grin, Jamie patted his pony's black mane. "Aye, let's race!"

"Be careful," Flora warned them. "You're going to get in someone's way." In her concern, she gave an unintentional jerk on her reins. Her blood bay sidestepped nervously, and she glanced at Lyon for help.

"You go on ahead with the ladies and the children," he told Rob, as he caught the bay's halter and calmed it with a pat. "I'll get the letters and catch up with you shortly."

"Right," his brother said with a quick nod. He whistled shrilly to his nephews. "Come on, ye twa loons. It's time to be going home."

Julie waited for a moment to see if Lyon would ask her to stay and ride with him. When he didn't, she drew White Thunder next to Flora's mare, and the family cantered across the meadow.

Holding Thor's reins in his hand, Lyon strode toward the gold and white striped tent. He would have to convince Julie that it was best for her to leave as soon as possible, yet somehow not make her feel rejected. He dared not tell her he loved her. If she knew how intensely he wanted to keep her with him, she might refuse to leave at all.

As Lyon stepped inside the Scottish National Society's

pavilion, he heard an ominous click. Someone held a double-barreled pistol inches from his head.

"Stand right there, MacLyon," the man warned with a raspy chuckle. "We wouldna want this gun to go off accidentally. That'd spoil all our fun."

Lyon understood now why Julie thought the tinker seemed familiar. The two men standing on either side of him were the same thugs who'd attacked him in Edinburgh.

"What do you want?" he asked.

" 'Tis yerself," the black-haired man chortled. "Me and Syme are takin' ye with us for a wee ride. There's someone that's wantin' to talk with ye."

The burly man signaled with a jerk of his head, and his lanky cohort unbuckled Lyon's shoulder holster and removed the Lancaster revolver. Then he unsheathed the dirk at Lyon's side.

"Ye willna be needin' these anymore," Syme said. He tossed the revolver and dirk atop a pile of ancient spears on the dirt floor. "Since I canna risk bein' caught with them, we'll just add them to the collection."

The large pavilion was in a state of upheaval. Pikes, spears, swords, poleaxes, and targes lay in haphazard stacks. Two men in MacDougall tartan were sprawled on the ground at the back of the tent, gagged, bound, and apparently unconscious. They'd been caught unawares while taking down the exhibit and packing the weapons.

"Me and Brodie have been waitin' all mornin' for ye to say farewell to yer loved ones," Syme said, his ugly, pocked face contorted with glee. "But dinna worry. There's a wee surprise waitin' for them up ahead."

Horror coiled its icy tentacles around Lyon's chest, squeezing the breath from his lungs.

Oh, God, no!

Not his family.

Not Julie.

With a smirk, Brodie jabbed his gun into Lyon's ribs. "Let's go, yer lairdship."

Lyon turned as though following instructions. But before Brodie could react he flung his arm upward, knocking the gun from his assailant's hand and sending it into a mound of halberds.

In the next instant, Lyon launched his well-trained body into a forward roll. He reached the nearest pile of armaments, snatched up a targe with his left hand and a basket-hilted broadsword with his right, and sprang to his feet.

Syme quickly armed himself with a pike. Flinty eyes narrowed, he advanced in a crouch and lunged. Lyon parried his attack with the round, wooden shield, and an agonizing pain jolted through his arm beneath the force of Syme's blow.

As his foe lunged again, Lyon brought the broadsword down on the pike's ash handle with such strength that he cut it asunder. Incredulous, Syme let the weapon fall from his numbed fingers.

Lyon sliced across Syme's chest on the return stroke, delivering a mortal wound, and with a final thrust, pierced his heart.

The kill had taken mere seconds.

Brodie grabbed a Lochaber ax and came at Lyon, swinging the long weapon with vicious skill. Lyon pivoted and dodged the slicing blade by less than an inch.

In an upward motion, Brodie caught the basket hilt of Lyon's sword with a hook on the poleaxe's five-foot staff. Giving a violent yank, he ripped the broadsword from Lyon's hand and grinned like a fiend from hell, as the bloodied steel went sailing across the pavilion to bounce off the canvas wall.

Lyon blocked the next strike with his targe, taking the shock of the blow on his weak arm. Lightning bolts of excruciating pain shot through his elbow.

Sweat pouring down his swarthy brow, Brodie struck again with such force that he buried the axe's broad blade in the wood and leather shield.

As Lyon toppled backward in the dirt, he twisted and

dove for a two-handed claymore. He rolled to his feet and recovered his fighting stance in one smooth movement. Just as his opponent jerked the Lochaber free, Lyon snagged the axe blade with the end of his claymore's large cross-guard.

At that moment, their gazes caught. The black-haired tinker looked into the face of death and froze in terror.

"This is for Neil and Jamie," Lyon said.

Yanking his huge, two-handed battle-sword back, Lyon wrenched the ax from Brodie's grasp and sent it soaring. With his return forward swing, he decapitated the man in one powerful stroke. Blood splattered over Lyon as the lifeless body sank to the ground.

Lyon threw down the claymore, snatched up his revolver and dirk, and raced from the pavilion. From his saddle, he shouted for those nearby to help the clansmen inside the tent. Then he galloped toward the village.

He reined Thor to a halt beside a MacDougall clansman walking along Strathbardine's main thoroughfare. "Find Dr. MacDougall," he called. "Tell him to go as fast as possible to Strathlyon Castle. Tell him to bring his medical bag. And tell him to come armed."

Then Lyon kicked the roan stallion's flanks and raced after his loved ones.

Chapter 23

High spirits radiated through the MacLyons' little group as the five riders climbed the steep slopes that rose from the sea loch. The Strathshire Gathering had exceeded everyone's expectations.

Juliette smiled to herself in secret enjoyment. The lingering bliss of her night with Lyon left her so buoyant, she felt she could float off her sidesaddle and fly back to the castle on imaginary wings.

Lyon had told her he loved her.

Granted, he'd spoken in Gaelic, thinking she couldn't understand. But armed with the knowledge of his love, there was nothing she couldn't face with complete assurance. She refused to allow his stern restraint that morning to perturb her. Their passionate mating had forged a bond that would last through eternity. He might *try* to send her away. He'd never succeed.

Flora's chatter interrupted Juliette's pleasant daydreams. "This morning, Lyon suggested I take the boys for a visit to their grandparents in Glasgow," she confided happily. "A short visit, but nevertheless, a trip home."

"I am very happy for you," Juliette said with a surprised smile. It seemed her talk with Lyon had done some good, after all.

"Not only that," Flora added, "but a gentleman I danced

with last night asked Lyon if he might pay a call on me at the castle. Lyon granted his permission.''

Juliette met Flora's sparkling eyes, and a feeling of joy and contentment wrapped around her like a warm buffalo robe. "Everything is going to work out for the best," she told Flora. "I am sure of it.''

Rob was in a rousing good mood, as well. He raced with Neil and Jamie, letting Neil win. The three MacLyon males then stopped and waited for the ladies to catch up. Beneath a delft-blue sky dotted with clouds, two heads of copper and one of inky black turned to watch their approach with typical masculine impatience.

Every time Rob met Juliette's gaze, he grinned jubilantly. Somehow, he'd guessed. She felt the heat of a blush spread across her cheeks, wondering if he'd seen her slip into— or out of—Lyon's room. If he had, he was clearly pleased with the notion of her joining the MacLyon family permanently.

They left the main roadway and turned up the winding lane that led to Strathlyon Castle. Ash, elm, hazel, and alders spread their branches above them, sprinkling their colorful foliage over the ground in a thick, rustling blanket. With a sudden whir of wings a bevy of grouse exploded from the underbrush, capturing everyone's attention.

In that instant a fusillade rang out. The entrapped riders, caught in a crossfire, milled about in turmoil. The frightened horses reared and plunged and whinnied. The children shouted in confusion, trying to keep their startled mounts under control. Juliette reached out and grabbed the reins of Jamie's pony. In the midst of the tumult, Flora toppled from her saddle without a sound.

"Go!" Rob shouted to Juliette. "Get the lads out of here." He jumped from his horse to help Flora, firing his revolver into the trees as he ran.

"Neil," Juliette called, "follow me!"

They galloped madly through the trees and broke into an open meadow, scattering a flock of sheep. She recognized a grove of birches from her morning rides and turned in that direction. A stream flowed through the birch woods to Strathlyon Glen.

The staccato report of gunshots echoed behind them. Once in the cover of the woodland, she dismounted and helped the boys down. "Come with me," she told them.

She led the youngsters to a stream bank covered with moss, rushes, and ferns. Working frantically, she dug a small cave in the soft ground with her knife in the old Cheyenne way. Her people had hid their helpless ones from the pursuing pony soldiers in just this manner. The dank smell of moist earth permeated her crimson riding habit as she knelt on its folds.

The two boys watched Juliette in silent terror, unable to comprehend what she was doing. At the sight of their innocent faces, fear sank its fangs into her like a wolf bringing down a doe, but she refused to give in to the panic. She would need all her warrior-woman training to get them out of this alive. If Rob could hold their attackers off long enough, she'd have a chance to save the children.

When she finished the hole, she crouched down in front of Neil and Jamie and placed her hands on their shoulders. "Listen carefully," she said. "You must do just as I say."

Too frightened to speak, they nodded mutely.

"You know I am a fairy, and that I have the power to make little boys disappear," she said in a confident tone. "That is what I am going to do now. I am going to use my magic so that the evil men will not find you. You must promise not to call out, not even to whisper to each other. For though they will not be able to see you, they can find you by the sound of your voices. No matter what happens, do not move from this place, unless you hear me or one of your uncles calling you."

"What if you don't come back, Miss Elkheart?" Neil's worried eyes reflected his mounting alarm. "We won't disappear forever, will we?"

Hope soared within her.

They believed her implicitly.

"No," she promised. "I will make the spell last only for twenty-four hours. If we do not come for you, stay here all night. Then very quietly creep away in the early dawn and go to Dr. MacDougall's house in the village. Do not try to walk back to Strathlyon alone."

Jamie's sturdy little body shook with fright. He wiped away his tears, but his voice broke on a sob. "What . . . what about Mama?"

"Your Uncle Rob will take care of her, Hehen," she told him tenderly. She stroked his plump cheek in reassurance. "Your mother would want you to stay here, where you are safe."

"And our ponies?" Neil asked. He was trying so hard to be brave, that Juliette pulled him into her arms and kissed his forehead. Jamie clung to her, and she kissed him in turn.

"I cannot make the ponies disappear, Maevess," she explained. "I need them to lead the evil ones away from here. But do not fret. They will not harm the horses."

She helped the boys get inside the damp earth cave. Then she hurriedly covered the front of it with the golden fronds of the ferns. She replaced the torn moss, uprooted rushes, and dry leaves, using a branch to remove all trace of their footsteps. Even from a short distance, no one would notice their hiding place. A searcher would have to ride directly over the top of the cave to ever find them.

Juliette gathered the ponies' reins in her hand and mounted Voxpenonoma, then rode to the edge of the birch woods. The gunfire had ceased, and the silence gripped her in its unnerving embrace.

Rob must have been hit.

She chanted a brave-heart song under her breath, the Cheyenne words filling her with courage and strength. Like her people's valorous Dog Soldiers, she would stand between the enemy and the helpless ones, even to the death. Neil and Jamie's lives were in her keeping. Nothing else mattered but that.

The sudden bleating of sheep carried across the meadow. Two strangers cantered their horses through the dry grass, searching right and left for some sign of her and the boys. The trail of broken stems cut a swath straight to the birch grove. She and the boys wouldn't be hard to follow.

With the trained patience of a hunter, Juliette waited for the riders to come nearer. They were big, brutish men armed with pistols. Ignorant men, who hadn't the least notion how to track. They kept riding back and forth, disturbing the signs.

She gauged the distance between them and the edge of the woodland, waiting until they were just out of pistol range, but close enough to spot her at the right moment. Then she struck the two little ponies on their rumps, sending them crashing noisily through the trees away from Neil and Jamie. The men looked up and gaped at her. She urged White Thunder in the opposite direction, leading the evilmakers further into the birch woods toward Strathlyon Glen.

Lyon found Rob and Flora sprawled in the roadway. There was no sign of Julie and his nephews—and no sign of their attackers. He could tell that Flora was dead. Her lovely eyes stared vacantly up at the heavens.

He dismounted before Thor came to a stop and raced to his brother, who'd fallen face down in the dirt. Dropping to one knee, Lyon gently turned Rob over and cradled him against his arm.

Rob's face was ghastly white, his lids closed. Lyon quickly examined the wounds. He'd been struck in two places, shoulder and thigh, but there was a steady pulse.

His brother's eyes opened slowly. "Two men," he gritted. "After Julie and the lads."

Removing his own plaid, Lyon opened Rob's jacket and pressed the blue and black wool against the bullet hole to staunch the bleeding. The sight of the bloodstained tartan brought the bitter taste of bile to his mouth. Memories of El Durman swirled before his eyes.

He hoisted his strong, athletic brother over his shoulder. The two hundred pounds of muscle and bone sent sharp jolts of pain shooting through Lyon's left elbow. He carried Rob to a nearby tree and propped him against its trunk, then crouched beside him.

"What the hell happened to you?" Rob asked with a groan.

Lyon glanced down at his own bloodied clothing. "I met the black-haired tinker who gave Neil and Jamie the poisoned sweets."

"I don't have to ask if you killed him," Rob said with a faint smile. "You're wearing the proof."

Lyon unpinned Rob's plaid from his jacket and used it to make a tourniquet for his thigh. He gave his brother a quick, encouraging pat on the shoulder before returning to the road.

Flora had been struck in the forehead. She'd probably died instantly, and for that much, Lyon was thankful. He bent and lifted his sister-in-law up from the dusty ground, her limp form such a slight burden in his arms that his throat constricted painfully. Laying her down on the grass near Rob, he tenderly closed her eyes and folded her hands across her waist.

Regret ate at Lyon's insides like a canker as he knelt and studied her peaceful face. All the times he'd lost patience with her flighty ways rose up to haunt him. She'd suffered a nearly incapacitating grief at James's death, a bewildered widow far away from her parents, with the responsibility of two lads to care for and raise to manhood.

His vision blurred as he brushed aside the ebony strands blown across her cheek by the autumn breeze. He glanced at Rob and found him watching with solemn eyes.

"Why couldn't I have been a little kinder, a little more understanding?" Lyon asked, his voice choked with remorse. "Flora's terrible headaches and bouts of depression surely were justified for a young woman who'd lost a husband who'd adored her.''

"She'd been much happier of late," Rob said quietly. "And she was thrilled that you were sending her and the lads to Glasgow for a visit.''

At the thought of her excitement that morning when he'd told her she'd soon be with her mother and father, guilt squeezed Lyon's heart. The remarkable change in Flora since Julie had arrived only showed how lonely and frightened she'd been in their midst.

"Why was I such a cold-hearted sonofabitch?" he asked with a low growl of self-contempt.

Rob's words were faint, but reassuring. "You were dealing with your own grief and guilt at the time.''

Lyon removed his jacket and covered Flora's head. Then he met his brother's glassy, pain-filled eyes. "I'm going to have to leave you here.''

"Just give me my pistol and go.''

Lyon looked around and saw the revolver close by. He retrieved the weapon and pressed it into his brother's palm. Despite his injuries, Rob's fingers curled around the handle in a firm grasp.

"Did you see which way they rode?''

"East, toward the glen.''

"Keir's on his way," Lyon told him. "He'll find you.'' He rose to his feet and glared down at his brother. "Goddammit, Robbie, don't you die on me.''

Rob managed a crooked grin. "Hell, I wouldn't miss the wedding for anything in the world.''

Lyon mounted and sent Thor crashing through the trees. He found the path of flight across the meadow, where the tall grass had been crushed beneath the pounding hooves. At the edge of Rothnamurchan Woods the trail split in two, heading in opposite directions. Torn, he gazed one way and then the other. There wasn't a sign of anyone.

With a rapid thud of hooves, two Welsh ponies broke from the birch trees and galloped wildly across the meadow toward the lane and home. A stranger chased after them. Unholstering his revolver, Lyon took careful aim and fired. The man's arms flew up, and he toppled backwards off his horse.

Rage seething inside him, Lyon rode to the crumpled figure and dismounted. He hadn't killed the miserable bastard, because he needed him alive. He picked up the man's powerful Horsley pistol and shoved it into the belt of his kilt. Then he grabbed a fistful of the man's dirty brown hair, lifted his head off the ground, and jammed the long barrel of his Lancaster into his mouth.

"If you want to live, you frigging better answer my questions."

The man's bloodshot eyes bulged. Sweat poured down his forehead and trickled along the bridge of his bulbous nose.

Lyon withdrew the gun just far enough for him to talk. "Where are the lads?"

"I dinna ken," he blubbered. "I dinna find them, only their wee ponies. They must be still with the lass."

Lyon recognized the peculiar, recitative accent of a Glaswegian.

"Where's your friend?"

"Lizars went after the lass when we thought they'd split up." He clutched his injured shoulder. Blood seeped through his fingers. "Ye maun help me, man, or I'll fairly bleed to death."

"Shut up," Lyon warned, "or I'll put you out of your bloody misery right now. Who hired you?"

"Some rich laird," he wailed. "I dinna ken his name. It's the gospel truth! I swear it, man! Grig Brodie said he'd pay us after it was all done. We're to meet the laird in an old broch in four days."

"Where's this broch?"

"It's on a cliff overlooking the village."

Lyon rose to his feet. "Take off your boots."

"What?"

''Take off your boots, or I'll shoot you in the goddamn foot.''

The wounded man hurried to do as he'd been told.

Lyon shoved the dilapidated work boots under the man's saddle, then struck the horse sharply on its flank. The animal took off in the direction of Strathbardine.

Without another word, Lyon clubbed the man over the head with his gun butt. When the bastard woke up, he wouldn't get far—not without his boots, and bleeding the way he was.

Lyon mounted Thor and galloped back along the edge of the birch grove, searching for the hoof prints that would lead him to Julie and the lads.

Juliette had to slow White Thunder to a canter several times to be certain the *veho* was following. He rode like a drunken mule skinner, whipping his horse viciously, cursing, and sawing on the reins. She led him deeper into the birch woods until she was certain that even if he found her, he'd never discover Neil and Jamie. He couldn't force her to divulge their hiding place, no matter what he tried.

Knowing the boys were safe, she felt calmer, no longer so frightened. But she reminded herself what Strong Elk Heart had taught her: never underestimate your enemy.

When she dismounted, she left her white mare sheltered in a clump of rowan trees dense with clusters of scarlet fruit. The Scots believed the rowan could ward off evil. Maybe its magic would protect her.

Juliette removed her half boots and dropped them on the ground. She ran across the carpet of fall leaves in her stocking feet, going as quietly and quickly as possible. She could hear the man's horse smashing through the undergrowth as he searched for her.

Juliette's riding habit was a deep, rich crimson, easily seen against the yellow leaves and silver bark of the birches.

She made a perfect target.

She took her jacket off as she ran and hung it on a low branch, where the white man would be sure to see it. Continuing to move through the woods, she unfastened her waistband, stepped out of her skirt, and let it fall to the ground. She headed along the stream bank toward the castle, leaving her white blouse and then her petticoat in plain view.

Once she'd discarded her outer garments, Juliette had the freedom of movement she needed. Her bronze skin and dark hair helped her blend with her surroundings, but the stark white of her chemise and drawers stood out like flags of surrender against the autumn foliage. She doubled back, moving from tree to tree in silent stealth. If luck was with her, the *veho* was as stupid as he looked. And the scattered female attire just might make him so anxious to find her that he'd become careless. His carelessness could save her life.

Lyon followed the trail into Rothnamurchan Woods easily. No one had made any attempt to hide their tracks.

He found a dun gelding tied to a tree, its coat lathered with sweat. It'd been whipped mercilessly. At his approach the horse shook its head, jingling the bridle. A soft nicker came in response, and Lyon spotted White Thunder, almost hidden in some rowans. The Arabian mare stamped and neighed at the sight of him. Dismounting, he patted her nose, soothing her into silence.

A dreadful fear seeped through Lyon's gut. Not far away, Julie's black kid boots lay on the ground. He withdrew his revolver, cautiously scanning the trees.

As Lyon moved through the grove, he discovered her jacket tossed carelessly aside. The dark red cloth, like a pool of blood on the golden leaves, was impossible to miss. The shock of finding it slashed like a knife at his vitals. Yet he dared not hurry too fast and risk overlooking some small sign. He couldn't take the chance of heading in the wrong direction.

He stopped and listened, straining to hear any telling sound. Not even the chirp of a wren disturbed the still woods. The unearthly silence throbbed out a warning, grim and sinister. Images of Julie being beaten and raped flashed though his mind, and for a moment, he could almost hear her sobbing.

The sight of her skirt lying in a heap on the ground ignited his cold, dark rage to the heat of a blast furnace. He'd beat the bloody, frigging bastard to death with his bare hands. He'd rip out his black heart and stomp on it.

When he heard the crunch of clumsy footsteps in the dry leaves, he moved quickly in their direction.

From behind a tree, Juliette watched the bearded *veho* jam his gun in his belt and stoop down to pick up her petticoat. He fingered the embroidered cotton as he grabbed at the crotch of his filthy trousers. He'd lost his hat, and his smooth, hairless scalp was the speckled brown and white of a lizard's belly. He brought her lingerie to his bearded face and chortled soundlessly, and she wondered if he thought she was trying to use her body to barter for mercy. She doubted that mercy was a commodity this man knew anything about.

Lizard Head was larger than she'd thought. He had a grossly distended belly, but his upper arms swelled with muscle. There was something intensely evil about him. He had the depraved look of a cunning predator, a *veho* who lived in the slums of a great city and would do anything for the white man's gold.

In cautious silence, she drew her knife and stepped from her hiding place. She stood only a short distance from where he crouched. Before he had time to rise to his feet and look around, she hurled the lethal weapon.

The Lizard must have caught a glimpse of her white drawers from the corner of his eye, for he moved at the last possible moment. The blade, which should have struck him in the neck, caught him instead on his shoulder.

"Bloody bitch!" he roared, as he lumbered to his feet and whirled to face her. Glaring at her in rage, he reached back, yanked the knife free, and threw it to the ground.

Juliette darted away.

With a blood-curdling howl, Lizard Head charged after her.

Branches caught at her hair and struck her face and bare arms. In her blind terror, she stumbled over a thick clump of shrubbery and fell on her hands and knees. The full weight of his huge body crashed down on top of her, knocking her flat on her stomach. Gasping for air, she struggled to crawl away.

The *veho* caught her chin in one hand and forced her head back. His other hand came around to grasp her breast and gouge her painfully with his thumb nail. His putrid breath sickened her.

Applying relentless pressure, he tried to leverage one beefy leg under her thigh and flip her over.

Fervent determination to fight him with every breath in her body pumped through Juliette's bloodstream, though she knew she'd never be able to match his brute strength. The more she fought, the more she incited him to murder—which was exactly what she wanted to do. Better a quick, clean death than one of lingering humiliation at the hands of an obscene animal.

Chapter 24

For the second time in her life, Juliette felt an assailant being lifted off her. She rolled to her side, dragging air into her starved lungs, just in time to see Lyon smash Lizard Head against a tree.

As his opponent lunged toward him, Lyon grabbed the handgun jammed in the man's belt and cracked him across the side of his head with the butt. Stunned, the Lizard fell to the ground.

Lyon pulled him up by the front of his shirt and kneed him viciously. The bearded man doubled over, howling in pain.

Lyon yanked him back up and ruthlessly struck him again and again in the ribs and paunch with his fist. The big-bellied man sagged, grunting beneath each punishing blow. A stream of blood trickled down his bearded chin.

It seemed Lyon intended to break every rib in his foe's body before he quit.

When Lizard Head staggered backward against a tree and slid down, Lyon refused to let him lie there. He grabbed the thug by the throat with both hands and dragged him halfway up. Gripping him in a merciless choke hold, he smashed the bald head repeatedly against the trunk.

Juliette scrambled to her feet. She watched, dazed, as the remorseless pounding went on and on.

All the suppressed rage bottled up inside Lyon was channeled into his powerful arms and hands. His fury wasn't just for her endangerment, but for Flora and Rob and the boys. For the ambush on the roadside, for the arsenic poisoning, for the lighthouse fire, and for the steamboat explosion.

His enemy must have been dead for several minutes before the Lion became aware of it. He stood over the battered corpse, slowly massaging his left elbow, as though disappointed it was over so soon.

When Lyon turned to Juliette, she stared at him, unable to say a word. He was covered with blood. It stained his shirt and kilt, his neck, hands, stockings, and buckled brogues. It was even in his beautiful hair. A look of utter ferocity hardened his scarred, rugged features into a murderous mask.

His furious gaze swept over her torn chemise and dirt-stained drawers, and the rage blazed in his eyes. She half-expected him to turn around and kick the dead man in the head one more time.

Instead, he came and gripped her shoulders as though she might be torn from his grasp at any moment. She could feel the savage energy pounding through him as his gaze swept over her.

"Did that bastard hurt you?" he rasped.

"No." Her lips trembled in belated reaction. "*Ahahe,*" she cried woefully. "I tried to kill Lizard Head with my knife, but I threw too late and missed. *Nihoe* would have been disappointed in me. Warrior-women are supposed to keep their wits about them in battle."

With a tender smile, Lyon brushed his lips across her forehead. "Where are the lads?" he asked gently

"They are safe." Juliette's voice quavered and broke. "What about Flora . . . and Rob?"

His mouth tightened grimly. "Rob's wounded, but I think he'll live." Lyon paused, and Juliette's heartbeat stuttered to a halt. "Flora is dead."

"Oh, no, no!" she cried, tears filling her eyes. Her lower

lip wobbled, as sobs shuddered through her. "Why? Why would anyone kill Flora? She never harmed a soul."

Lyon didn't answer her impassioned question. He just held her in a comforting embrace, rocking her back and forth as though she were a small child.

When Juliette regained control at last, Lyon kissed the top of her head and released her. Glancing around, he found her knife in the leaves, wiped the blade on the dead man's shirt, and returned it to her.

They gathered up her scattered clothing, and she dressed hastily. He listened in quiet amazement as she explained that she'd purposely removed her constraining garments to allow her more mobility and to fool her enemy. Then he washed the blood from his hands and face in the clear water of the burn.

They rode to the spot where she'd hidden the boys. Lyon looked around impatiently, worried the children were no longer where Juliette had left them.

The lilting song of a thrush drifted down from the branches overhead. The yellow birch leaves rustled. Along the gurgling stream bank, the leafy, golden fronds of the bracken fern trembled in the slight breeze. The place appeared to be deserted.

"Call them," she whispered.

Lyon scowled in puzzlement as his gaze swept over the peaceful scene.

"Go on," she insisted softly. "Call them."

"Neil! Jamie!" he roared in a voice that could be heard all the way to the castle.

The two little boys popped up out of the earth directly in front of them, covered with pieces of moss and fern and bits of shrubbery. Their grins shone white in their dirty faces.

Lyon climbed down from Thor and dropped to his knees. The children rushed into his open arms.

"Miss Elkheart put a spell on us and made us disappear," Neil told him excitedly. "She hid us in a fairy hill. No one else could see us, except you and Uncle Robbie."

Jamie curved his arm around his uncle's strong neck and spoke earnestly into his ear. "We disappeared, Uncle Lyon. Can you see me now?"

"Yes, I can see you," Lyon said hoarsely. "You look . . . *wonderful*." He kissed their grimy cheeks, as he hugged them tight. Then he looked across their tousled heads and met Juliette's gaze. Tears glittered in his eyes. "Thank you."

Juliette knelt beside them on the dry grass and put her hands on the boys' shoulders. "The first responsibility of a Cheyenne warrior-woman," she explained, "is to protect the young and helpless."

"What's the second, Miss Elkheart?" Neil asked. His eyes glittered with curiosity in his begrimed face.

"To never miss what she aims for. I am still working on that one," she conceded.

Lyon put his arms around the three of them and gathered them to him in a ferocious bear hug. "God damn," he said softly, "I don't know when I've been so scared."

"Don't be scared," Jamie told him. He patted his uncle on the shoulder reassuringly. "Miss Elkheart won't let anything happen to us. She's a fairy princess, you know. Her magic is stronger than any evil man."

Tears burning her eyelids, Juliette met Lyon's gaze, and her heart wrenched with sorrow. Together, they would have to tell the children the appalling truth.

Her magic had not saved their mother.

On the day of the funeral, nearly everyone in the region of Strathshire came to the castle to pay their respects. The large entourage followed the glass-sided hearse drawn by sleek black horses with nodding plumes on their heads. Black umbrellas bobbed and shifted like flotsam on the sea as the mourners filled the MacLyon family's burial ground. Amidst granite Celtic crosses and praying angels with eyes

cast heavenward, men stood hatless in the drizzle, black
armbands on their black sleeves.

Juliette stood beside Keir and Annie MacDougall. She
looked across the open grave at the five MacLyons, who
were huddled together in their terrible grief. Lady Hester
sat in a chair, her stricken face drained of color beneath the
black net veiling of her hat. Haggard and solemn, Rob sat
beside her, one pale hand clutching a cane. He was still
weak and unsteady from loss of blood, although Keir had
assured them the robust young man would make a full recovery in time.

Standing next to his younger brother, Lyon held his
nephews' hands. From his stony expression, Juliette knew
the thoughts that plagued him. The two boys had lost both
their father and mother, and as head of the family, Lyon
held himself responsible—just as he'd assumed the blame
for the annihilation of an entire battalion of Royal Scots at
a place called El Durman.

Flora Annabelle MacLyon was laid to rest beside her
husband, James. Disbelief on their innocent faces, the little
orphans wept inconsolably as their mother's casket was
lowered into the rain-soaked ground. A piper in the
MacLyon kilt and plaid played the haunting strains of an
old Scottish hymn. Even the most hardened men present
blinked back tears.

After the brief interment service, the people filed past the
family, bending to shake Rob's hand or to press a loving
touch on Lady Hester's shoulder. Flora had made many
friends since she'd come to Strathlyon, and all of them had
a tender reminiscence to share with her loved ones. The
chief of Clan MacLyon formally thanked each of the
mourners for attending.

Lyon had been reticent and subdued for the past two
days. Flora's black coffin, draped with an enormous spray
of white orchids, had sat in the castle's spacious gallery,
where clansmen and family friends gathered in quiet rev-
erence. Hour after hour, Lyon had stood vigil over his

brother's widow, accepting condolences with reserved dignity.

He'd noticeably favored his left arm since the day of the attack. In fact, he barely moved it most of the time. Juliette assumed he'd injured it further in his struggles with the evildoers, but she knew it would be useless to ask him about it. He'd only scowl and change the subject.

He'd offered the excuse that he might lose the use of his arm altogether as the reason for not having the surgery, but Juliette knew the truth. Lyon chose to suffer because he'd failed to save his brother and Flora. His crippled arm was to be his lifelong penance.

As the wailing of the bagpipes faded, Laird Macfie and his sister, Georgiana, joined the MacDougalls and Juliette.

"It's a sad day," Hamish said to Keir. He tipped his hat politely to the two ladies, then glanced back to the doctor. "I understand that one of Flora's murderers managed to get away."

"Yes," Keir replied. His fair features grew livid with suppressed rage. "Lyon succeeded in killing three of them, but the fourth was merely wounded. Shot from a distance, at that. Lyon had no choice but to let the man escape, since he still hadn't found his nephews or Miss Elkheart."

Georgiana dabbed at her watery eyes with her handkerchief. "What a terrible, terrible tragedy. My heart goes out to those poor laddies." She brought one gloved hand to her breast in heartfelt sorrow as the tears flowed freely down her cheeks.

Macfie patted his sister's shoulder consolingly. "It's a damn shame," he concurred. "Did MacLyon recognize the fellow that escaped?"

"Unfortunately not," Keir replied. Annie stepped closer to her husband, and he covered the hand she'd placed on his arm in a comforting gesture. "He was too far away. Lyon's not sure he could even identify him."

Hamish glanced over at the yawning grave and felt a twinge of regret. The one person he'd have preferred to survive the ambush was the only one who'd been killed. Flora and Georgiana had always enjoyed each other's companionship. The lively brunette's visits, accompanied by her two sons, had been a real solace to his childless sister.

Those idiots from Glasgow had botched everything—and he still had one of them to deal with. Jervis Stirton would be at Dubhgall Broch tomorrow, expecting his payment for shooting a helpless female. He'd get a payment, all right—but it would be delivered in lead, instead of silver.

Hamish looked at Miss Elkheart and smiled repentantly. "I was told that your bravery saved the lads."

She gazed at him with those mysterious almond-shaped eyes, and he had the eerie feeling she could read his thoughts.

He'd sent her a letter of profuse apology the previous day, asking her to forgive his insufferable behavior if only for Georgiana's sake. His sister dearly wished to attend Flora's funeral. Hamish explained that he'd allowed his temper to get the best of him the night he discovered her in his home. He assured Miss Elkheart he'd meant her no real harm.

"It was Lyon who saved us all," she replied modestly. Beneath her black umbrella, the travail of the past days remained etched on her face. Dark shadows under her eyes revealed two long, sleepless nights.

Georgiana clasped the young woman's hand. "I suppose you'll soon be going back to Edinburgh, now that the gathering is over."

"At the moment, I have not made any plans," Miss Elkheart answered in a noncommittal tone. But she smiled kindly at Hamish's sister, clearly not wanting to blame the soft-hearted widow for her brother's mistakes.

Macfie knew that many of the people present were angry that he'd kept his clan's duplicity a secret at the expense of the innocent Danielsons. Nothing could be done legally about a hundred-year-old crime, but only their affection for Georgiana made them hold their tongues that morning.

"We'd best be going now," Hamish said, as he took his sister's elbow. He nodded to the MacDougalls, and they withdrew.

The mourners gradually drifted away, leaving the family to comfort each other in the privacy of their home. Juliette assumed she'd ride back to the castle with Lady Hester and the boys in the closed landau, but at the last moment Rob took her place while Lyon escorted Juliette into the brougham. She placed her dripping umbrella on the farther side of the small coach and moved the heavy folds of her black dress out of the way so he'd have more room to sit down.

Rain pattered softly on the roof, as the footman hopped on back of the closed carriage and the coachman turned the horse in the castle's direction.

Frowning, Lyon rubbed his elbow absently. "I saw Hamish Macfie go over to talk with you and the MacDougalls. What did he have to say?"

Juliette resisted the impulse to ask if she could massage Lyon's injured arm with a special ointment she'd made, once they arrived back at the castle. She suspected he'd been unable to sleep because of the pain. For the past two nights, she'd lain awake worrying about him. And thinking of Flora.

"Laird Macfie wanted to know about the men who murdered Flora and attacked you in the pavilion," she replied. "He and his sister were terribly shocked by her untimely death, but then, so was everyone who came today."

Stretching his long legs out in front of him, Lyon moved restlessly on the seat. His severely tailored black coat and trousers emphasized his indisputable masculinity. An image of him in the shirt and kilt splattered with blood rocked her with its startling vividness. The rumor had surfaced that he'd beheaded the man who'd given Neil and Jamie the poisoned candy. She didn't doubt its veracity.

He regarded her now with a quizzical expression. "Nana

said you received a letter from Macfie yesterday.''

''Yes, he wrote to apologize for his behavior the night I broke into his home. Laird Macfie said his temper got the best of him when he found me pilfering his collection of documents, and that he was truly sorry. He begged me to forgive him for his sister's sake.''

Lyon cocked an eyebrow inquiringly. ''Which you apparently did.''

Wondering if he disapproved, Juliette toyed with the strings of the handbag on her lap. Lyon had come close to strangling Macfie to death that night. She wasn't certain how he felt about the man now.

''The letters are safe in Keir's hands,'' she said, ''and I am certain their authenticity will be proven. Since the papers will establish the innocence of Clan Danielson once and for all, there is no reason to upset Laird Macfie's sister any further. Georgiana is kind and sweet. I think she sincerely loves her brother and has no perception of his true nature.''

''Which is?''

She searched Lyon's grim visage. He had a specific reason for his questions, though she couldn't guess what it was—unless he wanted to punish Macfie for concealing his ancestors' treachery.

''Hamish Macfie has the eyes of a wolf,'' she said. At Lyon's evident surprise, she continued. ''Through the course of a Canadian winter, a wolf pack will harry and haunt a single herd of deer from the mountains and highlands down to the open plains. As the bitter season progresses, the wolves bring down the helpless fawns first, then the smaller does, and finally the exhausted bucks. Kill by kill, the pack feeds off the herd until it is completely destroyed. There is a ruthless calculation in Macfie's eyes that makes me think of a wolf.''

Lyon's brief smile lightened his drawn features. ''That's quite a character reference. I think I prefer being compared to a mountain lion.''

She tilted her head and peeked at him sideways. "Yes, *nanoseham*," she agreed with a teasing smile. "But although a mountain lion does not hunt in a pack, it is every bit as dangerous."

Lyon somberly took one of her gloved hands in his, and Juliette could feel tension vibrate through the closed coach. A foreshadowing of desolation deepened his rich, resonant baritone. "Julie, I'm sending Lady Hester and the lads to Glasgow for a visit. I'd promised Flora the children could spend some time with their grandparents. I regret now that I'd waited so long. If I had let her go there sooner, she'd be alive today."

"You must not blame yourself," Juliette insisted. "There was no way you could have known such a dreadful thing would happen."

Something in his gaze warned her there was more to come. And that it was much, much worse.

"Nevertheless, I regret my stubbornness. If it hadn't been for your bravery and quick thinking, Neil and Jamie would be lying in the burial plot beside their parents." He looked down and studied her fingers in the black leather gloves, as though measuring them against his own.

She shook her head in adamant disagreement. "You would have arrived in time to save them."

"Perhaps."

"When are they leaving for Glasgow?"

He raised his eyes to hers. His cold, unflinching resolve penetrated her chest like a spike of green ice. "Tomorrow morning."

She gasped in shock. Her frozen heart seemed to crack into slivers. "Tomorrow!"

"Yes," he said calmly. "You can accompany them on the train as far as Stirling. It's only a short distance from there to Edinburgh."

She lifted her chin in outright defiance. She wouldn't let him force her to leave, now that she knew he loved her.

"I will not go."

When Julie tried to pull her hand away, Lyon held it firmly in his grasp. He'd known this wasn't going to be easy. "What I'm doing is in your own best interests."

Blinking rapidly to ward off tears, she turned her head aside. Beneath the curved brim of her black velvet hat and half veil, her profile was achingly beautiful. Her adorable lower lip jutted out in obstinate rebellion, and her stiffened posture declared her absolute refusal to discuss the subject further. One of the things he most admired was her indomitable spirit. But this was one decision Lyon wasn't going to let Julie make.

"You're an impressionable lass suffering from an infatuation for a decorated soldier," he said softly. He offered her a placating smile. "It's not uncommon. It's usually fleeting. And it's hardly ever fatal."

Her head snapped around, and she glared at him. The tears that pooled in her angry eyes swamped his heart. Lyon felt like a drowning man, who'd grasp at anything to save himself from the approaching oblivion. But he wouldn't yield to her tears or her anger.

"What I feel for you is not infatuation," she stated with clipped resolution, "and you know it. I will love you with the last breath I take. And I will not allow you to send me away. Not tomorrow. Not ever."

"You have no choice," he told her, trying desperately to keep his tone rational and even. He had the upper hand. But God above, he didn't want to hurt her any more than was necessary. "You can't stay at Strathlyon after Nana leaves with Neil and Jamie. Not with just Rob and me there; it wouldn't be proper. Your uncle would be on the next train from Edinburgh to fetch you the moment he found out."

Teardrops glistened on Julie's impossibly long lashes. Her husky contralto pulsated with scorn. "And you would make certain he found out."

"I already telegraphed Dr. Robinson your expected time of arrival at Waverly Station."

Julie leaned toward him, her eyes narrowed. "Tell me you do not love me," she dared him. "Then I will go."

"Fine. I don't love you."

Lyon steeled himself, expecting her to burst into sobs of mortification. Instead, she glowered at him, her eyes darting sparks of wrath. The wee fairy princess looked furious enough to zap him into a toad or carve up his liver with her knife.

With a toss of her head, she gave him a sharp, supercilious smile that cut all the way to the bone. "Then you will not mind returning my hand, *veho*," she said coldly. She tried to yank her fingers out of his grasp.

He released her hand, and Julie turned to face the front of the carriage. She folded her arms across her chest with glacial contempt and proceeded to ignore him. He'd never seen her serene highness in a royal fit of temper until now. But infuriated as she was, there wasn't a damn thing she could do about it. She was leaving on that train tomorrow.

Lyon had expected Julie to cry and plead and try to change his mind with soft, tender kisses. Hell, he'd planned on it. He'd intended to savor every one of those sweet kisses; to use her tears as a balm to soothe his shriveled soul. If she had too much pride to beg, he wished to bloody hell she'd just accept his decision with trusting, female compliance. They had so damn little time left. The last thing he wanted to do was fight with her.

When Julie reached her bedroom and discovered that the maids had packed all of her belongings while she'd been at the graveside, she might even refuse to speak to him again before she left. He glanced out the window at the gray, murky drizzle. It matched the gloominess in his desolate heart.

The brougham came to a stop in the Strathlyon courtyard, and Lyon knew Grierson, the footman, would jump down and open the door at any moment.

"Julie," he said, gently touching her arm, "let's not part this way. I know why you're angry, and I take full responsibility for what happened between us. But compounding one mistake with another is not the answer.''

She rounded on him, just as the door swung open. ''Do you know why I am angry, Scotsman? I do not think so. So I will tell you: I am angry because you are *such a fool!*''

With the footman's assistance, Julie stepped down from the carriage. She popped her umbrella open and marched up the stairs without another word.

Davie Grierson stared straight ahead, a look of horror mingled with intense amusement on his handsome face. Everyone at the castle, from the lowliest bootblack to the head steward, would soon know exactly what Miss Juliette Elkheart had just said to The MacLyon, laird of Strathlyon, and marquess of Strathshire.

And Lyon didn't have to ask where their sympathies would lie. They respected and feared him. They adored her.

''God dammit,'' he muttered as he climbed out of the vehicle. ''Women.''

Chapter 25

∾⌒◯⌒∾

A golden eagle circled above the tall stone tower on the cliff overlooking the sleepy fishing village. Its piercing whistle of alarm carried on the coastal breeze as the great bird soared and hovered in majestic, broad-winged flight. It swooped and beat low over the ground as though to drop on its prey.

In the grass below, a mountain lion roared in frustration at the noisy display of diving and wing-clapping.

The russet cat was a large, adult male, weighing over two hundred pounds. From his nose to the tip of his long tail, he measured eight feet. The injured animal licked his torn, mangled flesh and tried once again to free himself. His left forefoot was caught in a vicious steel trap.

Through the dry autumn grass, a gray wolf made its solitary way toward the ancient ruin. Hungry and dangerous, it spotted the wounded lion and lowered its body to slink even closer.

The mountain lion's sensitive whiskers twitched as he caught the rank odor of wolf in his nostrils. He tried to spring away, but the trap's metal claws sank deeper into his swollen paw with every move.

Ordinarily, a lone wolf presented no threat to a powerful mountain lion. But the big cat had dragged the heavy trap across the rugged countryside for miles. Exhausted and *weak from loss of blood, he sank back down in the grass and snarled a warning.*

The wolf crept closer. Tail stiff, ears laid back, it watched the maimed cat, aware that he was still dangerous. One swipe with a muscular forepaw, and the lion's needle-sharp claws could rip the wolf open.

The cunning wolf wouldn't attack at once. It would circle the mountain lion, crouching and waiting throughout the day. When nanoseham grew weak and helpless, it would charge, deadly canine fangs bared.

The wolf tipped back its head and howled in the certainty it would gorge on its kill that night . . .

Juliette woke to feel her heart racing in silent terror. She scooted from beneath the covers and lit the gas lamp on the night stand. With shaking fingers, she picked up the porcelain clock and turned its face to the light. Two in the morning.

Sitting on the edge of the bed, Juliette buried her face in her hands. The vision had left her nearly paralyzed with fright. Now she knew why Lyon had questioned her so closely about Hamish in the carriage the previous afternoon.

Laird Macfie was responsible for the men who'd attacked them on the road from Strathbardine! Like a pack of wolves, they'd lain in wait, watching for the opportunity to murder the MacLyons. The fire in the lighthouse, the explosion on the paddle-wheeler, and the attempted poisoning of the children were all part of a diabolical plot.

The realization brought a flash of insight. *This* was the reason the spirits of her ancestors had brought Juliette to the Highlands. Not to exonerate Clan Danielson from a crime buried deep in the past, but to save the MacLyons in the present crisis. Even in death, the Danielsons remained true and loyal friends.

Somehow, Lyon had learned that Laird Macfie was the real culprit. That was why he'd decided to send his grandmother and nephews away on such short notice. If Rob were well enough, she knew Lyon would have insisted on sending him along as their escort.

From her vision, Juliette was certain Lyon planned to meet Hamish at Dubhgall Broch that very day. But Macfie was as crafty as an old wolf, and this time Lyon's injury could cost him his life.

Her frustration and anger at Lyon's stubbornness faded with the awareness that he was in mortal danger.

She opened the drawer of the night table and withdrew one of the pots of ointment she'd made for Lyon. Derived from wild plants, it was a soothing medicine that would alleviate the worst of his pain. It could also help him regain some use of his arm, if only temporarily. She'd planned to leave the jars with Rob before departing the castle, but there was no guarantee that Lyon would use the salve before meeting Hamish.

She had to do everything she could to help him, even if it meant swallowing her pride.

Lyon stood by his bedroom window and stared out at the starry night sky. The previous morning's cheerless drizzle had been blown away by westerly winds. For the fourth night in a row, he'd hardly slept. He paced the floor instead.

From the shoulder joint to the tips of his fingers, the persistent pain lanced through his arm like fiery spears. Keir had wanted to give him an injection of morphia that afternoon, but he'd refused. The vial of laudanum the compassionate doctor insisted on leaving stood unopened on the bureau. Lyon couldn't afford to be slowed down by any lingering effects of a drug. He needed to be alert for tomorrow's rendezvous.

Hell, pain or not, he wouldn't have been able to sleep, anyway—not knowing this was the last night Julie would spend in his home. It took all his willpower to keep from going to her bedroom. The longing to take her in his arms and wake her from slumber with tender kisses caused a torturous ache in his loins that made the pain in his arm seem a trivial nuisance.

Julie had been so infuriated with him that afternoon, she'd probably slip her knife between his ribs rather than welcome him into her bed. He smiled to himself at the thought of her vitality and spunk.

Lyon walked to the fireplace and tossed another log on the grate. The sheriff of Strathshire had come to the castle on the day of Flora's death. Together, they'd arranged to keep the identity and whereabouts of the fourth murderer a secret. The felon sat locked in the castle's cellar at that moment. A fitting place, since it had once served as a dungeon.

Keir had doctored Jervis Stirton and pronounced him fit for his execution. Then the three conspirators had purposely spread the rumor that the miscreant had gotten away. Lyon didn't want Laird Macfie forewarned. He, not Stirton, would meet Hamish at Dubhgall Broch that coming afternoon.

Lost in thought, Lyon stood gazing at the flames when his bedroom door opened. He felt Julie's presence like a bright swirl of fairy dust enveloping his senses, and turned in joyous welcome.

She stepped inside and quietly closed the door. She wore a flowing yellow robe tied with tiny white ribbons. Her dark hair tumbled over her shoulders and down to her waist. The tenderness that shone in her eyes bathed him in its soft glow.

"I came to say good-bye," she whispered. Barefoot, she crossed the room with a graceful rustle of satin. She touched his stubbled cheek, her thumb moving gently across his lips to forestall his objections. "Please do not tell me to return to my room."

Lyon put his sound right arm around her waist and drew her close. "I couldn't if I wanted to," he said. He bent to kiss her, but she placed her fingers against his mouth and shook her head.

"I have something to give you," she murmured. "This is for your arm. I know your injury pains you gravely."

For the first time, he noticed she was carrying a small jar in one hand. "My arm can wait," he replied with a crooked smile. "Another ache is craving your attention at the moment, *a ghràidh shìth*."

"Later," she promised. She slipped from his embrace and pointed to the wing chair near the fire. "Sit there and remove your shirt."

He shrugged out of the rumpled white linen and sank down on the striped cushion. Julie knelt in front of him, opened the lid of the blue jar, and placed it next to her on the floor. The sharp tang of evergreens permeated the air.

"I made this for you," she explained. "It will bring you some relief, so you can sleep."

"What made you think I couldn't sleep?"

At his scowl, a smile skipped about the corners of her mouth. "You have been a little grumpier than usual lately. I assumed it was because you had been deprived of your rest."

He gave a snort of self-derision. "I'm always grumpy. Ask anyone who knows me."

"Not always," she disagreed. "Sometimes you are the sweetest, gentlest man I have ever known."

She took his arm and rubbed a translucent salve along the cramped muscles of his wrist and forearm. The tingling sensation brought a sense of warmth and relaxation. As she slowly massaged his arm, the warmth turned to heat, radiating through the aching flesh to the tortured bone beneath.

"What is this?" he asked with a wary smile. "Something you concocted for old, spavined horses?"

She laughed softly. With deliberate precision, she moved upward to minister to his scarred elbow, then bicep and shoulder. The immediate cessation of pain was extraordinary.

"No," she replied, "this salve is for old, spavined warriors."

"Like me."

Her eyes sparkled with amusement. "My great-grandmother, Porcupine Quills, taught me how to make this recipe from alder leaves, juniper root, the inner bark of willow and larch, and the gum of spruce."

He sniffed appreciatively. "I thought it smelled like Yuletide."

She paused and settled back to look up at him. Her arched brows drew together in a frown as her tone grew serious. "This medicine will give you temporary relief only, *nanoseham*. You must still find a surgeon who can remove the bullet shard."

Cautiously, Lyon bent his arm. Amazingly, he had almost full use of his elbow without the agonizing pain that had tormented him since he'd fought his two assailants in the pavilion. "How often can I use this salve?"

"As often as you need to," she replied. "I will leave you more jars, if you promise you will see a surgeon."

"All right," he agreed reluctantly. "Next time I'm in Edinburgh."

"And you will do as he suggests?"

He traced the ruffled lace on the collar of her robe with the tip of one finger. "I'll consider it," Lyon compromised, as he pulled on a silk ribbon, untying the bow at her throat.

She rose, precious jar in hand, and replaced the lid. "Eventually you will run out of my medicine, *zehemehotaz*. Then you will want me to come back across the ocean to bring you more." She placed the jar on a nearby table. "That word means 'beloved,' by the way," she added with an entrancing smile. "You have my permission to use it anytime you wish. Now I need to wash my hands."

He gestured toward his dressing room and the bath beyond. "Through there."

The thought of Julie an ocean and continent away struck him with the sickening force of a knee to the crotch. How he'd bear the agony of losing her was more than he could comprehend. She'd become so much a part of his life. Like her marvelously soothing medicine, she had seeped into the marrow of his bones.

Lyon wandered restlessly about the room. He swung his injured arm in a wide arc and bent his elbow up and down, testing its unexpected mobility. Dazed by the miraculous improvement, he sat on the edge of his bed to wait for his magical fairy princess.

When Julie returned, she'd removed her robe and nightgown. Her slender nude form was revealed in the wavering light, her honeyed skin reflecting the warm glow of the flames. Warmth leapt to his groin, igniting a conflagration as pagan and primitive as the bonfires lit on the hillsides on Samhuinn. She came to stand in front of him, and he drew her between his thighs.

"You don't play fair, princess," he said, his words gruff with passion.

Every rapacious instinct inherited from his fierce Norse ancestors raged through his veins. Lyon slid his big, rough, conquering hands over the delicate curves of her hips and waist and greedily smothered her breasts. She was a Valkyrie sent to convey him to Valhalla, and he would ride her through the night sky with an unquenchable lust that would last through the ages.

"I cannot match your warrior's strength," she said softly. Her nutmeg eyes were dreamy and luminous in the dim light. "I have only the wiles of a woman."

The overwhelming love Lyon felt for her outweighed even the carnal flames that roared inside. "Julie," he whispered tenderly. "This will change nothing."

She brushed her lips against his forehead, then bent and breathed her answer in his ear. "If I must go," she said, "then let the place of our leave-taking be mine to choose. Let us say farewell here in this room, not at some noisy train depot where curious onlookers will watch and listen."

Tonight, there were no fumes of Scotch whisky to excuse his selfish behavior. Yet Lyon had neither the strength nor the will to refuse her. He wanted to make love to Julie this one last time more than he wanted life itself.

Let his black soul burn for all eternity.

He would have her now.

Her breath caught as he bent his head and laved her coral tips. Her lashes drifted downward, and she rested her elegant hands on his solid shoulders. She stood so quiet and still beneath his caresses, he could almost hear the thundering of their hearts.

Lyon brought her down on the bed with him and leaned over her. He traced his open mouth across her silken skin, tasting the golden flesh of her breasts and stomach and limbs.

He spoke to her in the Gaelic, telling her of his need. "You are like a ripe peach, succulent and sweet. From the moment I saw you, my darling, I wanted to feast on your delectable flesh. I wanted to devour you. To suck you and lick you." He smiled as he lifted her foot and kissed the high arch. "Even your toes."

Juliette caressed Lyon's hard, broad chest. She buried her fingertips in the crisp hair and traced the circles of his flat nipples. His incomparable masculinity heightened her awareness of their obvious differences. Her soft, female body had been fashioned by nature to cling to his lean, muscled strength. Her rounded curves accentuated his long, powerful limbs. The need to see him naked and aroused throbbed inside her like the steady beating of drums at a war dance.

"Take off your clothes," she urged.

Lyon responded with a wicked grin. "I thought you'd never ask, *a ghaolaich*." He rolled off the bed and quickly removed his trousers.

Juliette knelt on the mattress and admired him openly. Beneath her gaze, his manhood jutted out from its dark bronze nest, and the pleasurable ache of desire spread through her. His lean flanks and tight buttocks, his corded belly and sinewy thighs, revealed the strength and virility of a mighty warrior.

Lyon stretched out on the bed and lifted her on top of him. As she sank slowly down upon his massive shaft, the feeling of fullness brought a sigh of joy and awe.

She bent over him, her long hair forming a curtain to enclose them in their own private world. The fragrance of juniper and spruce swirled around them. "Does it always feel this special? This wonderful?" she asked.

Lyon bracketed her face in his large hands. "Only with you, sweetheart. Only with you."

They moved slowly, lingeringly, as though resisting the passage of time, trying to make the night last forever.

Lyon felt Julie's lips brush his, her fragrant breath fanning across his face. "I shall always love you, *nanoseham*," she whispered. "You are the voice of my heart. Your spirit has lived within mine, and mine within yours. Though we are separated by a distance of four thousand miles, we will be one, as we are one now. Always and forever."

Tears blurred Lyon's vision. "Ah, my darling, darling lass," he said in the Gaelic, "I would not be sending you away if I didn't love you so much."

"Tell me in English," she murmured.

"I'll miss you," he lied, "as much as you'll miss me." He kissed her deeply, his traitorous body unable to hide the unutterable love he felt.

Their spirits melded and fused as their bodies reached fulfillment at the same moment. Lyon poured his love into her soul as he poured the seed of life into her womb. He knew he would never be the same. Like a magical creature from the ancient Celtic ballads, she had changed some deep, unreachable, unknowable part of him. With her, he was whole. Without her, he was a hollow, depleted husk.

With a joyful sigh, Julie stretched out her small form on top of his big body in complete satiation, and they fell asleep in each other's arms.

*   *   *

The Dunstaff Railway Station stood on the southern shore of Loch Etive. The MacLyon family crossed the narrows of the sea loch on a ferry and arrived in the busy village of Dunstaff.

The servants who would accompany them to Glasgow unloaded the trunks and parcels from the flat-bottomed boat. Four footmen, a lady's maid, a maid to serve as nanny, Colin Dittmar, the boy's harassed and harried tutor, and the steward, Thomas Gairdner, who'd oversee all arrangements on the journey, made up the entourage. In respect for their recent loss, every member of the party was attired in black, and the men retained their black armbands.

Although they looked forward to visiting their grandparents, Neil and Jamie stayed close to the adults, quiet and subdued. Juliette had presented each boy with a dreamcatcher to take with him on their visit to Glasgow. She'd also fashioned a small medicine bundle to protect them and hung it around their necks before leaving the castle that morning.

Lyon never left Juliette's side for more than a few minutes at a time, and only when he was called upon to make decisions or issue directives. Everyone had taken a quick glance at his grim face that morning and sidestepped around him. All except Juliette, who knew the reasons for his ferocious expression and refused to be intimidated.

Rob had remained at the castle, exhausted by the ordeal of the funeral. When his shoulder wound started to bleed again the previous afternoon, Keir had prescribed complete bed rest for a week. So the travelers wished the invalid adieu in his suite of rooms.

Their farewell had been tearful. The boys hugged their red-haired uncle tight, as though fearing they might lose him, too.

"Ah, ye twa loons," he told them, as he chucked each boy under the chin. "I'll miss ye both like the very devil."

"I'll miss you, too," Neil said, brushing away a tear.

"Miss you, Uncle Robbie," Jamie added sorrowfully.

Rob took Juliette's hand with an endearing grin and squeezed her fingers. "I'll come to Edinburgh to see you as soon as I feel stronger," he promised.

While his older brother watched in stoic silence, she'd kissed Rob's cheek. "There will be ample time before I must leave to join Jennie and Grandpapa in London," she said with a grateful smile. "The *Etruria* doesn't sail for New York until the twenty-fifth of November."

Two private rail coaches now stood waiting at the Dunstaff Station, one for the family and one for the servants. The luxurious cars had been pulled off the siding earlier that morning and hooked onto the rear of the train.

Lyon scanned the bustling scene, making certain no one who looked suspicious lingered nearby. Passengers clustered in front of the depot, saying their last farewells to their families. Beside the puffing locomotive, the conductor discussed the day's timetable with the engineer, while several brakemen checked the couplers. The four tall, husky MacLyon footmen carried handguns and were fully aware they were responsible for guarding the women and children until they safely reached their destination.

"Do you like to ride on trains, Miss Elkheart?" Jamie asked with mounting enthusiasm.

"Oh, yes, Hehen," she agreed, as she stooped down to his level. She brushed back an unruly lock that had fallen over his forehead and smiled brightly. "Train rides are always fun, no matter how old you are."

Lyon found her blithe composure disconcerting. He'd told himself he wanted Julie to accept his decision with feminine acquiescence. But she seemed almost content.

Almost?

Hell, she *was* content.

Last night, Julie had sworn she'd love him forever. This morning she acted as though she were leaving on a brief shopping excursion and would be back in a few days' time to show off her collection of new hats.

He wished to God that were the case.

Granted, he wanted her to forget him and find happiness elsewhere. He just hadn't thought her change of heart would happen so suddenly.

They'd awakened at dawn and made love again. Intense and passionate, they'd clung to each other, their naked bodies pale in the faint morning light. When it was time for her to return to her room, Lyon had been prepared for pleading and female stratagems. But Julie never once mentioned the fact that she was leaving that day.

"Walk to the end of the platform with me," he told her now. He glanced at his nephews. "You lads stay with Nana and Mr. Dittmar. Miss Elkheart and I will be right back."

Julie slipped her arm in Lyon's and strolled beside him, remarking casually on the beautiful weather. If she was purposely trying to stomp on the few pieces left of his shattered heart, she was succeeding admirably. He felt as though he were walking around with a claymore stuck through his chest.

When they were out of hearing distance of the other passengers, Lyon turned to her, loosely clasping her elbows.

"Julie," he said in a hushed tone, "there's a possibility you could be with child. If you should discover that you are, I want you to send word to me immediately."

"Why?" she asked in surprise. "It is you who are sending me away. Why would you want to know that?"

He gripped her tighter, trying to keep the frustration from his voice. "Because I wouldn't let you go through it alone. Nor would I abandon my responsibility to the unborn child."

Her eyes grew wide. "You mean you would send money to raise your son or daughter? *Hesc!* Do not concern yourself about that. My grandfather is a wealthy man. And my parents' ranch house in Alberta is large enough to raise several dozen children. There would be no financial worries. Both the infant and I would be well provided for."

"I'm not talking about money," he said gruffly. "I'm saying I wouldn't let you face the ordeal of having a child out of wedlock. I would never let you or an innocent baby suffer for what is my responsibility.''

Lyon knew, deep inside, that a part of him fervently hoped and prayed she was pregnant at that moment. Fate, destiny, call it what you will, it would be the only excuse for keeping her with him that could assuage his tortured conscience.

Julie stared at him as though he were daft. ''My people do not hold a child's existence against it, no matter what written promises the parents did or did not make to each other.''

''Neither do the Scots,'' he said quickly. ''I'm thinking of when you return to America . . . to the college in Philadelphia.''

''If I am with child, I will go to my parents' home in Canada,'' she replied with unruffled serenity. ''A baby's birth is *always* a matter of celebration for the Cheyenne. Any son or daughter of mine would be accepted and loved by my family, regardless of whether or not I wear your wedding band. And if a warrior loves a woman, he is proud to claim her children as his own. There would be no shame, no punishment, heaped upon any child I might bear. So you have nothing to worry about, Lyon.''

The possibility of another man marrying Julie had been torment enough. At the thought of some sonofabitch claiming his child, Lyon felt as though he'd been kicked in the teeth.

''Promise me you'll send word if you're pregnant,'' he grated. ''I have a right to know.''

''Come to Edinburgh and find out,'' she suggested softly, her eyes shining with allurement. ''I will be there through most of November.'' The black plume on her hat fluttered into her face, and as she moved the feather away, she batted her long, gorgeous lashes seductively.

Exasperated, he drew her closer. ''You know what would happen if I came to Edinburgh.''

Julie gave him a radiant smile. "Yes, and I know what will happen if you do not."

He scowled, refusing to explore the obvious.

She told him, anyway. "You will be the loneliest, unhappiest man in Scotland."

The train whistle blew, and Lyon glanced up the length of the platform. Lady Hester and his nephews started moving toward the first private coach. Most of the servants were already aboard the rail car behind it. Neil motioned excitedly for Lyon and Julie to join them.

Lyon bent toward her, his raspy words betraying his misery. "Tell me good-bye, Julie."

Tell me you love me, darling.

Tell me you'll always love me.

She touched his cheek with her gloved hand. "I told you good-bye when we woke this morning, *nanoseham.* That is how I want you to remember me. Not here in this noisy place, but in your soft, warm bed."

He bent and kissed her cheek, her sweet scent bringing back memories of the intimacy they'd shared only hours before. Then he took her arm and led her back to Lady Hester and the lads.

Juliette stood beside a window in the Dunstaff Inn, as she watched the train pull out of the station to begin its journey eastward to Edinburgh. From where she waited, she could see Lyon still standing on the platform. He stared after the departing train until it chugged out of sight. Then he strode briskly to the ferryboat landing.

She'd had only a few minutes to kiss Lady Hester, Neil, and Jamie a hasty farewell in the rail coach, after Lyon handed them aboard. Then she'd slipped out the door on the car's opposite side.

While the boys bounced up and down on the seats and waved to their uncle through the window, Juliette hurried along the full length of the train, crossed the tracks on the far end of the depot, and entered the hotel lobby across the street.

That morning she'd confided in the dowager, telling her about the vision. Whether Lady Hester believed in Juliette's interpretation of the dream, she couldn't be sure. But the elderly woman promised to have one of the footmen stay with Juliette's baggage all the way to Waverly Station and inform Dr. Robinson of his niece's abrupt change in plans. For the sake of the children's security, their great-grandmother would still take them to Glasgow, far away from whatever might befall their uncle at Dubhgall Broch.

Juliette was afraid that if Hamish succeeded in killing Lyon, he would go after Rob and the boys. But without anything to offer as proof except a dream, she couldn't go to the Strathshire sheriff and accuse Laird Macfie of trying to assassinate an entire family.

Assuming an air of calm she didn't feel, she went into the inn's dining room and found a place at an empty table. She set her small valise down beside her chair, prepared to order tea. She couldn't risk starting out until Lyon was well on his way. Once she felt it was safe, she'd hire a hack at the inn's livery stable, cross on the ferry, and ride to the tower ruins.

Her fingers trembled as she laid her handbag on the tabletop. She straightened her spine and threw back her shoulders, determined to ignore the debilitating fear that gnawed in her belly.

Juliette took a deep breath and prayed to Maxemaheo she'd be on time.

Chapter 26

⟨⟨⟨◦◦◦⟩⟩⟩

J uliette reined in her tired mount as she came to the edge of the woods. On the grassy knoll above her, Dubhgall Broch rose up against the sky. Not knowing who might be waiting inside the stone tower, she planned to approach it on foot, moving as soundlessly as possible. She sent a prayer to the Great Creator Above that she hadn't arrived too late.

Just as she was about to dismount, she heard a horse's soft snort and the faint jingle of its harness. She looked cautiously around the wooded glen. At that moment, Hamish Macfie appeared from behind a screen of rowan branches. He'd apparently heard her coming through the pine trees and hid till she appeared. He urged his dappled horse closer and grabbed her hack's halter before she could kick her heels against its lathered flanks.

"Planning to break into someone's home, Miss Elkheart?" he asked with an ugly leer. "I see you're wearing men's clothing again. You must have burglary in mind for your evening's entertainment."

"Laird Macfie, how nice to see you," she said with an ingratiating smile. "I was just enjoying an afternoon ride."

"To Dubhgall Broch?" he asked sardonically. His disdainful gray eyes raked her. "Well, well, my conniving little redskin, if you are near, can MacLyon be far away?"

She looked up at the tower. "I was not riding to the old

ruins,'' she denied. ''I have been there before, and there is little to see. In fact, I was just about to turn around and go back to the castle.''

''You're not going anywhere,'' Hamish said. He leveled his pistol at her with a sneer. ''You're coming with me, bitch. Now, give me that knife.''

Juliette had changed from her traveling suit to a jacket and breeches in the Dunstaff Inn's retiring room, knowing she'd make better time riding astride. Consequently, the bone-handled knife fastened to her belt was in plain view. She withdrew the weapon from its sheath and handed it to him.

''Get down,'' he ordered, as he shoved the blade into the wide leather belt at his waist. ''We'll leave our horses in the trees and walk the rest of the way.''

Since there was no alternative, she slid from the saddle.

Macfie tied their horses to a branch, then grabbed Juliette's arm in a painful hold. With brutal force, he whipped her around to face the broch. ''Let's go see if the chief of Clan MacLyon is up in that tower waiting for me.''

''I am certain Lyon is not there,'' Juliette said. ''When I left Strathlyon, he was with his brother and the doctor.''

''Too bad Rob didn't die like he was supposed to,'' Macfie snarled. He dragged her up the steep, grassy slope. Jerking her to a momentary halt, he pressed the gun against her side. ''One word of warning, and you'll never speak again.''

She scrambled up the rise beside him. When she stumbled on a hidden rock, he yanked her viciously to her feet and shoved her onward.

The round stone tower appeared deserted. In the unnatural silence, an eagle circled the broch, then glided away.

Only a few yards from his goal, Hamish slowed, his breath raspy and short. The rigid tension in his thick arms and fingers revealed his uncertainty. He was sweating profusely, and Juliette could smell his fear. Strong Elk Heart

had taught her that a frightened man was the most dangerous kind because of his unpredictability.

Juliette remained calm. The last thing she wanted to do
was startle Macfie into making some rash move. As they
stepped inside the tower's open doorway, he held her in
front of him like a shield, one hand clamped on the back
of her neck. He pressed the cold tip of the barrel against
the underside of her chin.

Lyon stood waiting for Macfie's arrival with his gun already drawn and aimed at the entrance.

"If you make a move, MacLyon," Hamish grated, "I'll
blow her head off. Her brains will be spattered all over
these stones before you can take a second step."

The stunned look on Lyon's face as he met Juliette's eyes
threatened to destroy her hard-won composure. He'd
thought she was miles away, safely on her journey to Edinburgh.

He pointed his powerful Lancaster revolver at Macfie's
head. "Let her go," he said evenly. "She's not a MacLyon.
She has no part in your plan."

Hamish chuckled with sadistic pleasure. "So you figured
it out," he gloated. "There'll be no more MacLyons. After
I leave here, I'll make damn sure of it. And you can take
that thought to the grave with you. You'll be the last chief
of your clan. I can swear to it on your exalted lineage."
He motioned with a jerk of his head toward Lyon's weapon.
"Now throw the gun over here, or I'll pull the trigger."

"He will kill me anyway, *nanoseham*," Juliette said
placidly. "Better that one of us should live, than both die,
while the wolf goes free to devour the sheep."

Lyon's gaze locked with Julie's. He knew she was telling
him that Neil and Jamie were still on their way to Glasgow
with Lady Hester. For their sakes, Lyon, not Hamish, must
be the one to walk out of this tower alive. He could read
the unspoken message of love and self-sacrifice in her beautiful eyes. She was prepared to die, but she didn't want to
die needlessly.

Lyon had no intention of letting Macfie harm a hair on her precious head. Without a word, he tossed his revolver at Hamish's feet.

Macfie kicked the gun, sending it spinning through the doorway. "Now the dirk in your boot," he said. "Remove it slowly and carefully and toss it over here."

Lyon pulled the dagger from his riding boot and threw it across the broch's dirt floor.

Hamish kicked the weapon outside and grinned fiendishly. "Since the pretty redskin means so much to you, MacLyon, I'm going to let you keep her. You can take the bitch with you. Maybe you can spawn the next MacLyon heir in hell."

He shoved her brutally, and Julie sprawled on the ground at Lyon's feet.

Lyon bent over her in a seemingly automatic reaction, and scooped up a handful of dirt. Rising from his crouch in lightning reflex, he threw it in Hamish's eyes.

Blinded, Hamish roared and shot wildly as Lyon charged him. Snatching Julie's knife from Macfie's belt, he plunged the double-edged blade into the man's stomach. Ripping upwards through the vulnerable flesh, Lyon gutted the bastard.

The pistol discharged a second time in Hamish's death grip, and an agonizing pain exploded in Lyon's head. Blackness swirled before his eyes as Lyon collapsed on top of his enemy.

Juliette sat in the chair opposite Lyon's bed, her gaze fastened on his beloved face. The bandage, covering the burns the gun powder had scorched on his temple, cut a swath of white across the red-gold hair framed by the pristine pillow.

His blunt, rugged features were ashen. The broken nose, the scarred chin mocked the fragile, antiseptic aura of the sickroom that surrounded him. An invincible warrior sprung from the loins of Norse kings, he seemed too mighty, too fierce to be brought down by any human hand. But the pagan gods of old had intervened, callously deciding the fate of a mortal by the casting of the bones. In a room as silent as snowfall, life and death hung in the balance.

"You must wake up, Lyon," Juliette pleaded hoarsely. "You cannot let Macfie win in the end. Please, please, *zehemehotaz*, wake up and talk to me. I love you so much."

Her entreaties were useless. Except for his faint, shallow breathing, Lyon lay as still as a corpse. Not an eyelash flickered. Not a muscle twitched.

Juliette pressed her hand to her heart, as though she could ease the fear that squeezed her ribcage like a tight rawhide band with the continuing hours of dread and mounting despair.

Four days had passed since the meeting at Dubhgall Broch. Lyon had never awakened from the concussion caused by the force of Macfie's exploding pistol.

Annie MacDougall quietly entered the room. She drew back the velvet drapes to let the faint morning light stream across the rug, then turned down the gas lamp on the night table.

"You need to get some rest," she chided with a gentle smile. She bent over the wooden chair's tall back and touched Juliette's shoulder. "It's past dawn. Go to your room, dear, and get some sleep. I'll stay here while you're gone."

Juliette's throat ached from weeping. She pressed a fist to her mouth and swallowed before trying to speak. "I cannot," she croaked. "I cannot leave him."

"What good will it do Lyon if you collapse of exhaustion?" Annie coaxed. "When he comes to, you'll want to take care of him. And you'll be in no fit shape the way you are."

Juliette met Annie's clear hazel eyes and recognized the grave concern for her, as well as Lyon. The affectionate, warm-hearted woman had stayed at the castle for the past three days, giving help and support with unstinting generosity.

Reluctantly, Juliette rose. Smoothing her hand across her brow, she pushed aside the loose wisps that drooped from her braided chignon. "I will lie down for a short while," she conceded. "But if I do fall asleep, be sure to wake me when Keir comes."

She bent over Lyon, watching the nearly imperceptible rise and fall of his chest beneath the coverlet. His thick straight lashes deepened the shadows under his eyes. Yet even in his unconscious state, his soldierly presence dominated the room.

The evidence of his past military life was all around. His shoulder holster and pistol straddled the arm of a wing chair. The dress sword and scabbard of the Royal Scots hung above the fireplace. His dirk lay on the marble mantel. A large, glass-fronted cabinet displaying rifles, shotguns, and carbines stood directly across from the foot of the huge bed. An ancient targe adorned the far wall with the MacLyon clan slogan embossed on its leather covering.

Duinealachd.

Manliness.

Juliette touched his bearded cheek. Four days of luxuriant growth attested to his virility. Yet Keir had warned her that Lyon's heart could stop without his ever regaining consciousness. The possibility that he might slip away screamed through her terrified mind.

No! No! No!

He could not leave her.

She would not let him.

Just as Juliette was about to bend down and kiss Lyon's brow, Rob and Keir entered the room. At their questioning looks, she sadly shook her head.

"There has been no change," she told them.

Rob's handsome face was marked by the sleepless hours he'd spent with Juliette keeping vigil over his brother, when he should have been flat in bed himself. His worried gaze swept over Lyon's immobile form as he limped across the carpet with the aid of a cane. "I've received word from Glasgow," he quietly informed her. "Nana and the lads are on their way home."

Blinking back tears, she clamped her hand to her mouth and smothered a sob. Annie put her arm around Juliette's shoulder and squeezed her comfortingly. The three friends watched in stricken apprehension as Dr. MacDougall examined his friend.

Keir and Rob had arrived at the broch only moments after Macfie fired his gun. They'd brought John Woodburn, the Strathlyon gamekeeper, and his staff with them, all heavily armed.

Juliette later learned the doctor had stopped at the castle to check on Rob's progress and found the ill young man in a state of frenzy. Lyon had left a note, explaining where he'd gone and why—in case he didn't return. He had wanted Rob to know what he'd learned from Jervis Stirton. Hamish Macfie planned to kill every male heir to the MacLyon chiefship.

When Keir completed the examination, he returned his stethoscope to his bag and asked Annie to remain with the patient. Then he walked into the suite's sitting room with Rob and Juliette, where they could hear his prognosis.

"His pulse is fainter," he told them. "The breathing more shallow." The doctor's blue eyes were filled with sorrow as he met their frightened gazes. "It doesn't look good."

Propping his hands on his hips, Rob stared up at the ceiling in consternation. "I don't understand it. Lyon's as strong as a bull elephant."

Keir placed his bag on a low table. His forehead furrowed in a thoughtful frown as he folded his arms across his chest. "The problem isn't his strength. He's simply not fighting."

"Is that why can't he regain consciousness?" Rob asked. "He's not trying?"

"Maybe he doesn't want to," Keir replied with a speculative lift of his brows. "Maybe Lyon thinks he has no reason to live, now that he knows Macfie is dead and no longer a threat to his family."

Rob threaded his long fingers through his unruly hair. "My God, I can't believe that! Lyon's so much in love with Julie, he doesn't know up from down or left from right. He has every reason in the world to live, and she's standing right here in front of us." He clasped Juliette's hand and drew her closer. "He didn't have a reason before you came," he told her emphatically. "But your arrival changed everything. My brother loves you with every fiber in his being. He's just been too damn stubborn to admit it."

Tears streamed down her face. She sniffed and wiped them away with shaky fingertips. "I know that he loves me," she confessed. "He told me so. Only he told me in Gaelic. He never knew I understood every word he said."

The two men gaped at her.

"You have the Gaelic?" Rob questioned in amazement.

Wretched, she lowered her head in remorse. "I should have told Lyon. But I was afraid he would be angry because I kept it a secret for so long. And I hoped, one day, he would admit his true feelings openly."

"I spoke to Lyon on the afternoon of Flora's funeral," Keir said. "After the burial, I came back to the castle and examined his arm." The doctor's fair features softened with compassion as he met Juliette's gaze. "Lyon was convinced you'd be throwing your life away to marry him, despite anything I could say to the contrary."

"*Hesc!*" she exclaimed. "That is such foolishness! And even if I were to throw my life away, it would be my decision. That should be obvious to anyone."

Rob shook his head glumly. "Not to a man who thinks he's responsible for the world. Or at least, his part of it."

"Is there anything more we can do?" Juliette asked in desperation.

"Talk to him," Keir replied. "Call him by name. Assure him you're here. Other than that . . ." He shrugged in defeat. "Wait and pray."

Juliette immediately returned to the bedroom. Frowning with determination, she dragged the ladder-back chair closer and sat down. She grasped Lyon's hand and bent forward to talk directly into his ear.

"You think you got what you wanted, don't you?" she said in Gaelic. "You think that now your family is safe, I will return to Edinburgh. You think I will go back home with my sister, and in a year or two, I will meet a man and fall in love and get married. But you are wrong, MacLyon. There will never be another man in my life. Never."

Juliette wiped away a teardrop that plopped on his still hand. She knew Rob and the MacDougalls stood behind her, listening in mute stupefaction, but she didn't care that they must think her crazy. She was too furious at the intractable, pigheaded Scotsman in front of her.

"And . . . and you are wrong about another thing, too," she continued through the sobs that choked her. She jabbed her finger repeatedly against his chest. "I am *not* leaving the Highlands. I am staying right here at Strathlyon Castle and helping Nana and Rob raise Neil and Jamie. I am going to . . . to move into this room . . . and every night I am going to sleep here . . . alone . . . in this big bed."

Juliette's voice grew thicker and huskier as the tears streamed down her cheeks and splashed on the coverlet like raindrops. "And your ghost will . . . will haunt this castle, MacLyon," she warned him angrily. "You will come into this room and see me lying alone in your bed, and . . . and you will remember the night we spent in it together . . . And you will have the rest of eternity to . . . to regret what you threw away."

She collapsed on Lyon's chest, her hands clenched in despair. Great, heaving sobs shook her, their ache scalding her throat and making it impossible to go on. How could she live without him?

As she lay weeping, lost in dark misery, the frozen place inside her slowly began to melt like snow in the springtime. With dawning wonderment, she slowly became aware that one of his big hands had crept up to cover hers.

"Since you refuse to sleep anywhere else but in my bed, princess," he murmured in an exhausted voice, "I think we'd better get married."

Juliette's heart bounded with joy. She jerked upright, staring at Lyon in breathless wonder as she took his bearded face in her hands. "I think that is a marvelous idea!" she said, laughing and crying at the same time as she covered his face with kisses.

"When the hell did you learn the Gaelic?" he growled in her ear.

"Long before I came here," she admitted.

"Then . . . you understood . . . ?" The shocked accusation in his gaze made her want to crow out loud with happiness.

"Yes," she whispered, refusing to be contrite. Her lower lip trembled as tears of joy slid down her cheeks. "Every word you said to me, *nanoseham*. I purposely kept it a secret."

He released a long, incredulous groan. "I don't believe it."

She leaned even closer and mischievously repeated several picturesque phrases he'd unknowingly used to seduce her, her words barely a breath in his ear.

Lyon's hand lifted slowly, till his fingertips rested on her cheek. One corner of his mouth turned up in a lopsided grin. This time he spoke in plain Cheyenne. "*Namehota, Vehona*. I love you, my wee, fairy princess."

Epilogue

November 1886
Strathlyon Castle

Neil and Jamie rolled around on the rug in front of the fire, their collie puppies yipping excitedly. Aggie Dowel and Grizel Conacher had presented the lads with two of Sweetie's litter over a week ago. Neil had named his brown and white pup Bruce, and Jamie called his sable and white one Wallace, or Wally for short.

Julie sat on the floor with them, enjoying the fun. She braced her back against the sofa on which Lyon relaxed, his stocking feet propped on a cushion. He lazily stroked his fingers through her unbound hair, enjoying the silken feel of the glossy strands and the heavenly scent of wild roses and violets that drifted around him.

Heat stirred in his blood at the thought of taking his wife upstairs and laying her down on their big, soft bed—the bed she'd insisted she was going to sleep in for the rest of her life. On their second night of marriage, Julie had discovered her dreamcatcher hidden under Lyon's pillow. The feathered hoop now dangled from the ceiling overhead, bringing them both the most wonderful dreams. But no dream could be more wonderful than his life now. Julie hadn't realized it yet, but he was certain she was pregnant.

In her wing chair by the fire Nana plied her needle,

glancing up every so often to smile at the lads and offer a comment. Rob lay sprawled on the other sofa, reading *The Scotsman.*

Lyon glanced restlessly at the clock on the mantel. It was early in the evening. Too early, really. But hell, he'd waited long enough. An ache of anticipation tightened the muscles of his abdomen and thighs. The familiar heaviness in his groin reminded him just how pleasurable it was to undress his wee, bonny wife each evening and smooth his hands across her luscious honey-gold skin.

He stretched and yawned convincingly. "Well, I think I'll head for bed," he announced, as he shifted to a sitting position on the sofa. "We'll have a busy day tomorrow."

Neil paused in his roughhousing with his brother and the energetic puppies and looked up at him in surprise. "Are you going to bed early again tonight, Uncle Lyon?"

Rob snorted behind his newspaper.

"Won't you stay and play cards with us?" Jamie asked. His eager eyes shone hopefully. "You haven't played rummy with us since the wedding."

Lyon met his nephew's expectant gaze and ignored the sliver of guilt that pricked his conscience. It'd only been a week, for God's sake. The lad made it sound like a year.

Lyon and Julie had been married in the Kirk of St. Columba, with Annie MacDougall as bridesmaid and Rob as groomsman. Julie's uncle, Dr. Robinson, had come from Edinburgh to give her away.

Miss Juliette Evening Star Elkheart had made an exquisite bride in her ivory doeskin dress, with a beaded, feathered ornament twinkling in her hair. At Lyon's insistence she'd worn her long tresses loose and flowing, except for two narrow sidebraids tied with white fur. At Julie's insistence they'd spent their wedding night at the Dalriada, in the same room where, she claimed, she'd seduced him. Their wedding trip to Paris had been postponed till the spring for several reasons.

"I'll play cards with you on the train tomorrow morning,'' Lyon promised the lads. "In fact, I'll challenge you both to a tournament.''

"How about you, Aunt Julie?'' Neil asked. He shoved his unruly locks off his forehead and sent her an engaging smile. "Would you like to stay up for awhile and play rummy with us?''

Lyon buried his hand in his wife's thick, lustrous hair and squeezed the nape of her neck gently in warning. "Aunt Julie's tired, too,'' he said, before she could get a word out.

Folding the newspaper, Rob swung his long legs down from the sofa and sat up. "I'll play with ye twa loons,'' he offered with a knowing grin. "Your Uncle Lyon is a married man now, which can be a very exhausting proposition. Marriage brings lots of responsibilities.''

"What kind of responsibilities?'' Jamie asked, hugging the black and white collie. He nuzzled Wally's long, dense fur, and the puppy licked his young master with unstinting enthusiasm.

"Well, for one thing,'' Rob replied in a serious tone, "keeping your new bride happy.''

The lads looked at Julie expectantly.

"Are you happy, Aunt Julie?'' Neil asked, while the frisky brown and white puppy chewed on his fingers.

"I am very happy, Maevess,'' she replied. "But we are leaving for Edinburgh in the morning, and I will soon be visiting with my family. So I think I shall retire early, too.''

Juliette glanced up at her husband and met his smoldering gaze. His goal of getting her upstairs, undressed, and in bed flared like a brilliant green flame in his eyes.

Once Lyon decided they were to be married, he'd had no intention of wasting any time. While he recovered from the injury he'd sustained at Dubhgall Broch, Juliette had explained the rules of Cheyenne courtship. He was supposed to send gifts to her parents and wait patiently for their permission to wed their daughter.

But once back on his feet, her future groom wasn't about

to wait any longer than it took to arrange a ceremony at the church. The only concession he'd made was to send a profusion of gifts along with his personal resume and war record as a wedding announcement to his future in-laws. Just to be safe, he'd included a listing of his many decorations for valor on the battlefield to impress her warrior father. And he'd chosen Davie Grierson to accompany the thoroughbred horses, furs, and guns all the way to Medicine Hat. Juliette realized, belatedly, that she should never have called the poor footman by his first name in Lyon's presence.

"Will we meet your twin sister in Edinburgh, Aunt Julie?" Neil asked, scooting across the carpet to sit beside her. Bruce followed, nipping at his trouser cuffs.

"Yes, and my grandfather, too," she said patiently. He'd already known the answer before he'd asked the question. "And Jennie's new husband, as well."

In the midst of the wedding preparations, she'd received word from Uncle Benjamin that her sister had been married in Istanbul—to an English duke, no less. Juliette had quickly telegraphed her congratulations and that she'd meet the bridal couple in Edinburgh. She'd kept her own news for a surprise.

While he was at Strathlyon for the wedding, her uncle had examined Lyon's arm. Surgery to remove the bullet fragment had been scheduled for the week after next at the medical university in Edinburgh.

Jamie came over and dumped a squirming Wally in Juliette's lap, then crouched down in front of her. "Does your sister look just like you, Aunt Julie? Just *exactly* like you?"

"Exactly," she said with a laugh, as she scratched the wriggly puppy behind its ears.

Neil peered at her dubiously. "How will we tell you apart?"

"Perhaps you will not be able to," she warned him.

"Oh, that would be something!" Nana exclaimed with

a tickled, little laugh. "Not being able to recognize your own aunt."

Neil looked over at his eldest uncle in obvious concern. "What about Uncle Lyon?" he asked Juliette. "Will he be able to tell you and your sister apart?"

Juliette met her husband's gaze and flashed him a teasing smile. "Yes, I think he will . . . unless I purposely try to fool him."

"Could you do that?" Jamie demanded. "Could you fool Uncle Lyon?"

"Never," Lyon stated unequivocally, as he rose to his feet. "Julie could never fool me."

He offered his hand to his wife and drew her up from the floor. Standing behind her, he wrapped his arms around Julie's waist and pulled her close. The feel of her lithesome form pressed against him raised his body temperature several degrees higher. He radiated more heat than the blaze in the fireplace.

With the plump, wiggling puppy captured in his hands, Jamie cocked his head thoughtfully. "Not even with magic?"

"Not even then," Lyon declared with imperturbable male confidence.

Julie leaned her slight weight against him and shook her head, telling him it wasn't so. She could fool him, if she wanted to. The playful light in her eyes sparkled with the potency of an aphrodisiac. Every erogenous region of Lyon's big body lit up like rockets exploding in the night sky.

He had to get her up to their bedroom.

Now.

When he'd mentioned to his wife the previous evening that the first time she'd seduced him hadn't been at the Dalriada Inn at all, but in her makeshift tipi, she'd insisted on building one in their bedroom and spending the night in it. Memories of last night now burned in his brain. The laird of Strathlyon Castle could get very used to sleeping on the quilted floor of a fairy house.

"Before you go to bed, Uncle Lyon, can we ask Aunt Julie one more riddle?" Neil queried.

Jamie nodded emphatically. "Please, Uncle Lyon! Just one more riddle!"

"Oh, I don't know if that's such a good idea," Lyon replied in a somber tone. He planted a kiss on the top of his wife's head and frowned in deliberation. "The fairy princess belongs to me now. I can't be letting you lads try to enchant her. What would I do with a wife no bigger than a butterfly? I'd have to carry her to Edinburgh in my pocket."

"We won't enchant her," Neil promised solemnly. "We just want to see if she knows the answers to the last two riddles in the ballad."

"Go on, let them ask her," Rob urged with a canny grin. "See if Julie can do it one more time."

"Yes, let her try," Nana encouraged. She smiled at Lyon over the top of her spectacles. "We won't let the lads cast a counterspell on your new bride if she doesn't guess correctly."

"All right," Lyon agreed, as though with the greatest reluctance. "One riddle each."

"Maevess may go first," Julie said. Her low, throaty laughter sent bubbles of heady expectation cascading through Lyon's veins like champagne frothing over the neck of an uncorked bottle.

Neil's blue eyes gleamed with confidence, certain this time that he'd fool her. "What is heavier than lead?" he asked with a grin reminiscent of his Uncle Rob's charm.

Julie nodded to the youngest MacLyon. "Your turn, Hehen."

"What is better than bread?" Jamie questioned, giggling ecstatically.

Lyon cuddled his wife to him as she pretended to ponder the riddles. The ravenous hunger rising inside him could only be allayed by her sweet kisses and caresses. If he didn't get her upstairs and in bed soon, he'd frigging starve to death.

"Hm," she mused, apparently in no hurry whatsoever. "Heavier than lead . . . better than bread." She touched a fingertip to her upper lip and gazed at the ceiling in prolonged contemplation.

"Come on, Lady MacLyon," he growled impatiently, "the lads can't wait all night."

"And neither can their Uncle Lyon," Rob added. His eyes glinted with amusement.

Lyon shot him a warning glance.

"Very well," Julie said with a dramatic sigh. "I will take a guess." She smiled enchantingly at her two nephews, then spoke in Gaelic. "Guilt is heavier than lead, and the blessing is better than the bread."

The lads gaped at her in astonishment, their eyes enormous in their round faces.

"You spoke in the Gaelic, Aunt Julie!" Neil cried in awe.

Jamie squealed in amazement. "Did you know you spoke in the Gaelic?"

"No! Did I?" Julie glanced at her husband with an air of enchanting innocence. "Now how do you suppose that happened?"

Lyon grinned. "Tell everyone goodnight, sweetheart," he said, "in whatever language you'd care to use."

"*Pavetaeva*," she said in Cheyenne and threw them all a kiss.

"We'll see everyone bright and early in the morning," he told his family, as he ushered his little bride to the door. "Don't stay up too late."

"Good night and sweet dreams," Nana called, barely able to smother her laughter.

The two lads hurried to stand beside Rob, seated on the sofa.

Neil put a hand on his shoulder. "Did you hear Aunt

Julie speak in the Gaelic, Uncle Robbie?'' he asked softly. "Did you hear her?''

Jamie crept closer to whisper in his uncle's ear.

"She really is a fairy!"

Dear Reader,

If you're looking for a sensuous, utterly romantic historical love story, then look no further than November's Avon Romantic Treasure *So Wild a Kiss* by Nancy Richards-Akers. It's filled with all the unforgettable passion you're looking for! A young woman needs protection and help to keep her family together, so her little brothers and sisters arrange for her to drink a love potion—and it seems to work when a dashing man enters her life...and steals her heart.

There's nothing like a sexy lawman to steal a working woman's heart, and in Cait London's Avon Contemporary romance debut, *Three Kisses*, you'll meet Michael Bearclaw, the strongest man in Lolo, Wyoming. He sweeps Cloe Matthews off her feet...and together they discover the secrets of Lolo. Learn why *New York Times* bestselling author Jayne Ann Krentz calls Cait, "...An exciting, distinctive voice."

Lovers of historical westerns won't want to miss the latest in Rosalyn West's exciting series, *The Men of Pride County: The Rebel*. A former Confederate soldier travels west, and finds love in the arms of a Union colonel's daring daughter.

And Danelle Harmon's delicious de Monteforte brothers make another appearance in *The Beloved One*. An English officer spirits a young American woman to his English home, only to discover he feels much, much more for her than he ever dreamed.

You'll find the very best romance here at Avon Books. Until next month, happy reading!

Lucia Macro

Lucia Macro
Senior Editor

AEL 1098

Avon Romances—
the best in exceptional authors and unforgettable novels!

THE HEART BREAKER   **by Nicole Jordan**
78561-7/ $5.99 US/ $7.99 Can

THE MEN OF PRIDE COUNTY: **by Rosalyn West**
THE OUTCAST   79579-5/ $5.99 US/ $7.99 Can

THE MACKENZIES: DAVID   **by Ana Leigh**
79337-7/ $5.99 US/ $7.99 Can

THE PROPOSAL   **by Margaret Evans Porter**
79557-4/ $5.99 US/ $7.99 Can

THE PIRATE LORD   **by Sabrina Jeffries**
79747-X/ $5.99 US/ $7.99 Can

HER SECRET GUARDIAN   **by Linda Needham**
79634-1/ $5.99 US/ $7.99 Can

KISS ME GOODNIGHT   **by Marlene Suson**
79560-4/ $5.99 US/ $7.99 Can

WHITE EAGLE'S TOUCH   **by Karen Kay**
78999-X/ $5.99 US/ $7.99 Can

ONLY IN MY DREAMS   **by Eve Byron**
79311-3/ $5.99 US/ $7.99 Can

ARIZONA RENEGADE   **by Kit Dee**
79206-0/ $5.99 US/ $7.99 Can

Avon Romantic Treasures

*Unforgettable, enthralling love stories,
sparkling with passion and adventure
from Romance's bestselling authors*

❄❄❄❄❄❄❄❄❄❄❄❄❄❄❄❄❄❄❄❄❄❄❄❄❄❄❄❄❄❄

MY WICKED FANTASY *by Karen Ranney*
79581-7/$5.99 US/$7.99 Can

DEVIL'S BRIDE *by Stephanie Laurens*
79456-x/$5.99 US/$7.99 /Can

THE LAST HELLION *by Loretta Chase*
77617-0/$5.99 US/$7.99 Can

PERFECT IN MY SIGHT *by Tanya Anne Crosby*
78572-2/$5.99 US/$7.99 Can

SLEEPING BEAUTY *by Judith Ivory*
78645-1/$5.99 US/$7.99 Can

TO CATCH AN HEIRESS *by Julia Quinn*
78935-3/$5.99 US/$7.99 Can

WHEN DREAMS COME TRUE *by Cathy Maxwell*
79709-7/$5.99 US/$7.99 Can

TO TAME A RENEGADE *by Connie Mason*
79341-5/$5.99 US/$7.99 Can

We've got love on our minds at
http://www.AvonBooks.com

Vote for your favorite hero in "HE'S THE ONE."

Take a romance trivia quiz, or just "GET A LITTLE LOVE."

Look up today's date in romantic history in "DATEBOOK."

Subscribe to our monthly e-mail newsletter for all the buzz on upcoming romances.

Browse through our list of new and upcoming titles and read chapter excerpts.